Praise for the Dune series

"The magic lingers, even when the final chapters have already been written."

—*Kirkus Reviews* on *Mentats of Dune*

"A fun blend of space opera and dynastic soap opera."

—*Publishers Weekly* on *Sisterhood of Dune*

"Delivers solid action and will certainly satisfy."

—*Booklist* on *The Winds of Dune*

"The saga continues to embroider the original works with intelligence and imagination and also a stronger role for women."

—*Booklist* on *Mentats of Dune*

"Fans of the original Dune series will love seeing familiar characters, and the narrative voice smoothly evokes the elder Herbert's style."

—*Publishers Weekly* on *The Winds of Dune*

"This sequel to *Paul of Dune* is an important addition to the Dune chronology and will be in demand by Herbert fans."

—*Library Journal* (starred review) on *The Winds of Dune*

"Characters and plot are beautifully set up, the timing is precise . . . The universe . . . is so vast, complex, and fascinating that the magic lingers."

—*Kirkus Reviews* on *Sisterhood of Dune*

THE DUNE SERIES

BY FRANK HERBERT

Dune

Dune Messiah

Children of Dune

God Emperor of Dune

Heretics of Dune

Chapterhouse: Dune

BY FRANK HERBERT, BRIAN HERBERT,
AND KEVIN J. ANDERSON

The Road to Dune
(includes the original short novel *Spice Planet*)

BY BRIAN HERBERT

Dreamer of Dune
(biography of Frank Herbert)

BY BRIAN HERBERT AND KEVIN J. ANDERSON

Dune: House Atreides

Dune: House Harkonnen

Dune: House Corrino

Dune: The Butlerian Jihad

Dune: The Machine Crusade

Dune: The Battle of Corrin

Hunters of Dune

Sandworms of Dune

Paul of Dune

The Winds of Dune

Sisterhood of Dune

Mentats of Dune

Navigators of Dune

Tales of Dune

Sands of Dune

Dune: The Duke of Caladan

Dune: The Lady of Caladan

Dune: The Heir of Caladan

Princess of Dune

PRINCESS OF DUNE

Brian Herbert

and

Kevin J. Anderson

TOR PUBLISHING GROUP

NEW YORK

This is a work of fiction. All of the characters, organizations, and events portrayed in this novel are either products of the authors' imaginations or are used fictitiously.

PRINCESS OF DUNE

A Tor Book
Published by Tom Doherty Associates / Tor Publishing Group
120 Broadway
New York, NY 10271

www.torpublishinggroup.com

The Library of Congress has cataloged the hardcover edition as follows:

Names: Herbert, Brian, author. | Anderson, Kevin J., author.
Title: Princess of Dune / Brian Herbert and Kevin J. Anderson.
Description: First edition. | New York : Tor, 2023. | Series: Dune
Identifiers: LCCN 2023033330 (print) | LCCN 2023033331 (ebook) | ISBN 9781250906212 (hardcover) | ISBN 9781250906267 (ebook)
Subjects: LCGFT: Science fiction. | Novels.
Classification: LCC PS3558.E617 P66 2023 (print) | LCC PS3558.E617 (ebook) | DDC 813/.54—dc23
LC record available at https://lccn.loc.gov/2023033330
LC ebook record available at https://lccn.loc.gov/2023033331

ISBN 978-1-250-90629-8 (trade paperback)

Our books may be purchased in bulk for promotional, educational, or business use. Please contact your local bookseller or the Macmillan Corporate and Premium Sales Department at 1-800-221-7945, extension 5442, or by email at MacmillanSpecialMarkets@macmillan.com.

First Tor Paperback Edition: 2024

Printed in the United States of America

0 9 8 7 6 5 4 3 2 1

by Brian Herbert

This book, like so many others I have written individually and in collaboration, is for my beautiful, intelligent wife, Jan Herbert, who has dedicated her entire life to me. I can think of no one else as deserving of my humble words of praise. I remember well the first time we met as teenagers, and how that initial spark has lasted through fifty-five incredible years of marriage, to the very moment when I am writing this tribute to her. With Jan it is always a grand adventure, and I am eternally grateful to her for everything.

by Kevin J. Anderson

In a book about princesses, how can I not think of my little sister, Laura? So, from me, this book is dedicated to Laura Anderson, who had to grow up with a brother who was always shut in his room pounding on the typewriter or off with his friends doing nerdy things. She wasn't exactly a princess, and she grew up to be a big reader. I think she turned out pretty well.

10,189 A.G.

Two years before House Atreides
arrives on Arrakis

Two women were critical in shaping the pivotal events of our time—Princess Irulan, firstborn daughter of Padishah Emperor Shaddam IV, and the Fremen Chani, daughter of Imperial Planetologist Liet-Kynes. They came from opposite ends of the political and economic spectrum, but their lives hurtled on collision courses with Paul Atreides, the legendary Muad'Dib.

—Imperial Archives on Kaitain

Certain things about Navigators and foldspace mechanics must never be revealed to outsiders.

—NORMA CENVA, genius Rossak scientist and first Navigator, written before her transformation into the Oracle of Time

In a prominent viewing stand, Princess Irulan sat beside her father, Padishah Emperor of the Known Universe, surrounded by opulence but without any Imperial entourage. They were extremely honored guests; historically, spectacles such as this one were for the eyes of the Spacing Guild only.

The funeral of a Navigator was a rare and solemn event.

Amid the exotic lights and sounds, the regal pair gazed across the immensity of the Junction spaceport and its array of enormous landed Heighliners. The Guild held its secrets.

Irulan and her father wore fine but tastefully subdued garb: the Princess in a dark dress and minimal jewelry with her blond hair neatly coiffed, and Shaddam IV in a dark robe of state with little adornment. Guild dignitaries filled the other seats of the viewing area.

It was an overcast day on the central Guild planet, warm but not humid. Breezes whisked away industrial odors from the presentation complex, and a haze of artificial lights filled the air. At the entrances to the restricted viewing area, Imperial Sardaukar stood at attention, and more of the Emperor's elite soldiers remained back at the luxurious Imperial frigate, awaiting Shaddam's return to the spaceport.

Irulan's father had grudgingly agreed to the security restrictions, after Guild reassurances from their high-level representative, Starguide Serello. Now the Starguide sat on the other side of the Emperor in the viewing stand, and he had presented guarantees from his superiors that the Corrino guests would be safe, and a Guild guarantee was not given lightly. In this ultra-security zone, Irulan felt assured that she and her father need not worry.

The Padishah Emperor and his eldest daughter were the only outsiders allowed to see this celebration of a Navigator's life. To Irulan's knowledge, such an honor had never been granted in the millennia of cooperation between the Spacing Guild and House Corrino.

The invitation included her, rather than the Empress, because Shaddam was currently without a wife, having recently lost his latest spouse, Firenza Thorvald. Irulan, at twenty-six years old, was the Princess, his most important child. In her position, Irulan had traveled on diplomatic missions and visited many worlds, but she had never been to the Guild's headquarters. Few outsiders saw any part of Junction, the nexus of all galactic spacefaring routes. Even her father, for all his grand importance, had never been here.

Ahead of her on the presentation field, the vast array of Heighliners filled her with awe. The enormous ships landed on no other planet, and now hundreds of them covered the ground as far as she could see—all to memorialize one of the powerful, mysterious Navigators.

Her father seemed pleased to witness the event. He leaned close to her. "Most impressive, isn't it? This will be noted in my official biography." He kept his voice to a whisper out of respect, although even a shout would have been swallowed by the immensity.

The handsome Starguide glanced at the visitors, noting the whispers, but his expression remained stony and unreadable. Serello had a solid jaw and a thick head of dark, wavy hair; his eyes were a startling deep black. A man of illustrious credentials and reputation, he reported directly to a small cadre of Guild leadership; an hour ago, he had met Shaddam and Irulan at the Imperial frigate and escorted them here for the event.

The ceremony unfolded, and the Imperial guests watched with rapt attention. Despite her Bene Gesserit upbringing and long years of practice maintaining a calm demeanor, the Princess felt a rush of excitement just to be here.

Thousands of uniformed Guildsmen gathered in the foreground below, making little noise despite their large numbers. The Guildsmen displayed a variety of body shapes, but they all wore similar gray uniforms. Many looked ordinary to Princess Irulan, but others had physical deformities, which gave them an alien air.

Nearby, shielded and murky tanks held Navigators, altered humans who guided the great Heighliners safely through foldspace. Preparing for this event, Irulan had studied diligently, utilizing secure Imperial and Bene Gesserit documentation, to learn what was known about Navigators, despite the Spacing Guild's mystique.

Each Navigator had an enormously expanded consciousness and prescience, by which they chose safe pathways through space. Due to lifelong immersion in spice gas, Navigators typically lived for centuries, and thus the death of one was a momentous event. The name of this fallen Navigator had not been revealed. Irulan wondered if the mutated humans even maintained their original names.

In the wide assembly area below, the motley assortment of Guildsmen encircled a clearplaz globe mounted on a towering column. Serello had explained to them in an awed whisper that the hypnotic orb contained the Oracle of Time, an entity said to be thousands of years old. Irulan found the globe compelling, magical.

Within the sphere and pedestal of the Oracle, lights flickered, then fell entirely dark, as black as deep space. Irulan covered a quiet exclamation so as not to call attention to herself.

Serello leaned over and whispered to the Emperor. The two men rose together and walked to a speaking bubble at the head of the viewing area, while Irulan remained in her seat. Her father was tall, but the Starguide loomed half a head over him.

The Guild representative spoke first, his voice carrying out over the vast assemblage, and all faces turned in his direction. "We are honored to be joined by Emperor Shaddam Corrino IV, as well as his daughter Princess Irulan. His Imperial Majesty will address the loss of our Navigator comrade, who served the Guild and the Imperium so well."

The big Starguide stepped to one side, and Shaddam moved with Imperial grace to the center of the speaking bubble, his head held high to display his aquiline nose and classic facial features. He looked as dignified and somber as Irulan had ever seen him.

"We offer heartfelt condolences to those who knew this fallen Navigator. The Spacing Guild is an essential partner to House Corrino in commerce, military affairs, and so much more. On behalf of the Imperium, we express our deepest gratitude for his long years of service." He bowed his head enough to show his respect for the Guild, though she knew it went against his proud nature. The Emperor exited the speaking bubble, and both men returned to their seats.

The field erupted with glowing colors, like an aurora awakening within the globe of the Oracle of Time. The sphere rose from its pedestal, as if borne on suspensor engines. The round chamber lit up with a rainbow of spectacular streaks of color, and Irulan smiled in delight.

Now the sturdy support column illuminated a fiery orange to reveal that the pedestal itself was a tank of spice gas holding a floating, misshapen form—motionless except for the natural eddies in the tank's gas. Above, the Oracle sphere dimmed so that all eyes focused on the Navigator's tank.

Inside, a hypnotic display of gases swirled and lights flashed. The dead figure—a grossly distorted humanoid body—seemed to move of its own volition, like a last burst of life before the end.

In the air outside the tank, a parade of immense holograms was projected, a record of the dead Navigator's life. At first, he appeared as a normal child and young man, dressed in clothing that had gone out of fashion centuries ago. This was followed by his metamorphosed form inside a tank, and then a huge Heighliner moving away from Junction orbit and out to open space.

A funeral dirge came from orchestral instruments, a haunting tune with a slow, regular beat.

Hovering in the air above the immense field, the Oracle of Time brightened, while the coffin tank dimmed to conceal the floating figure. Bursts of light from the Oracle's globe lit the area.

An eerie, all-encompassing genderless voice filled the air, accompanied by the sphere's pulsing. Then shimmering ephemeral shapes surrounded the globe as the Oracle spoke. "Hear my words. Our blessed Navigator's body will return to the source of the spice."

The globe went dark again, still suspended in the air.

Irulan and her father exchanged curious glances.

Now the darkened tank, like an alien sarcophagus, rose from the ground and floated beneath the globe. As if linked by unseen wires, both objects drifted toward the field of Heighliners.

The Emperor looked at Serello, as if to ask a question, but the Starguide announced in a voice that allowed no discussion, "It is time for you and the Princess to return to Kaitain. The Guild is grateful for your attendance."

Not accustomed to being dismissed, Shaddam persisted, "I would like to ask—"

"Sire, the rest of this sacred ceremony is strictly confidential. Please understand and respect our ways. We are honored that you attended."

Shaddam was startled by the attitude. Bowing, the Starguide departed quickly after signaling the Sardaukar to come and escort the Corrinos back to the Imperial frigate.

The desert holds many secrets. And the Fremen know only some of them.

—REVEREND MOTHER RAMALLO, Sietch Tabr

The open sky of Arrakis was wide and clean, with high dunes stretching to the horizon. A smudge of blown dust rose into the air like a primitive marking on the sky.

Seeing such vastness made Chani, daughter of Liet and Faroula, think of freedom. She and two companions had traveled far out into the open bled, telling Naib Stilgar that they were on business for the sietch, but the young Fremen were merely wandering the desert. *Their* desert. These places, still untouched by the Harkonnen overlords, reaffirmed her belief that the Fremen people would never be conquered.

They had been on their own for four days. Chani and her companions would summon a worm, ride all day, then make camp in the rocks before departing with the next sunrise. She traveled with her older half brother, Liet-Chih (known by his Fremen name of Khouro), along with Jamis, the oldest of their band, who had been on more razzia raids than either of them. But Chani was only fourteen, and she had time to gain in experience.

On the morning of the fifth day, after the trio awoke in stilltents tucked among the rocks, they watched the sunrise. Jamis shaded his eyes and stared at the undulating dunes. He sniffed the air and frowned, then removed a pair of oil-lens binoculars. He turned to Chani and Khouro. "Do you smell it? It's far away, but even here . . ."

Chani closed her eyes and inhaled a deep breath, concentrating on the subtleties in the dry, dusty air. "Spice chemicals, raw vapors. Harsher than a normal melange field."

Her brother's blue-within-blue eyes shone with eagerness. "We should investigate."

Chani would not be rushed into rash action. "You are always in a hurry, Khouro." She took her time to consider. The chemicals were faint as they wafted toward them. Yes, she detected the hint of an alkaloid scent. "A pre-spice mass nearby, within a few kilometers."

Chani's father, Liet, served as the Imperial Planetologist on Arrakis. He would explain science to his daughter, imagining that someday she would be his successor, just as he had served after his own father was killed in a cave-in at Plaster Basin. Though she had no interest in serving the Padishah Emperor, Chani did want to learn ecology, as it would be useful for the Fremen dream of a green Arrakis.

She took the binoculars from Khouro and adjusted the focus. Far off, she could see a rounded bulge under the open sand unlike the swell of a dune: an expanding bubble of carbon dioxide in the underlayers as organic matter from the Little Makers mixed with a trickle of buried water, as well as the pooled detritus from sandworms. She saw the copper-colored tracery of spice, like burst blood vessels on an old Fremen's face. Rising fumes addled the air above the swell as chemical reactions churned and changed, molecules interlocking in an ancient mystical puzzle.

As if the decision had already been made, Khouro stuffed his belongings into his Fremkit and was ready to go. He adjusted his stillsuit, and Jamis did the same, as if it were a race. Chani realized they would have little time.

The brooding power of the spice blow fascinated her. Such events were rarely witnessed from this close. She and her companions had come out to scout, possibly to observe illicit Harkonnen spice operations, but any occurrence important to the desert was important to the Fremen.

The pre-spice mass was close enough that they would not summon a worm. "We have to cross open sand," she said. "But worms won't go near a brewing spice blow."

"I will lead like a wisp of dust blown on the wind," Khouro said as he scrambled down the rocks. He had taken his private name from the Fremen word for a wind that lifted a transient skirl of dust, like a phantom flitting across canyon floors. He had announced the choice after his first successful razzia against a Harkonnen spice factory, and he prided himself on leading his life that way, like a *khouro*.

When they reached the base of the rocks, the trio set off across the sand, walking with uneven footsteps. Before they had gone twenty paces, Chani heard a distant, out-of-place hum, more a feeling than an actual sound. She raised her hand to signal a halt. Her companions froze, looked for any sign of danger. Pulling out the binoculars, she scanned the sky and tried to track what she heard. High against the dusty yellow sky, she saw a black speck growing larger. "A ship."

Without a word, the three bolted back to the shelter of rocks. As they retreated, Chani brushed their tracks to erase the abbreviated trail.

Back in the safety of shadows, she watched the strange vessel approach. They could all hear the hum of its engines now. Khouro said, "Not an ornithopter, and not Harkonnen."

She scanned the sturdy craft, noting that it was not built for sandstorms and abrasion—a vessel designed for space. "It's a Guild ship!" She tightened the focus, made out no markings on the hull. "It's going straight for the spice blow."

"Do they not know the danger?" Jamis said in a mixture of scorn and disbelief. "If they're caught in the explosion, maybe we can salvage something from the wreckage."

Her brother stared, intent with anticipation. A kilometer away, the Guild ship hovered above the increasingly obvious bulge of the pre-spice mass. As more gases escaped, Chani could smell the bitter chemicals plainly in the air.

"They're using suspensor engines," Khouro said. "They'll be lucky if they don't draw a worm and drive it into a frenzy."

"Strangers do many foolish things." Chani passed him the binoculars. "But who can explain offworlders, and especially the Guild?" Her father had told her about his few dealings with Guild representatives and claimed they were always unsettling encounters.

The hovering vessel was bigger than a spice factory, with heavy engines and bulbous nodules on its sides, dotted with small windowports. Chani wondered how many strange people were inside looking out.

Jamis shook his head. "I give that spice blow less than an hour."

Chani considered what her father would do. "Maybe they are performing experiments." Liet-Kynes and his father before him had studied spice blows in an attempt to understand how melange was linked to the life cycle of sand plankton, sandtrout, and the worms.

But the mysterious ship was not performing experiments. A lower hatch opened, and six uniformed Guildsmen crowded a suspensor platform, which descended toward the trembling sand above the mass.

"Suspensors again," Khouro muttered with deep scorn. "What are these intruders doing?" He stared through the binoculars before passing them to Jamis, who eventually returned them to Chani.

The suspensor platform hovered just above the swollen sands, and the Guildsmen shifted position to reveal another form that lay motionless on the deck. Chani zoomed in, saw a naked figure with grayish skin, distorted head, angular limbs—a body that did not look quite human.

Her brother nudged her for the binoculars, and she passed them, while shading her eyes to discern the distant figures in the mirage-rippled air. Khouro let out a surprised grunt. "They brought a corpse with them!"

When Chani got the instrument back, she watched the Guildsmen lower the gangly cadaver to the trembling sands near the red cracks of fresh spice. She realized what they were witnessing. "See the reverence in their movements. They are placing that body on top of the spice blow—a funeral." She remembered what her father had told her. "The Spacing Guild reveres spice. Their Navigators are saturated with it." The malformed body must be one of the mysterious creatures that guided Heighliners through space.

Leaving the body on the sand bulge, the six Guildsmen returned to their hovering platform, which rose to the looming ship.

"They use our world as a graveyard!" Jamis sounded offended.

Chani frowned. "Many bodies are buried in the sands of Dune."

Humming, the Guild vessel climbed away from the imminent spice blow, leaving the discarded body. The ship dwindled to a speck in the sky.

Chani's half brother moved even before she could speak. "Quick! Whatever that body is, the Guild considers it valuable. We must see for ourselves." Showing no caution, he bounded out onto the sand. "That secret could be vital."

Jamis ran after him. "Look at the swell of the pre-spice mass."

Khouro ran, not bothering with the careful sandwalk. There would be no worms, not now. Chani's wiry legs were strong from the rigors of a life walking the sands. As she followed them, she felt the ground vibrate with energy and thought of the roiling chemistry deep underground, the buildup of heat and pressure.

"Is a dead body worth it, Chih?" she called, preferring to use that name.

Her brother didn't look back. "A dead Navigator body."

Raised as a Fremen, she was accustomed to danger. At all times out here, she needed to be alert for wormsign, and she could summon a worm herself if needed. She understood Shai-Hulud, knew his moods and habits.

A pre-spice mass, though, was unpredictable. Chani warily eyed the curvature of the swell, saw that it had doubled in size since they'd first left the rocks. When the chemicals began to mix deep underground, the reaction could take hours, even days, to reach its explosive climax. She didn't know how long this blow had been building up.

Her brother and Jamis thrived on risk. She'd seen it before, but nothing like this. They crossed the sand and climbed the crumbling slope, which was like the windward side of the steepest dune.

Chani panted through her nose filters as she joined the others on the swell, pawing their way to the misshapen corpse. Sand grains popped and rattled, vibrating from deep below. The pungent cinnamon smell filled the air, stinging her eyes.

The dead Navigator lay sprawled and naked, its long arms bent in the wrong places. The hands were webbed, the head swollen and misshapen. The open, dead eyes stared into infinity—as Navigators were said to do even in life.

Khouro bent to touch the ribs of the body. "This creature was once human, but the Spacing Guild changed it hideously."

Chani said, "Father says they use melange to alter the adaptable candidates."

The spice fumes were so thick in the air, she felt she could slice them open with a crysknife. The rumbling of the pre-spice mass made the sand jitter, and the vibrations caused the Navigator corpse to shudder and twitch as if eerily alive. Jamis retreated in superstitious horror, making a warding sign with his fingers. "The spice has brought this monster to life."

Chani grabbed her brother's arm. "There, you have seen it! We will all be dead if we don't leave soon. The mass will blow in minutes."

Khouro bent down and reached under the dead Navigator's arms. "Help me!"

Jamis picked up one of the ankles, but as they lifted the body, Chani could see they would never make it. "Leave him, the blow is coming! You know it!"

Her brother grimaced down at his prize specimen, then dropped the corpse. "Our father would probably just dissect it anyway. Run!"

Jamis and Chani did not need to be told twice. They bounded down the swelling surface, slipped and tumbled, rolling as fast as they could. When they reached the bottom of the main swell, they began to run as if pursued by an oncoming worm.

Halfway back to the rocks, Chani heard a deep-throated rumble underground like a growling beast trying to claw its way up to the air. The stability of the rocky ridge still seemed many kilometers away, and the sand pulled at her feet as she ran.

Jamis tripped and sprawled on the ground. Racing past him, Khouro reached down to grab his friend's hand and pulled him to his feet without pause. The rumble had turned into a roar.

When Chani heard a new buzzing in the air, she wondered if it was static electricity or hissing fumaroles of escaping spice gases. Turning, she was astonished to see another aircraft racing low over the dunes, so close to the ground that its wake picked up a trail of dust. The vessel was sleek and unmarked, built like an insect.

They were completely exposed out on the sands. "Ship!" Chani shouted. By now they might be safe from the spice blow—but they wouldn't be safe from marauders.

Khouro and Jamis spun about. They were still about two hundred meters from the shelter of the rocks.

"They've seen us!" Jamis said.

"They won't take us alive. We'll fight." Khouro touched the crysknife at his side. "We can kill them all."

"They don't want us," Chani said.

The ship burned a hard, braking maneuver above the bulge of the spice blow, hovering over the sprawled Navigator body. The ship reminded her of a cliff wasp, naturally adapted for stealth and speed.

The lower hatch of the marauder vessel opened above the corpse. Suspensor fields thrummed, and the body twitched and drifted up off the jittering sand. With limp arms, the body looked like an ascending spirit as it rose into the strange ship. The hatch closed, and the ship streaked away with a roar of heavy acceleration, tearing up a trail of sand and dust in its wake.

Then the spice blow erupted. The bubble of sand burst open with a fury of released gases, converted spice. The geyser shook the ground and cracked open the dunes like a gaping wound.

Chani sprawled onto the sands and kept scrambling forward, trying to get farther away. Within moments, sand and dust pelted down on them, and they covered their heads as they rushed to the stark ridge.

With her back against solid rock again, Chani turned to see the pillar of dust tinged with rusty melange thrown high into the air. The sand cloud widened, blotting out the sky—and she could see no sign of the mysterious marauder ship through the haze.

The Guild had deposited their revered corpse here, expecting it to be swallowed in the spice blow. They would never imagine that someone might steal the body at the last minute. The marauders believed they had gotten away with their scheme unnoticed—but Chani and her companions had witnessed it.

When does a boy become a man?

—PRINCESS IRULAN as a child, private journals, writing about her father, Emperor Shaddam Corrino IV

Once they had returned to the Imperial Palace on Kaitain, Irulan sat beside her father in the Imperial Audience Chamber. Shaddam would rather have had sons, but she played her role as Princess Royal perfectly. Her seat was smaller than her father's, a ceremonial chair normally reserved for the Empress, but Irulan considered her companion throne imposing enough, as befitting the firstborn and favorite daughter. She was regal, her blond hair lush and perfectly styled, her gown magnificent.

The Golden Lion Throne was far more impressive, a massive block of green Hagal quartz carved into the Emperor's seat. Shaddam sat there as he held court, looking across the vast chamber. On both sides of the room, the walls were lined with dozens of dark wooden chairs for daily functions.

Two of her younger sisters, Wensicia and Chalice, sat across from each other on separate sides, flanked by court functionaries. The lesser princesses often attended the Imperial Court, but they observed from the periphery. Chalice was always atwitter with gossip and fashions, but Wensicia—Shaddam's third daughter—watched with intense concentration and hungry eyes.

Shaddam had explained to Irulan the benefits of observing the day-to-day court as supplicants presented their various reports and requests. Irulan had been trained for all this during her years at the Bene Gesserit Mother School, and here on Kaitain the court instructors drilled her on every aspect of etiquette. Now, after the recent loss of Empress Firenza, whom her father had greatly disliked, Irulan was more frequently invited into the center of court activity. Her own mother, Shaddam's first wife, Anirul, had been dead thirteen years now.

As the eldest daughter, she had a close relationship with her father, spending much more time with him than did her four younger sisters. Great opportunities were open to Irulan, and she was resolved not to let the Emperor down, or the Imperium.

Shaddam seemed satisfied with her dedication to the role, but he acted as if all aspects were new to her, even after she had been fully instructed. Irulan suspected his mind was so full that he lost track of what she had already learned, and he would repeat himself. She let it pass, not wanting to add to his stress. It was no easy thing to be the Emperor of a Million Worlds. . . .

Balut crystal glowglobes floated around the chamber, set to simulate the time of day and weather outside—right now, the morning sun of a warm summer morning. Through the towering open windows of the great hall, she could hear the faint, haunting music of the Imperial Entertainment Troupe practicing stringed and wind instruments in the courtyard for their next nightly appearance before the Emperor and his guests.

Chamberlain Beely Ridondo stepped forward, a gaunt, skeletal man with yellowish skin and a high forehead. Head bowed, he climbed the dais steps to hand an oversize message cube to the Emperor. "Today's agenda, Sire."

On its glowing face appeared a written summary of business, white lettering against a black background. Irulan glanced over to read the cube display along with her father, flash-memorizing the details. The schedule listed a number of noble representatives who had requested a court appearance. First on the list was a man not allied with any major noble house, however, but rather a military officer named Moko Zenha.

"Who is this?" The Emperor turned the cube and wagged a finger at the name. "What does he want?"

Stepping close, Chamberlain Ridondo spoke in a low voice. "I placed him first on the agenda rolls so you could see him for only a few minutes before moving on to more important matters. Fleet Captain Zenha is a talented and ambitious officer in your Imperial Guard. He asks to speak with you on a matter of utmost personal importance. His record is exemplary, Sire, and he has distinguished himself in numerous fleet exercises. Considering his humble background, he is an impressive individual. It may be worthwhile to indulge him, if only briefly. I suspect he wants to point out some aspect of the guard that can be improved."

Shaddam frowned. "Likely at additional cost."

Ridondo acquiesced. "In our rushed schedule, I did not press him for further details, Sire. Would you like me to cancel him today?"

With a glance at Irulan, the Emperor sighed. "No, let's get it over with, whatever it is. Every subject is important to me, although if this is a military matter, he should observe the chain of command." He sat back on the Golden Lion Throne and brushed a hand through his red-gray hair.

When Zenha's name was called, he marched into the audience chamber, his boots clicking on the gleaming floor. Tall, broad-shouldered, and ruggedly handsome, he wore the scarlet-and-gold uniform of Shaddam's Imperial Guard, with officer's epaulets on the shoulders and tiny golden lions on the collar. He presented a spotless, impeccable appearance, every medal and button shiny. His gaze was fixed on the Padishah Emperor as he walked at a precise cadence toward the dais, though when he reached the lower step, his gaze flicked over to Irulan. She noted his attention, and found it peculiar.

Zenha removed his brimmed cap and bowed before returning to a ramrod-straight posture, looking at the Emperor. When Shaddam granted him leave to speak, the Fleet Captain said, "Thank you for seeing me so quickly, Majesty." He turned and focused his hazel-brown eyes on Irulan. "Princess." His manner was certainly unconventional as he addressed her rather than the Emperor. "I am Fleet Captain Moko Zenha, second-in-command in your father's Imperial fleet, Kaitain squadron."

Irulan gave a slight nod to acknowledge him, but Shaddam snapped, "You will address *me* directly, not my daughter."

Zenha composed himself and stood at attention. "Yes, Sire. I meant no disrespect."

Irulan noted that his uniform bore the scroll emblem of his noble family, a Minor House on a world known for producing fine editions of official documents. Though Shaddam did not seem to recognize the family name, Irulan had heard of him, one of the few competent officers in the bloated Imperial military force. Zenha had moved up in the ranks through hard work and dedication. Unlike many higher-ranking commanders, Moko Zenha had received his appointment through skill rather than patronage or nepotism.

She wished the chamberlain had given them more forewarning, so she could have researched Zenha's record more deeply. She sifted through her memory, things she had heard and filed away, using techniques she had learned on Wallach IX. She recalled that this man was widely admired in the ranks, especially by the secondary officers and the soldiers themselves, though not so much by the noble leaders, with whom he had little in common.

The awkward silence stretched out, then the officer gathered his courage and addressed the Emperor. "Sire, I have carefully considered what I know of the Imperium, its politics, its commerce, and its military. I believe I may have a wider and more important role for the continued stability and greatness of House Corrino."

Shaddam pursed his lips, pleased by the words, but waited for the man to get to the point.

Zenha straightened even more. "Sire, I humbly request the hand of your daughter Princess Irulan in marriage."

From the secondary throne, Irulan involuntarily jerked her head back. Shocked mutters rippled through the chamber, followed by titters. She spotted her sisters, looking scandalized in their seats against the wall.

The Fleet Captain pressed on. "I present my full credentials and pedigree." He offered a dense sheet of ridulian crystal.

Shaddam's face reddened, and Irulan could see that he was about to say something in anger, but for some reason, he controlled himself and changed his mind. He said to the audacious man, "Step back. I wish to speak with my daughter."

Obediently, Fleet Captain Zenha retreated from the dais, out of listening range.

Leaning toward her from his massive throne, the Emperor whispered, "Worry not. He may look gallant in that uniform, but that man is in no position to offer himself to you. His Minor House has few assets. He would be a bad match, especially considering how many other options I have for your husband. But I will not crush him just yet."

Irulan was surprised at how well he controlled his temper. "As a political matter, it is best to deliver him a graceful denial, Father. This man has a bright military career, and we must encourage his service."

A troubled expression crossed the Emperor's face, and she could see he was thinking something entirely different. Still, he replied, "Yes, a graceful denial, but we must also demonstrate that any arrogant popinjay cannot stride into my throne room and ask to marry one of my daughters! I will explain my full reasons later."

She saw Chalice covering her mouth with a thin hand as she leaned closer to her friends at court, whispering furiously and giggling. On the opposite side of the chamber, Wensicia looked surprised and annoyed.

Straightening in her chair, Irulan directed an unreadable stare at the impertinent officer, concealing her own emotions and thoughts. Despite his immaculate uniform, he seemed less than polished in these ostentatious surroundings, a fighting man more accustomed to the company of soldiers than noble courtiers.

Even so, she was impressed at his boldness and courage. Obviously, her father was correct, that the marriage of the firstborn princess must be granted to only the most suitable candidate. But looking at Fleet Captain Zenha, she couldn't help feeling some sympathy for him. Surely the man must have known he'd be rebuffed?

As Zenha waited in the drawn-out silence, he seemed increasingly uneasy, shifting on his feet. The courtiers continued their incredulous murmurs.

After an interminable moment, Shaddam turned back to the officer. "Step forward and state your case. Bear in mind that my time is extremely valuable."

Irulan was curious. Why would her father even let him think his proposal might be considered?

Looking suddenly confident, Zenha delivered his words in a quick, efficient manner. "Throughout my career, I have distinguished myself in your service, Sire. My noble family, while not a Major House, is on the ascent due to our well-run business operations. If my humble request is granted, Sire, be assured your daughter will live in sufficient splendor." He scanned the ornate chamber around him. "Though not at the level of Kaitain, of course."

He listed his military accomplishments, his conquests, and emphasized how well he got along with other officers in the Imperial fleet. He described how his troops held him in high esteem, as if that might bolster his case with Shaddam.

Slipping a glance at her father, Irulan detected thinly veiled distaste as he listened. She could tell he had something else on his mind, some way to capitalize on this situation?

Irulan had always known she would be a pawn in Imperial plans, eventually married off to the most important and advantageous suitor. But she was twenty-six, well past the age when she'd expected to be betrothed. The Padishah Emperor had turned down many proposals over the years, though he sometimes strung along the supplicants . . . as he was doing now. She knew he would ultimately deny Zenha, since Shaddam would never let his firstborn princess marry a mere military commander, regardless of his accomplishments.

Why didn't he just turn the man away now, and be done with it?

She knew of seven previous applicants for her hand—and possibly many more in quiet back-channel requests. How long could her father draw out the game, using her as a lure to make treaties and political gains?

What benefit could Fleet Captain Zenha possibly bring to House Corrino?

She looked at her sister Chalice, a vapid, pie-faced young woman, who wore a sapphrite-studded necklace and matching bracelets. Chalice was enamored with trappings over substance, and she always overdressed for daily business at court. But her sister didn't have the capacity to deal with a complex web of nuances and subtleties; Shaddam's second-born daughter simply adored pretty things. She accepted superficial gossip as fact, and shifted her opinion according to the last thing she had heard.

On the opposite wall, however, Wensicia watched with razor focus. She was four years younger than Irulan, and far prettier than Chalice. Her heart-shaped face and lavender eyes veiled a sharp mind. Wensicia was a student of Imperial history and politics, absorbing and retaining information in clear contrast to the shallow Chalice.

Now both of her sisters sat in obvious disbelief, each reacting in her own way. The background noise of the court audience grew progressively louder.

Zenha was still making his case when the Emperor raised a hand and interrupted him. "A most impressive story. I will give your application due consideration, Fleet Captain. For now, report back to your unit and await my formal decision."

The officer seemed surprised, but guardedly optimistic. He gave a graceful bow, then marched out of the chamber with perfect strides, his chin held high.

As he departed, Irulan whispered to her father, "Why did you even listen to him?"

"I have something interesting in mind, daughter. We must make a point of this." He patted her forearm. "Do not worry yourself over the matter."

Despite hearing this, Irulan could not help feeling uneasy.

One must pay for anything of great value, but few understand the extent of the cost.

—Fremen saying

Arched above the dunes, the sandworm plowed across the open basin. The long wake it left in the sands only hinted at how far they had come.

Chani sat secure on one of the rough ring segments. Although any offworlder would have considered it a horrifyingly dangerous situation, most Fremen learned how to ride a sandworm by the time they reached adulthood.

Higher up on the huge head, her half brother stood tall, his spiked boots anchored onto the fleshy surface. He grasped ropes attached to the ring segments by hooks, using a long goad to steer the beast.

Stilgar, the Naib of Sietch Tabr, crouched beside Chani, ready with a spreader to expose the sensitive flesh should the worm turn unexpectedly. Behind them sat her father, Liet-Kynes—the Imperial Planetologist, but also revered among the Fremen because he shepherded the long-term dream of turning Arrakis into a verdant paradise.

Chani, Jamis, and Khouro had returned to the Fremen community only a week ago, excited with their recent adventure, but now her father called them to another important mission. It would be Chani's first time meeting with a Spacing Guild representative.

Although the others rode in determined silence with nose plugs in place, Liet-Kynes kept his mouth exposed so he could express his observations—always teaching. "For all his years on Arrakis, my father never learned how to call a sandworm."

Stilgar glanced at his companion. "Umma Kynes was so focused on important, world-scale matters that he did not trust himself with everyday things."

"I never knew my grandfather," Chani mused.

Liet looked at her. "He was not a warm and loving man. His priorities lay elsewhere."

At the head of the sandworm, Khouro made a scoffing noise, implying that he didn't consider Liet, his stepfather, to be a warm and loving man either.

Ignoring him, her father glanced across the empty dunes. "Continue this direction for now, Liet-Chih, but soon we take a more easterly course to reach the meeting place."

"I know where I'm going." The young man used the goad to shift the worm's path. "And *Khouro* is my Fremen name. Liet-Chih is not a name I chose." His resentment made Chani uncomfortable.

Liet did not respond to the antagonism, but reminded him with great patience, "Your mother chose the name of Liet-Chih for you."

That comment silenced her brother, and the worm churned on across the basin.

For generations, the Fremen had paid an exorbitant amount of spice in a secret deal with the Guild to keep observation satellites out of Arrakis orbit. It kept the prying eyes of the Harkonnens and Imperial spies from watching Fremen activities in the desert. Not even weather satellites were permitted, to the consternation of the spice harvesters, the planetary governors, and the rest of the Imperium. The Guild, however, did not deign to answer questions. They honored their deal with the Fremen—so long as they were paid in spice.

The Fremen had made the deal to keep outsiders ignorant about their plantings, the faint green coloration in portions of the isolated wasteland. Such lack of observation also aided the Fremen in their desire to be free of the hateful Harkonnens.

Among the tribes, it was considered an honor to deliver the Guild spice bribe. As the daughter of Liet, Chani was held in certain esteem among her people, but she had also proved herself an accomplished fighter who excelled in desert skills. She had participated in raids against Harkonnen operations, spice factories, carryalls, scout ships. So, despite her youth, her respect had been earned.

Khouro eventually drove the first worm to exhaustion after crossing the basin. Near sunset, Chani and her companions gathered the packages of condensed spice and their Fremkits. After Khouro moved the hooks and Stilgar retracted the spreaders, they sprang off the weary beast as it wallowed into the sands. Out in the open dunes, there was no obvious shelter, so they deployed their camouflaged stilltents and camped, resting and eating.

"I will set another thumper when the second moon rises," Stilgar said. "If we ride through the night, we can be at the meeting point by dawn, a day early."

"We will be ready in case the Guild representative betrays us," Khouro said.

Liet frowned at the young man. "The Guild has honored our agreement for generations. Why would they betray us now?"

"Who can understand offworlders?" Khouro said, then shot a glance at Chani. "Especially the Guild, with its freaks and strange ways." They had not told anyone what they'd seen at the spice blow, not the dead Navigator, nor the unmarked marauder ship.

As they ate honeyed spice wafers and sipped water from catchpockets in their stillsuits, Liet mused, "The first time I delivered a spice bribe, I was about your age." He glanced at Khouro. "I went with your father, Warrick. He and I were such great friends . . ."

With another quiet snort, the young man turned away.

Showing no reaction, Liet turned instead to his daughter, although she had heard the story before. "Warrick and I rode through the storm zone to the south polar regions. Back then, the Fremen used an intermediary with the Guild—Rondo Tuek, a water merchant with extraction operations in the cold zone." He grimaced. "That man betrayed us and betrayed the Fremen, which is why we now deal directly with the Guild. During that trip, the two of us found Dominic Vernius and his group of smugglers—"

Khouro cut off his stepfather's familiar story. "I'm going to sleep." He crawled into his stilltent and sealed the sphincter opening.

Now Liet did let his disappointment show, but he said nothing. Chani was annoyed by her brother's rudeness.

Stilgar broke the awkward silence. "We should all rest."

When they had settled into their places for the night, Chani lay in the enclosed darkness of her tent, listening to the sound of her own breathing. She used the privacy to sort her thoughts, excited about their mission, considering what she would say to the Guild representative. She also mulled over her half brother's attitude. Khouro had confided in her many times, but she didn't agree with his opinion of Liet. What had happened to Warrick, his real father, long ago was not Liet's fault.

Chani wished her brother would direct his anger toward the Harkonnens. She loved and respected her father, although even she was uneasy with Liet's partial loyalty to the Imperium. Chani was too pure a Fremen to understand how he could serve two masters, but he was still her father.

She snatched a few hours of rest before Stilgar woke them. Chani sipped the water that had gathered in her catchpockets, then crawled out of the tent. After packing up, the four of them moved off to find a good dune, where they could plant a thumper and summon another worm.

They rode off under the starlight toward the rendezvous point.

ONCE IN PLACE, they hid in the rocks and kept watch, but the Guild sent no scouts early, nor did they attempt any trickery.

During their quiet waiting time, Khouro and Stilgar tossed tally sticks into a pocket of sand in the rocks. Chani knew the game made her father uncomfortable, reminding him of how he and Warrick had decided which one of them would have shelter from an oncoming sandstorm.

At the appointed time, a bulbous, reflective vessel appeared in the sky, similar to the ship that had secretly deposited the Navigator body. Liet and Stilgar stood out in the open, waving to draw the ship's attention.

In the jumbled line of rocks, the large vessel hovered silently above them. Chani smelled ozone in the air, felt the vibrations and energy of suspensor engines. An open platform dropped down to meet them, holding three gray-uniformed Guildsmen. Two were bald androgynous figures with unsettling features, misaligned eyes, and distorted skulls that looked as if someone had softened the bones and resculpted them.

The man in the center, though, was quite tall and handsome, with dark hair and heavy eyebrows, a strong jaw, and a prominent widow's peak. "I am Starguide Serello. I have come to accept your payment."

Taking charge, Liet gestured to the heavy packages they had brought. "Our payment is freely given for the services the Guild offers to the Fremen."

The Starguide gave a slow nod. "Our long-standing business relationship is mutually acceptable. In exchange for spice, your people may keep their secrets and their privacy."

"And our security," Stilgar said. "We want no prying Imperial spies, no Harkonnen eyes."

Khouro brashly interjected, "We want no prying Guild eyes either."

Serello directed an empty gaze at her brother. The side of the man's mouth twitched, turning part of his face into a grimace, as if he had lost control of those muscles. "The Guild has no interest in spying on your people."

Chani felt she had to support her brother. "We've seen what you do in the desert. You think the Fremen don't know, but we witnessed it ourselves."

Serello turned his strange gaze toward her, and Liet stepped closer, breaking the awkward silence. "This is Chani, my daughter."

Her brother broke in. "And I am Khouro. Recently we watched a Guild ship out in the open desert, the Fremen desert. We saw you drop the body of one of your own on top of a pre-spice mass."

The dour Starguide replied in a flat voice, "Our ships do not go into the desert." The two silent and misshapen Guildsmen looked at him but said nothing.

"But we saw one," Chani insisted, "and it had the look of a Guild vessel. It placed the corpse of what we believe was a Navigator, just before the spice blow. We saw it."

"You are badly mistaken." Serello was implacable. "We come here to receive your spice payment, and then we leave." His two silent companions stepped off the hovering platform and retrieved the packages of compressed spice.

Stilgar flushed with anger, insulted by Khouro's rudeness.

Liet said, "My daughter and stepson go many places, but the desert holds its mysteries. Plumes of dust and heat ripples in the air can create false impressions."

Chani was indignant that her father wouldn't support her claim. "We did not see a mirage. You left a Navigator's body on the sands, where you knew it would be destroyed in the spice blow. You didn't expect any Fremen to witness it, but we were there."

The two Guildsmen finished loading the spice onto the hovering platform. Serello acted as if she had said nothing at all, and Chani could see the annoyance build on her brother's face. Before he could take ill-considered action that might endanger the agreement with the Spacing Guild, she blurted out the last piece of information.

"Perhaps we were mistaken," she said without sincerity. "But if you did not drop a Navigator body in the sands, then you would not be interested to know that after your ship departed and before the spice blow occurred, another unmarked vessel swept in and stole the body."

A flare appeared in Serello's impenetrable eyes as if a tiny star had exploded there.

"I saw it, too," Khouro insisted. He turned toward Liet and Stilgar. "And so did Jamis. Would you disbelieve all of us?"

The Starguide's jaw muscle twitched and distorted one side of his face again. He addressed Stilgar and Liet, as if the two young people weren't there. "Your payment has been received. We will arrange to pick up the next quarterly allotment when it is time."

Taking the packages of spice, the hovering platform rose back into the bulbous ship. Chani watched the Guild vessel rise away into the dust haze of the sky.

Now, she would have to explain everything in full to her father.

Little is known about the formative years of Irulan, first daughter of Shaddam IV, other than comments about her intelligence and beauty. After her training at the Bene Gesserit Mother School, the golden-haired Princess became an astute student of Imperial history, with a talent for documenting the events of the day. In particular, she chronicled the lives of her father, the Emperor of the Known Universe, and of Paul Muad'Dib. As time passed, Irulan became an unofficial historian and biographer, submitting her writings to Imperial scholars for editing and additional commentary. Later historians would praise her keen observational skills and writing abilities. Most telling, even her father valued her as an adviser.

—*A History of the Imperium*, updated and annotated

At a private luncheon the following day, the Emperor explained how he planned to deal with the upstart military officer who had asked to marry the Princess Royal. In the throne room, Shaddam had quelled his instinct to quash the man, even arrest him for the insult. He had other plans.

"There are opportunities in such a situation," he said to Irulan with a paternal smile. "It is important that we send a message, so no one else dares to make such an unworthy suggestion again."

She observed and learned, which was what the Emperor asked of her.

At lunch, he instructed her to attend that afternoon's meeting in the Imperial War Room and dress as if she were going to a gala event. "Fleet Captain Zenha will also be summoned to the meeting, and he needs to be aware of the significance of the assignment I will give him. You are a prize he can only attain through the success of the mission."

Irulan covered her irritation, knowing it was just a ploy, but the answer would give the impertinent officer hope, and a goal. And she was sure success would be as unattainable as she was. Her father would plan it that way.

Nevertheless, she returned to her suite and enlisted the ladies-in-waiting to dress her with glitter, finery, and ostentatious fabrics. She selected a light makeup treatment to enhance her green eyes and patrician features, and wore a jeweled pearl-white gown that was simultaneously modest and enticing. Her coiffed and braided hair was adorned with a white-gold tiara encrusted in priceless stones. In all, it was intended to make her look breathtaking—and all the more desirable.

To emphasize her importance (as her father had instructed), Irulan timed her arrival in the War Room so that she entered last. The windowless room was large enough to accommodate fifty attendees, with a long central conference table and viewing screens mounted on three walls.

When Irulan passed through the door, leaving her group of courtiers behind, she looked at no one, betrayed no emotions, and took a seat opposite the Emperor. For this important meeting her father wore a gray Sardaukar uniform with a Burseg's gleaming black helmet. Protocol ministers and military advisers sat in other chairs; Sardaukar guards lined the sides of the room. Chamberlain Ridondo was busy arranging documents on Shaddam's right.

At the front of the room, Fleet Captain Zenha was made to stand at attention until Irulan took her seat, whereupon he bowed and chose one of several available middle chairs. As he placed his officer's cap on the table in front of him, he acknowledged the Emperor, "I am honored to be here, Sire."

Shaddam didn't answer. The helmet on his head and the fierce Corrino lion insignia made him look quite stern.

Cool and formal, Irulan acknowledged the young officer, knowing that he must be curious about what the Emperor had in mind by summoning him to the War Room. Obviously, this would be a test of Zenha's worth, though surely the assignment would be rigged against him. Love often did turn into a form of war.

Shaddam gave a terse signal to begin the meeting, and the lights dimmed. Projected images appeared, split among the three wall screens—an astronomical chart on one, videos of violent street unrest on another, even the burning of a ruling family's palace.

"This is planet Otak in the Ramiran star system," Shaddam explained. "It is a resource-rich world with mining, crystals, rare foodstuffs, and pharmaceuticals." He sniffed. "Navachristian fanatics have taken over the government and vowed to secede from the Imperium."

Zenha gave an angry snort. "An outrage!"

"Their leader, a former mercenary who calls himself Qarth, says that I, the Padishah Emperor, hold no authority over their world. I tell you this:

The people of Otak are uncivilized and poorly equipped, but they are an embarrassment to the rule of order, a thorn in my side."

Seeing where the briefing was heading, the Fleet Captain brightened. "Someone should teach them a lesson, Sire." He didn't apologize for his outburst. In fact, Irulan thought he looked more polished and confident than before. "Otak must be brought back in line with the Imperium."

Her father offered a sharp smile. "And you are the person to do so, Fleet Captain Zenha—or I should say, you could be that person."

The officer's eyes glistened with the opportunity. He glanced at Irulan. "It would be a clear demonstration of my abilities, Sire."

Shaddam nodded. "You will lead the task force and take care of the Otak rabble."

Zenha blurted out, "I shall be in command? Are you giving me a promotion, Sire?"

"Promotions must be earned."

Zenha could barely contain his excitement. "I will accept my promotion only after I clean out that nest of vipers. When I return successfully, perhaps . . . as a colonel?"

Irulan could tell her father was struggling to control his anger. "You have not yet met the challenge."

Despite his obvious ambition, she found the officer likable. In the past day, she had studied his background and realized that he could indeed become even more successful and influential in the future, given his charisma and leadership abilities—if he had support, a career nudge at the right place and time. Irulan wasn't certain her father saw it, though.

Zenha was clearly enthralled with the opportunity, his face flushed, a hint of perspiration on his brow. He looked at her in a moment of hope, but she responded with a blank face, offering no encouragement.

"That's enough for now, Fleet Captain," Shaddam said, tapping his fingers on the table. "Chamberlain Ridondo will provide a complete dossier of all that is known about Qarth and his fanatic rebels. Prove yourself to me, and then we'll discuss if you've earned the right to marry my daughter."

Zenha leaped to his feet and saluted. "I won't let you down, Sire!"

Nodding, the Emperor removed his helmet and placed it on the table. "I know you won't, young man."

But the Fleet Captain wasn't finished. "I have my own talented division, officers and soldiers I've led for years on various missions and maneuvers. They will be perfect for this mission. How many additional Sardaukar will I command for the assault?"

Shaddam scowled. "No Sardaukar at all. I require these special troops here to protect the capital world. You will not need them for such a minor operation anyway—unless you are less skilled than you claim? With the ships and personnel in your own task force, you should be able to mop up a few troublesome rebels." His expression darkened further. "If you cannot take care of this little flareup, then I will send in my Sardaukar to clean up the mess."

Zenha's brown eyes flashed. "I understand, Majesty, and I accept your challenge with gratitude." He picked up his officer's cap. "I will not fail this test."

The Emperor gave him a dismissive wave. "That will be all. Read the dossier my staff provides." He smiled at the officer without sincerity. "Now be on your way and get ready."

The Fleet Captain turned for a final bow as he exited the War Room. "Thank you for this opportunity, Sire." He looked at her. "And Princess."

After Zenha had left, a protocol minister closed the door behind him.

"This will teach him not to behave so impertinently," Shaddam muttered with a chuckle, "if he survives the mission."

Though she understood what her father was doing, Irulan found his smile cruel.

We are each wise in our own areas of expertise, and we build impenetrable barriers to keep others safely ignorant.

—STARGUIDE SERELLO, Spacing Guild internal advisory memo

Though he traveled from system to system representing his masters in the Spacing Guild, Starguide Serello considered Junction to be his home.

The spherical buildings, silver monoliths, and bustling transport-authority portals thrummed with activity, a fantastic array of geometric shapes to emphasize mathematical precision. Huge cubes signified the main business and administrative offices, distinguishing them from other buildings. Large melange silos, the Guild's own stockpile, were kept at the edge of the expansive landing field that had recently held the spectacle of the Navigator's funeral.

The dead Navigator . . . Serello's great-grandfather.

His primary office was a penthouse enclosure with curved, prismatic windows. He stared out at the view and contemplated the troubling comments from the Fremen youths on Arrakis. As a Starguide, his enhanced brain used myriad neural pathways supplemented by Guild training, as well as specialized Mentat instruction, which was quite rare for a Guildsman.

Serello's thoughts were a tapestry of decision trees, of choices and possibilities, some of which led to dread consequences. He was still grieving in his own way after the death of the revered Navigator, not only because of the loss to the Guild, but because his great-grandfather was the last of the Serello bloodline to have achieved the transformation. Others in the family tree had tried and failed—his grandfather, parents, sister, and himself.

Statistically, most candidates did not succeed in becoming Navigators, so Serello should have felt no shame. He should have been proud of the position he currently held. Very few became the Starguides who served as the Guild's public face—intermediaries who operated within the framework of the Imperium, House Corrino, and CHOAM, since more advanced Guild intellects could not communicate with mere mortals.

After prior generations failed, Serello and his sister had been the family's next hope. In their younger, malleable years, they had studied intensely, learning Imperial history all the way back to when Norma Cenva became the first Navigator. Serello had absorbed all information the Guild considered necessary, and his sister had been even better at performing complex computations.

Sufficiently prepared, he and his sister were taken to a sterile facility, where they saw Mentat observers sworn to serve the Guild, Suk doctors with medical apparatus, and hopeful Guild officials who assessed the candidates as if they were no more than laboratory specimens.

A Starguide had also been there—the first one Serello had ever seen in person. Such beings were inferior to Navigators, but still powerful, influential, and revered. At the time he had never imagined the possibility of becoming one. Serello wanted to be a Navigator like his great-grandfather—the pinnacle of human evolution. He wanted to use his mind to see countless paths into the future.

He and his sister had been sealed into separate transparent cylinders, naked. Standing there nervously, Serello had blocked out the statistical fact that most candidates failed the test, and many perished. There had always been rivalry between the siblings, while both were confident they would become Navigators. They would restore family honor after two generations of failures.

In a monotone, one of the Guild observers had announced, "Your body will be exposed to a high concentration of melange gas. This is to judge your physical suitability for longtime immersion and metamorphosis."

Next to him, a grim Suk doctor added, "You undergo this test voluntarily."

Serello had acknowledged this, as had his sister. Then the rush of potent, acidic cinnamon poured in through ducts in the floor. Orange vapors engulfed him. He had sampled melange in small doses to enhance his mental acuity and sharpen his physical reflexes, but this was an assault on his senses, on his mind. His eyes burned, and tears streamed down his face, but he could see nothing. The spice gas smothered him.

At first, he had tried to control the effects, but more and more permeated him. He couldn't exhale. He choked. The spice gas filled his lungs, his nostrils, his throat—then it began to roar through his bloodstream. His brain lit on fire with thoughts he could no longer contain. He coughed and retched as he tried to escape, but the melange was everywhere like ignited fuel. His brain screamed, and he could feel his neurons twisting, tangling, spreading out like spiderwebs, and questing.

Then each path ended in a black dead end, and the darkness reflected back, filling his mind with oblivion. He'd lost consciousness.

When Serello came back to himself, the spice gas had been drained from the cylinder. He slid down the curved wall as the hatch opened to spill him out. Standing over him, the Suk doctor wore a sour look.

At a second station, two workers dragged a limp body out of a cylinder. His sister. Her once-confident eyes were red with hemorrhages. Her mouth was slack with a drool of vomit down the side of her face. She was dead.

Seeing her lifeless, Serello's mind had been afire with thoughts, and he'd realized that the loss of his sister was just a data point, one infinitesimal incident in a vast galaxy. He'd channeled his emotions elsewhere as his thoughts blossomed.

He blinked up at the uniformed Starguide observer, who stared at him with dark, strangely distant eyes. "Did I pass the test?" he croaked. "I can feel the difference! My mind's capacity is so much increased. Will I be a Navigator?"

The Starguide gave him a withering frown. "No, you failed, as I once did. Your body rejected the quantities of spice necessary. But unlike your sister, you survived. And if the millions of unused neural pathways in your mind are now accessible to you, perhaps you can be useful to the Guild after all."

Serello had been forever altered by that day, and he learned how to excel in ways that benefited the Guild. Eventually, he became a Starguide and reached his own pinnacle. . . .

Now he stared through the transparent walls of his high office. He scanned a report of space traffic, saw that a Heighliner had just arrived. Through the prismatic window film, he watched an enormous globe-shaped vessel descend into the heart of Junction. An official diplomatic transport. Serello was expecting it.

The wall thrummed with a message for him. "CHOAM Ur-Director Malina Aru has arrived and will be escorted by transport pod to this building."

"I am ready for the appointment," he replied. He waited for his counterpart from CHOAM.

Because of the extreme importance of treaties between the CHOAM commercial empire and the intertwined transportation obligations of the Spacing Guild, the Urdir had come here personally. In his own position, Serello could countersign the treaties. A Starguide could *see* connections and possibilities, political chain reactions, consequences of the simplest choices. He knew all the Heighliner routes, and he understood how CHOAM worked.

His office was expansive but austere, with an oval polished desk that rippled like quicksilver and could display any image. Though Serello preferred to stand, he extruded a pair of comfortable chairs made of polymer foam and pliable metal. He summoned refreshments, because the Guild kept a dossier on the Ur-Director's preferences.

A subtle signal on the transmission wall informed him of Malina Aru's approach. He fashioned a practiced smile to be ready for her.

The Ur-Director of CHOAM, one of the most powerful people in the Imperium, came without an entourage, accompanied by only two pets—needle-furred spinehounds, fiercely loyal and deadly.

Serello was not intimidated. "Ur-Director, I am pleased you came here in person. A face-to-face meeting shortens the distance between personalities."

"All business arrangements are personal, Starguide, whether we recognize it or not," she said. The slender Urdir had short, dark brown hair, perfectly in place. Her dark brown business suit was unadorned, but cut from the most expensive fabric. She moved with an animal grace. "I could have sent my son Frankos as my representative, but it has been some time since I visited Junction."

"The CHOAM President would have been an acceptable delegate," Serello said. He drew upon the information he had studied. "You have a daughter as well, who serves as the Baroness of House Uchan? And another son?"

Malina frowned. "Frankos is the CHOAM President. My other son, Jaxson, is being trained on Tanegaard, and we expect to find an appropriate CHOAM position for him. My daughter is well settled in her own role." She gave an impatient sniff. "But let us not concern ourselves with family trivialities. We have business."

His jaw muscle twitched, a neurological aftereffect of his exposure to the spice gas in the testing tank. The Suk doctors could find no direct cause for it and suggested that it was in his mind. He focused on controlling it.

Refreshments arrived, but Malina paid no attention to the silent servants, nor did she partake in any of the food or drink. "Shall we get down to the matter at hand?"

Serello waved a hand over the polished desk surface, and images of the documents appeared. "The treaties, as negotiated by our delegates. Ready for us to place our marks."

Malina inspected the crisp holographic projections. "Acceptable. CHOAM and the Guild will continue as always."

Serello affixed his digital genetic signature. "As will our coordination with the Imperium."

Malina frowned. "The Imperium is an old construct, but it serves its purpose for now . . . even if House Corrino has outlasted its usefulness." Without further comment, she affixed her genetic imprint.

The Urdir's unexpected words made questions expand in Serello's mind. *House Corrino has outlasted its usefulness?* He had heard of a quiet rebel movement circulating throughout the Imperium, the Noble Commonwealth—outspoken critics making plans to dismantle the Corrino stranglehold. He decided to pay more attention now.

Only after the documents dissolved again into file storage did Malina indulge herself with a sweetened pastry. Serello noted which one for future reference.

But the Ur-Director was not done. "There is one other matter I wish to bring to your attention—an item of information freely given, in hopes that the Guild will remember and reciprocate."

"The Spacing Guild has a long memory," Serello said. "Now, I am intrigued."

Malina patted her pets, stroking the needle fur. "These spinehounds, Har and Kar, are perfect specimens, the result of much trial and error in the Tleilaxu breeding tanks."

Serello's jaw muscle twitched at the mention of the vile Bene Tleilax. "You do business with *them*?"

"Out of necessity—as does the Guild. Have you ever . . . touched a member of their race?"

He suppressed a shudder. "I have had minimal dealings with Tleilaxu Masters, but as a Starguide, I must represent the Guild to all peoples. A year ago I met a Master Giblii. Those people avoid being touched by outsiders, whom they call 'filthy powindah,' but Master Giblii made a point of shaking my hand." He recalled the loathsome grayish skin, the oddly abrasive touch of the Tleilaxu Master's grip that made Serello feel as if his palm had been scraped. "He said he was doing me a great honor by allowing the contact. Why do you ask?"

"I have had my own private dealings with the Tleilaxu," Malina said, "and not just to procure spinehounds. One of the Masters made an unwelcome offer to CHOAM, which I declined."

Serello was instantly alert. "What offer?"

"He asked if CHOAM might find a market if the Tleilaxu offered an alternative to a Navigator's mental and prescient abilities."

Serello could not keep the shock from his face. "An alternative to our Navigators?"

The Ur-Director gave him a coy smile. "I thought you might wish to know. Are the Tleilaxu attempting to create their own Navigators?"

"That . . . would not be possible," he said, but it was an automatic response.

Having triggered her dangerous land mine of information, Malina Aru turned to leave, calling her spinehounds. Now Serello suddenly remembered the two Fremen youths claiming that a mysterious ship had stolen his great-grandfather's body.

It was common knowledge that the Tleilaxu performed horrific genetic experiments. They had been known to grow gholas in their tanks . . . clones from the cells of a dead body.

Perhaps a Navigator's body was one of their top projects.

Consequences ricocheted like fireworks through his mind. Serello barely managed to partition his moods and maintain his calm diplomatic appearance as he bade the Urdir farewell.

Ceremony and formality are essential elements in Imperial order.

—EMPEROR SHADDAM CORRINO IV

Floating inside a suspensor-bubble high over the capital city's central plaza, Irulan and the Emperor observed the spectacular military parade, flowing ranks of uniforms with variations of the basic crimson-and-gold Imperial colors and banners of numerous houses, army divisions, fleets, brigades, planetary and sector military detachments. Tamed (or drugged) beasts plodded ahead of the marching troops to add to the spectacle.

These uniforms represented the primary worlds that comprised the vast Imperium, with minor changes allowed according to the varied cultures, but all under the banner of House Corrino. It had been the same for millennia, a sprawling and often ceremonial Imperial defense force like a security blanket over the galaxy.

Small observation drones flew over the marchers, operated by Imperial security units. High-resolution images appeared on the walls of the Emperor's floating observation bubble, but Shaddam peered through the plaz to see with his own eyes.

"I so love these ceremonies," he said to his daughter. "This demonstrates the magnificence of our Imperium, so many components keeping the peace and stability."

But Irulan noted something different in this show of force. Despite the colorful spectacle and the sheer number of marching troops, she sensed a grudging participation among these people, a weakness in the ranks, and that might ultimately affect her father's hold on the throne.

In the streets around the Imperial plaza, gaudily uniformed noble officers marched in front of their units, some of them waddling due to their weight. All wore medal-bedecked dress blouses with gilded ceremonial swords at their sides—weapons few had ever used in combat. One elderly nobleman—long past his prime, if he'd ever had one—could not even walk on his own, and his bulk was carried in a chariot drawn by stallions. Making a fool of himself, he clumsily flourished his sword from side to side.

Shaddam navigated the bubble over the parts of the parade and exhibition he wanted to see. Above the crowd noises, Irulan barely noticed the smooth purr of the suspensor mechanism. They drifted along the main parade route and descended for a better view.

Despite her father's enthusiasm, she expressed her concerns. "I'm not so certain, Father. Look at those foolish marching nobles. They are clearly not in fighting shape, and most of them have no experience in command. They secured their ranks through bloodlines or bribes, not skill." She wasn't convinced he would heed her advice, though.

He frowned at the criticism. "Not that subject again. You'd rather see commanders like that upstart Zenha? Those officers below have the most impeccable breeding."

She persisted anyway. "I respect you more than anyone, Father, but during the decades of your reign, and your father before you, our Imperial military has grown languid, overconfident, and content. Too many commanding officers are bloated and rich, merely figureheads. They wouldn't be worth anything in a real fight."

If the two of them hadn't been sealed alone in the observation bubble, Irulan never would have spoken up. But she had studied Imperial military history in great detail, and feared that her father did not see the larger picture. The Princess had even discussed such concerns with her sister Wensicia, who was also fascinated by military annals.

Shaddam touched her shoulder reassuringly. Patronizingly. "You worry too much. I've already taken this into account. I cannot upset the Landsraad and all those families who think an honorary military rank is their due, but your point is well taken. At Count Fenring's suggestion, whenever a division is led by an obviously unqualified noble military officer, I have installed a competent second officer who rose through the ranks on merit. Rest assured that the pompous fools are supported by strong, capable officers."

"Such as Fleet Captain Zenha," she said.

"Yes, the upstart." Shaddam frowned. "He is too ambitious, I fear, and we must clip his wings."

Irulan could not allay her concerns. "That may help behind the scenes, Father. But in a military parade such as this, your subjects see only these uniformed blockheads on display." She pointed. "Just look out there."

His brow furrowed as he expanded the view of two front-line officers who could barely keep up with the rest of their troops. "Well, perhaps some of them should not be in parades in the future."

"And who do the competent officers report to, if they are merely in place to prevent embarrassing missteps from their superiors? Where do they file a grievance if their own commanding officers are fools?" Irulan asked.

"They follow the chain of command."

"Competent officers should report directly to you, Father, and not be in fear of speaking the truth. As it is now, their unqualified superiors can whitewash whatever their subordinates say."

Though the Emperor scowled, she could see that at least some of her words were sinking in. Even he could see the unintended buffoonery.

But Irulan knew that his mood would turn if she kept pressing, so she changed the subject, cooling the tension with superficial matters. Ultimately, she and her father were close, and he usually did consider her advice. But the Padishah Emperor had numerous advisers, and not all of them agreed with her. Imperial systems were entrenched and difficult to change.

She had done some investigating on her own, noted that Fleet Captain Zenha had taken his task force assignment seriously, sending requisitions and preparing Imperial troops to put down the Otak uprising. She wondered if her father would actually give him a chance to succeed. From what Irulan could see from the briefings, the fanatic rebels did not seem like a particular challenge. She wondered what else her father knew that he did not put in the formal mission briefing.

In her private rooms at the Imperial Palace, she had delved into Zenha's bloodline, his lackluster house. She was impressed by the heritage of honor she found—loyalty to one's comrades in battle as well as absolute allegiance to the Emperor. This intense sense of connection often led to heroic, selfless acts. Even with his lesser family name, he had indeed excelled, but clearly he was aiming too high when he tried to marry the Princess Royal.

Having studied various personality types with expertise the Bene Gesserit had taught her, Irulan felt that Fleet Captain Zenha had the potential to become a hero if properly groomed.

Zenha fit neatly into his niche in the modern Imperial military—a highly competent second officer, performing duties that his noble superior could not. Did that make up for the harm caused by the figurehead officers, who were often foolish and bullheaded? Could the steady decline of the Imperial military be reversed? Maybe with people like Moko Zenha.

But there was only so much even an Emperor could do in an entrenched system, and for the firstborn princess, it was even more true. Irulan was the eldest daughter, a bargaining chip. She had even less influence over history.

What if Zenha did manage to put down the Otak rebellion and returned victorious? It didn't seem that difficult a task. What would her father do then, if the young officer claimed his promotion and her hand in marriage?

Four security drones surrounded the observation bubble, and Shaddam smiled at her. "Note that I have heightened the protection around us, here and throughout the palace, until the Otak rebellion is resolved."

"Very wise, Father. Very wise, indeed."

Escorted by the drones, the Emperor guided the observation bubble to the top of a palace tower, where he brought it to rest. The drones buzzed off, and Shaddam was excited to prepare for a gala military banquet after the parade. Irulan knew she would endure many hours of inept, drunken officers telling one another how great they were.

Our people have a long memory for pain—and we keep score. For every harm inflicted upon us, we return that pain tenfold, no matter how long it takes. The Harkonnens, and whoever comes after them, will lose.

—LIET-CHIH, also known as Khouro, Fremen writings

As the wrecked spice harvester burned, black smoke mixed with rust-colored dust, too far away for Chani to smell the spice. Even so, she felt a great sense of triumph.

Jamis whooped from the top of the dune, where they observed the glorious sight. Not caring how much noise he made, he waved his crysknife, slashing invisible enemies. He pranced about, knowing that his vibrations were insignificant compared to the rumble of the collapsing harvester and the thump of detonations beneath its massive treads.

Shading her eyes in the bright sun, Chani could see tiny figures of the spice crew scrambling out of escape hatches. They looked like scorpions startled from under a rock.

Their massive machine had driven along the rich spice field, sifting out the melange, vomiting away undesirable dust and sand. The people were arrogant and confident, acting as if they owned all of Dune. Until they had hit the mines.

Now they were not so powerful, not so safe, defeated by a handful of Fremen. Chani did not understand Imperial economics, nor did she value their solari coins, but she knew this attack would cost the Harkonnens dearly. And she and her companions would keep making the oppressors hurt.

Three patrol 'thopters raced in, their articulated wings buzzing in the air. The aircraft would try to evacuate the spice crew as they ran from the burning spice harvester.

Chani scanned the line of dunes, watched her brother and two companions, Rona and Adamos, rise from where they were camouflaged in the sand. They held rocket launchers, and Khouro coordinated their shots. The bright flares of projectiles spat out from the tubes and arced toward the oncoming aircraft.

The first missile struck the underbelly of the lead 'thopter, and the flyer turned into a dying, burning bug in the air. Wreckage fell toward the ground.

The second projectile struck the wing assembly of another 'thopter. The aircraft huffed and coughed in the air, spinning. The pilot could not regain control, and the flaming craft smashed down onto the damaged spice harvester.

Jamis let out another hearty laugh and grinned at her.

The third projectile missed as the remaining 'thopter swerved into evasive action, and then the vengeful pilot swung around to target where her brother and his companions had fired upon them. Even from a distance, the 'thopter's lasbeams strafed the dunes, leaving a line of glassy sand.

Chani yelled an unnecessary warning. Khouro dove to the side, as did the man on his left, but their other companion was cut in half by the beam. Since Harkonnens knew that Fremen did not use shields out in the desert, they were free to use lasguns.

While his companion scrambled to hide in the sand, Khouro raised his rocket launcher again and shot another projectile. This rocket struck the hapless 'thopter, blowing it out of the sky.

He and his surviving companion sprinted across the sands, instinctively using an erratic pattern of footsteps. Shai-Hulud would come soon enough and help them erase all trace.

THIS TIME, THEIR group had tried a new tactic—Chani's idea. When Harkonnen patrols spotted a large unmined spice field, the Fremen scouts knew that crews would come back with one of their huge harvesters.

So Chani and her companions made their plans. At night, aware that the factories would arrive the next morning, the Fremen had sprinted out onto the spice field. Digging deep, they planted a line of explosives across the path the factory would surely take. They buried the mines far under the sand, then retreated to take up their positions.

"This is an ambush the Fremen will talk about for years," Jamis crowed.

"Just one of many," replied Khouro. "And we will keep doing them."

Proud of her new tactic, Chani had told her father about it, thinking he would be pleased. Liet-Kynes was not a Naib like Stilgar; he didn't lead the tribes or mediate feuds among the Fremen. To him, all the people of Arrakis were an army for ecology.

His own father had reshaped the Fremen dream for Dune, but Pardot Kynes was a visionary, not a war leader. Liet-Kynes was different. He understood the violence that might be necessary to achieve their aims. House Harkonnen, CHOAM, the Spacing Guild, and the Imperial throne all depended on spice. All were parasites! Liet had raised Chani and even Khouro to be firebrands, active soldiers, but the most difficult task was to measure out balance and patience. To awaken Dune would require many generations.

She, Khouro, and their friends didn't want to wait that long, and so they struck blows where they could.

"We will make spice operations so difficult for the Harkonnens that they will leave Dune," she had told her father. "For every new spice factory they bring, we will destroy two, forcing them to flee in shameful defeat and leave us alone."

Liet had given her a proud but sad smile, shaking his head. "You've lived in the hard desert for so long, my daughter, that you don't understand *weeds*."

"Weeds are hardy plants that survive anywhere," Chani said, squaring her shoulders. "Is that not a good thing? Does it not help our plans?"

Liet sighed. "But weeds are not desirable plants, and if you pull one up, another grows in its place—one that might even be worse than the previous one. That is what you do when you attack the Harkonnens. Look what happened when Fremen fighters drove out House Richese long ago." He clucked his tongue. "That did not give us freedom—it merely brought in Harkonnens instead. What will happen if we get rid of them? The Emperor will bring in a new House that could be even more brutal."

Chani was disappointed that he showed no excitement for her new tactics. "Your attitude is defeatist, Father. If we do not strive for a better world, why would any of us bother to live at all?"

Hearing that, Liet-Kynes had given her a warm smile. "You speak the truth. Make your attack and do your harm, so the Harkonnens don't take us for granted. But as planetologist here, I am the one who has to deal with the consequences of your rash actions."

When all the preparations were made, she and Jamis had hunkered down in the sand and watched the spice factory lumber out on the desert. It moved toward the line of explosives. She did not consider this a rash action. She felt it was necessary.

At the proper time, the deep charges had detonated, shooting fire and smoke into the air right under the enormous front tread. The explosion damaged the big machine, but more importantly, the blasted pit in the sand was a trap, and the factory slid into it, wallowing and unable to move. More explosives breached its underbelly and ripped open the cargo chamber, spewing melange everywhere. What a glorious sight!

When it was all over, her brother and his surviving companion Adamos huffed up to join them, exhausted after running across the sands. Despite the energy of victory, Khouro hung his head. "Rona is dead from the cowards' lasbeams. We will retrieve her body when we pick up the pieces here." He swung his gaze toward the burning hulk and drew his crysknife. "But we can go now and slay some Harkonnen workers."

Jamis raised his own milky blade. "The sands are thirsty for blood."

Chani scanned the surrounding dunes, spotted oncoming ripples from the southeast. "No time. Wormsign." The others turned toward the ominous vibrations. "Shai-Hulud will have to finish the killing for us."

Jamis frowned. "I would rather have done this in a personal fashion, so I could see the terror in their eyes."

"Dead is dead," Chani said. "The Harkonnens will just bring in more offworld spice workers, more Harkonnen troops."

"Then we will kill more of them," Khouro said. "And more." He rammed his crysknife back into its sheath. "My arm will not grow tired."

The last fleeing workers spread out like ants, running as far as they could, but the desert was already churning in a deep whirlpool as the sandworm dug deeper for its attack. In the dry air, Chani could hear faint shouts of dismay and panic. The spice workers knew they could not run far enough, but still they tried. Even if a few managed to escape the sand vortex, then what would they do? Left alone and without resources in the deep desert, they would die slow, agonizing deaths.

Chani and her companions stood in the open and watched, none of them worried about being seen.

The churning sand began to sink into a crater with the wrecked spice harvester at its center. With astonishing grace for something of such tremendous size, the sandworm rose up, its maw open wide to swallow the offending machinery. The tiny black figures tumbled down the slope into the gullet. Shai-Hulud engulfed every trace of the invaders, closed its huge mouth, and slithered under the sands again.

"Bless the Maker and His water," Chani murmured.

Jamis picked up the prayer. "Bless the coming and going of Him. May His passage cleanse the world."

Khouro finished, "May He keep the world for His people."

They watched in solemn reverence as the sands settled back into the calm desert. Their desert, Chani thought. Fremen desert.

I have made many critical decisions in my life, and not all of them good. Those, I try to keep to myself.

—REVEREND MOTHER GAIUS HELEN MOHIAM

The Reverend Mother played two roles that were usually in harmony, but not always. Gaius Helen Mohiam served as the Emperor's Truthsayer, providing advice and identifying falsehoods, but she was also an emissary for the Bene Gesserit, performing high-level special assignments for the Mother Superior.

Today, she was focused on her latter duty. She intended to remind Shaddam's eldest daughter of her true loyalty and her duties, which she had been neglecting.

The old woman's long black robe rustled as she made her way along a central path into the Imperial gardens, her shoes whispering on slate pavers set in gravel. It was a cool morning, with thin clouds fleeting across Kaitain's pale blue sky.

Emerging from a section of ornamental trees where the path skirted a meandering brook, she saw Princess Irulan ahead at the edge of a miniature flower-filled meadow. In a white dress with black ribbons around the collar and sleeves, Irulan tossed tiny objects out in the field, one after another. Seeds? No, Mohiam saw they were rainbow butterflies that, once released, fluttered over the meadow to explore the flowers.

When the Reverend Mother greeted her, Irulan glanced up without being startled. Alert to her surroundings, the Princess had already been aware of her approach. Mohiam pressed her lips together in a smile, remembering the young royal student who had excelled in her teachings. "What are you doing?"

Even with the butterflies darting around in the calm garden, Irulan seemed troubled. She let out a slight sigh as she lifted a flat clearplaz container that held many more trapped butterflies. Irulan pressed on one end of the container, and a butterfly emerged onto her palm, opening and closing its wings before flying away. Mohiam noticed that many of the butterflies were motionless in the container. Dead?

"My sister Chalice did a bad thing, and I scolded her for it," the Princess explained. "She took this trap from the Imperial science lab and collected fifty-two rare butterflies, then placed them into suspended animation."

The Reverend Mother was surprised. "The Imperial science lab? Suspended animation? Chalice has never shown any interest in science . . . or any kind of complex thinking for that matter."

Irulan released another sluggish little creature. "She loves butterflies and says they're pretty." She shook her head. "I don't believe she meant any harm, but it disturbs me. I don't know where she got the idea." She continued setting the rainbow insects free. "Perhaps Wensicia put her up to it."

The colorful butterflies spread out over the little field, drawn to the flowers. Bees buzzed around as well, hovering, pollinating and moving on.

Irulan glanced at Mohiam. "Chalice wanted to release them all in her private quarters to impress her friends, then she was quite distressed when I told her the fragile creatures would not survive. I'm letting them return to their natural habitat."

Mohiam pursed her wrinkled lips. "They are just insects, child, with brief, transient lives. They would die in a few days anyway."

"But they are rare specimens, Reverend Mother, and should be protected as much as possible—even if only for a short time." The Princess released the last of the butterflies and, holding the empty trap container. she turned to the old woman. "We are just people, Reverend Mother—trillions of us across countless planetary systems. Our life spans aren't so long either, in a cosmic sense. It's a matter of perspective . . . and respect."

Mohiam remembered the deep philosophical discussions she'd had with this young woman during her years on Wallach IX. Unlike Shaddam's other daughters, Irulan had received the deep indoctrination into Bene Gesserit ways. "You are applying our teachings."

"I am trying to be a good princess and a wise adviser." She glanced up at Mohiam. "Within the narrow parameters of what I'm allowed to do."

The two strolled into a willow grove, where they enjoyed the shade. Irulan seemed relaxed. "I always value our conversations, Reverend Mother, but I know that you never come to me for an idle chat." She let the unspoken question hang in the empty pause.

Mohiam chuckled. "Someday I will surprise you . . . but you are correct. I am a very direct person, with little patience for small talk."

Irulan smiled. "After the blur of nuances and subtleties in tedious court conversation, I rather like that you don't waste my time."

"I don't do this to be liked." Mohiam kept her face stony, then softened her expression. "Rather, I come to remind you of your obligations to the Bene Gesserit." She lowered her voice, as if concerned about listening devices. "You received our most careful training and advanced indoctrination so that one day you might become a Reverend Mother yourself. A princess of the Imperium who is also a Bene Gesserit Reverend Mother! Think of the possibilities."

Irulan's green eyes flashed with concern rather than anticipation. "That particular decision, ultimately, will be mine."

"True enough, but if we do not first give our approval, you will not have the option."

Irulan gave a resigned sigh. "By then, I will be married off to some lordling. Many decisions in my life, maybe even most of them, are made by others, for political reasons. Not *my* reasons."

"Or the Sisterhood's," the Reverend Mother said. "You may feel like a pawn, but we have ways to adjust the game board so you can be moved wherever we want you to be."

Irulan seemed frustrated. "It's not pleasant to be a pawn of the Sisterhood."

"But you *are* the Sisterhood, child. Never forget that." Mohiam's voice became sterner. "I've observed you, and lately you seem distracted from your duties for the Mother School. You have not submitted reports for weeks, and you rarely wear our formal robes or insignia to remind the court of your ties to the Sisterhood."

Tossing her head back, Irulan said, "I am the Emperor's daughter, the Princess Royal. That role is a more ostentatious and colorful one, requiring certain actions and appearances. But I know full well that I am also bound to the Sisterhood."

Mohiam stared hard at her, measured her own words. "I understand split loyalties myself, but the Sisterhood must always come first, regardless of your other duties."

Standing under one of the feathery willows, Irulan turned to face the Reverend Mother, her eyes flashing angrily. "With all due respect, what have I done to earn your criticism? How have I raised concerns about my loyalty to the Bene Gesserit?"

Mohiam decided it was best to be blunt. "You spend an unusual amount of time with your father, seeking to please him too much."

The young woman's expression was incredulous. "Too much time with my own father?"

"With the *Padishah Emperor.*" Mohiam sat on a bench under the tree, while Irulan remained standing, indignant.

The Princess took a moment, obviously considering her words. "My duties pull me in different directions—political duties, spying for the Sisterhood, maintaining the prominence of House Corrino, remaining available for my own marriage prospects to make the most significant match."

"The Sisterhood must have input in your choice of husband." Mohiam's voice was cold. "We will look at the bloodlines and compare with our breeding index."

Irulan's expression darkened, but she composed herself and closed her eyes, obviously running through calming techniques. "Each day, each moment, I attempt to pay equal attention to my duties as a Sister and my duties to my father and the Imperium. As a natural circumstance, from time to time I may focus on one more than another. Review the long arc of my behavior, and you will see that it is balanced."

"Balanced to an outside observer, perhaps. But your unquestioning loyalty should be to the Sisterhood."

"I am as loyal as you are."

"That's saying a great deal and close to impertinence." The old woman's sternness shifted to a soft smile. "However, you make a very good point about the long arc of your behavior. Perhaps I don't need to send a warning to the Mother School. *This time.*"

FROM THE PALACE steps, Wensicia watched her eldest sister approach, walking alongside the slightly shorter Reverend Mother. The two spoke in low voices as if engaged in some conspiracy. Soon Mohiam left her, choosing a different path out to the courtyard, while Irulan approached the stone steps where Wensicia stood. She gave her sister an automatic smile.

"The old witch doesn't look pleased," Wensicia said. "Another homework assignment for the Sisterhood?"

"Reverend Mother Mohiam never looks pleased," Irulan said. "Besides, I am done with my schooling on Wallach IX."

Wensicia followed her as she tried to walk past. "You know I have a great interest in the Imperial military. I've done some research into your would-be suitor, studied his service record. Would you like to know what I found?"

Irulan looked at her younger sister in surprise, her interest piqued. "I studied his record as well."

Wensicia continued with an edge in her voice. "Despite his humble background, Zenha is quite impressive. He has the chance for a very illustrious career and the ambition to accomplish it—if he gets the right opportunities."

"You could be right." Irulan paused to stare up at the enormous palace looming above them. "But your interest is a waste of time. Fleet Captain Zenha and I will never marry."

"He is not suited to you?" Wensicia saw the answer in Irulan's eyes, which revealed a moment of regret.

"It does not matter what I think. Father would never allow it. As the Princess Royal, I am too valuable a bargaining chip to be wasted on some military officer from an unimpressive house." Resentment filled her voice.

"Considering his skills and potential future, if he had the right connections and the right catalyst, that officer could become a significant figure. Perhaps our father is too dismissive of him. Moko Zenha would make *someone* a competent and admirable husband."

Irulan immediately caught her meaning. "You?"

Wensicia sniffed. "I'm twenty-two, and by tradition, the third Imperial daughter marries a military commander, while the firstborn—you—is matched for political reasons. And the second daughter, Chalice, usually goes to some wealthy merchant or CHOAM administrator."

"That is the tradition." Irulan's distracted smile showed her amusement. "Chalice would be starstruck with any gaudy nobleman who showered her with fine things." She glanced into the shadows of the entryway, and her expression warmed. "I am already twenty-six. Father is obviously in no hurry to marry me off—but I can wait."

Wensicia watched as her sister glided ahead to meet a handsome, discreet young man who emerged to accompany her. Irulan's male concubine, Aron, had been waiting for her in the main parlor. A muscular man with a wide, pleasant face, he was a head taller than the Princess Royal, who was herself a tall woman. Wensicia knew that Aron was very protective of her, though his role required him to studiously remain in the background. As he escorted her into the palace, neither of them gave a glance in Wensicia's direction.

Feeling dismissed, Wensicia quelled her annoyance and impatience. Of the five Corrino daughters, only Irulan had undergone full Bene Gesserit instruction on Wallach IX, a secretive program that Wensicia suspected included sexual training and the art of seduction. She and Chalice, and their younger sister Josifa and certainly not little Rugi, had received none of that instruction, only the ordinary curriculum from tutors here on Kaitain. In-depth Bene Gesserit teaching was not considered necessary for any of the Corrino princesses with the exception of the Princess Royal, but Wensicia was hungry to learn, and she wished she'd had the same opportunity. She buried herself in her own studies, seeking to compensate as much as possible.

The Mother School kept a hundred or so male consorts, and Irulan had grown fond of one of them during her years of training. Upon returning to Kaitain, she had brought Aron with her, to a minor scandal that quickly died away. Now he was the Princess's available male companion, as was accepted practice, though Irulan did not allow herself to become too attracted to him. If Wensicia so chose, she could have selected her own male concubine from the local stock of candidates, but so far, she had no interest.

Remaining behind in the palace foyer, Wensicia considered ways to increase her own possibilities, so she wasn't just a middle daughter of five, an afterthought of House Corrino. She did love her sisters, but could not help resenting Irulan's close bond to their father, as well as her obvious importance to the Sisterhood.

Wensicia was determined to find her own way. She was tired of waiting for whatever crumbs her father and Irulan tossed her way.

IRULAN LED ARON to her private dining room for a late breakfast of guinea hen eggs, spicy green sausages, and melon. She appreciated the male concubine's reassuring presence, and she occasionally used him as a sounding board for her ideas.

As she sat across the table from him, she admired his physique, high cheekbones, strong chin, alert blue eyes. He had an intelligent and insightful mind. The Mother School selected their male candidates carefully. Aron had learned to understand Irulan's moods well; now, he obviously recognized her preoccupied thoughts, so he offered quiet company and nothing else. It was one of the reasons she liked him; he knew how and when to give her space.

Though Aron was a reliable companion, as she needed, she had never imagined anything resembling love between them. The Bene Gesserit had taught her to protect herself from those emotions. That was not why she kept him.

As she ate, Aron reassured her. "I am grateful to serve you, Princess, and I will do so as long as I continue to hold your interest." His voice was warm and carefully modulated, and she noted hints of the training he had received.

Irulan responded as a friend to another friend. "You still hold my interest, Aron, and you keep me from unnecessary distractions by other men."

He served coffee, placed spice pastries on a plate for her. "Yet, I always want to improve."

She looked past him out the wide open windows to the gardens and the grassy hills beyond. Despite the calm opulence around her, Irulan felt pulled by storm winds in several directions. The Emperor, the Sisterhood, court expectations, the needs of her sisters, even this military officer who wanted to marry her for political reasons.

Wensicia's suggestion of being a better match for Fleet Captain Zenha, so that she could mold and uplift him into an important figure, was a good one. Unlike Chalice, Wensicia was smart, even crafty in troubling ways. Was it narcissism, or naked ambition?

Irulan had much in common with her middle sister and needed to make sure that she was her ally—otherwise, Wensicia might be a dangerous foe. Her disarmingly benign appearance and pleasant cooperation at court were only a façade—and though she could not influence Irulan, Wensicia had been known to manipulate others, especially Chalice.

Irulan wanted to be her own woman, and she intended to maintain and enhance her personal dignity and pride at all times, in all of the significant decisions she made.

More battles are won with cunning than with a cudgel.

—A saying of the Bene Gesserit

Specially commissioned by the Imperial defense fleet, the Heighliner entered orbit over Otak. As the huge vessel loomed above the intransigent world, Fleet Captain Zenha's task force dropped out of the hold: frigates, dreadnoughts, destroyers, and three large troop carriers, emerging as if the Guild ship were giving birth to them. The warships descended in battle formation, their weapons panels flashing on.

Zenha had studied the briefing materials about the Navachristian fanatics, so he knew the basic situation, as well as the population centers of Otak, the flash points of unrest from the rebels, and the lackluster ruling noble family. But that was all dry, secondhand data. He had developed an action plan in his private stateroom during the voyage, but wanted to get the lay of the land before implementing any specific orders.

The Heighliner remained in orbit above, not interfering, not dispatching any shuttles or commercial ships that would normally be scheduled for Otak. The Guild remained carefully, sometimes maddeningly, neutral in all conflicts in the Imperium.

During the controlled descent in his dreadnought flagship, Zenha matched what he saw below with the materials he had read in the briefing dossier. The capital city of Lijoh had been built on a strategic point on the western coast, and an unusually large number of smaller cities spread out to the east and southeast across an agricultural plain. Growth to the north was bounded by a mountain range, honeycombed with lucrative crystal mining operations. Much farther to the east were dense forests, whose trees and bark extracts provided rare pharmaceuticals. Because of

Otak's significant natural resources, Emperor Shaddam could not ignore a revolt here.

The Minor House that ruled Otak for more than a century had recently been ousted by the fanatics. The briefing packet stated that the nobles had withdrawn from Lijoh and retreated into self-imposed exile, gone into hiding with the family atomics secured.

Surely, the fanatics realized the Imperium would retaliate decisively. The Navachristians had interdicted all interstellar commercial operations, but normal trade would open up again as soon as Zenha rooted them out. Once his assault force secured the rebellious cities, he would send in a separate unit to find and, if possible, rescue the ruling family.

Zenha's task force continued to descend in comm silence, though once it was in positon, the Fleet Captain would make a public declaration. According to the battle plan, he directed his troop carriers to land in three strategic sites around the outskirts of Lijoh—by the spaceport, in an industrial and warehouse zone, and in an area of parks that the ruling family had established.

On board the flagship, his second-in-command, Leftenant Pliny, sat beside Zenha, watching video feeds as they came in. "So far, the spaceport is the only area that seems to have defensive weapons." The leftenant's contralto voice sounded almost feminine.

Zenha and Pliny had served together for nearly two years now, and Zenha felt a close bond with the slender young man. Pliny had been raised in a poor family, but was quite brilliant and had proven himself worthy of his Fleet Captain's trust, though he often paid insufficient attention to personal appearance. Even now, bushy blond hair stuck out from beneath his officer's cap.

"Focus more of our support firepower against that area," Zenha said. "Neutralize those defensive batteries before they become a problem."

"Oh, they won't become a problem, sir." Pliny put out the order, and a wing of gunships altered course to close in on the spaceport. When the approaching vessels laid down suppressing fire on the entrenched rebel facilities, the Lijoh defensive batteries responded with little more than a whimper and a fizzle, inflicting hardly any damage.

With the spaceport defenses neutralized, Zenha's vessel set down near the capital city. The other two troop carriers were already down and unloading, and as his flagship flew low over his forces, Zenha was pleased to watch his soldiers, groundtrucks, and mobile cannons pouring out to secure Lijoh. It was a very efficient and inexorable operation. Emperor Shaddam would be impressed.

As their commander, Zenha was proud of his fighting teams, though he would have liked a legion or two of Sardaukar for shock and awe. Even so, he anticipated an easy victory. The Emperor hadn't really given him much of a challenge, but he hoped that a quick success here would pave the way for marrying the Princess Royal. That was more important to his career and family legacy than a formal military promotion.

In the past five years, Zenha had been involved solely in defensive operations as an officer in the Imperial fleet, establishing measures to prevent lone assassins or terror cells from threatening the Corrino family. Prior to that, he had served as a junior officer on assault squads to discontented worlds, eliminating any firebrand leaders before their unrest grew too great. In each of those preemptive strikes, at least a few Sardaukar had led the charge, with Zenha's forces going in afterward for mop-up operations. He was familiar with Shaddam's take-no-prisoners, zero-tolerance retaliations, and he knew they kept the Imperium secure.

This assault on Otak was different, though—a test of his abilities. Zenha was leading the operation with no Sardaukar support, but his intelligence briefing indicated that the fanatics numbered only in the hundreds. He did not need the Emperor's elite troops.

As Zenha coordinated his task force, his dreadnought closed in on the city, while the rest of his force encircled Lijoh. The rebels had taken over the capitol building, and ousted the ruling family, but he needed to have more detailed information before he tightened the noose. Prudently, he dispatched small plainclothes reconnaissance teams to investigate, coordinated by officers who had experience in infiltration.

The Navachristians weren't going anywhere.

After landing the flagship and setting up a command hutment, Zenha began receiving video feeds from the ground operatives. The unruly religious rebels had occupied the government buildings in the city center. Guards wearing crudely tailored uniforms with prominent Navachristian symbols patrolled the entrances, on high alert.

Zenha saw without surprise that Imperial markings had been removed from government buildings, statues of Shaddam defaced. Disturbingly, recon patrols reported that the ordinary citizenry seemed haughty and defiant as well, spitting on broken statues as they walked by. Others shouted curses against the Imperium.

So, Zenha realized, the unrest extended beyond the extremists. Maybe it would not be so easy to extract a few troublemakers and return Otak to Imperial rule.

"Troop carriers unloaded, sir, and all soldiers prepared to move against the city center," Pliny reported. "They await your signal."

Zenha paced restlessly inside the command hutment. "Hold back half our forces and keep them around the perimeter of Lijoh in case we need a second wave. Tell the others to prepare for a hammer blow. I intend to do this quick and hard."

Pliny dispatched messages to the units, moving troops and equipment into position. Zenha's soldiers converged on the city center from different directions, using ground vehicles for part of the way, then proceeding on foot. They encountered little resistance as they closed the net, no more than token weapons fire that soon dissipated. Rebels and unruly citizens melted away, opening up clear routes to the capitol. Numerous buildings bore prominent, freshly painted Navachristian symbols.

Watching the ease and speed of the advance, Zenha felt exhilaration mixed with unease. He sent an alert to prepare the second wave waiting on the perimeter, while his initial assault force of four hundred fighters marched into the capitol zone. They broke into teams and entered the government buildings, meeting some resistance, taking prisoners, and marching them out into the streets.

Most of the large government buildings, though, held no rebels at all, even though surveillance overflights had clearly shown them to be present.

"Where are they hiding, sir?" Pliny asked.

Zenha opened the comm to the advance team's ground commander. "Find the leader of the fanatics and arrange for me to speak with him. What was his name? Qarth." He paused, then added with a smile, "Oh, we need to learn the whereabouts of the ousted noble family, rescue them from exile."

"We can track them down later, sir, after we deal with the primary threat." Leftenant Pliny's brow furrowed. "If you deign to speak with the rebel leader, does that not give him undue prominence? His actions make him guilty, and he must be executed."

"My instincts say he won't resist the chance to grandstand before an Imperial audience, and the invitation might flush him out. My instincts have never failed me. Have our advance crew broadcast the announcement so that everyone hears, then go yourself, find the bastard, and set up a meeting."

Pliny departed on a groundcycle with a military vehicle escort, speeding toward the city center. Half an hour later, the adjutant's voice contacted the command hutment. "We have identified Qarth's location, sir, though I have not seen him in person. The leader is barricaded inside the former parliament building, with no hope of escape. I demanded that he send out any hostages as a gesture of good faith." Pliny paused. "He replied that we could have the burned ashes of the former rulers, if we wish."

Zenha's heart sank. "The ruling family? But our intelligence says they are safe in exile."

"Qarth claims the entire noble house has been assassinated, even the small children murdered. He could be lying, but he seems to be flaunting the act as a matter of pride."

Zenha drew in a long breath. "That is a significant flaw in the information we were given." His brow furrowed. "That also tells me much about Qarth's personality. I see no rational way to deal with such a man."

Pliny continued, "The man refuses to talk with you anyway. He says that you are too unclean for him, and that all Imperials are beneath him."

Zenha sighed. "Return to the command hutment, Leftenant. There will be no negotiating. I'll send the second wave of troops into the city center for a full assault."

While waiting for his adjutant to return, the Fleet Captain dispatched his assault teams into the capitol zone for a full sweep. But this time when they charged the government buildings, they found no sign of any rebels. After combing the empty structures, scouts discovered a network of underground passages.

Zenha muttered, "Like rats in the sewers. This is going to require a more thorough assault than I anticipated."

When Pliny returned, the second-in-command gave a quick debriefing, then as he glanced at the recon screens, Zenha suddenly recoiled in alarm. He looked at the readings scrolling up from sensors the scout teams carried with them. "Radiation detected in the capitol building? Is that where the noble family stored their atomics? Right here in the city?"

A new voice suddenly broke over the open comm band. "I, Qarth, shall bask in the glory of the light rather than the shadow of Imperial corruption." He paused, as if to let the import of his words sink in. "That is all."

"Damn!" Zenha's blood turned to ice. "He's taken control of the house atomics! He lured us into the city center." He hammered down on the comm, activating the troop frequency. "Withdraw! This is a trap. All personnel return to your ships immediately!"

Pliny looked around the hutment, barked orders of his own to a smaller group. "Return to the dreadnought! Troops, back aboard the flagship!" He flashed an urgent glance at Zenha. "Fleet Captain, we must get you to safety."

Zenha resisted as his junior officer dragged him by the arm. Shouting, the soldiers raced back to the flagship. The second wave of soldiers at the city perimeter retreated in perfect formation. "Get aboard your troop carriers! Take off as soon as all personnel are loaded!"

The core assault force raced out of the city center, but were far behind the other soldiers. Zenha ordered one troop carrier to remain on the ground for them. Though sickened, the Fleet Commander was rushed aboard his flagship by his command crew. Even before he had made it to the bridge, the dreadnought rose from the ground.

The Navachristian leader hadn't spoken again, but his threat resounded through the city. "Would he really use atomics, sir?" Pliny asked, his face flushed as they finally reached the bridge. "It makes no strategic sense."

"A fanatic leader doesn't have to be logical—that is why they're called *fanatics*." Zenha felt tension building in the air, saw the eerie emptiness of the city center. He yelled his reluctant orders. "All troop carriers! Get away as soon as possible!"

The three large vessels were only half-filled, waiting for the assault groups to retreat. The flagship rose up and away, leaving the abandoned hutment on the ground outside the spaceport. More warships lifted away, but the bulk of the Imperial force kept loading soldiers at the perimeter.

Suddenly, the sky over Lijoh lit in a white-white flash. Seconds later, even though they were kilometers away and ascending rapidly, the blast wave slammed Zenha's flagship and knocked him sprawling across the deck. Instinctively, he threw an arm across his eyes to shield against the atomic flash. He groaned in dismay and pain as he and his bridge personnel were thrown about like leaves in the wind. His ankle caught on a chair stand and twisted, but he was in too much shock and horror to feel his injury. Another officer helped him up, and they all stared at the now-filtered screen.

Pliny's voice sounded thinner than usual. "Fleet Captain, despite your orders to only have one troop carrier on the ground, none of them managed to launch in time. All . . . all personnel in the main task force presumed lost."

Fierce waves of fire rolled over Lijoh, and a boiling pillar of smoke and ash climbed into the sky from the city center. When filters resolved the images and blocked the blinding glare, Zenha saw the disaster. "They wiped out their own capital city, rather than surrender! All those people!"

His left ankle throbbing from being tossed about, Zenha slumped into his command chair, head spinning. The Emperor's intelligence report had been filled with misinformation on the unsecured family atomics and the level of fanaticism from this splinter group.

"Reports!" he snapped. "I want damage assessment reports."

The numbers were agonizingly slow to come in. Most of the ships in the assault force had been caught in the nuclear shock wave. Of the 4,000 troops he had brought with him, he would return to Kaitain with only 248, most aboard his flagship. No other capital ships had managed to escape.

After Qarth's martyrdom and the obliteration of Lijoh, angry sparks of rebellion—planned ahead of time?—were flaring up in other cities across Otak, but he could do nothing to put them down right now. He didn't have enough personnel or other assets. His task force had been gravely wounded.

He could not imagine a worse outcome. His career lay in ruins like the city below, his reputation destroyed, and thousands of lives lost. His soldiers, the fighters he loved!

How could he have been sent here so woefully unprepared? He had studied every detail in the dossier, but it had been incomplete, even criminally flawed, and he'd been given inadequate support for his mission. If only he'd had a Sardaukar division, or a clearer assessment of this rebel movement.

He realized those all sounded like excuses. *He* had been in command. *He* was Fleet Captain. The blame would be squarely on his shoulders, a crushing blow.

Some memories last longer than a lifetime, and significant actions can have repercussions for centuries.

—REVEREND MOTHER RAMALLO, Sietch Tabr

Back inside the cave community after their attack on the Harkonnen harvester, Chani was surrounded by the smells of home: the thick musk of bodies, the sharp hint of bitter cinnamon, lingering chemical derivatives from base melange material converted into plastics, fabrics, even explosives. The Fremen sietch design provided ventilation, but moisture-sealed doors locked the air in. It was different from the open breezes out on the sands, but comforting in its own way, even when stale.

Right now, with the news of her mother's condition, Chani needed to feel comforted. There wasn't much time.

She heard the chatter of voices, Jamis and Khouro boasting about their exploits. The women, weaving fabrics in the sietch, sang traditional Zensunni songs. An old man played a stringed instrument he had purchased in an Arrakeen bazaar, though he had never spent money on lessons.

Without taking time to converse with other members of the community, Chani went directly to her parents' living quarters. The rough rock walls were adorned with woven hangings. On a low table rested an expensive ornate coffee service Liet-Kynes had obtained from traders.

The sietch's ancient Reverend Mother sat watch inside the chamber by the bed. When Chani entered, Ramallo straightened from her cushion on the stone floor. She wore an expression of grave concern. On a low bed, Chani's mother lay deep in sleep.

When Ramallo rose, she flinched with body aches. The old Reverend Mother's blue-within-blue eyes showed sadness as she glanced at the gaunt, ill woman, then back at Chani. "We have done what we can to make her comfortable. She sleeps now."

"But does she rest?" Chani smelled strong aromatic herbs and incense, chemical infusions wafting up from the teacup next to the bed.

"She will rest soon enough," said Ramallo, and Chani nodded.

Faroula was decades younger than the sietch's Reverend Mother, but looked exhausted beyond her years. Her face was hollow and her mouth slack, as if all the life and youth had been drained from her.

She had been a striking beauty at Chani's age. A holo-image still adorned their quarters, because her father reverently kept it there. As a young woman, Faroula had attracted many men, flirting and tempting them with saucy behavior, but she'd always had clear thoughts and made wise decisions. Liet had been one of those suitors, as well as Khouro's father, Warrick, and each man had married her in their time.

Now Faroula had very little time left.

Chani looked at her mother in dismay, thinking of the sickness that spread inside her like an invading army, despite all the healing herbs and potent melange in her diet. Spice could not cure everything. Faroula was still young, but the wasting disease did not care.

Old Ramallo murmured a blessing and left the chamber, pulling shut the woven hanging at the door to give them privacy. Chani did not speak, but merely watched Faroula sleep, not wanting to disturb her in her bone-deep pain. Yet the teenager was also thirsty for every possible moment with this woman who had given birth to her, who had raised her and taught her to be a Fremen woman, while others taught her to be a Fremen fighter.

Kneeling on a cushion, Chani tenderly stroked her mother's forehead, pushed aside a strand of brittle hair. Faroula once had a thick head of raven-black hair, but much had fallen out. As Chani regarded the sunken cheeks, drawn lips, and shadows around painfully closed eyes, she still pictured her mother as beautiful. She could imagine why her father and his best friend had accepted the challenge of a sandworm race across the open bled, just to win her hand. . . .

As if sensing her presence, Faroula stirred, and her eyes flickered and opened, staring into emptiness for a few long seconds, before they focused on Chani. A smile crossed her dry lips, and the expression of pain lessened. "Ah, daughter, you are not a dream. You really *are* here."

Chani squeezed her mother's hand, though the answering grip was weak. "I am not a dream, Mother. I'm here, with you."

"You are always with me, child . . . as I will always be with you. Remember that when I am gone." The frail woman squeezed harder.

"Let us talk about *now*," Chani said, avoiding the discussion of Faroula's imminent death. Her mother stirred, and the young woman helped her sit up. Her body felt like an empty bag of rattling bones that weighed almost nothing. Chani propped cushions behind her.

"Give me my tea." Faroula flicked a finger toward a medicinal cup at the bedside. "It makes me feel better. My own herbal recipe . . ." Chani lifted the cup so her mother could take the smallest of sips, all she had the energy to do. Faroula sighed with relief. "I was the best herbalist in Sietch Tabr for generations. I wrote down all my discoveries, all my mixtures." Her voice rose in intensity. "They did not help with this damned sickness, but I want to pass my knowledge on to others."

"We'll make sure everyone has your records," Chani whispered to her. "Your knowledge will be shared."

Her father had taken a scientific approach, documenting the pharmaceutical properties of the various plants, roots, and blossoms that Faroula used to treat ailments, and Chani and other young Fremen women would pass on the common knowledge.

She heard the rustle of door hangings and glanced over her shoulder to see Liet-Kynes arrive. On her deathbed, Faroula noticed him, and her expression lit up. "Ah, my love!" she said in her quiet, raspy voice. "If you and Chani are both at my side, then I must be near the end."

Liet's expression darkened. "Don't think like that! Fremen know one thing above all—never to give up hope."

Faroula let out a soft chuckle. "Fremen also know when to be pragmatic."

Liet pulled up a cushion for himself and sat next to Chani. He looked with loving care at his wife and whispered, "How is she?"

"She rests. I hope the tea gave her strength."

Liet clutched Faroula's other hand, since Chani refused to relinquish her own grip. "You were always so lovely; you still are."

"If all you intend to say are beautiful words, you may as well sing Zensunni poetry," Faroula said.

Despite his own obvious pain and grief, Liet-Kynes smiled at her. "I would do that, if you wish."

"No, beloved, I have heard you sing."

Growing more serious, Liet said, "Please, we must take any possible opportunity to make you well. I have Imperial solaris, could find a Suk doctor in Arrakeen. Maybe he can do a miracle treatment."

Faroula's expression became more pinched. "Offworlder medicine is not for me. I don't care about your science, beloved. Being so close to the Harkonnens would be like poison for me."

Chani knew they'd had this same discussion many times over the past year as Faroula's health declined. Now Liet said, "Science is what we use to change the face of Arrakis. Science is how we build the catchtraps and store water in our great cisterns, how we organize our plantings, how we terraform the desert. You believe in that dream, my love." He clutched her hand even tighter. "Why will you not listen to science now when it could save your life?"

Faroula's eyes drifted closed. "Because I understand things you do not, husband. I know what is inside me. I am the one who is dying, and I accept it. You must find acceptance as well." She opened her eyes and turned to Chani. "And you, daughter, must help him to do it."

"She doesn't want to go to Arrakeen," said a hard voice from the doorway. "If our enemies are the ones who save her, then is she saved at all?" Khouro entered. "I will support you, Mother, whatever you wish."

"Ah, Liet-Chih!" she said. "We are all here."

Chani saw her brother flinch as Faroula used his given name, but then his expression changed to one of desperation and love.

"I want to know that we have tried everything," Liet-Kynes said.

"She doesn't want Imperial medicine," Khouro insisted.

"You are all here . . ." Faroula said. "Do not quarrel. Let me have and hold this memory."

Chani touched the hilt of her crysknife, looked at her half brother and father, then relaxed her hand.

Khouro took a cushion on the other side of Chani, and all three of them remained at Faroula's bedside in their deathwatch.

THE FUNERAL WAS a somber procession through twilight as the skies turned purple and shadows deepened in the narrow, rocky defile. Faroula's body had already gone to the deathstills, and her valued water had been rendered for the tribe.

Chani and her brother walked together at the front of the group, with her father immediately behind them. The trio carried heavy literjons on their backs as they walked to the sealed cave deeper in the canyon. Eerie chanting in Chakobsa echoed off the high walls. The entire tribe mourned the loss of their revered companion and herbalist. Fremen men and women alike joined those carrying the water that had comprised Chani's mother, though she had wasted away for so long that very little of her was left at the end.

Khouro was dour and resentful, but Chani knew the young man grieved in his own way, as did her father. She wrestled with her own emotions. Faroula had wanted Chani to become a good, obedient Fremen wife, to learn the lore of herbs, to understand the songs of the women, the history and culture they had carried from generation to generation. Chani had indeed learned all those things, but she also felt the burn of the long-standing Fremen fight for survival and success, and vowed to carry on that struggle. Chani wanted to be more than just one thing—and her mother had respected that and loved her for it.

The procession reached the end of the defile, and Stilgar opened the camouflaged door with quiet reverence . . . out of respect not just for Faroula, but for what the grotto contained. Carrying the literjons of Faroula's water, Chani, Khouro, and Liet entered first. Stilgar activated glowglobes to illuminate the large polymer-lined cistern chamber.

Preserved and sacred, the still water in the reservoir was an unimaginable treasure that filled each Fremen with awe. The amount seemed incalculable, liquid wealth beyond imagining, yet every drop had been carefully measured and accounted for.

Stilgar raised his voice as the people gathered around. "Faroula was a woman of our tribe, an accomplished herbalist and much more. Out of love she bore two children. She worked hard in the sietch, and we all honored her kind personality, gentleness, wisdom, and readiness to help others. May her water remain among us and continue to flow." He nodded to Chani. She unslung the literjon from her shoulders and stepped to the cistern's intake pipe.

"Faroula was my beloved mother," she said, and the words caught in her throat, tumbling together as she thought of many different stories to tell: The time Faroula taught her how to weave patterns into spice cloth; how to play an ancient tune on a bone-and-brass flute. She remembered how Faroula had taught her the ways of womanhood when her monthly flow first started, then patiently described the joy of how men and women shared their bodies in lovemaking. Chani had already heard such explanations from other young Fremen, and she had struggled not to show her embarrassment, awkwardly letting her mother finish her dutiful maternal lecture.

But none of those stories came out of the young woman's throat now as the rest of the tribe watched and waited. After a long silence, Chani finally said, "She was my mother, and that reality holds all the stories."

She opened the literjon and poured its contents into the intake pipe, which fed into the cistern.

Khouro stepped forward next. "Faroula was my mother, and she was a dreamer. Once, she tended me after I ate toxic berries I found on scrub bushes. They gave me the flux and terrible cramps, but she knew the right herbs to ease me through it. The worst part of my ailment was that I wasted so much of my body's water."

Some of the Fremen chuckled. Her brother grew more serious. "She told me wonderful stories about my real father, Warrick." Hearing this, Liet-Kynes closed his eyes, looking uncomfortable. "She talked about how my father won her hand by besting Liet in a challenge. And she told me how much she loved my father, even after he returned to the sietch grievously wounded, half of him scoured away in a sandstorm. And how he died . . . following his own vision and drinking the Water of Life."

The Fremen muttered, and Chani was upset with him for bringing up such painful memories now. Yes, those were true stories of their mother, but Khouro's recitation now would only serve to enhance his own father, and hurt hers.

Finishing, Khouro said, "She was my mother." He poured his water into the intake pipe.

Now all eyes turned toward Liet-Kynes. Though the man had faced Imperial councils and stood before the Emperor's throne, though he had done business with Baron Harkonnen and Count Fenring, he now seemed diminished, crushed.

Her father came forward, cradling the last literjon of Faroula's water in his arms. "Faroula was my wife," he said, "the only woman I ever wanted—and the only woman Warrick ever wanted." When he looked over at his stepson, his face held love and patience, not resentment. "We would have done anything for her, and she called us to a challenge. Warrick and I raced sandworms across the desert to where she waited for us in a distant cave. Whoever got there first would win her hand . . ."

The words choked in his throat, and he took several deep breaths. "Warrick bested me, and the two were married. They had a son—Liet-Chih." He intentionally didn't use the young man's Fremen name.

"But Warrick and I remained best friends. We delivered our spice bribe to the Guild. We journeyed to the polar regions to bring our melange to the smugglers there, but one time the desert turned against us in a great sandstorm, and we were exposed, surely to die. We found a tiny shelter." Liet closed his eyes, as if drowning in the memory. "It was only large enough for one of us. Warrick and I threw gambling sticks. That time, I won . . ."

The grotto was utterly silent except for a faint drip of water. The Fremen didn't move.

"And after he died, Faroula accepted me as her new husband, her second choice. But she was always my first love, and I loved her with all my heart, just as I love the daughter we had." He held up the literjon, opened its sealed spout. "Faroula was my wife," he repeated. He stared at the container of water, as if the literjon had adhered to his hand and he could not release it.

Chani saw him trembling. He whispered so only she could hear, "I cannot bear to do it. It is too final."

She stepped forward to take the container out of his hands. "That's the Imperial side of you speaking, Father. This is a Fremen place and a Fremen need. Mother's last dream would be to have her water benefit the tribe. You know this."

Liet's fingers clung to the literjon, but then he released it to Chani. She poured the water into the cistern, and the rest of the funeral procession let out a sigh of relief.

Stilgar announced, "Faroula's body yielded twenty-eight liters and nine drachms of the tribe's water."

A watermaster came forward and extended a handful of metal rings to Liet in compensation for the water, but he just shook his head. "Put it into the treasury of the sietch. I have my sweet memories of Faroula, riches enough for any man."

Crestfallen, he turned and made his way through the other Fremen as if they were a gauntlet.

Long ago, a charismatic leader of Old Earth observed that life is not fair. He was right, and at a young age, he was assassinated.

—*A Study in Human History*, Imperial Archives file, coded

It did not seem fair to her.

Except for an accident of birth, Wensicia knew she was most qualified to be the Princess Royal, but in a cruel turn of fate, she was the third of Shaddam's five daughters: insignificant in the scheme of things, facing only a lackluster future, no matter her ambitions or capabilities. In importance, she was behind even the foolish Chalice, who would arrive in just a few moments for a "cheery visit" in Wensicia's private outdoor viewing box.

At least Wensicia had some level of influence over her weak sister, who was two years older, but far behind in intelligence, maturity, and motivation. Chalice had a stubborn streak and an often misplaced feeling of independence, and she required constant and careful handling on Wensicia's part.

Waiting for her sister to arrive, she sat at a bistro table that looked out on the grass-covered glowball field, where a match was about to begin. The viewing stands were full, and the crowd of well-dressed fans made a great deal of noise. Chalice loved such silly diversions.

Saddled players sat astride bulky but agile nar-beasts, maneuvering them into position. Each of the noble players, dressed in house colors and emblems, wielded a long stick to hit the small, bright glowball, a shining red orb that now floated in front of a uniformed official, who prepared to release it onto the field. The beasts grunted and snorted, flashed their deadly tusks.

Wensicia had changed into a crimson blouse, still feeling the sore muscles and perspiration from a rigorous exercise session. She kept herself in good shape, more athletic than any of her sisters. Irulan was also trim, though her good health came naturally to her without effort. Wensicia shook her head, chastising herself for resentment over what was not her sister's fault. She did love Irulan and the others, no matter how much they grated on her in different ways.

Outside the private viewing box, her personal servants greeted Chalice and escorted her to the table. Wensicia smiled and gestured for her to take the seat across from her, so they could both see the match.

As usual, her sister had overdressed, wearing a long black gown with a lace collar and an expensive rubine necklace, along with matching bracelets and rings. Her brown hair was secured in an elaborate bun, with a sparkling jewel in front.

Wensicia complimented her appearance, but added a bemused expression. "This is only a sporting event. You look like you're dressed for something more."

"And you are dressed for something less?" Chalice chuckled, pleased by her clever retort. Wensicia let her have that, to maintain her good mood. "One never knows when a charming suitor might see me in public," she added. Then Chalice gathered her skirt with a swish and took a seat at the little table.

Wensicia maintained a warm expression, though her thoughts soured. Emperor Shaddam and his key advisers would be the ones to choose her sister's best match; it would not come from any chance encounter at a social event. "You've been searching for some time for a husband, dear sister. Have you found your Prince Charming yet?"

Chalice responded with a sly smile. "Maybe."

Wensicia knew she had small delusions. "Would you like to tell me who he is?"

"Well, there is a wealthy jewel merchant I like." She held up one hand, displaying her rings and bracelets. "He admired these when he saw me wearing them. He is so perceptive he could name the planet on which each one was mined. He stroked my hand as he took a closer look, then even identified the maker who designed the settings! Who knows if he was telling the truth?" She giggled, then lowered her voice. "I think he was looking at me most of the time."

Out on the field, the glowball was in play, floating a meter off the grass and spurting this way and that. The mounted players were lined up, thundering away on the heavy beasts. The glowball had shifted to green now, and riders spurred their mounts. The first player, leaning forward in his saddle, reached the orb and struck it with his stick, attempting to guide it toward one of the four goalposts around the field.

Chalice squeaked in delight as a rival player closed in on him, using his nar-beast to slash with a curved tusk that cut the first rider's saddle straps. The crowd roared its disapproval as the rider tumbled to the ground, barely protected by a personal shield as he rolled away from the hooves.

Calmly returning to the conversation, Wensicia said, "I've seen you making eyes at CHOAM President Frankos Aru, even though he's twice your age. Whenever he comes around, you flutter close to him and say silly things."

"I do not!" Another smile. "Well, I mean for it to be enticing conversation. And he *is* very handsome."

Wensicia pointed to the stands on the right. "I believe he's in attendance today, right over there."

"I hadn't noticed." It was a lie of course, and Chalice tried to change the subject. "That Fleet Captain Zenha is handsome, too. Do you think Irulan will fall in love with him?"

"Father will never let him marry Irulan," she said, a little too abruptly. Privately, Wensicia thought the Emperor had been dangling the Princess Royal for his own purposes for far too long. "Maybe Zenha will be available for you after all."

Chalice took on a petulant expression. "A military officer? You think I want to lead an armed forces life?"

"More likely, Father will choose an important government official or wealthy merchant for you. Don't worry, you will have a perfectly acceptable match."

"I hope you're right." Her sister frowned, preoccupied, and leaned forward for a better view—not of the game, but of the stands, probably searching for the dapper CHOAM President.

Wensicia kept her thoughts to herself, but she found Fleet Captain Zenha attractive enough, or at least intriguing. She could envision ways to increase his importance so she could advance her own fortunes. First, though, she would need to get him promoted to a higher rank with far more influence. His house had little significance in the Imperium, but at least he had noble blood.

"I just wish I knew my future," Chalice said, and her voice had a whining undertone. "I'm twenty-four. I should already have my own household and be starting a new royal line . . ."

"Let me keep an eye out for you, Chalice. I'll see what can be done for you. I'll even speak to Father at the first opportunity." Seeing her sister's eyes light up, Wensicia gave her a reassuring smile. "I always have your best interests in mind."

As the crowd roared with another turn of the glowball game, servants delivered white tea in separate pots and little sweet cakes for the center of the table.

Out on the field, medics ran to help the fallen player, who had been injured despite the body shield.

Wensicia changed the subject. "I heard that Irulan was displeased about your butterfly trap." She frowned. "That did not go well for you. Do you know why?"

Flushing with embarrassment, Chalice stared at her tea, shook her head.

"Because you didn't ask me for advice. It seemed a lovely idea to you, but it was impractical and poorly executed."

Her sister looked like a child being scolded. "I promise to ask you next time."

Wensicia drove the point home. "And if you had asked me, I would have said what Irulan told you, that the butterflies will die if you try to keep them inside your apartments."

"Then I would have had dead butterflies all over my rooms, the furniture, the floor!" Chalice was kindhearted, Wensicia knew, but had no grasp of consequences or ideas that required very much scope. "I never wanted to hurt them."

Chalice sipped her tea, but did not take cake, as she was always vain about her weight. Wensicia did not point it out. The current situation called for reassurance, not criticism.

"The butterflies are free in the gardens again. You can see them whenever you like." Wensicia shifted the conversation again. "Even though Irulan was right this time, she does like to feel superior to us because she's the oldest. It's you and me against her."

Chalice chewed her lower lip. "She did scold me."

"I'm your only real friend in the palace. You know that."

"I know it. And I promise to do better."

Wensicia gazed out on the grassy field, paying little attention to the glowball match or crowd noises. Then, leaning across the table, she said, "And don't ever let anyone tell you you're not smart. I heard Irulan say that more than once. She had no right to make such awful comments—you and I don't say bad things about her."

Chalice looked perplexed. "Aren't we doing that now?"

Wensicia laughed. "See, I told you you're smart." She extended the plate of treats. "Have a little cake. I know this is your favorite."

Her sister demurred, then accepted one enthusiastically. Wensicia kept her expression warm and comforting, but she secretly resented Chalice for being closer to the Imperial throne by virtue of birth order rather than merit. At least Chalice was easily influenced. It was almost a game for Wensicia to see how much she could get her vapid sister to swallow . . . and do for her.

"Did you notice the new lady-in-waiting? Duchess Festa?" Wensicia watched her sister's eyes brighten with the potential gossip. "She's from the north country, but such a scandal! She has to work because her father squandered the family fortune with gambling losses. And I hear there is an issue of paternity . . ."

Chalice's eyes lit up. "Really?"

Wensicia smiled inwardly. Very little of this story of Festa and her father was true, but with each tale she told, each conversation she had with Chalice, she was grooming her sister as an important ally.

In the vast Imperium, very little is actually as it seems.

—PRINCESS IRULAN, unpublished notes

At the proceedings scheduled against Fleet Captain Zenha, Irulan asked not to sit beside the Golden Lion Throne. Shaddam was surprised at her attitude, expecting her to feel smug along with him, but he allowed her to sit in one of the two viewing galleries, so long as she was visible to the large audience, as well as the disgraced officer.

Irulan sat erect and alert in a modest white dress with a golden lion crest on the breast. As Princess Royal, she showed no emotion while analyzing every detail, as the Bene Gesserit had taught her to do.

In one of his impressive robes of state, the Padishah Emperor emerged from a side door after introductory fanfare, and the audience fell into an awed hush. He strode toward his Hagal quartz throne and seated himself before the large and restless audience. Irulan did not see the Emperor's Truthsayer present, nor was Chalice there—it was too early in the morning for her sister, she supposed—but Wensicia sat in the opposite observation gallery, keenly interested in the officer's fate. Also in the audience, she noticed the poised and lovely Lady Margot Fenring, wife of Count Fenring, the Imperial Spice Observer on Arrakis. Lady Fenring was spending a month or so at court, away from her husband, and she had been visible in many prominent events. She would not miss such a spectacle as this.

Given his disastrous and very public failure, Fleet Captain Zenha's punishment seemed certain, even preordained. But when the officer was summoned, he did not look like a disgraced commander whose battle group had been virtually wiped out. He strode forward and stopped in front of the dais, proud in his full dress uniform, his medals brightly polished. He had a slight limp, reportedly from an injury in the Otak debacle. One of his feet was medpacked and in a special boot.

The onlookers fell into a hush. Zenha's gaze was fierce as he glanced around the large room, then removed his cap and focused on the Emperor. From her near vantage, Irulan studied him carefully. She could not take her eyes from him.

While the officer maintained a stony expression, the Emperor allowed his anger to show, as if this man's failure were a personal affront. From the immense throne, Shaddam spoke in a withering voice. "I have been fully briefed on the Otak incident. I know your numerous, inexcusable errors, which cost the lives of almost four thousand soldiers. Your arrogance and miscalculation destroyed the capital of one of my worlds. The fanatics did not receive the justice they deserved, and the uprising continues across the planet." His nostrils flared. "At least you did not attempt to flee from justice, nor did you take your own life in a cowardly attempt to shirk responsibility."

"I make no excuses, Sire. I willingly accept any penalty you impose." He straightened even further. "But the disaster on Otak did not need to happen. My decisions and reactions were hindered by a lack of accurate military intelligence. I was not apprised of the number of rebels, nor that they had acquired atomics. We were given false information that the ruling family was safely in exile. My briefings did not suggest the level of fanaticism, nor that the Navachristians would use these forbidden weapons."

Shaddam stared coldly at him. "So on one hand you say you accept any penalty without excuses, and on the other hand you argue your case? You blame your ineptitude on inaccurate information? A good military commander should be prepared for everything, yet you failed to take uncertainties into account."

But Zenha remained resolute. "I mean only that after you have imposed your punishment on me, Sire, you should also investigate your own intelligence operatives. I was given grossly inaccurate information and provided with inadequate support." He drew a breath and spoke clearly. "I believe I was set up to fail, Sire."

His words resounded throughout the opulent throne room. Irulan sat straighter, considering. Was he accusing the Emperor? She knew her father wanted to dispense with Zenha's audacious proposal. Would he really have sacrificed so many loyal Imperial troops just to humiliate and destroy a promising officer? To intimidate any other unacceptable suitors who might come forward?

The Emperor glared at him, turning white. "Look at the courage you display now, but you didn't stay behind with your troops. You ran away while they died."

The Fleet Captain looked up. "Sire, if I could have given my own life on Otak, I would have done so. Once the presence of atomics was known and that the fanatic leader was ready to use them, I ordered an immediate retreat and evacuation. I saved the warships and crews that I could."

"No matter how you try to cast blame, Fleet Captain, Otak was no shining moment for your career. Since the insurrection continues on Otak, I must dispatch Sardaukar forces to take care of the rabble and finish the mission you left incomplete."

"With all due respect, Sire, I did request Sardaukar for backup, but my request was denied."

Shaddam raised a hand to command silence. "Your defeat has emboldened the rebels and increased their uprisings in outlying cities. Because of your failure, now we *need* Sardaukar in what should have been a minor mop-up operation!"

The Emperor summoned his Sardaukar commander, and a gray-uniformed officer marched in from the wings, where he had been waiting. Crisply attired and without a wrinkle in his clothing, the dark-complected man removed his officer's cap and took a position one step ahead of Zenha. "Major Bashar Kolona, Sire."

Shaddam rose from his throne. "Prepare your troops for an immediate punitive attack against Otak—exterminate all rebels and prepare the planet for resettlement with worthier citizens. Give no warning. Do not offer them the option of surrender. Just use overwhelming force to obliterate resistance, so we can remake Otak. Do you understand?"

"I will begin immediately, Sire."

The Emperor dismissed Kolona with a wave of his arm, and the Sardaukar marched off, leaving Zenha still standing exposed in front of the large, muttering audience.

Daring to fill the moment of silence, Zenha spoke. "Might I accompany the force back to Otak, Sire? In any capacity you command."

"You've already caused enough damage there," Shaddam snapped. He towered over the officer at the base of the steps below. "I must conclude your punishment here, before this audience."

The Fleet Captain looked up at the Emperor with dignified defiance, waiting. Through subtle indications, Irulan could tell he was a broken man. His hope seemed to be that he would be sent off to battle again, not in an attempt to redeem himself or salvage his reputation, but to die in a more honorable way than a public execution.

Shaddam's voice dripped sarcasm. "What to do with you now? Your request to marry my daughter is out of the question, considering that you have disgraced your uniform and ruined your reputation."

Zenha flinched, but remained locked in place. Irulan noted that Lady Fenring was watching him intensely with her blue eyes.

Shaddam descended the steps, pushing aside his ornate robes to reveal a ceremonial dagger at his side. The Emperor faced the unmoving officer and slid the dagger from its sheath. "You insulted me when you asked to marry the Princess Royal. You were obviously unworthy of my daughter, but I gave you a chance to prove yourself anyway—a chance you failed miserably."

Irulan couldn't believe the personal venom she heard in her father's voice.

He placed the razor-edged dagger against Zenha's throat. Whispers and gasps rippled through the audience, but the officer didn't cringe, didn't beg for his life. Instead, he simply met the Emperor's gaze.

Shaddam seemed flustered by the man's cool composure. He pushed the blade enough to nick Zenha's throat, just a little, and then withdrew, leaving a spot of blood on the skin. "The deepest cut of all is total disgrace."

He used the knife to slash Zenha's rank insignia and cut off the epaulets, which he threw to the throne room floor in disgust. Next, he sliced away the medals and discarded them, finally removing even the markings of Zenha's house and family. Then, as if discarding garbage, he kicked the items away on the polished kabuzu-shell floor around the dais.

After the humiliation was over, the Emperor's demeanor shifted. "But I do not entirely waste resources, Moko Zenha, and your past record showed some promise. You will remain in service to the Imperial military, but as a fourth-level middle officer, stationed with the Imperial battle fleet at Chado under Duke Bashar Gorambi. Dismissed!"

Zenha reeled as the information sank in, but accepted his dismal fate, even managing a bow. With his uniform in tatters, he turned and left, not nearly as proud as when he'd entered, and he walked with a more pronounced limp than before.

Irulan assessed what she had witnessed. Duke Bashar Gorambi was one of the wealthiest and most purebred of all noble military commanders—the perfect example of a foppish poseur who did not belong in his position. The man had somehow gotten himself commissioned to a rank traditionally reserved for Sardaukar, but for him, it was only an empty title. Gorambi was one of the useless stuffed-shirt officers Irulan had complained about to her father.

She permitted herself a small smile as she considered the punishment. Even though the demotion had been degrading for Zenha, she thought his competence might prove useful under Gorambi. He would be low in the command structure, but at least his talents would not be entirely wasted.

If only Zenha had asked to marry someone else, he would not have inflamed her father's ire. In a small part of her mind, however, Irulan was relieved not to be trapped in a betrothal.

There are many who watch, yet few who actually see.

—Fremen aphorism

The articulated wings made the 'thopter vibrate, but Chani drew confidence from the thrumming as she held the controls. She concentrated on maintaining the flight path, watching readouts for the engine, fuel level, sol-battery packs, and weaponry. A phantom gust of wind pushed the craft to the side, but she corrected course and kept flying.

"Stay low," Stilgar warned. In the copilot seat, he monitored the controls as well. "We are far from Harkonnen territory, but it is good to practice keeping beneath any sensor nets."

To demonstrate her proficiency, she abruptly dropped altitude and skimmed only a few meters above the rolling dunes. She hugged the undulating surface, then climbed as a high dune appeared in front of her.

Stilgar tensed but did not criticize. He could have taken control of the aircraft, but trusted the young woman. "You're a good pilot, Chani. You don't need to flaunt your skills to impress me."

Her brow furrowed. "I'm not flaunting. I need to practice desperate moves if I'm to fight against Harkonnen 'thopters."

"Practice is one thing," Stilgar said in his deep voice. "Cockiness is another."

"*Confidence* is a better word," Chani retorted, though she relented and rose another few meters above the desert surface.

She found the endless emptiness around them comforting, uninterrupted sand extending to the horizon—golden waves similar to the oceans on other worlds that her father had described to her.

"Besides, this is a Harkonnen 'thopter," she pointed out, not yet willing to relinquish the subject. "We would be equally matched against another one in a firefight—except I am a better pilot."

"You are *learning* to be one," Stilgar said, then muttered under his breath, "Cockiness!"

Chani grinned. This 'thopter had suffered some damage when it was seized on a razzia raid. The enemy soldiers were killed, their bodies rendered for water as a small repayment for the long-standing blood debt. Harkonnens preyed on the "desert rabble" whenever they could, but also underestimated their enemy.

Liet-Kynes had helped the tribes put preparations in place for the eventual liberation of planet Dune. Every Fremen needed to be trained and ready. Chani had begun her own flying lessons at only eleven years of age, and had taken to them with great fervor.

A rippling desert thermal rocked the 'thopter, but she flew through it, relaxed despite the buffeting. As she sat in the cockpit, the ornithopter seemed like her extended body, and her instincts flowed into the articulated wings. The lasguns and projectile launchers were like extensions of herself, her own claws.

Chani smiled as she flew in a tight circle around a dust devil. This angry brown column wasn't big enough to be a *khouro*, but it still made her think of her brother.

Stilgar laughed. "I admit that you no longer need my lessons. You have proved yourself, child."

"Then don't call me *child*," she said. "And tell my father of my skill so that he no longer thinks of me as a mere girl."

The Naib gave a serious nod. "Liet needs to have an accurate assessment of the resources he has."

Chani would rather be thought of as a tribal *resource* than a child. "My next real training will be when we attack the Harkonnens, and I look forward to it."

They had learned Harkonnen comm frequencies, including special bands reserved for warfare, though the Fremen did not know their enemy's secret battle language. Harkonnen markings could be repainted on the 'thopter's fuselage, although the disguise would last only so long. Chani hoped she was there when the Fremen used it.

When it came to combat, she was more than a pilot. She had trained in crysknife fighting, engaged in countless duels with Jamis on the cave's sandy practice floor. She beat him half the time, although he still treated her with inadequate seriousness. To compensate for his comparative size and strength, she had studied his fighting techniques, learned his habits, and used them against him.

Chani also possessed a maula pistol, a spring-loaded projectile weapon. The simple clockwork device was used by bandits, though not effectively against Harkonnen soldiers, who tended to wear body shields. In addition, her late mother had shown her many poisons to use against an enemy, if subtler ways were called for.

Chani, daughter of Liet, was ready to fight for her people. She was ready to kill Harkonnens.

Stilgar looked grim and troubled, and she expected he would speak soon enough. They had a long flight ahead of them, and eventually, the Naib's words would come to the surface. She did not prod him.

At last, he said, "You know the ways of the desert, but Liet thinks you should learn more of the ways of the Imperium."

Chani scoffed. "To what purpose? I am *Fremen*."

"As am I," Stilgar said, "but Liet is Liet, and you are his daughter. Therefore, you must be more than Fremen."

She did not like this conversation. "What is wrong with just being a Fremen? I don't need an Imperial stink about me."

"It may be good to have Imperial knowledge, because knowledge is power, and the Fremen need power to win our freedom."

Chani flew on in sullen silence. Her father had already suggested expanding her education beyond the desert ways she knew so well. "He wants me to attend an offworld Imperial school," she muttered, knowing Stilgar could hear her even over the throb of 'thopter wings. "I told him I still have much to learn about Dune. How can one person know even this planet in a lifetime? Why should I study other worlds that mean nothing to me?"

"Liet serves two masters," Stilgar said, "and he uses that service to strengthen his role here. As Imperial Planetologist, he can help in ways the rest of us cannot."

Chani's disbelief was tinged with annoyance. "He believes mistakenly that I will be the next planetologist!"

"Liet took the role after the death of his father. There would be no dishonor in it for you."

"And would the Imperials ever accept a woman in such a position, even if I did have the schooling and the training?"

Stilgar gave a quick shrug. "The ways and traditions of the Imperium are different. I do not pretend to understand them." He turned to her. "But you would make a good successor to Liet."

She cut off further discussion. "My father is still young. There is no need to worry about his successor."

After a quiet moment, Stilgar pointed to the south in the direction they were heading. "A large dust devil. Stay clear."

The pillar of sand was higher than the one she had dodged earlier. At this distance, it posed no threat, and she could easily evade it.

But when she looked past the dusty column, she saw specks in the sky, a trio of dark aircraft. They flew in formation, widely separated. Her attention was suddenly focused, and she dismissed the unsettling conversation. "What are those?"

Stilgar countermanded his earlier caution. "Fly low. Keep as close to the dunes as you can. If they are Harkonnens, it is better that they don't see us."

"I could shoot them down." Chani activated the sensor array and directed the cockpit's magnifying scopes until the dusty screens showed the mysterious ships more clearly. She wondered if they might be connected to the unmarked marauder that had stolen the Navigator's body.

"You cannot shoot down three of them," Stilgar warned. "No matter how good you are." He leaned closer to the cockpit windowscreen.

Chani realized those were not Harkonnen vessels. They were swift and bulbous, with rounded blisters housing the suspensor engines.

"Look at the pattern of their movement," Stilgar said. "They're flying an organized search grid over the desert. Long-range spice scouts? But if they are not Harkonnen . . ."

"Spacing Guild," Chani said. "Similar to the one we saw above the pre-spice mass. If we were closer, we would see the markings."

Stilgar's expression darkened. "We pay the Guild a large bribe to keep prying eyes away from our desert."

"Maybe the Guild believes they are exempt from their own agreement."

"We pay so that *no one* watches us," he retorted. "Why are they scanning the desert, mapping our secret places?"

"More importantly, what are they looking for?"

Stilgar made a rude noise. "On Dune, what does anyone look for? *Spice*, I'm certain. It is the only thing valuable on this world. The Guild should honor their agreement with us." He growled under his breath. "I intend to speak to the elders about this."

Chani adjusted course away from the Guild craft. She used the dust devil as cover to remain unseen. A tan haze spread into the sky as the whirlwind whisked across the dunes.

The unmarked Guild ships clearly weren't searching for any stray 'thopter. Chani flew until they were out of range, while behind them the strangers continued their methodical search patterns. She still had no idea what they were looking for.

Jealousy is a particularly ugly emotion, often not well concealed.

—Suk medical school manual, psychiatric maladies

Reverend Mother Mohiam was stern and serious in all things, including her role as the Emperor's Truthsayer, but this morning she felt particularly sour as she waited inside a classroom on the palace grounds. Most of Shaddam's daughters were late.

The old educational building was a remodeled guesthouse that stood on the shore of a pond covered with flowering water lilies. This main classroom had a high ceiling like a gymnasium, with four acrobatic bars dangling high overhead and a Holtzman safety field shimmering beneath them.

Up there the youngest Corrino princess—thirteen-year-old Rugi—swung back and forth in an athletic slimsuit, leaping from bar to bar. The physical training honed muscles, balance, and reflexes, but the slender girl took such delight in the activity it might as well have been play. Rugi was in excellent shape and participated in a variety of athletics.

Mohiam had asked all five of the Corrino princesses to come at the top of the hour, but so far, only Rugi was here. The girl continued to swing back and forth overhead, increasing her speed and effort.

"Come down now," Mohiam called in a sharp voice, then reminded herself not to take out her annoyance on the one daughter who had done as she was told.

"As soon as I see my sisters." Defiantly, the girl began a new routine.

The whole situation irritated Mohiam, who valued her own time. Of course, Irulan, Chalice, Wensicia, and Josifa all had high royal stations, but clearly they needed to remember their Bene Gesserit ties and obligations as well. Especially Irulan.

Mohiam had already felt glum and edgy since rising from bed at her customary time. With deep introspection, she tried to identify the reasons for her mood, but they were not obvious even to her. She recalled snippets of a bad dream in which her female ancestors kept calling out to her, but the details slipped into the vagueness of memory. Sometimes she was better at analyzing other people than her own actions.

The Reverend Mother calmed herself, waited. The others were ten minutes late now.

Finally, she heard voices outside, and presently Irulan led Chalice, Wensicia, and Josifa into the class chamber, unhurried. The Princess Royal said, "We were delayed by a succession of distractions at court, Reverend Mother. The blame is all mine." The young woman showed just the right amount of contrition to dissipate the matter, and Mohiam did not make an issue of it.

Rugi dropped onto the suspensor field and then slid down a rope to the floor, joining her older sisters. She pulled a blue robe over her exercise slimsuit.

The Reverend Mother indicated half a dozen chairs in a circle, and they all took seats. Pursing her lips, she concentrated on the two youngest girls, Josifa and Rugi. "I must review some important matters with you all. It is a time of change. Your older sisters will know what I mean."

Josifa, the second youngest, was six years older than Rugi—a lovely young woman with dark hair and soft features. She was the calmest and most patient of the Corrino daughters, and thus far she had shown little interest in young men at court, even though she was nineteen. She would need to marry well, in a match recommended by her father and by the Sisterhood, but tradition gave the fourth daughter more choice in the matter.

Looking at the two youngest princesses, Mohiam said in an authoritative voice, "Josifa and Rugi, your father is sending both of you to the Bene Gesserit Mother School on Wallach IX. Over the course of the next year, you will receive basic training in the ways of the Sisterhood, just as Irulan did."

Irulan was surprised. "Both at once? Their ages are quite different, Reverend Mother."

"Their minds need to be shaped and disciplined. Wallach IX is the best place for that."

Wensicia looked envious. She and Chalice had received instruction from Bene Gesserit tutors in the palace, designed to benefit them in many aspects of life and politics. Irulan, however, had undergone far deeper training at the Mother School itself. She had spent several years in a very rigorous curriculum.

Shaddam had not considered additional instruction for her necessary, nor did the Sisterhood. The ambitious third daughter had, however, continued intensive studies on her own using palace resources.

Rugi did not look pleased, while Josifa took longer to consider how she felt. Either way, it did not matter; they were going. The pronouncement should not have been a surprise to them.

"Why isn't Father here to discuss this with us?" Rugi demanded. "Did he command it?"

"Certainly he must have approved it," Josifa said.

With a wry smile, Mohiam responded, "I am merely the messenger. One does not *discuss* such matters with the Padishah Emperor. One listens to his commandments. And it is his desire that you prepare to travel immediately. Your Heighliner will arrive in two days."

Chalice seemed delighted for her sisters, while Wensicia showed a hint of resentment.

Irulan offered the younger girls a calm smile. "It is for the best, as you will see. The Mother School will open new lines of thought for you. Rugi, you will especially appreciate the physical prana-bindu training."

"What will this course of instruction include?" Josifa asked, still reluctant. "Can we not get the same training in the palace, from our own tutors? Like Wensicia's? They can teach prana-bindu here."

Wensicia stiffened. "My instructors are my own choice, as are the subjects I study."

Mohiam nodded to the Princess Royal, designating responsibility. "You will both be instructed in the ways of the Sisterhood. If you meet the stringent standards, you will be asked to remain on Wallach IX for more thorough training, such as Irulan received. Maybe someday you could even pass the most difficult of tests and become a Reverend Mother, like me." She said it as both an enticement and a warning.

Irulan spoke up, highlighting subjects that she knew would interest her sisters. "At the Mother School, you will learn martial arts, as well as perfect control of your body, all your individual muscles. You will learn the simplest breathing exercises and calming techniques that are required for clear thinking."

Surprisingly, Chalice spoke up with a giggle. "That would be useful during long and boring meetings or ceremonies!"

With a petulant expression, Rugi looked away.

Mohiam turned her attention to Josifa. "You are almost too old for effective training. Perhaps your father could have sent you sooner, but he has his reasons for doing so now, and Mother Superior Harishka has granted a special dispensation."

"You'll do fine," Irulan said. "You have a clever mind."

Josifa glanced at her younger sister, who still seemed displeased. "It will be a good opportunity for us, Rugi. I just wish we'd been given more warning, considering all of our activities at court." She put an arm around her little sister, who pulled away.

"And friends," Rugi said. "Can I refuse?"

"No," Mohiam said, careful not to make it sound like a rebuke. "But you may ask questions if you wish, or save them for Irulan. It is a great honor and privilege to be invited to the Mother School."

"It doesn't feel like an honor," Rugi said, then her eyes brightened. "But I would like to learn how to fight like a Bene Gesserit . . ."

Mohiam rose from her chair, feeling the age in her joints. "That is all I have to say for now." She moved toward the door, heard her own robes rustling. "Josifa, Rugi, please go about your business now. I have things to discuss with your older sisters."

Perplexed and unsettled, the girls left the education building together.

When they were gone, Irulan said, "This is rather sudden, isn't it? Bene Gesserit are usually better at planning."

Mohiam scowled. "It has been decided that the girls must go to Wallach IX for their safety, as a precaution. Political and potential military matters are brewing, and your father does not want the girls used as pawns."

Chalice exclaimed, "For *their* safety? What about *ours*? Are we in danger here?"

Mohiam said in a serious tone, "As the Emperor's daughters, you are always in danger."

Wensicia's expression sharpened. "What are you not telling us?"

"Only that you should all be vigilant, perhaps more than usual."

Wensicia shifted in her seat. "This brings up some raw wounds. As Corrino princesses, we should be as prepared as possible, ready to meet any challenge or threat." She sniffed. "I should have received full Bene Gesserit instruction on Wallach IX, to learn as much as Irulan did. Instead, I had to arrange my own private tutelage here."

Mohiam scowled at her. "It was not deemed necessary for you, Wensicia." None of them looked at Chalice.

Irulan spoke to Wensicia in a comforting tone. "There are many duties in the Imperium that we must accept, as our noble birth requires. Sometimes we never learn the reasons."

"You *would* say that," Wensicia said. "You, who have our father's ear and advise him on political matters. He never asks for my counsel."

Mohiam gathered her robes and turned to the door of the educational building, while Irulan said to her sister in barely a whisper, "Maybe he should."

TWO DAYS LATER, on a chilly early morning, Josifa and Rugi prepared to board an Imperial shuttle on the palace's private landing field.

As the girls' traveling things were loaded aboard—only small packs despite their yearlong trip, because the Mother School would provide whatever they needed—Irulan, Wensicia, and Chalice came to bid their sisters farewell.

Josifa was calm, having accepted the sudden change, and now she looked forward to studying on Wallach IX.

Thirteen-year-old Rugi was crying. "Do I have to go?"

"It has already been arranged," Wensicia said in a hard voice. "Appreciate the opportunity."

"You'll both love it there," Irulan promised. "And you'll learn so much. You will come back home as much stronger princesses."

Chalice said, "I wish I were going along. It sounds exciting."

Rugi wiped at her face, looked past Irulan toward the Imperial Palace. "Where is Father? Why isn't he saying goodbye to us?" The tears kept coming.

"The Emperor has many important matters this morning," Mohiam said, although she knew Shaddam was handling only routine business in his office.

Now both of the younger girls looked troubled as they boarded, while their older sisters remained on the landing field. Mohiam wished she could go back to Wallach IX now as well, but she had too many duties and obligations here that took precedence.

Competence breeds competence. Unfortunately, the reverse is also true.

—Sardaukar instruction manual for officers

It was only a rudimentary mess hall, a cafeteria for enlisted men, with plain plaswood tables and mismatched metal chairs, some with cushions and others without. After Zenha's fall from grace, this was the best facility his well-wishers could obtain for his farewell gathering, a crowded room with at least forty people and only a token amount of celebratory food.

At least they were Zenha's friends. For the occasion, they would spend more time drinking than eating, and he was fine with that.

For this somber departure celebration for the banished former Fleet Captain, the men had rearranged the simple furnishings to their own needs. The demoted officer sat at a makeshift head table between two of his closest friends in the service, Staff Captains Sellew and Nedloh, both of whom had traveled to Kaitain from their planetary assignments. Sellew was a young officer with intense blue eyes, while Nedloh was an old veteran with a battle scar on the side of his face. Everyone present at the sullen gathering knew how to manipulate the military bureaucracy to accomplish what they needed, since no official going-away party would have been sanctioned.

Commiserating with him, these boon companions were ordinary officers wearing Imperial uniforms, none of them members of the elite Sardaukar troops, nor of the noble high command. This group had advanced through the ranks with Zenha through hard work and competency, with no advantages of important bloodlines. They were all adjutants to showy, inept figurehead officers. They knew their places.

The pompous figureheads refused to be seen with the disgraced officer, but his friends didn't abandon him. Most of these soldiers traveled extensively around the Imperium in fleet detachments aboard Guild Heighliners, leading peacekeeping forces for the Emperor. When word got out about what had happened to Zenha, they rushed to his support.

The former Fleet Captain had accepted his fate with grace, rather than sniveling shame. He wore his new leftenant uniform without any ribbons or medals, but he had promised himself he would earn them all over again, no matter how long it took. He would make up for those thousands of lives lost under his watch due to criminally faulty information provided to him. His injured ankle felt much better after the medpack and special boot, and now he could walk without a noticeable limp.

Listening to the subdued conversations, Zenha sipped a drink and pretended to enjoy himself. He greatly appreciated the presence of these people. Most of his friends were in dark moods because of how poorly he had been treated, yet they also honored the fallen soldiers on Otak. Zenha would never forget the blood of all those losses on his hands. The mission would have been so different if he'd had accurate information beforehand.

"Worst part is that now you're serving under Duke Bashar Gorambi," said Staff Captain Sellew. "'Duke Bashar'! What a ridiculous made-up rank! At least my own commander is oblivious enough that I can fix problems and keep the fleet detachment running without him interfering. Gorambi, though, is *actively* incompetent! He's a very pushy man."

Nedloh nudged Zenha in the ribs. "Moko will have him wrapped around his finger."

"What an injustice, assigning you to that fool!" grumbled another officer, a big bearded man. "Gorambi puts his troops in one stupid debacle after another."

Zenha forced a smile for all of them. "I will do my best, as always." He refrained from drinking to excess, wanting to keep his head about himself. Now he looked to the back of the room, where a supposedly unobtrusive but painfully obvious Imperial aide sat in a chair by himself. The dark-haired aide held a shigawire recording device, no doubt for a report he would make; he had taken no noticeable food or drink. The man had an unremarkable appearance, dressed in an Imperial business suit. He did not seem to be enjoying the party any more than Zenha.

The noise in the room grew louder as his friends drank more, gradually raising their voices to be heard over other slurred comments. One of the officers seated at a nearby table, Captain Horon, stood up and raised his glass. "A terrible thing was done to you, my good friend. They threw you into a static-storm of an operation, with a reeking pile of misinformation. How were you supposed to succeed? It was like dumping you on Arrakis with furs and arctic gear!" Horon continued ominously, "And all because you dared to ask for a princess's hand in marriage."

"Should have aimed lower, Moko," Nedloh said with a snort.

The men all agreed, generating a hostile clamor of noise. A big officer boomed out, "Imagine that! One of *us* asking to marry the Emperor's daughter!"

"Damned Shaddam could have just said no!" Sellew said.

Self-conscious, Zenha looked back at the suspicious Imperial aide, sure that all this would be reported to the palace. He was surprised to see the man switch off his shigawire recording device and disconnect the uptake spool, no longer interested in the proceedings.

Whether or not the spy was paying attention, Zenha had a great deal to say and didn't care who heard it. Gathering his courage, or maybe his foolishness, he called out directly to the aide. "Why not turn your recorder on, so the Emperor can hear what I have to say in my own words?"

A smile curled at the corners of the aide's mouth.

Frustrated with the presence of the spy, Staff Captain Sellew marched to the back, grabbed the recorder, and smashed it on the floor, then stomped on it for good measure. The nondescript aide stood up, unbothered.

Then Sellew grinned and clapped a hand on the spy's back. "Moko, meet my adjutant, Leftenant Bosh."

Zenha was surprised. "He wasn't sent as a watcher for the Emperor, then?"

A wave of relief rippled through the room, and laughter among those who had known in advance. Sellew seemed very proud of himself. "No, but the man has contacts, and he managed to get hold of one of their trademark business suits. Bosh can set up anything, fix anything! Through his other contacts, he arranged for us to have complete privacy in this gathering. There are no recording devices here, no hidden microphones or spy-eyes. We can say whatever we want."

"Nice to know," Zenha said, "but I had planned to say whatever I wanted anyway."

"And we want to listen!" Nedloh yelled, scratching the scar on his face.

The handful of loyal, trusted people pounded the tables in approval. Zenha felt the vibration around him like armor. Though the collective mood began to lift, he still felt the terrible ache of losing his troops, reliving the orders he'd given, second-guessing himself. Three troop carriers lost! So many lives!

Now that he had their full attention, Zenha rose to his feet, leaving his drink on the table. "I expected the Emperor to put me to death, but he thinks that serving in disgrace is a worse punishment. I still intend to make a difference. I can be a good leader *in spite of* the people I have to serve!"

"Hear, hear!" the men said, and they drank more.

"Assigning you to Gorambi is like a death sentence," Captain Horon said with a snort.

No one laughed. The room grew silent, except for rustling bodies and tinkling glasses.

The bearded man continued, emboldened by the brash actions of Sellew and the spy Bosh. "Duke Bashar Gorambi is probably the biggest fool of all the noble popinjays. Have you ever heard him speak of military matters? He's like a child moving toy soldiers around on his bedroom floor."

Bosh joined other officers at one of the tables, though his clothing made him stand out.

Shaking his head in dismay, Zenha said, "The Emperor *needs* us, because we are the competent ones, and he knows it. We may criticize the peacock officers because their foolishness is a detriment to the Imperium, but we remain loyal to the Imperium. Would any of you deny that?"

A murmur of concurrence passed through the room.

"Everyone knows we are the capable officers, that we hold everything together. With that in mind, and in honor of the oaths we took, I say this to you this evening—" Now Zenha reached down to take his drink. "Even after what has happened to me, I still give this toast to our Emperor Shaddam Corrino. And to the Imperium, may we always serve honorably and bravely."

After a moment of awkward hesitation, Staff Captain Nedloh returned to his place with Zenha, as did Sellew and Horon. Patting Zenha on the shoulder, Nedloh said, "This is the bravest man of all of us. Who among you would have dared to ask for the hand of Princess Irulan?"

Laughter and applause filled the air. "For all the good it did him!"

"Our friend here was sent woefully unprepared to Otak, without the military intelligence or forces he needed. He accepted his assignment out of duty, then returned to take responsibility for his failure and face punishment. Moko Zenha is not a man who runs from anything."

"Well said!" a man shouted. "Give that man a promotion—again!"

"Give us all promotions!" shouted another to louder laughter. "That way, we'll outrank the popinjays!"

Zenha knew they all secretly wanted to keep the useless superior officers occupied at gala military balls and showpiece parades, so long as they could make no decisions where actual lives were on the line. The audacious idea of outranking them generated even more applause, along with foot stomping and shouts for more drinks, and stronger ones.

Then Bosh rose to his feet, showing clear military bearing even in his civilian clothes. "Leftenant Zenha, by rights you should hold a substantially higher rank—even higher than Fleet Captain. I applaud your actions, and we are inspired by your grace in accepting your demotion and censure. But there is something I must tell you."

Now the room grew quiet, as if the men already knew something Zenha did not.

"As Staff Captain Sellew told you, sir, I am an arranger, a fixer, and I have many contacts at all levels of government and the military services." He paused. "This does not come easily, but it must be said. And you must know."

A chill of dread went down Zenha's spine.

"I found intelligence files regarding the situation on Otak that were not revealed to you before you left—the number and status of the rebels, a complete psychological profile of the Navachristian leader Qarth, and a full analysis of the level of fanaticism, the number of deaths already recorded in prior uprisings on Otak." Bosh's expression was stony. "And intelligence reports that prove it was known the ruling family had already been captured and likely killed, not in safe exile, and that the fanatics had stolen the family atomics."

Zenha gasped, but could find no words.

"This information was intentionally redacted from the dossier you were given. The summary with which you prepared your task force was inaccurate and misleading."

Zenha's throat went dry. "So the dossier I read was worthless."

"You were given a severely abridged document, with information that was missing, or willfully incorrect. Emperor Shaddam sent you to Otak so you would fail and, presumably, all your troops would die."

"Just because . . . because I asked for his daughter's hand." His heart was pounding. "Thousands of our soldiers died, not to mention all the inhabitants in the capital city. And now Sardaukar are using my failure as an excuse to launch a bloody punitive strike, which will kill countless more, obliterate other cities."

"The punishment for being impertinent," Horon growled. Others muttered in horror and disbelief.

Zenha sat down, enraged and indignant. "You merely confirmed what I already suspected." He knotted his fists, inhaled deeply, exhaled. His vision was filled with black static, but he forced it to clear. He said in a deep, steely voice, "We are Imperial military officers, and no matter what, we keep our sacred oath to the Imperium."

He got up and left his party, the thoughts roaring in his head. The words of the oath sounded hollow, but he had pointedly not said he would keep his oath to *the Emperor himself*.

Violence begets violence, but peace does not always beget peace.

—Imperial archives, *Lessons of History*

Wensicia moved toward her restricted suite in the southeast wing of the palace, her own private domain where she could make personal choices without bowing to politics or expectations.

This wing of the palace had been reconstructed six centuries ago following a devastating fire that killed the Emperor's beautiful concubine and a Sardaukar officer. Their bodies had been found in bed together. Always fascinated by history, Wensicia had studied the scandalous details in a narrated filmbook and was both shocked and titillated to learn that her own bedchamber was where the illicit lovers had died, though the rooms themselves had been remodeled since then.

As she entered her personal reception area, she was surprised to see Chalice waiting for her.

"Oh, Wensicia! I need your help!"

Wensicia struggled to keep the annoyance from her face, forging a friendly smile. She had left her sister only an hour earlier, after the droning chatter gave her a headache. "I told you earlier, dear, I don't feel very well, and I have many things to get done." She just wanted time alone to study more filmbooks.

"I'm so sorry, but this will only take a few minutes. It's extremely important."

Wensicia quelled her exasperated sigh, but did not invite her sister inside the main chambers. She needed to maintain strong ties and a solid alliance with her, but Chalice was becoming too clingy, begging Wensicia's help to lay out a personal schedule, and even to select her daily attire, jewelry, and perfume. Wensicia had been supportive, providing proper guidance to her older sister, but that had worked *too* well, and Chalice felt increasingly uncertain of even the most innocuous decisions.

Wensicia did not bother with an opinion on every imaginable detail. Now she blocked her sister from entering the bedchamber. "You have to make some decisions for yourself. What could possibly be so important?"

Chalice beamed as if she were in her own world. "I might ask Father if I could have a pet. Don't you think a dog would be nice to have around?"

"Father used to have a little dog himself, so I'm sure he wouldn't mind. But why don't you ask your head lady-in-waiting? She'd be the one to take care of an animal for you. Or maybe one of the chamberlains? Such a decision need not go to Father."

Asking the Emperor of the Known Universe about a dog!

"An excellent idea! I hadn't thought of that." Chalice gasped. "What do you think is the best breed? How big a dog? Should I get a male or a female, and—"

Wensicia placed a finger on her sister's lips, forcing her to stop talking. "Choose one of each, if it makes you happy. But I really do have a terrible headache and just need to rest."

Chalice dithered. "Should I bring some of your favorite pastries to help you feel better?"

"I had enough to eat at breakfast. Now if you will please excuse me—" She ducked into her main chambers and closed the door firmly but softly, then headed straight for her private study. Her purported headache immediately felt better once she was away from Chalice's constant chatter.

The spacious room had a large window with a view of the ornate Lion Fountain outside, four gleaming golden lions circling a pool, spewing water from roaring mouths. She let out a long sigh as she turned to face her library of filmbooks, ridulian crystal volumes, and shigawire spools.

For years, she had studied Imperial records of the Butlerian Jihad and the thrilling military history from thousands of years ago, the old battles of Faykan Butler and his brothers—great heroes of the Jihad who led the overthrow of thinking machines and founded the Corrino dynasty.

Even though she hadn't received Irulan's deep Bene Gesserit training, Wensicia made up for it by learning everything she could in other ways. She had often used her special Corrino access to look into deep classified files, which made the most interesting reading. In the process she had discovered numerous details censored from official Imperial military history and command systems. She didn't think even her father had bothered to dig deep enough to find the loopholes and truths.

Finally alone, she decided to learn more about the old story of the tragic fire in this wing. She found the right shigawire spool, which she had extracted from dusty and long-sealed records in an archives vault, and spun it up on the reader. Here were the names of the two victims, and she saw clear images of their burned bodies. The Emperor's concubine, Triga Yan, and her lover, the Sardaukar Burseg Hindor Evoc. Some details of the scandal had been muddied intentionally at the time, but part of the sealed chronicle implied that the lovers were murdered by a jealous cuckolded Emperor, who had sent a team of henchmen to assassinate them, then set fire to the chambers. Since both the concubine and the Sardaukar came from powerful families, some nobles raised a great hue and cry.

The scandal pitted the hedonistic Emperor Sheff Corrino II against a Landsraad military alliance that threatened to attack the capital world if a trial were not held. After two inconclusive deep-space skirmishes, the Emperor acquiesced and granted a trial. During the court proceedings on Kaitain, Sheff presented evidence that his own Empress, Akkana, had started the fire in a rage against the adulterous concubine, a woman she believed her husband cared about too much. Despite Akkana's protestations of innocence, as well as threats of military retaliation from her own influential noble family, the Empress was convicted and publicly executed.

Wensicia kept digging into the story. Many decades after those dramatic events, rumors surfaced that Akkana had been wrongfully accused, that the Emperor had fabricated evidence and used his Empress as a convenient scapegoat, but by that time, any trail of clues had grown cold. And they were even colder now.

It all made Wensicia wonder what had truly happened so long ago. The bloodline of Empress Akkana and Emperor Sheff Corrino carried through to her and her sisters.

She mused that another Corrino "love story" had just gone awry, although she knew there was more of politics and ambition in Fleet Captain Zenha's marriage proposal than romance. Still, she hoped for the ambitious officer's sake that he did not lose more than Irulan's hand.

With enhanced prescience, a Navigator can explore the infinite web of possible futures that spread out as consequences from any event. But one does not need prescience to imagine dire troubles ahead. One only needs a healthy level of skepticism and paranoia.

—STARGUIDE SERELLO of the Spacing Guild, internal memo

At Arrakis, the Heighliner prepared to receive House Harkonnen's regular shipment of spice, which included a substantial payment to the Guild and significant tonnage to CHOAM. Another portion of the cargo was designated for Imperial taxes and tariffs. The wealth was enormous, and the people's craving for spice was even greater.

Once the enormous vessel settled into stable orbit, Starguide Serello boarded a small spherical ship, which he sometimes used for his own purposes. Receiving coded clearance, he dropped out of the Heighliner hold so he could travel by himself, unnoticed. A Starguide was often the center of attention, the diplomatic face of the Spacing Guild, but now he was insignificant among the flurry of frigates, cargo haulers, and crew transports filled with new indentured spice workers. With two small Guild corvettes flying nearby to protect him, he guided his private ship away from the traffic, to where he could more easily observe Arrakis.

He watched as whalelike water tankers dropped out of the open hold, filled with a resource that was almost free on many planets, but here every liter of water was worth its weight in solaris. The supply ships descended under heavy military escort to be delivered to Carthag and the older city of Arrakeen. Smaller portions of the liquid cargo would be distributed to outlying towns and cities.

The shipments of melange, also under heavy guard and worth even more than the water, rose from the surface to be taken aboard.

Serello piloted his ship to a higher, empty orbital lane, where he would be undisturbed. As he peered through the curved windowports, a plaz focal layer magnified the view so that he could study the hellish arid lands.

At the equator, he saw swirling Coriolis storms, monstrous dry hurricanes that ripped across the desert and threatened spice-harvesting operations.

A network of weather satellites would have made operations much more efficient, allowing Harkonnen crews to predict the dangers and reroute their excavations, but thanks to the Fremen spice bribe, Arrakis remained one big, arid blind spot.

Serello honored the long-standing secret agreement. The Fremen paid the Guild more than the Harkonnens did, and the Fremen would always be there, while the ruling noble families shifted according to Imperial whim.

With his hyper-focused mind, Serello analyzed the landscape, tracing lines of storm systems. He saw deceptively soft tans in the vast sea of dunes, interspersed with mountainous lines like black scabs. He concentrated, using new pathways in his mind, following thoughts and consequences. With the whole desert world below, he received insight and a general sense of inspiration, but no further answers to the mystery that troubled him.

What had those Fremen youths actually seen?

As the culmination of the solemn funeral, the Navigator's body had been delivered to this sacred place, the origin of spice. His great-grandfather's melange-saturated body had joined a pre-spice mass, where his flesh could become part of Arrakis. It upset Serello that outside eyes had witnessed the ceremony, but he should have realized that the Fremen had eyes everywhere on their desert.

Far more disturbing was the idea that an unknown marauder had stolen the Navigator's body. Incomprehensible, and unconscionable! Outwardly, Serello had hidden his reaction when the boastful young Fremen reported what they had seen. He doubted their claims, but had a way of testing them.

Many years ago, after surviving his ordeal and emerging with an expanded mind, Serello had trained at the Mentat school under the auspices of the Guild, learning Mentat techniques, how they were able to organize data and make projections. Because of his partial spice transformation, Serello could supplement their human-computer calculations with faint Starguide prescience, thus developing accurate extrapolations and better views into the future. After two years, though, the Mentats could teach him no more, and Serello had returned to Junction, where he became fully ordained as a Starguide.

At first, the story of the young Fremen had seemed improbable, maybe even impossible . . . but why would they make up anything like that? Using his enhanced Mentat skills, he analyzed all available data (including the manner of speaking and demeanor of the desert people), and determined that it was indeed possible. The body had been stolen! But who had done it, and why?

Now as he stared down at the desert planet, he revisited his Mentat skills, going an important additional step. He let his eyes roam over the swirling storm systems and asked the question and tested many different answers. Who would have taken a Navigator body, and for what purpose?

Recently, he had dispatched a group of discreet surveillance ships equipped with the best Ixian technology. Using methodical search patterns, they combed the vast wasteland of sand and rock, looking for any evidence of a secret facility that could hide the mysterious thieves. But the Guild scout ships had not found any evidence.

From orbit, Serello could see no hidden facility, but with his Mentat projection abilities and his limited prescience, he *knew* it had to be down there. Somewhere.

He lifted his private craft higher from the shipping lanes and in doing so passed unexpectedly close to an unmarked and unidentified satellite. He lurched as he avoided the obstacle, then approached for a better view. It was a sphere coated with stealth alloys and sensor-blurring projectors. Though his controls gave only uncertain readings, Serello had his own senses.

The Guild strictly prohibited observation satellites over Arrakis! This construct should not be here.

With the two small corvettes still nearby, he maneuvered his craft closer to the mysterious satellite, which hung in orbit like a cancerous tumor that needed to be removed. Serello's ship had minor defensive capabilities, but he needed one of the corvettes to do what he had in mind here. He took numerous images as he circled the large secret satellite. He would need to show his superiors the proof when he brought this back to Junction.

In total concentration, Serello concluded that the enigmatic construct was a communications recorder, an unsophisticated satellite that could receive coded transmissions and store them for later retrieval. Numerous lenses and observation systems, even Richesian mirrors, were directed down at the desert.

At first he wondered if this might be a secret observation device launched by Baron Harkonnen. His House had the most to gain from being able to observe the desert planet, to map the weather patterns and also document smuggler traffic out in the open bled. Serello knew the Baron's ambition and ever-increasing need for profits, as well as his complete lack of morals.

But this did not feel like a Harkonnen thing. Serello studied closer.

Applying Mentat abilities, he recalled details that he knew from thousands of academic routines, and thus concluded that the design was of Tleilaxu origin. Somehow, the vile Tleilaxu had put this unauthorized satellite in orbit over Arrakis.

Now his Mentat projections clicked into place.

CHOAM Ur-Director Malina Aru had provided the fundamental clue. He once again recalled his meeting with Tleilaxu Master Giblii, and the man's unorthodox insistence on shaking Serello's hand, the roughness of his palm, as if the contact had scraped some of his skin loose.

Scraped . . . to obtain a cell sample?

Serello was from the same family line as the dead Navigator. As a Starguide, he himself was enhanced. Did the Tleilaxu intend to use *his* sample cells to grow clones? To develop enhanced human beings? For what purpose?

His anger grew quickly.

The Tleilaxu genetic wizards could have performed experiments with an intact Navigator body. Would they do biological research, brain mapping the enlarged cerebrum once they cut it out of his great-grandfather's skull?

Worse, would they try to grow a ghola, a clone in a vat, using the cells from the corpse? What could they do with the ghola of a Navigator?

Projections continued to roll through his mind. The Bene Tleilax did nothing that did not benefit them. Was there a commercial reason? Would they try to sell Navigator gholas? To whom? Would they contrast his own cells and his great-grandfather's to filter their mingled DNA and develop something more?

As his thoughts spiraled outward, Serello felt ill. Could the Tleilaxu possibly have designs on building their own space vessels and crew them with their own ghola Navigators to be independent of the Spacing Guild? To travel the stars wherever they liked, without paying for passage, without being watched?

Were they perhaps designing a military force of twisted Navigators, the way they twisted Mentats and Swordmasters?

None of the possibilities were good.

He had to destroy the satellite.

Serello's hands moved, virtually connected to the systems in his bulbous ship. He contacted the escort corvettes to eradicate the unauthorized satellite. Suspecting that the stealth satellite might be shielded, he told one of the mercenary corvette pilots not to use lasbeams, but to launch an explosive projectile. Moments later, the corvette fired, and a projectile struck the hovering construct. The satellite exploded, breaking into hot wreckage.

Large chunks of debris were knocked down into lower orbit, spiraling in an ever-narrowing ellipse. The ruined pieces would graze the atmosphere and then burn up in the skies of Arrakis.

Serello had all the images and proof he needed. Now he had to go back to the council on Junction and lay out the numerous crimes the Tleilaxu were committing. He adjusted course and flew back to the waiting Heighliner.

The desert is the heart of the Fremen soul. Blowing winds may alter the pattern of the dunes, but the desert remains eternal, as do the Fremen.

—STILGAR, Naib of Sietch Tabr

Chani closed the moisture-seal door and stepped out onto a wide rock ledge that served as a lookout point. Today it would be a private balcony for her meeting. Cushions and a low table had been placed there by attendants, but Chani carried the spice coffee set herself.

The ornate design of the pot, the two small cups, and the silver tray reminded her of sleek spaceships and Imperial palaces. The letters engraved across the tray were arcane to her, in a language she could not read—it was neither Chakobsa nor Galach. Her father had acquired the coffee set from a Carthag merchant who wanted to bribe the Imperial Planetologist. Liet-Kynes accepted the expensive gift, but had felt no obligation to provide secret knowledge in exchange. When the merchant complained, Liet had merely shrugged and spread his hands. "The desert is there for all to see. Learn how to see, and you will know as much as anyone else."

For the special meeting today, Chani chose this particular coffee set because she knew its intrinsic value to her father, and she wanted to impress Reverend Mother Ramallo.

The old woman already sat on the low cushion at the table, under a camouflage awning. As she waited for Chani, Ramallo stared out at the rolling dunes. As the young woman emerged, she, too, paused to appreciate the beauty of the sunset and the day's cooling into twilight. As the smell of spice coffee tingled her nostrils, she watched the arid sky bleed into a flourish of colors, deepening reds and purples that spread out like a painter's palette.

"The desert is beautiful tonight, Reverend Mother." Chani set the spice coffee tray on the table, then shifted into a comfortable position across from the old woman.

Ramallo kept staring outward from the shade. "The desert is always beautiful. A spectacle such as this can be appreciated even by offworlders. But we are the ones who know how to see the desert and all its value."

"We will preserve and save it," Chani vowed. She poured the Reverend Mother a demitasse of the potent coffee, then one for herself. The moisture door separated them from the bustle of the sietch, so they could enjoy a moment of quiet peace without being disturbed. "Teach me how."

Ramallo turned her deep blue eyes toward her guest. Her face was full of wrinkles as incomprehensible as any sea of dunes. She held the coffee in front of her lips, but just inhaled the rising vapors. "Shouldn't your father be teaching you that? There is much to learn from a planetologist."

Chani sighed. "Yes, my father teaches me science, and I listen to him. He even tries to make me understand the mad ways of offworld thinking. He says I don't have to believe as they do, but I should consider them a tool."

"He is correct." The old woman seemed comfortable on her cushion, though she was well over a century and a half old. She exuded the vast wisdom of age. Ramallo had lived her life among the desert people, knew their religion, and had advised Sietch Tabr since before Chani's grandmother had been born.

"But that is not all I wish to learn, Reverend Mother. Aside from my father's dream, I need to know more about being a Fremen, how to listen to Shai-Hulud and do what is best for our people."

"Isn't your father's dream what is best for our people? All the plantings, the nurturing of ecosystems, the storehouses of water? That is what we aspire to."

Chani drank her bitter coffee, lowered her gaze. "He taught me well, just as my mother taught me herbal lore, but you understand things they never could, Reverend Mother. You understand things that I do not. Teach me the philosophy behind our prayers and Fremen dreams. Teach me about the Mahdi, and Shai-Hulud."

"Surely you know much of this already?" Ramallo set her coffee cup on the tray and looked at the deepening sunset. "Every child among us is taught the same thing."

Chani tried not to sound impatient. "I know what I was taught, but I want to know more."

The ancient woman's eyes sparkled. "Ah, you want to become a Sayyadina! Can you be both a Sayyadina and a planetologist?"

Chani looked formally at the old Reverend Mother. "I am Chani, daughter of Liet. I can be many things, but most of all I wish to be Fremen."

"Ah, a most important question—and you have delivered the correct answer." She nodded slowly. "I will teach you what I can, but I have no doubt that you will learn more on your own."

Both moons of the desert planet rose early, and Chani watched the bright disks climb over the horizon. As the sky deepened into a vault of stars, the pair sat together in silence, drinking spice coffee, feeling alone and at peace.

Chani knew that high overhead in orbit many ships cruised along, and she was disturbed by their intrusive presence. She tried to drive away her uneasiness and treasure this memorable moment. She was here with the sietch's Reverend Mother, trying to resolve deep questions about her place in the universe and who she was.

Suddenly, high in the dark sky an orange fingernail scratched a line, followed by a blur of shooting stars. Twin meteors flared bright as they burned down through the atmosphere.

Chani caught her breath, and Ramallo saw the cosmic display as well. Overhead, the debris of whatever it was tumbled as it burned up. The chunks flared bright and flickered out long before reaching the ground.

"I wonder what that was," she said.

Ramallo finished her tiny cup of coffee and sat back on the cushion, satisfied. She folded her gnarled hands in her lap and looked at Chani. "A sign, child, for you to interpret."

The teenager wasn't certain how to read the phenomenon, but knew she had made the right decision about who she was and what she wanted to do.

I pledge to devote my entire life to the goals of the Mother School, putting the Sisterhood above any personal or familial concerns.

—From the Acolyte's Oath

Two robed women—one young and one very old—descended to a subterranean level of the palace to a private chamber, with swollen, convex aquarium walls. It was an eerie, quiet place lit with blue light, where the pair could talk without fear of eavesdroppers. Reverend Mother Mohiam had scanned thoroughly to make certain there were no listening devices. She wanted no one to overhear what she had to say to Princess Irulan.

Large predator fish swam around them on all sides, brushing against the clearplaz walls with soft thumping noises. With a sidelong glance, Irulan noted that the old Truthsayer seemed agitated, while trying to cover her emotions. Mohiam had said little to the Princess during their descent to the underground levels, giving no reason for this isolated meeting, but when the Reverend Mother spoke, her former student was compelled to obey.

Yet Irulan reminded herself she was also the Princess Royal. As the two women entered the transparent walkway between two large tanks, she spoke up. "You have something on your mind, Reverend Mother—as do I."

Mohiam seemed surprised that Irulan would break the heavy silence. "Impatient child. Very well, tell me what is on your mind first. The matter I wish to discuss will surely take longer."

Out of respect, Irulan ignored her teacher's condescending, dismissive tone. Instead, she drew upon her own court training, remembered who she was, and reminded herself that she was no longer a mere acolyte at the Mother School. "I am convinced my father caused Fleet Captain Zenha to fail in his mission to Otak. Since he did not consider the man a worthy suitor for me, he decided to make a point. He did not think it sufficient just to turn him down, but he needed to crush the man's reputation and leave him in utter, public disgrace, even if it cost the lives of thousands of loyal Imperial soldiers."

Mohiam gave her an appraising look. "You're saying the Emperor would do that?"

Having already considered the matter, Irulan answered quickly. "Yes. And I want to know if you had anything to do with the cruel debacle."

The Reverend Mother arched her eyebrows. "Why would I interfere in such a thing?"

"Because you monitor the Bene Gesserit breeding index, and you would not have considered Moko Zenha an appropriate genetic match for me, the wrong bloodline. You could have encouraged my father to quash the possibility of a marriage to me. You are more than the Emperor's Truthsayer; he values your advice a great deal."

The old woman let out a rasping chuckle. "True enough, but in this case, I did not need to interfere. Zenha's proposal was absurd from the moment it crossed his lips, and the Emperor took care of the matter in such a way that other unacceptable suitors would never dare to ask for your hand. I was not worried." She narrowed her dark eyes. "I had nothing to do with it, though had your father asked for my advice—which he did not—I would have told him the Fleet Captain is not an acceptable match for the Princess Royal, or for any Bene Gesserit Sister."

Though Irulan was not a Truthsayer herself, she did not believe Mohiam was lying. "You confirm that I am on the Mother School's breeding charts, then?"

Mohiam's smile stretched deep-set frown lines around her mouth. "Every Sister is on one breeding chart or another. You are the eldest daughter of Shaddam Corrino and Lady Anirul, a Bene Gesserit of Hidden Rank. Of course your bloodline is of special interest to us. Certain standards must be met."

"So, Zenha was doomed to fail from the moment the idea entered his head."

Mohiam gazed at the wall of the aquarium, watched a spiny fish glide by like a soldier on patrol. "He is fortunate your father did not simply execute him."

"I would not call him fortunate. He was expected to die during the disastrous mission, along with all those other unfortunates."

Together they watched as another troop of sea predators looked at them through the curved glass and opened their jaws to display flesh-ripping teeth. One creature slammed against the tough clearplaz, as if to ram the two women. Neither Irulan nor Mohiam flinched, and the menacing predator swam on.

The Reverend Mother turned to her, dismissing Irulan's concerns. "Now then, I must discuss a more significant matter with you, to make certain you understand your role and your obligations. You received years of training on Wallach IX for one purpose. You are the highest-ranking Bene Gesserit in the Imperial Court. You have great responsibilities for the Sisterhood. Do not get distracted."

Irulan stiffened. "By virtue of my years of training at the Mother School, I owe a great deal to the Sisterhood. In my position at court, I represent the Bene Gesserit order—in part." Now her expression hardened, and her gaze became as sharp as one of the predator fish. "But I am not your puppet, Reverend Mother. As the Princess Royal, I have loyalty to my father and the Imperium on one side, and equal loyalty to the Sisterhood on the other."

Mohiam was startled by her changed mood. "Child, the Imperium is just an artificial construct of government that has grown too large and too ancient to match its former effectiveness. Your father and his spies do not even see the constant small weaknesses and rebellions, nor does he put together the larger tapestry of unraveling threads. We, the Sisterhood, continue to pull the strings. And you are a key part of our order, by virtue of your birth and proven skills."

Irulan bit her tongue. Using Bene Gesserit skills to subdue her true feelings, she said nothing to counter what she was hearing, but her old teacher was adept at reading body language.

"You have nothing to say?" Mohiam demanded.

"You give me much food for thought, Reverend Mother. My loyalty is pulled in two directions, but I must always keep in mind that House Corrino has ruled the Imperium for ten thousand years."

I also have my own plans and desires, Irulan thought, but did not say so aloud.

Out of habit, she nodded in deference, caught the old woman's determined glare. Mohiam turned about, and with a whisper of her dark robes, she ascended alone from the aquarium level, leaving Irulan to stare at the rare, languid fish, who knew nothing about the Imperium of which they were a part.

A school of silver darters streaked past like sparks from a grinding wheel, pursued by a translucent Cala squid. Irulan wondered, *How can I possibly serve two masters?*

And she knew full well that she served another as well—perhaps even more important than her other obligations or her personal desires—she served the people of the Imperium. She had to help maintain the stability of all those populated worlds that House Corrino ruled, to maintain peace and order, without allowing fanatics like the ones on Otak to catapult civilization into chaos.

To maintain the illusion of control and contentment, Irulan had to accept her father's sometimes-harsh methods. The Bene Gesserit had taught her to see the overall landscape of the Imperium and the history of humanity, rather than focus on one person or one event.

As she gazed at the hypnotic swimming creatures, large and small, a pair of squidfish drifted close, peering at her with dark, intelligent eyes, as if sensitive to her emotions and thoughts.

Irulan was the Princess Royal, and the Imperium was of paramount importance, while the Bene Gesserit Sisterhood was an essential pillar holding up civilization. She had to balance these needs, and the future of civilization.

That meant setting aside her own needs, if necessary.

There are instances in Imperial history where a single assassination has had consequences for the entire galaxy.

—PRINCESS IRULAN, unpublished notes

Designed to impress visiting dignitaries, the spaceport terminal on the industrial planet of Chado was more sprawling than the central spaceport on Kaitain. Duke Bashar Wilhelm Gorambi maintained a luxury penthouse office in the structure's top level, linked by skyway to opulent apartments in an adjacent palatial structure. With the success of House Gorambi's manufacturing operations over the centuries, the man could afford to build whatever he wished, wherever he wished.

It was utterly unlike what Moko Zenha expected from the supreme commander of an important division of the Imperial military. Nevertheless, he had settled in to this new assignment, which was meant to belittle him.

Having been summoned by his superior officer, Zenha entered the exotic building, which seemed to have forgotten the utility of what a terminal should be. Carrying his duty case for unscheduled overnight trips, as he'd been instructed to do, the demoted officer took a lift to the top level and emerged into the noble commander's breathtaking office: expensive furnishings and paintings from across the Imperium, banks of windows that looked out on the departures and arrivals of shuttles. Gorambi's penthouse office suite was as large as the barracks Zenha and his classmates had shared in the military academy, and as opulent as anything the Emperor possessed. Zenha could only imagine what the adjoining apartments must be like.

Some visitors might have been impressed by the grandeur, but Zenha had gotten to know the Duke Bashar himself, and that soured his appreciation for the Chado fleet-command operations. Now he watched the nobleman strutting around the office in a Sardaukar-inspired uniform festooned with medals and ribbons, along with a ceremonial blade at his waist. A large man with a thick brush of gray hair, Gorambi even brandished an ornamental riding crop. He enjoyed the whipping sounds it made in the air, and was known to strike subordinates with it, on a whim.

The pompous man was the second son of his powerful House, and his wealthy father had made the appropriate payments to let him play toy soldier. The Duke Bashar's entire demeanor spoke of narcissism, overindulgence, even sadism, and Zenha used all of his military discipline to hide his distaste.

Reporting as ordered, Zenha set his case on the office floor and saluted, but did not remove his officer's cap, as tradition dictated. In the month he had served at the Chado fleet headquarters, he had noticed that other officers—at least, the handful he liked—also made quiet gestures of disrespect. Gorambi was too much of a fool to even know the protocol.

The Duke Bashar snapped his riding crop back and forth as he stepped up to the junior officer. Zenha stared straight ahead, showing no fear of the flickering whip. The crop's tip stopped right in front of his face, but Zenha did not flinch. It was clearly some sort of juvenile test or intimidation.

Gorambi responded with a smirk, and lowered the crop. "You came here in disgrace a month ago, Leftenant, and I accepted your assignment only as a personal favor to my close friend, the Padishah Emperor. But you've proved yourself to be surprisingly capable in your position. Saves me a lot of work here, when I am already overwhelmed with responsibilities." His face was florid.

"Thank you, sir."

"I've decided to give you a battlefield promotion, Leftenant. How do you feel about that?"

Zenha knew the Duke Bashar did not possess a shred of generosity. "That depends, sir."

"Upon what?" Perturbed at the reply, Gorambi tapped the riding crop on his own open palm. "You should be pleased. You fell a long way after the Otak disaster, and you have a long way to climb back up!"

Zenha found the courage to smirk a little. "If it pleases you, then I am pleased, sir. But a battlefield promotion? What battle? I have been engaged entirely in administrative duties since my arrival here at Chado."

The Duke Bashar strutted about. "Well, I consider it battle enough for me to send my flagship on an important mission, and the two officers ahead of you have fallen mysteriously ill, which moves you up to First Officer on my crew."

Zenha narrowed his gaze in surprise. "LeftMajor Astop and Staff Captain Pilwu? *Both* are ill?" He liked the two officers, both of whom were willing to show their little signs of disrespect, so he felt a solidarity with them. In private, the pair had whispered about how the noble fool was crushing the morale of the force, making him wonder now if their sicknesses might be convenient and feigned. What did they know about this mission that he didn't?

"No doubt some plague they picked up from a local whore," Gorambi said dismissively. "They are easily replaced. You can fill their role—First Officer Zenha."

Zenha did not feel good about this, but he pressed the opportunity. "A clarification, sir. Am I to be *Acting* First Officer, or the actual First Officer, from now on?"

The Duke Bashar froze, and his riding crop stirred. Anger flushed his florid face an even deeper red, and then he burst out laughing. "I've heard you are an outspoken one, Zenha! Your ambition continues to get you in trouble. Asking for the hand of Princess Irulan in marriage!" He chuckled again.

Zenha remained icily calm. "About that rank, sir? Acting First Officer, or First Officer as a permanent rank? Since it is a . . . battlefield promotion."

"Which would you prefer?"

"I hold no animosity toward my fellow officers, but I can do a good job as First Officer." He drew in a breath. "As you say, I have a long way to climb back up to my former rank."

"Very well, I'll make it permanent, then." The close-set eyes gleamed in folds of fat on his cheeks. "Until I change my mind. I can always demote you later."

Through the insulated clearplaz viewing windows, Zenha heard the roar of an engine and turned to see a large passenger liner rise up from the industrial spaceport and lumber into the sky.

The Duke Bashar made an impatient sound. "Well, let's be off, Leftenant. Or should I say, First Officer?" He pointed to documents on his desk. "These are your briefing materials—take them. My flagship awaits! We will use my private lift and ground transport."

With riding crop in hand, as if he meant to beat anyone he encountered, the nobleman led the way.

ONCE THEY BOARDED the flagship, Zenha marched straight to the command bridge even before an aide scuttled up to deliver his new rank insignia. Gorambi dithered and moved more slowly, but the First Officer was required to inspect the command crew and join them for a basic briefing before their imminent departure on the field mission. Zenha hadn't even had a chance to review the orders himself yet.

Battlefield promotion . . . He decided to do something with this opportunity, no matter that it came from a noble buffoon who had little interest or experience in running the fleet.

Since his reassignment, Zenha had already served on three practice missions for Gorambi. Despite the buildup about this particular field mission, he guessed it would just be another training flight, something the bored Duke Bashar considered a waste of time. Or might they be called to put down another rebellion? To perform general peacekeeping duties?

Gorambi's task force—a flagship dreadnought, two cruisers, a score of fighter craft, and seven frigates—left the Chado spaceport and rendezvoused with the waiting Heighliner. The separate ship pilots remained in direct communication, coordinating their movements as they entered the maw of the huge transport craft, which would deliver the battle group to their destination. From the flagship bridge, Zenha scanned the military formation inside the Heighliner hold, anchored at mooring buoys, along with numerous other vessels.

Still waiting for their actual commanding officer to arrive, First Officer Zenha scanned his bridge crew. Several crew members acknowledged his arrival, some with open smiles of relief. He nodded to reassure them. The bridge crew rattled off a series of reports, and he saw that everything was in order, though he still didn't know what the mission was.

Finally, the Duke Bashar arrived and looked around. Satisfied that his new First Officer had all operations firmly under control, he took his seat in the command chair as if it were a throne. Zenha stood at his side, alert.

A civilian he did not know was preoccupied at a bank of recently installed instruments, with temporary connections and linkages still showing. The setup included five projection screens, along with digital and analog meters and control panels. Instead of a military uniform, the stranger wore a bright smock and an unusual cap, both with astronomical designs. He was talking to two men and a woman, who helped him set up the equipment. None of them paid attention to the general operations on the bridge.

Gorambi saw his interest and was proud to explain. "That's Tanak Riyyu, the Emperor's top astrophysicist, an expert in esoteric celestial theory. You've heard of him, of course?"

"I'm afraid not."

The Duke Bashar was clearly disappointed. "Well, I will introduce you later. Best not to bother him when he's focused on mission preparations. The Emperor placed him under my care for a special scientific undertaking, and his team needs to have their instruments prepared by the time we reach the flare stars. The Guild ship has been diverted for this very purpose, to drop us off."

Before Zenha could ask for more details, a pair of men stepped onto the bridge, both looking cowed and uneasy. He was surprised to recognize the supposedly ill officers, Astop and Pilwu, the former tall and awkward, the latter a small dark-skinned man. Appearing defeated, they acknowledged Zenha and went to take up separate stations on the bridge.

He turned to Gorambi, who sat smugly in the command chair. "I thought they were both on medical leave, sir?"

"They were only sick in their imaginations, so I ordered them to report for duty—as your subordinates." He showed a little smirk. "As I said, your new rank is now permanent."

Zenha did not feel particularly victorious and intended to discuss the matter privately with both men at his first opportunity. He wanted to know what was really going on.

UNDER A DIRECT dispensation from Emperor Shaddam IV, the Guild redirected the Heighliner to transport Gorambi's task force from the Chado system to a cluster of flare stars that constantly dimmed and brightened. The unstable stars made the system uninhabitable, though Zenha found the astronomical anomaly intriguing.

He was surprised the Emperor would dispatch such a research mission, since Shaddam showed little interest in pure science. Duke Bashar Gorambi was proud of his assignment, which seemed showy enough to meet his own expectations of grandeur. As with the Otak operation, however, Zenha felt unprepared and poorly briefed for the situation. At least this time he would not be facing an army of fanatics in control of forbidden atomics. He tried to get up to speed as quickly as possible.

Gorambi's full task force, each frigate equipped with newly installed analytical equipment and staffed with a technical assistant, departed from the Heighliner in the vicinity of the throbbing stars, closely packed furnaces surrounded by a debris cloud of metal-rich rocks blistered by the chaotic surges of solar flares.

"We have planned this research trip for a quiescent time," said Riyyu, the eccentric astronomer, addressing a point somewhere in the air between Zenha and Gorambi. "Still, the patterns are poorly understood. One star could release a surge of neutrinos and trigger an unexpected flare. From remote observations, we know that this cluster can erupt daily . . . or remain calm for months. We need to understand more about this."

He nodded, as did his assistants. Then with extreme intensity, they turned back to the instruments. A Mentat had also been assigned to the astronomer on board the flagship.

"Yes, we need to understand more about this," the Duke Bashar repeated.

Zenha remained puzzled. "Why? What is to be gained here to benefit the Imperium?"

Tanak Riyyu turned in a full circle, looking at the entire bridge, as he considered an answer. "I assumed it was obvious. Look at all the planets and asteroids in complex orbits. Frequent flares have cooked the rubble down to valuable heavy metals. Once we understand the flare patterns, as well as the precise orbits and compositions of these celestial bodies, the Imperium could reap great profits by deploying mining operations at an appropriate lull to extract enormous wealth, to be shipped away before the next flare storm." The astronomer tapped a finger on his lips. "And there is the pure science, of course."

"And the pure science," Zenha agreed.

The angry stars roiled in front of the task force ships. Although Riyyu and his team found them hypnotic and fascinating, Zenha now thought they seemed ominous.

"We are left here alone to do research for the time being. The next

Heighliner comes to retrieve us in three days." Gorambi slouched back in his command seat. "We may as well enjoy our relaxation time."

Riyyu seemed very excited. "It is even more fascinating now that we are here." He looked at his instruments rather than the stellar glare through the windowport. "I need the seven frigates deployed to strategic positions around the core stars. We must have accurate readings." He added with a grateful nod to the Duke Bashar, "All the equipment was installed in these ships at the Chado spaceport, thanks to you, sir."

The noble officer gave a pleased but dismissive wave. "The Emperor was explicit that I must do everything to get you the data you need." With a grunt of effort, he lifted himself out of the command chair. "First Officer Zenha, I leave you to oversee the operations. I shall be in my stateroom working on important correspondence."

After the rotund commander left, Zenha quickly reviewed the briefings and the mission parameters. Fortunately, the lower-ranking officers had each been given a specific protocol for their part of the operations, so they were able to comply with the research program, while Zenha tried to grasp the overall mission.

The flagship dreadnought hung near one of the largest planet-size rocks, while the seven frigates moved on separate paths, rising above or dropping below the orbital plane, where their sensor readings would not be obstructed by the numerous cratered planetoids.

The flare stars oscillated brighter and dimmer as Zenha studied them. Riyyu and his assistants aboard the flagship seemed pleased with their initial data. The science adviser on each of the scout frigates also reported continued success. In his role as First Officer, he felt in control, glad that the operation was running smoothly, although he did feel alone in this distant uninhabited system, with no Heighliner due to arrive for days.

Following orders, the frigate commanders headed out into open space above the cauldron of unstable stars. They spread out in their preassigned paths, deploying a rugged sensor network installed in their ships. None of the captains particularly knew how to use the network, but Riyyu's teams took control and did not ask for assistance.

From the flagship's bridge, Zenha monitored the overall operation, but pressed his lips together, again reminded of the lack of preparation and the careless command attitude. It was as if they were all doing their duties blindfolded.

When the Duke Bashar returned after six hours, it was clear that the officer felt this was the most glorious mission ever and he was already taking credit in his own mind. The nobleman had changed out of his formal uniform and now wore even gaudier clothes that prominently showed the crest of House Gorambi. He even carried his silly riding crop.

In a booming voice, the Duke Bashar demanded a report from his First Officer. Zenha provided a crisp, efficient summary and read from it, but the commander's eyes glazed over and he only pretended to listen. Excited, Tanak Riyyu chattered details about the importance of the sensor mapping, the uniqueness of the flare-star cluster. Although he smiled and nodded, Gorambi seemed uninterested in the astrophysicist.

The dreadnought hung in the shadow of the large planetoid, while the seven frigates continued their dispersed work under the glare of the stars. "The perspective is perfect," said Riyyu, and his assistants nodded. "The data array will soon be in place, and we can acquire our information. We are performing an invaluable service for the Imperium."

Abruptly, the sensor readings flashed and flared, and a rush of data scrolled up on the readouts. From the buzz of excitement and dismay, Zenha immediately demanded to know what was wrong. "Neutrino burst from the core of one of the stars," Riyyu said.

His female assistant barked out, "A precursor. It will trigger sympathetic flares."

Gorambi leaned forward in the command chair, showing no alarm. "Interesting, is it not?"

The astronomer looked unsettled. "A flare storm will be powerful enough to burn out our sensor systems, destroy any primary circuitry! No shielding will be sufficient!"

Zenha immediately felt cold. "And what does that mean for the frigates? All the people aboard? They don't have shielding for that kind of storm." He ran numbers in his mind. Two to three hundred crew on each vessel, seven frigates. . . .

Riyyu blinked at him. "Was I not clear? *All* electronic systems will fail, including comms, radiation shielding, and life support."

"Well, the Heighliner will be back in two and a half days to retrieve us," said Gorambi. "Will that be soon enough?"

Zenha spun to him, appalled, then he did what needed to be done. He stepped in front of the command chair, snapping orders to the bridge crew. "Take the flagship full into the shadow of the planetoid. Once those flares start, it will shield us from the burst of high-energy particles."

At their stations, the bridge crew jumped into action, operating the controls. He could already feel the big vessel begin to move. The helmsman and the comm officer looked to him, waiting for further instructions.

The next step was obvious. Zenha barked out, "Contact all seven frigates and have them withdraw immediately. Tell them to find any large asteroid or planetoid they can hide behind. Use those rocks for shielding before the first wave hits." He paused, then shouted, "Now!"

On the main screen, he saw the flare stars roiling, grumbling, brightening.

In the command chair behind him, the Duke Bashar growled, "We are the Imperial military. We do not hide. They must continue their mission."

Zenha whirled. "Sir, you heard the astronomer! The frigates will be roasted once those flares erupt. Eighteen hundred crew, and the scientists!"

"The Emperor himself insisted that we obtain these readings, and he gave us the equipment to do so," Gorambi said. Without rising from his command seat, he waved a manicured hand. "Carry on with the mission as planned."

Several bridge crew members froze, but Zenha didn't hesitate to defy the nobleman. "Countermand that order. Instruct all frigates to withdraw immediately! Lives depend on it." He could only think about the troop carriers he had left behind on Otak, thousands of soldiers with no forewarning and no chance. He wouldn't let it happen again.

"Acknowledged, First Officer." The comm officer began shouting into the voice pickup.

"But . . . we must collect data until the last minute!" Astronomer Riyyu cried.

Gorambi was on his feet. "How dare you, First Officer! I do not tolerate insubordination."

Zenha had reached the breaking point. "And I will not let my soldiers be massacred through your gross incompetence."

On the screens all seven frigate captains acknowledged and began to race back into the planetary belt and shelter in the shadow of asteroids.

"First Officer Zenha, you are relieved of command!" Gorambi said. "I knew you would show your cowardice if given the chance. LeftMajor Astop, take over Zenha's position. Give the order."

But Astop remained at his station and stubbornly refused to move. Gorambi turned red. "Very well, Staff Captain Pilwu, I restore *you* to position of First Officer. Finish this mission for the glory of the Emperor. We must not disappoint him."

Pilwu looked directly at Zenha and shook his head. "No, Duke Bashar, I cannot do that. Lives are clearly at stake."

Shaking but relieved, Zenha concentrated on the immediate emergency, ignoring the stuffed shirt behind him. He could be court-martialed later, once everyone survived. Calm but determined, he shouted another round of orders, helping to locate likely sheltered spots for the frigates. By now, the flagship was deep in the shadow of the huge planetoid.

He felt a *crack* on his back, a sharp blow, and again on his neck. Jerking back from the unexpected pain, Zenha whirled to see the noble commander thrashing him with his infamous riding crop. Zenha instinctively activated the shield belt at his waist, and as the florid Gorambi continued to thrash him, the riding crop glided aside, which frustrated the incompetent nobleman to no end.

"You are a disgrace!" he roared. "I will not let you ruin this prestigious mission."

On the screen, the first flares blossomed on the unstable stars. Deep crimson arcs boiled up like spouting blood. The first wave of high-energy particles had already washed through the sector, no doubt damaging some of the lagging frigates' systems before they managed to get into their shelter.

Spluttering with rage, Gorambi pulled out his ceremonial dagger. "I declare your life forfeit, traitor!" The Duke Bashar lunged with the jewel-encrusted knife, but he wasn't holding it right, and it was obvious the nobleman had little experience in personal combat.

Zenha deflected the sharp edge with his pulsating shield and reached out to grab Gorambi's plump wrist, pressing his fingers hard to deaden the nerves. The man's hold on the knife loosened, and Zenha snatched the blade away. In an angry impulse, he plunged it straight into the nobleman's heart.

A thunder of silence filled the bridge, and Zenha heard nothing but the pounding of blood in his ears. Then the clamor of radiation alarms and sensor alerts came rushing back.

With a grunt, Gorambi collapsed into his command chair as if the effort of getting up was too much for him. Zenha released the dagger and straightened, suddenly expecting guards to rush forward, seize him, and haul him off to the brig.

But the bridge crew just gaped at him. No one said anything.

After a long moment, Zenha spoke in a hoarse voice. "Status update from the frigates. Are they safe?"

Astop altered the display screen to show glowing indicators where the frigates had retreated. Two of the exposed ships were damaged from the initial radiation burst, but they managed to get to shelter in time. The others were safe.

One of the frigate captains opened a channel from his shadowed bolthole. Red hazard lights glowed on the screen, but the captain and his crew looked relieved. "Thank you, First Officer. You saved our lives."

The other six captains checked in and acknowledged their situation. Zenha had accomplished what he needed to do.

Collapsed in the command chair, Gorambi let out a gurgling death rattle, and blood rolled out of his gaping mouth.

Zenha turned to Pilwu, who opened a channel to all seven frigate captains. "Remain where you are. We'll wait for the flare storm to die down. In the meantime, make any necessary repairs. Strengthen your radiation shielding, if possible." He swallowed hard, feeling numb, but forced himself to continue. "When conditions return to normal, make your way back to the main task force. There has been an . . . incident aboard the flagship. I need to call a meeting of all subcommanders as soon as possible." He closed the channel and slowly turned to look at the bridge crew.

The astronomer and his assistants were appalled and terrified. Astop and Pilwu got up from their stations and moved to the command chair and Gorambi's dead body. They grabbed him by the arms and dropped him heavily to the deck, then dragged him away.

Astop said, "We'll get this garbage off the bridge, sir."

Zenha was astonished to see the other officers nodding. What had he done?

But did he have any choice? If he had not acted, all seven frigates would have been destroyed. He could not have allowed the deaths of all those crews so that Duke Bashar Gorambi could have parade glory.

Right now, Zenha couldn't believe the extent of the hatred for the nobleman he saw in the eyes of the bridge crew. He said, "It will be two days before the Heighliner returns for us. We have that long to figure out what to do."

You may think you have eyes on the desert, but the desert has eyes of its own.

—Fremen warning, recorded by LIET-KYNES

Relaxed and comfortable, Chani and her companions set up a desert camp, far from any known Harkonnen operations.

The stain from the planetary overlords was ubiquitous. The great harvesting machines seemed to appear everywhere. Chani hated them, and she worried that no matter how much damage her people caused, the Harkonnens would never go away. Her father had warned as much. She saw the continued Fremen resistance as *hope*, but sometimes it felt more like foolish stubbornness.

She, Khouro, and Jamis had left the sietch on another scouting mission. It was an exercise to hone their desert skills, ostensibly to collect blown deposits of melange to fill Fremen stockpiles. Chani was adept at finding corners and protrusions that diverted the breezes and caught the powdery melange. In reality, she simply liked to be out with her friends, to remind herself that the desert was theirs.

Each night as they sought shelter in remote rocks, they would split up and search in the natural pockets at the edges of sand and stone. Now, just after sunset while Jamis set up the stilltents, Chani stumbled upon a small mound of trapped reddish spice with an aroma so strong it stung her eyes. Not enough that any Harkonnen spotters would have noticed the melange from above, but clean and concentrated, and easily gathered so they could carry it home.

With her nose plugs fitted into place, she shrugged off her lined pack, then emptied her Fremkit to allow more space. She could carry the tools separately, or share equipment with Jamis and her brother, so long as they brought this abundance of spice back to Sietch Tabr. Stilgar would know what to do with such wealth.

Scooping with her bare hands, she felt a tingling on her palms and in her blood. Out in the vast Imperium, countless nobles, merchants, rulers, and poseurs paid dearly for the tiniest spoonful of this substance. They mixed it in coffee, sniffed the rust-red powder as a drug, took it to extend their lives. The demand never abated, and this addiction opened the floodgates for greedy offworld invaders, for their factories and harvesters, their storage silos, and their cargo ships. Cities such as Arrakeen and Carthag grew like infected boils on the skin of the sacred planet. Chani had seen the wide scars left in the dunes by lumbering factory crawlers, and felt only small satisfaction when she watched the blowing winds erase all marks of their passage. Or when she and her companions destroyed one of the huge machines.

She hated them.

She scooped more loose powder into her pack, pressing it down with her hands to compact it, then added more on top. Close exposure to so much raw melange, absorbing it through her pores, made her pulse race, increased her metabolism, awareness—and joy.

Carrying the full load on her back while holding the loose Fremkit items in her hands, she climbed back among the sharp rocks, nimbly reaching the outcropping where Jamis and Khouro waited by their stilltents. She heard the other two engaged in a gambling game, complacent and secure in their shelter.

Grinning, Chani crept up to them, taking advantage of the lengthening sunset shadows. She startled them. "While you two were playing, I did the real work." She swung down her heavy pack.

"The way it usually is, sister," Khouro joked.

Jamis said, "You managed to creep up on us, girl—you're getting better."

Chani retorted, "And you're getting lazy and complacent."

Khouro peered at the pack. "What have you found for us?"

"More spice in one place than we gathered on our last two scouting ventures." She dropped her Fremkit items with a clatter on the rocks: baradye pistol, thumper, sandsnork, stillsuit repair pack. "You'll have to help carry my kit. The melange is my trophy." She opened the pack, and the redolence of packed spice rose up for them to smell.

She suddenly felt a crackle of awareness, a rush of alarm and warning.

Perhaps her senses were enhanced by the spice in the air. She turned about, listening. "Something is coming."

All joking aside, Jamis and Khouro stood back-to-back and put their hands on their crysknives. Chani joined them in a three-pointed defensive configuration.

"What is it?" Jamis said in a hush.

From the far side of the rocky ridge, where the upthrust barricade blocked their view, a rounded vessel rose up with only a faint thrum of suspensor engines. In the deepening dusk, yellow lights outlined the bulbous curves of its hull. The glow of engine pods looked like eyes. She spotted the infinity symbol of the Spacing Guild on the hull plates.

"They've seen us," Chani said, alarmed that the vessel had been able to approach without them being aware. "No point in running." The ship drew closer.

"There—another one!" Khouro pointed to the west, where an identical ship streaked in over the rock line. Both vessels hovered over the young Fremen.

Jamis and Khouro both drew their crysknives, but Chani doubted they would have a chance if it came to a fight.

"I've heard that Guild ships snatch Fremen and take them offworld for their own purposes," Jamis said.

"As slaves," Khouro said.

"That's nonsense." Chani straightened to watch the thrumming ships that loomed above them. She could smell ozone in the air from the crackle of their engines, overwhelming even the melange from the open pack. She muttered under her breath. "What do you want?"

A circle illuminated on the bottom hull of the first ship as a platform lowered toward them, bearing a single tall Guildsman with thick, dark hair, a long and handsome face, heavy eyebrows—Starguide Serello. This time, he came to speak to them alone.

With her brother at her side, Chani faced the Guildsman, while Jamis crouched, ready for a fight. She remembered what her father had taught her about dealing with Imperial representatives. Serello was an important man, and he obviously wanted something.

"We searched the desert," Serello said, "and now we have found you."

"Why were you looking for us?" Khouro demanded. "We've paid our spice bribe."

The muscle on the left side of the Starguide's jaw twitched and tightened, turning his firm lips into a grimace. He did not answer.

"We saw Guild ships searching the desert," Chani said. "Many vessels flying low in a tight grid pattern. Spying! You broke your agreement with the Fremen. Perhaps we will stop paying you our melange every year."

"Apparently, you see many things, Chani, daughter of Liet," said Serello. She was surprised that he remembered her name. "And you, Khouro, also known as Liet-Chih. Yes, I did want to find the two of you in particular, because of what else you saw."

Chani sniffed. "So you believe us now?"

"I believe you, though I don't want to. Now I need to understand what it means. An unmarked ship stole the body of our Navigator and flew away before the spice blow. Unexpectedly devious. Evidence points to the Bene Tleilax as the responsible party. They are known for their unorthodox genetic research." Anger laced his tone. "They cannot be allowed to continue."

Jamis was flippant, possibly to disguise his uneasiness. "Your indignation is misplaced. You left a dead body in the dunes. Anyone can claim whatever they find in the desert."

The Starguide raised his voice. "Not the flesh of a Navigator! If the Tleilaxu are running experiments to unlock our secrets, to grow their own Navigators for whatever purpose, they must be eradicated."

The Guild ships loomed above them, and Chani thought she saw their running lights brighten, as if to reflect Serello's anger.

"The Spacing Guild can impose our own punitive measures, possibly even interdict the planet Tleilax. We suspect they are keeping the Navigator body here on Arrakis in some hidden research facility, close to the spice."

Chani narrowed her eyes. "We have heard of no such facility."

Serello turned his black-void gaze toward her. "We want you to find it. Our ships combed the desert unsuccessfully, searched all obvious places—but you are Fremen. You see things others do not. You find things."

Khouro squared his shoulders with pride. "If it exists on Dune, we can locate it."

"That is why I came to you," said Serello. "If the Tleilaxu are here on this world, their facility must be found." He paused a beat. "And destroyed."

"And why should we do this for you?" Chani asked.

The Starguide stared into the empty distance. "If the Fremen complete this task to our satisfaction, then the Guild will forgive your spice payment for a period of six months."

"A full year," Jamis blurted out.

Serello considered as he stood on his hovering platform. "Very well, one year. But only if you *find and destroy* the Tleilaxu facility."

Chani looked at her companions as they considered the offer, and in unison, they nodded. She said, "We are Fremen. We know the desert better than anyone."

The Guildsman said nothing more, and his levitating platform rose into the air, then reattached to the hovering ship. The two vessels separated and streaked off into the desert night.

In Imperial history, the biographies of the greatest leaders are improbably packed with so many significant events that they could not possibly fit into the span of a lifetime.

—From a filmbook lesson, Imperial Palace tutelage series

The flare stars erupted for more than a day, keeping all seven frigates to remain separate and hunkered down among the large asteroids, sheltering from the radiation storms. All of Gorambi's battle group was paralyzed, forced to wait . . . and consider consequences.

In that time, First Officer Zenha's life changed. The future of the Imperial military changed.

Thanks to open comm channels throughout the unexpected event, the Duke Bashar's grossly negligent, dangerous orders had been witnessed across the task force. Nedloh and Pilwu had more volunteers than they needed to carry the body of the cruel nobleman to one of the airlocks. Gorambi was ejected out into the roiling radiation storm, where he could drift forever among the rubble and flare stars.

Astronomer Riyyu and his technical assistants were taken to secure quarters and held in isolation, where they would be no impediment to whatever Zenha decided to do.

When the seven frigates finally did return to the main group, with their captains fully aware of how they had been sent out to die in the cosmic disaster, the crews were outraged and sickened, their loyalty shaken to the core.

The captains unanimously expressed their gratitude for First Officer Zenha's bravery and the decision he had made, even in the face of court-martial and, given his previous disgrace, almost certain execution once he returned to Kaitain. He had saved the lives of eighteen hundred crew members.

After long consideration, while waiting for the scheduled Heighliner to come and retrieve the task force, Zenha announced firmly to the group of ships, "I am not returning to Kaitain. I know you are all loyal to the Imperium, and you swore oaths to Emperor Shaddam. You agreed to follow all lawful orders . . . and you all witnessed that Duke Bashar Gorambi did not deserve your loyalty. He was venal, self-centered, and took actions that were clearly destructive to his troops.

"I considered it my moral duty to countermand his orders and save the frigates, their captains and crews. My duty was to prevent the unnecessary loss of lives through the stupidity of a shortsighted commander." His anger grew. "Duke Bashar Gorambi did not deserve your loyalty, but he *did* deserve his fate."

He could hardly believe the words he had just uttered, but he had already thrown his career off an infinite precipice. Zenha was pleasantly surprised to hear a smattering of cheers. He had worried that they would take him into custody to await his fate.

"Gorambi wasn't the only one," growled Pilwu, and others on the bridge crew began to mutter. "Rot and pompous stupidity is rampant throughout the noble officer corps."

Zenha decided he had to tell them everything. "And there is more. You all know my fall from grace that led to my assignment under the Duke Bashar. I was blamed for the debacle on Otak, most of my own strike force killed by fanatics." He lifted his chin. "Under normal circumstances, I should have been the man responsible, as their commanding officer. But I have since learned that I was given intentionally incomplete and inaccurate information about the rebels. I was set up to fail. Thousands of my soldiers were doomed, because Emperor Shaddam wanted to make an example of me." His voice was only a hoarse whisper. "I have proof of this, if anyone cares to see it."

Shocked whispers rippled throughout the bridge. Zenha decided to reveal everything, making available the complete analysis Leftenant Bosh had given him. Everyone would be able to see that the Padishah Emperor had sent him to die on a vindictive whim, just as Gorambi had sent the seven frigates to their destruction.

"I wish other First Officers had your courage, sir," said Nedloh. "Countless task forces are commanded by vapid stuffed shirts like Gorambi, nobles who bought their commissions rather than earned them as we did." More cheers.

"You know it as well as we do, First Officer," said Pilwu with a growl. "All the idiotic commanders deserve to die . . ."

Zenha's stomach roiled. Nedloh lowered his voice and asked sincerely, "Can you disagree with us, sir? You know it to be true in your heart."

Indeed, Zenha did. And so it began. . . .

SOME OF THE mid-level Imperial officers in the task force objected to the outright mutiny. They issued their complaints and resisted at every turn. Zenha had them confined to quarters; some were put in the brig.

He refused to execute the doggedly loyal officers, however, nor any ordinary crewmen who wanted no part in what circumstances had forced him to do. Unlike the Duke Bashar, Zenha was not a monster, and he asked two of his coconspirators to search library records aboard the flagship and find some out-of-the-way place where they could drop off the astronomer's crew and any determined loyalists, quietly marooning them on a backwater planet until they could be rescued.

When the Heighliner arrived on schedule to retrieve them from the flare-star cluster, Zenha's battle group lined up to enter the enormous ship, as expected. First Officer Zenha issued the proper commands, sent the expected transmissions. The Spacing Guild suspected nothing.

By ancient treaty, since the formation of the Guild ten thousand years before, Imperial military ships were granted passage aboard Heighliners and taken to their destination. The Guild did not ask questions of the Imperial military, and the Emperor did not ask for details on Guild routes or cargoes. It was a long-standing balance of secrets and obligations.

Zenha's adjutants filed the appropriate documents, and the Spacing Guild was none the wiser—if it even cared.

WHEN THE HEIGHLINER stopped off at the mining planet of Uthers for brief unloading operations, Zenha used Imperial military authorization to circumvent the standard paperwork. Erasing records behind him, filing exemptions with the Guild, he took the bulk of his battle group down to the rugged planet. The dreadnought flagship and four frigates flew down to a dry river valley, followed shortly afterward by the remaining cruisers and fighter craft from the task force, including nearly three thousand soldiers.

Three frigates remained aboard the Heighliner, however, their shaken captains determined to support and protect this new movement. None of them used the word *mutiny*, but they harbored no delusions about what they were doing. Astop and Pilwu also remained aboard the Heighliner, with plans to return to the larger Imperial military, where they would quietly spread word among Zenha's close friends and allies.

Resentment and distrust ran deep among the second-line officers who had spent their careers bolstering inept noble commanders. Zenha remembered his somber farewell party on Kaitain. From personal experience, he did not doubt that others would see a similar flash point.

He and his followers were outlaws now, but perhaps they could gather enough momentum to implement change.

Over the next few days, Zenha established a small military settlement on Uthers, with all the supplies and support from the large task force. His ships remained hunkered down, and his representatives told the local miners they were on a confidential Imperial mission. Such words were like a magic spell, and no one questioned the statement, seeing the uniforms and warships. The locals even contributed food, water, and other supplies to augment what Zenha's small force already had.

But he felt terrified of what he had begun. With his reassignment and exile as a fourth-level officer to serve on Chado, he had merely wanted to prove his abilities and maybe rebuild his career, but now he saw that competence and integrity were not sufficient in the suffocating military bureaucracy. Was there a way to salvage the ancient galaxy-spanning government he had revered all his life? Or did the corruption extend to every aspect of the nobility, the bloated military, the Landsraad, even the Emperor himself? If so, Moko Zenha could not possibly abide by that.

On the morning of the sixteenth day of their lockdown on Uthers, he received notification that the usual Heighliner was scheduled to arrive. He considered taking his splinter battle group on board and moving about to continue their supposed "secret mission." But where would he go next?

Soon after the Heighliner arrived, however, the sky of Uthers filled with numerous Imperial warships—an overwhelming fleet of armed vessels—and as soon as he saw them appear in the thin, cold air, Zenha knew he could not put up a fight against them. The warships arrayed against his splinter group were three times his number. He could not let all of his soldiers face execution for the rash decisions *he* had made.

Shaddam's retaliation had come swifter than he expected. Again facing defeat, he stepped outside into the cold air. As he gazed up at the amassed fleet overhead, Zenha refused to scramble his own task force, nor did he prepare his weapons. He would not turn his followers against other Imperial soldiers who were just doing their own duties.

Assuming the worst, he stood beside the landed dreadnought and watched as troop carriers and smaller assault craft set down in the canyon around his own ships. In a symbolic gesture, he removed his personal weapons—dagger, flechette pistol, and even the ceremonial riding crop he had taken from Gorambi—and placed them on the ground in front of his flagship. It was not in his nature to surrender—far from it—but he had to think of others now, and did not want his impetuous nature to cost the lives of more soldiers. Once again, he would face the consequences of his own actions.

Two more cruisers, each as large as his own, landed on the canyon floor in front of his flagship. Uniformed Imperial officers marched out of each, heading straight toward him like an execution squad.

He was startled to recognize some of his closest friends—LeftMajor Astop and Staff Captains Pilwu, Sellew, and Nedloh. All were smiling, and in unison, they presented him with a crisp formal salute.

"We brought you fifteen hundred more soldiers and seventy warships," Astop said. "All are now under your command."

"We were very convincing to them," said Pilwu, with a grin. "And the popinjays—bad actors that they were—had already made our arguments for us."

Sellew gave a formal bow. "We also brought along a couple of captive noble officers who came with the flagships we decided to repurpose for your mission, sir. They might come in handy as bargaining chips."

Zenha had to catch his breath as he absorbed what they were saying.

"Awaiting your orders," said Staff Captain Nedloh. "This is your victory, sir. You inspired us, and we are pleased to bring you the news."

Finally, Zenha returned the salute as he regarded all the ships in the sky above him. "This is more than I expected. Give me time to assess what we have, and what we need to do next."

"You require an appropriate rank for the new situation, sir," Astop said. "You were Fleet Captain before Otak, and then you were Leftenant and First Officer . . . before this mess."

"Since no one recognizes our fleet division anyway, I can make up my own rank," Zenha said with a sigh. "But it has to mean something to my followers . . . for as long as we survive."

"Gorambi called himself Duke Bashar," said Pilwu.

"I am no Duke. My noble house has the honor, but not the wealth or influence to throw around titles like that."

"Then you should just call yourself *bashar.* This is your fleet, sir. And it will grow as word spreads," Sellew said.

"Bashar Zenha." Nedloh nodded. "We are not Sardaukar, but perhaps our mission is as important."

"A Sardaukar rank does not sound right to me," Zenha said, concerned. He paused. "I'll be Commander-General Zenha."

The officers liked it.

Before long, his officers brought forth nine captive noblemen who had wallowed in their pompous ranks. Armed soldiers escorted the disgraced, indignant men forward. Their uniforms were scuffed and rumpled; their wrists bound with shigawire, their faces red and swollen.

Zenha recognized the infiltrator Leftenant Bosh among the guards standing on one side; he wore a military uniform now. The spy caught his gaze and responded with a nod, but made no comment.

Nedloh asked, "What do we do with the incompetent officers, sir?"

Zenha scowled. "We could leave them here on Uthers to work in the mines, but they might cause more trouble."

Staff Captain Pilwu muttered, "They're flabby idiots, couldn't even do manual labor."

Zenha's officers chuckled.

AS HIS MOVEMENT germinated, Zenha's mind spun forward, imagining his next moves. The resentment over so many lives lost and careers ruined due to incompetence ran far deeper and more poisonous than he had imagined. Now he unexpectedly found himself representing what many wished had happened long ago.

That made him consider intriguing possibilities.

Soon enough, under the cold skies of the mining world, Zenha developed a way to neutralize more of the incompetent noble leaders, and that would build his fleet's momentum, expand his footprint.

Utilizing the captive noble officers, he forced them to call a meeting of their fellow stuffed-shirt commanders. The rest of the Imperium still had only the barest inkling of what Zenha had already accomplished. The reluctant officers requested a routine meeting to discuss ship-deployment patterns, to be convened over the Imperial prison planet, Salusa Secundus. It was considered a safe and secure rendezvous spot.

Using Imperial access codes and classified permits, Zenha's rebel fleet traveled to the blasted world, the site of an ancient nuclear holocaust during a disastrous rebellion millennia ago. In light of what had occurred on Otak, Zenha found it appropriate. Below, exiled Imperial convicts either perished, or were recruited to become hardened Sardaukar.

Flagships from Zenha's growing fleet waited in orbit over Salusa when the next scheduled Heighliner arrived, carrying twenty Imperial warships in its hold for the ostensibly innocuous meeting of officers. The dreadnoughts and diplomatic frigates dropped into orbital space and joined Zenha's ships, entirely unaware of the threat awaiting them. On threat of death, the disheartened captive officers among the mutineers pretended to be in command in their initial welcome transmissions. Though they did his bidding, Zenha scorned them as cowards.

Linked together by a common, secure communication system, the meeting was projected across the command bridges of the representative ships. Zenha did not show himself, even after the meeting began. He watched as the nine captive noblemen spoke their scripted words to deceive the other equally incompetent commanders, each man saying what he was told to say, all spineless, all weak.

As instructed, Url Dabbar, one of the noble commanders, called the session to order, his voice quaking with anxiety. The other commanders didn't seem to notice at first. Finally, one of the visiting noblemen demanded, "What's wrong over there? Are you all right?"

"Of course," Dabbar said, his gaze flicking out of the video frame, then he found some reservoir of courage and blurted, "Beware! Mutiny—"

The man barely got his words out before the blade of a long sword sprouted from his chest. His companion hostage on the command bridge was garroted by Leftenant Bosh in full view of the shocked Imperial commanders.

Simultaneously, aboard the unsuspecting newly arrived Imperial ships, the spluttering noble commanders were assaulted and put to death by any means their secondary officers possessed. The bloodbath was over swiftly.

After the violence, three of the astonished noble officers were spared, men who had been reasonably well liked by their subordinates. They were not as bad as their peers, but even these captives no longer commanded anything. Zenha did not expect them to willingly join his movement.

On every newly subdued ship, a capable officer took charge—leaders who had previously been forced to serve as second officers to incompetent commanders who had never deserved their positions.

Across the comm rose a rallying cry. Zenha shouted, "For the martyrs of Otak!"

They all shouted in unison: "For the martyrs of Otak!"

Above the night side of Salusa Secundus, only a few lights flickered on the planet below. As the captured Imperial ships continued to orbit, the rebels cleaned out the last holdouts among the officers and crew. Upon orders from Commander-General Zenha, bloodshed was kept to a minimum, and many loyalists were taken hostage. The worst offenders and most hated officers were ejected from airlocks like garbage.

When it was over, Zenha looked down at the blistered world, where gray dawn light began to spread over the surface. He considered all the Sardaukar training camps below.

He smiled. "Now let's go down and get more fighters."

My father, Liet-Kynes, often says he serves two masters, the Padishah Emperor and the Fremen. But I have watched him and heard him speak, and I know that above all, he serves the greater calling of his own father, Pardot Kynes—the magnificent dream for Dune. The Emperor and the Fremen are but tools for Liet-Kynes to achieve this destiny.

—CHANI, daughter of Liet

Scattered across the wastelands of Dune were dozens of old botanical testing stations, hardened laboratories established during an early period of Imperial expansion and exploration, even before the value of spice was known.

In the past five years, Chani had visited all of them, or at least all that were known. Most of those facilities had fallen into disrepair, lost from Imperial records, but the Fremen had poked into every cranny of the desert and found them, stripped them of any useful materials, and brought some of them back online.

Her grandfather Pardot Kynes, the Imperial Planetologist assigned here by Emperor Elrood IX, had adapted those testing stations for his work. Now, her father used the stations not just as laboratories, but as hideouts and base camps.

After the Guild Starguide tasked Chani and her companions with locating the secret Tleilaxu facility, she wondered if the devious Tleilaxu might have commandeered an old, undiscovered botanical testing station. That morning, she had posed the question to her father, enlisting his help.

Troubled, Liet asked her to travel with him to one of the distant botanical laboratory fortifications, where he had established a main suite of offices. "You accepted an important mission from the Guild, daughter. I can help, but I also have more work for you to do."

They flew together in an ornithopter piloted by Chani, and she landed in a prepared hangar area under a grotto overhang. The ancient testing station had armored camouflaged entrances to shield the place from prying eyes, whether smugglers, or Imperials, or Harkonnens. Fremen scouts would watch for Guild ships or spies. As soon as their 'thopter folded its wings and shut down, Fremen rushed out and unrolled a loose net with desert-colored sensors to mask the hangar opening.

After he climbed out of the dusty craft, Liet-Kynes stretched his arms, rolled his shoulders, and adjusted his stillsuit. He pulled back his hood and removed the nose plugs, then allowed himself a long sigh. "I have work to do as planetologist, and this seems the best place to do it." He narrowed his dark-eyed gaze at her. "The Imperium demands that I compile and deliver regular reports. I must write down what they wish to hear." He shrugged, gave her a smile. "It feels more appropriate to do that away from a sietch."

Chani furrowed her brow, wary. "You don't give the offworlders our Fremen secrets?" She thought of all their hiding places, their desert techniques. "I've noticed that sometimes you call our world by the Imperial name of Arrakis, instead of Dune. That suggests you are thinking more as one of them than as one of us."

Her father led her through a second moisture-seal door into the main part of the station, a bright, sterile chamber filled with terrariums. Chani could smell moisture in the air. Here were Liet's private gardens, tended and nurtured by Fremen workers.

She had seen sample trays before and, of course, the larger plantings down in the south, but here she admired the colorful flowers, feathery leaves, and delicate stalks of water-rich plants that were not hardy enough to survive on Dune. They seemed alien here.

Next to the terrariums was a long desk covered with shigawire spools and spice-paper pads. Her father sat down, opened one of the thick notebooks, and picked up a stylus. He finally answered her hanging question. "It is true that I sometimes use the name Arrakis, but that is because of the reports I must submit. It does not mean I sympathize with the Imperials. The reports I file consist of my observations about Coriolis storms, how the winds distribute spice deposits, my conjectures about the sandworms, as well as my opinion on the Harkonnen spice operations—everything from an objective, scientific point of view." He tapped the paper with the tip of the stylus. "I prefer to submit thick handwritten reports, not records on ridulian crystals or shigawire spools. This demonstrates that I have put great care and attention into my work." He gave her a wry grin. "It also ensures that few will read them, especially not the Emperor."

She leaned over the desk to scan his tight, neat handwriting. "And what other information do you tell them?"

"Oh, I document desert villages out in the graben, even encounters with a few rumored Fremen." He chuckled. "I purposely overestimate the amount of accessible spice so that the Harkonnens look inept in their efforts to harvest it, but not by so much that Emperor Shaddam brings in more harvesters to exploit the treasure. I exaggerate the dangers of the environment, while I undercount the projected number of Fremen. My reports get sent off to Kaitain, where they are promptly lost in the bureaucratic shuffle."

"Then what is the point?" Chani asked. "Is there no real worth in understanding the spice, the weather . . . and the Fremen?"

"Such knowledge is of great value to us, daughter, and I make certain that our people receive all the information they need."

Chani shook her head, still not entirely understanding. Liet wrote more in the logbook, filling the bottom of a page with some fabricated account. His writing was swift and well practiced.

As he worked, Chani wandered among the sample plants, saw insects moving in the mulch, climbing the stalks, pollinating the flowers. She remembered her real purpose in coming with him and asked, "The Tleilaxu lab we're looking for—do you have any idea where it might be?"

Her shook his head. "None whatsoever, but it is of grave concern. I have not heard so much as a rumor, which means that either the Bene Tleilax are adept at hiding themselves even from us, or their laboratory does not exist."

"I hope it does exist." Chani's response drew a look of surprise from him, and she added, "Because then we can destroy it, and the Guild will pay us a large reward."

Liet smiled and went back to his writing. "I like your optimism, daughter."

In the chamber, she studied the cacti and agave, some of which had been genetically modified to withstand extremely arid conditions. In surprising defiance, as if just to prove that he could do so, Liet had planted a delicate Ostinian rosebush that now displayed pretty yellow blossoms.

A Fremen worker came in with a spice coffee service. "For you, Liet." He bowed and backed away.

Chani poured them each a cup and sipped the strong coffee. Her father didn't seem to notice the taste as he continued writing.

After an hour, she was bored and wondered why he had brought her along. He'd said he had work for her to do, but gave her no real task. Leaving him preoccupied, she explored the testing station, walked the rock-walled passages, peered into the records room, admired a water tank fed by hundreds of catchtraps. Impatient, thinking of all the things she could be doing for the sietch, she came back to ask him directly.

Liet finished his notation, closed the notebook. "There, now we are ready."

"Do we go back to Sietch Tabr?" Coming out here seemed pointless.

"No, my report is complete, and now I must deliver it. I have a deadline to send this to Emperor Shaddam."

"You said the Emperor never reads them."

"That does not change my deadlines. What the Emperor does after he receives my reports is none of my concern."

"Then where are we going? How does it get delivered to him?"

Liet rose. "Tomorrow, you and I will fly off to Arrakeen. Count Hasimir Fenring is the Imperial Spice Observer, and he is my conduit to Kaitain. I will do my duty."

"Your *Imperial* duty," she said.

"My Imperial duty." He nodded. "But you will accompany me as my assistant. Count Fenring will no doubt hold a banquet for us."

Chani's stomach tightened. "Arrakeen! I do not like cities."

"Since when do Fremen shy away from things they don't like? I have a standard field uniform you can wear over your stillsuit. We will tuck your hair inside your hood, and they'll assume you are a teenage lad."

Chani snorted and saw that he was serious.

"Do it for your own reasons, not theirs," her father said.

AFTER THE ORNITHOPTER landed in the Arrakeen spaceport, Chani and her father emerged onto the plascrete apron. They had fitted themselves out in standard desert clothes, and now Liet wore prominent Imperial insignia, which he did not show when he was out among the Fremen. Chani wore her own stillsuit like a second skin, covered with a tan desert cloak and a scientific utility belt. She had even hacked off her long, dark hair, and now she tucked the remaining ragged locks inside her hood. Her hair had grown unruly anyway. Her voice was husky enough to pass as a young man's when she barked orders for the landing field operators to check the 'thopter's engines and recharge the fuel cells.

Liet-Kynes handed the workers a chit that held more solaris than he would ever need. "This Imperial account will pay for everything."

Chani watched the heat ripples that shimmered up from the tarmac and the curved, smooth buildings. The Arrakeen structures were solid and geometrical with pale neutral colors to reflect the heat, and windows covered with locking shutters. The doors were low and hooded with extended lintels to keep out blown dust.

Though it was midafternoon and the hottest part of the day, when sensible Fremen hid in shadows and waited for the coolness of evening, people still moved in the streets, going about their business. Some hurried to avoid the pounding heat, while others moved lethargically.

Liet turned to her. Under his arm he carried a valise that held the thick spice-paper report he had compiled. "Welcome to Arrakeen."

Chani fitted her nose plugs and covered her scowling mouth, but the glare in her eyes would still reflect her mood. "I have been here before," she reminded him, "and I did not like it."

"You don't have to like it this time either. Follow me to the Residency so we can do our business with Count Fenring. I want you to lay eyes on him, and there is someone else I'd like you to meet."

"For what purpose? When will I ever come back here again?"

"You never know." He touched her shoulder and directed her into the main thoroughfare, away from the noisy spaceport. "Someday, you, too, might serve as planetologist." He raised his hand to cut off her objection. "Someone will serve in that role, daughter. Would you rather it be an offworlder, a person with no connection to the Fremen at all? Consider the big picture."

She didn't like the answer, but understood.

The crush of people in the open air disturbed and disappointed her. So many had sloppy water discipline and poorly fitted suits. This was greatly different from living in a crowded sietch, where everyone knew that even the tiniest decisions, the smallest amount of waste, might be a matter of life or death not only to themselves, but to the entire tribe.

As they walked at a brisk pace, she heard water sellers calling out, saw beggars in alleys, noticed rough-looking spice workers crowding through a tavern door that sealed behind them. Hard-faced men and women stood in the shadows ready to offer their services, or perhaps to slit a throat and steal water.

Chani was so busy looking at the activity around her that she was startled when her father tapped her shoulder and pointed. The Arrakeen Residency rose in front of them, an ornate and imposing fortress flying the crimson-and-gold flags of House Corrino.

In front of the main gate, she saw a line of astonishing palm trees—tall yet fragile-looking growths like monoliths of hope. Desert people crowded against a fence, staring up at the palms as if they were objects of worship.

"Palm trees," she whispered to her father, remembering their hidden plantings in the south. "But these are so tall . . . and exposed!"

"They make a point," Liet-Kynes said. "Those trees grow only because of our protection and our sacrifices. I doubt Count Fenring feels any sort of wonder at the prospect, but these palms remind me of my father's dream."

She stared, but he moved her along to a small side entrance rather than the tall main door. "I've made arrangements," he said. "And we do not want to draw any attention to ourselves. The Count has been informed of our arrival, and he will no doubt make a show, while you must remain unobtrusive." He rang a signal at the side door and waited, pressing himself into the thin line of shade. "Once you are noticed, your options will be fewer. We'll take advantage of that. Everyone already knows who I am."

When the door opened, a short-statured Fremen woman stood wearing drab household garb. She had leathery skin, deep blue eyes, and a compactness about her. She glanced at Chani, but focused on her father and said, "Liet . . ." The word sounded more like a reverent title than a name.

Her father slipped inside to the cooler shadows of the entryway. After removing his mouth covering and nose plugs, he said, "This is my daughter, Chani. And this is the Shadout Mapes, who has served in the Residency for many years. Her eyes and ears have seen and heard valuable things, and her mouth has whispered them to me."

Mapes swept Chani inside and sealed the door. They were surrounded by the cool relief of shadows. "The household is busy today, Liet. The Count prepares for your arrival, and he will host a dinner this evening, though not an extravagant one." She lowered her voice. "His Lady Fenring is still on Kaitain, so he is all alone here. His mood is harder than usual."

Her father chuckled. "Count Fenring is not a lovestruck schoolboy!"

"He has schemes enough to keep himself occupied," the old shadout said, "but the Lady's presence often softens him around the edges and makes him safer for others to be around."

Liet-Kynes lifted the valise with its report. "I must do my business. I will sign papers and perhaps speak to the Count. Meanwhile, take this opportunity to show my daughter around the Residency. She is very observant, and I'll want to hear her impressions."

Leaving her behind, Liet strolled down the corridor and vanished into the cavernous building.

Shadout Mapes turned to her. "Daughter of Liet, come with me, and learn."

Any system left unchanged for too long begins to rot and fall apart. It can only survive by continually adapting to new conditions.

—From the report of a long-dead Imperial Planetologist

Irulan emerged from her private dressing room into the bedchamber, followed by a statuesque lady-in-waiting who had been dithering too much over her appearance. Early afternoon sunlight streamed through high clerestory windows, which gave a cheerful atmosphere to the Princess Royal's apartments.

As the lady-in-waiting straightened the bed coverings and adjusted a plush reading chair, Irulan heard Aron enter the apartments from the outer hall. Her male concubine had lunched with friends from court, and he often returned with new gossip for her.

Calm and handsome, Aron stepped into her bedchamber without being invited, and she read the barely concealed excitement on his face. Since he clearly had news to share, Irulan dismissed her lady-in-waiting. When the woman had closed the door behind her, leaving them alone, Aron burst out, "The court is abuzz with rumors about that officer who asked to marry you—the one your father doesn't like."

Irulan gave him a teasing smile. "You don't like him either."

His brown-eyed gaze sharpened. "No, Highness, I do not, but I know my place in your life."

She gestured for the concubine to sit on the bed beside her. "Fleet Captain Zenha was demoted and sent far away more than a month ago, to serve under Duke Bashar Gorambi." She frowned with distaste. A part of her wished she'd gotten to know the ambitious officer better. "What else is there to know?"

Aron gave his report concisely, as the Bene Gesserit had taught him. "This comes from a friend of mine, Comte Difio, sixth son of the Duchess from House Difio. It seems Zenha has created another scandal, disobeyed orders . . . murdered his commanding officer!"

Irulan snapped straight. "You must be mistaken—or there must be some reason, extenuating circumstances?"

Aron nodded. "Indeed, some are even calling his actions heroic, but it is still mutiny, and murder. Details are very sporadic. His entire task force has gone missing."

She spoke in a sharp, serious tone to focus his thoughts. "Tell me all you know." Trained at the Wallach IX Mother School, her male concubine knew how to observe and report.

According to what he had heard, a small group of indignant officers and scientists had been rescued from an outpost on the fringe of a mining system where they'd been marooned, and they reported what Zenha had done. Aron summarized how the idiot Gorambi had foolishly placed his ships and crew in danger from a flare-star outburst, how Zenha had countermanded orders and saved the ships—then violently seized command. Irulan frowned, easily believing that the Duke Bashar could have done something so thickheaded and stupid; indeed, a great many of the talentless noble commanders had demonstrated their ineptitude. But now Zenha and his mutinous followers were dangerous armed outlaws, loose out in the galaxy, and Irulan knew her father would issue orders to have him hunted down.

Irulan spoke aloud, since Aron served as a good sounding board. "I've made no secret of my criticisms about the unqualified nobles being given command over important military fleets. But my father can never allow a deadly mutiny to stand, no matter how it was provoked. What does Zenha expect to do with a small battle fleet? Go renegade? Run and hide?"

Aron lowered his gaze, concentrating. "Morally, he may have made the correct decision in saving those crews, even if it meant killing his commanding officer. But afterward, he should have surrendered himself to court-martial."

Irulan frowned. "I cannot know what went through his mind, but when Zenha chose to seize those ships and recruit others into his rebellion, he changed everything."

"Agreed, Highness."

She gave him a soft smile. "When we are in private conversation, you know you may call me *Irulan*."

His expression remained unreadable, another sign of his Bene Gesserit instruction. "I do not want to let myself slip." She brushed a hand along his arm and gave him a smile. Aron continued, "I wanted you to know right away. Perhaps you wish to join the Emperor for the strategy session?"

She rose from the bed. "Once again, you prove your worth—in so many ways."

WHEN SHE LOCATED her father in his palace office, Shaddam was already upset, having heard about Zenha's debacle. "Gorambi's entire task force has vanished! And witnesses report that Moko Zenha murdered him in cold blood, right on his own command bridge! I should have executed that disgraced officer instead of giving him a second chance!" He shook his head. "Now I've received reports that other ships have gone missing as well."

Irulan stood in front of the massive, ornate desk. "Given Fleet Captain Zenha's exemplary past record, Father, you should not have underestimated him—or *wasted* him. He had so much potential." Despite her sympathy, though, she knew that Zenha had crossed a line and could not be forgiven. She didn't point out that her father had created this explosive situation in the first place.

Shaddam's expression darkened as he reread the briefing packet. "Despite his outspokenness and ambition, I never imagined that man would be so blatantly treasonous. I must call an emergency session of my commanding officers."

Irulan drew her eyebrows together, knowing those top officers were exactly the ones least capable of handling a complex, delicate situation such as this.

"I suspect it's more than a rumor, Father, and we have a dangerous, growing rebellion on our hands."

She could see the frustration boiling inside of him. "Then we must quash it. No one must be allowed to think they can get away with mutiny! It's a small group of ships. We'll root him out and put an end to this nonsense."

THE EMPEROR'S TOP Imperial officers and bureaucrats were summoned to a meeting in the War Room, including his Sardaukar commander Kolona. The blond Princess was allowed to attend, but she sat quietly on an uncomfortable divan to one side, drinking in details, analyzing. She would reserve her advice for later, preferring to give it to her father in private.

She tried to block out the bustle and distractions as the attendees arrived, some indignant, some wearing showy uniforms as if this emergency meeting were a grand social event. In her mind, Irulan reviewed the data, using Bene Gesserit projections. Bits of information began forming around a core idea and confirming it. She filtered the data through what she knew of Moko Zenha's personality and past actions. He had boldly stepped before the Imperial throne and asked to marry the Princess Royal, surely knowing he would be rejected. It showed that he was impulsive and highly confident, willing to face impossible odds, believing his abilities and his record would put him on equal footing with countless other high-ranking nobles. According to unverified reports, Zenha had expressed private contempt for noble-born commanders who had not earned their commissions.

But he did not seem to be a schemer, a lawbreaker, a man out to disrupt the Imperial order. Given the proper set of circumstances and provocations, though, she could believe he had been pushed into an untenable situation.

But even if Zenha had felt forced into refusing a terrible order, what about those other officers who had thrown in with the mutiny? Could there have been so much dissatisfaction among the second-line officers under Duke Bashar Gorambi? She remembered the supercilious nobleman and believed that might also be true.

As the gathered officers in the War Room received their briefing, Irulan noted Anford Iglio, the slender Imperial Mentat, who sat on the opposite end of her divan. She watched him roll his eyes and go inward, performing his own mental projections with the data as it unfolded.

"There must be another explanation," said General Xodda, a rotund man whom Irulan considered pompous. "A lowly, disgraced officer could not possibly take over an entire battle group. The other loyal officers aboard would arrest him. Every Imperial military ship has the highest security, especially a dreadnought flagship."

"How right you are!" exclaimed another loud officer. "A mutiny simply could not have occurred in our Imperial military."

Xodda laughed nervously, looked at the Emperor. "We should directly question those rescued astronomers and humiliated officers. I'm sure they have greatly exaggerated the incident. Perhaps Duke Bashar Gorambi died of natural causes, a heroic death in the face of a cosmic disaster!"

The other commanders muttered and nodded, convincing themselves. Irulan could see they couldn't accept any explanation that involved the violent uprising of underlings—not wanting to imagine it could happen to them, too.

"But what if it is true?" asked a young Captain named Patra, a noble-born exception who had risen through the ranks largely on the basis of merit.

Irulan caught her father's eye and spoke up. "Permission to speak frankly, Sire?" She rose from the divan and took a moment to look at the noble officers, all of whom swiftly fell silent to hear the Princess Royal. "It is as if all of you cannot see how you created this situation through your own flaws. The system of appointing leaders on the basis of birth and wealth, rather than merit, is fraught with problems. If not Zenha, then it would have been someone else pushed into a corner like this."

Though General Xodda looked angry, he managed to refrain from making an outburst.

Irulan continued, "What if word spreads that the Duke Bashar knowingly sent his entire task force into certain death out of stubbornness and an idiotic failure to consider the dangers of the mission? What if even more of the competent second-line officers oust their figurehead commanders? In many fleet divisions, the secondary officers already manage the primary work and shoulder leadership responsibilities because their commanders are not trained or experienced in the necessary duties." She did not point out that the case referred to many here in this room, but this was obvious anyway, and she didn't care. "What if other inexperienced noble commanders decide to issue orders with disastrous unintended consequences? Orders that unnecessarily place their entire battle groups into harm's way? Would the doomed crews remain blindly loyal?"

"Of course they would! They are Imperial soldiers!" exclaimed a thin, florid commander.

"Would they indeed?" interrupted the Imperial Mentat, dropping out of his trance.

Irulan saw that the Emperor was deeply disturbed. "Mentat?" he prodded. "Speak."

Anford Iglio turned to Shaddam and spoke as if there were no one else in the room. "Given the current information and eyewitness accounts, Leftenant Zenha likely did save all those soldiers and commandeer the task force. There is also a viable possibility that additional second-line officers might see the opportunity to do the same, if word were to spread."

"If more upstarts turn against me, I always have my Sardaukar." Shaddam smiled, as if he had been keeping additional news in reserve. "I call Major Bashar Jopati Kolona, with a new report from Otak."

The War Room doors opened, and a powerful officer strode in. As always, the dark-skinned Kolona looked impeccable in his gray uniform, as if it had been freshly cleaned and pressed, though he'd just returned from a military operation.

He stood before the Emperor, glanced emotionlessly around at the gathered nobles. "Sire, as you requested, I took a legion of Sardaukar to the rebellious planet Otak. We decisively ended the matter that Fleet Captain Zenha allowed to get out of control. We provided a lesson for all the Imperium to see."

Using a handheld device, Kolona activated a set of wall screens to display a parade of horrific images. "The capital city of Lijoh was earlier obliterated by the Navachristian atomics, but other flash points of rebellion continued across the planet's surface in many major cities. The people of Otak flouted their obligations to the Imperium. They thought they were safe."

Kolona played more images of towns massacred by the Sardaukar, leveled buildings, burned bodies, a crushed and dispirited populace. "But they were not safe from *us*. Otak is now free. You may send in new colonists, new reconstruction teams and investors, as you see fit, Sire."

Shaddam looked pleased. "So you see, the Imperium can exert authority with an iron hand. Otak is a valuable world with many resources. It has now been purged of rebellion, and we can bring in new settlers, reward truly loyal noble houses, dispatch a comprehensive rebuilding operation with the assistance of CHOAM." He rubbed his hands together. "We will let the entire Imperium know, and the message will be clear."

General Xodda also looked impressed. "We have nothing to worry about from an upstart military officer who has fallen from grace. Look what our Sardaukar can accomplish!"

The room filled with self-congratulatory muttering. Irulan watched them all, looked at Major Bashar Kolona, even the Mentat. No one spoke aloud the obvious fact that these stuffed-shirt noblemen were not Sardaukar themselves. Not a single one of them.

I cannot remain long in this terrible place. If I do not find a way to escape, I shall go mad. Each day I wonder if this will be my last—my own death by violence—or if I will kill another prisoner instead.

—KIA MALDISI, secret notes to herself

Salusa Secundus was a harsh, inhospitable world. The desolate landscape looked as if it had been cooked from the inside out, then discarded into the universe. Once, Salusa Secundus had been the lush capital of the early Imperium, but long ago, it was devastated by an interfamily nuclear holocaust.

The planet had three principal climate zones, like tiers of hell, and only the hardiest human beings could survive in any of them. Little vegetation grew in the hardscrabble soil, except for the toughest plants, such as shigawire vines. The animals and insects were the most ruthless species, becoming tougher over time. Laza tigers, brought here thousands of years ago, were now apex predators, hunting anything that moved.

Salusa made for a perfect prison planet, a purgatory to test those who could fight and survive. Though the truth was hidden from the rest of the Imperium, classified reports available to military commanders suggested that the blasted scab of a world was a sieve, from which the Emperor filtered the toughest of his Sardaukar recruits.

Moko Zenha was not Sardaukar, so he had never been to Salusa Secundus before. But he knew what to expect, and found the possibilities intriguing. He could find the most motivated and vicious warriors here for his expanding movement. He knew he would have to fight for what he intended to accomplish.

With the other commandeered military ships still in orbit, Zenha ordered his flagship to descend, scanning for camps or settlements in the most inhospitable climatic zone. He had a plan.

He glanced up to the bridge bulkhead, where Duke Bashar Gorambi's riding crop had been mounted on display, with the admonition painted below in red letters. "Never Again." All of his crew drew determination from the bold statement.

As the dreadnought dropped through the rough atmosphere, dodging angry clouds, lightning, and dust storms, Zenha kept his eyes on the site he had chosen—a camp where brutalized recruits would be eager candidates to hear his proposal.

It was the most rugged and basic of all prisoner settlements. Reinforced shelters were scattered in a haphazard manner, joined by guarded supply hutments and medical tents, near expansive graveyards. Many of the prisoners exiled to Salusa did not survive daily life for very long, much less the rigors of Sardaukar indoctrination.

Formal training centers were located in the more hospitable zones, places where Sardaukar officers could drill candidates they had drawn from the prison population. Zenha knew, though, that this particular settlement was not for active training. It was a dumping ground for those who had the strength and resources to survive, but were deemed unworthy to become Sardaukar. Zenha could take advantage of that. The ruthless fighters there would be looking for a way out, but would likely resist command or discipline. He would make the effort.

Zenha's bridge officers wore pale blue uniforms with black trim, with no previous insignia, no sign of the Corrino lion. LeftMajor Astop and Staff Captain Pilwu ran their scans as the flagship closed in on the survival camp.

"No air-defense systems for us to worry about, Commander-General," Astop reported. "The prisoners won't be shooting at us."

"Sardaukar would never bother with basic defenses," Zenha said. "Who would be insane enough to travel to Salusa by choice?" It was just another part of their enemy's overconfidence.

"The camp inhabitants have seen us, sir," Pilwu reported, adjusting the screen to magnify the squalid view. "Fighters forming below."

As part of their training, these prisoners were often harassed by superior military might, hunted down by Sardaukar recruits. "They must be used to practice attacks. We'll offer the people something different."

He sought ruthless fighters to join him, desperate men and women who had scraped out an existence here. He would offer them an alternative to their harsh exile. None of these hardened, bitter people had any reason for loyalty to the Padishah Emperor. They had been deemed to be of inferior quality, undisciplined and expendable. But Zenha knew they were tough.

The flagship came down outside the camp, with ship's defenses active and shields ready. The refugees made their way forward, cautious but hungry, clearly looking for any opportunity to attack. Watching them from the bridge screens, Zenha imagined their hard-bitten lives, how they would fight to scavenge any scraps, but they must know they could not win against an Imperial warship.

He deployed soldiers around the dreadnought to maintain a perimeter against attacks. A crew of engineers pulled out ground machinery and prefab structures to set up a small encampment in front of the flagship. Zenha needed an open place where he could meet with prisoner representatives. He hoped they would listen before bloodshed was necessary, but he might have to kill a few of them first, to make a point and get their respect.

When he was ready, he donned his First Officer uniform. The red stains from Gorambi's assassination had been laundered out. He emerged from the flagship and stood in the middle of his guarded camp, then dispatched an armed messenger, inviting representatives from the prisoners to come speak with him.

"Commander-General Moko Zenha calls for volunteers. You are all fighters or you would not still be alive. You received some Sardaukar training, but you were disposed of here. Would you like an opportunity to leave Salusa Secundus? Join the Commander-General in his own fight against Imperial corruption, and you will receive passage away from Salusa. New uniforms. Food. A new chance. But you must be willing to fight against Emperor Shaddam IV—the man who sent you to this place."

Zenha had timed his next move with the delivery of the message. Two large troop transports landed adjacent to the dreadnought, waiting to be filled with eager recruits. He stepped down the boarding ramp to face them himself, gazing around the landscape. He smelled the sour air, noted the ominous clouds in the skies—and saw the squalid camp where the survivors eked out a miserable existence.

Within an hour, after dark had fallen, the boldest prisoners cautiously approached from the camp, clearly suspicious that this was some Sardaukar trick. One muscular warlord with a battered training sword threw himself on one of the perimeter guards, and Zenha's men resoundingly cut him down, then drove back several other surly prisoners, killing everyone who came up against them.

Zenha stepped into the bright lights of his camp, and shouted through a voice amplifier. "I have made my point. I want you to fight. I need you to fight. But do not try to kill those who offer you a way off this planet. You'll have a chance for a life of fighting with my troops—a battle you have a chance to win! Not these rigged training debacles that have already killed so many of you."

Zenha walked closer to the perimeter, while his guards kept their weapons ready. He could see the menacing Salusan survivors gathered outside their camp. He squared his shoulders. "Now, who wants to prove themselves?"

Before long, seven of the toughest-looking men came forward, still suspicious, but their eyes held a glimmer of hope as well as anger. Zenha watched them demonstrate their prowess, showing how they could fight with the weapons they had used in their survival camp. He had them face off in hand-to-hand combat, and observed closely. Their techniques were brutal and unpolished, but violently effective. He called a halt, although they looked perfectly willing to murder each other.

"Save your killing for later," he warned.

The fighters were not entirely convinced of his reasons for coming here, nor did they believe what he offered them. They had survived on Salusa for this long, and they had the potential to become Sardaukar, but he was giving them something the Sardaukar corps did not—a degree of freedom, and a promise of even more if they fought at his side. He offered them hope for new lives.

As the demonstrations and questioning continued, Zenha heard movement from the opposite side of the camp, a much larger group of hard-core survivors led by a pair of muscular scarred men who wore patched and ill-fitting Sardaukar uniforms. They both carried long, well-maintained swords, while most of the others bore only repurposed or patchwork weapons. The two aggressive leaders approached the perimeter, glowering scornfully at Zenha and his uniformed men. "Imperial swine!"

More of Zenha's forces emerged from the dreadnought, armed with blades, flechette pistols, and even a few lasguns. None of these ragged survivors would be wearing a personal shield. The flagship's mounted weapons warmed up, swinging about to target the oncoming, menacing group.

But Zenha raised his hand to cut off any initial action from his own people. "We are not Imperials!" he shouted back. "Not anymore. And neither are you—no matter the Sardaukar uniforms you wear."

One of the two burly uniformed men snorted and plucked at his old uniform, no doubt taken from the body of a fallen officer.

Zenha continued, "Our goals and yours are aligned. Join us and fight against those who abandoned you here. We know the Sardaukar tried to train you and then dumped you in the wasteland. Use what you learned—and turn it against them. Blame the Emperor. He threw me to the wolves, too. I'll give you a chance to slap him in the face."

The approaching pair of warlords laughed. Leading their group of fighters, they moved to the perimeter, very close to Zenha's guards.

The ferocious-looking giant at the forefront had piercing black eyes. He strode up to Zenha and looked down at him. "We should fight for you? Are you worthy?" He sniffed, stepped to the side, noted the lack of insignia on his uniform. "I could crush you in a minute."

Zenha didn't flinch. "It might take longer than that, and don't expect to come away with no wounds of your own."

The big man guffawed. "I am Kenjo the Magnificent! Be afraid of me, little soldier! Do you know the reputation of the Sardaukar?" He pounded the ill-fitting uniform on his chest.

"Fear has nothing to do with anything I do. I do not back down." Zenha drew his own sword, held it ready. Kenjo was talking too much, not fighting. He was all bluster, testing how Zenha would react.

"Why would I join your army? I am a ruler here, a warlord—a Sardaukar officer!"

Zenha noted a black smear on the shoulder of his uniform shirt, sloppy for a true member of the Emperor's elite troops.

A woman in the group called out, "He's not really Sardaukar." She stepped forward wearing a tattered camouflage blouse and trousers, and a tilted beret over matted red hair. Her wide belt carried an assortment of small but deadly weapons—a stunner, two daggers, a cluster of throwing stars, and a garrote with tiny needles on the strand. She gripped a short sword in her left hand. "He just stole the uniform off a dead body. So did his henchman Ritt'n there."

The other man in Sardaukar uniform flushed deep red.

Zenha regarded the woman's broad, hardened face, noting that the underlying beauty in her features was overshadowed by a lifetime of pain and hidden by grime.

The warlord glowered at her. "Kia Maldisi! I'll kill you and dry your salted flesh to eat during the next cold snap!" He brandished his sword at her.

Ignoring him, Maldisi pushed her way forward, and the other fuming fighters flinched. Perhaps she was one to watch.

"They failed to be real Sardaukar," the woman continued, "though we have all learned to fight and survive. Kenjo likes to intimidate, but he doesn't like to actually fight." She sneered at him. "It is boring." Aloof, the woman turned back to Zenha. "You look more interesting. I might like to join your game."

"You would not have a chance!" The warlord puffed up his chest, but even he seemed to show a flicker of uneasiness near Kia Maldisi.

Half a dozen more women emerged from the group, looking almost as tough as Maldisi. "We want to join, too!"

Kenjo guffawed, while Zenha inspected the women. "And can you fight?"

Insulted, Maldisi raised her chin. "We survived on Salusa, haven't we? We're not the usual prostitutes in the prison districts, not the women who follow trainees around in the dark. And we certainly aren't the high-toned courtesans of Sardaukar commanders!" She let out a bitter chuckle. "You might not be able to handle us, little soldier."

Her companions chuckled.

"He wants fighting *men*, not whores!" roared Ritt'n, the henchman.

"Consider my application to join your forces and get off this world," Maldisi said, glancing at Zenha, then turning to the two big men in salvaged Sardaukar uniforms.

Kenjo and Ritt'n both drew their swords, but Maldisi strode abruptly toward them—and the men balked.

She chuckled. "There, see the fear in their eyes? The prisoners here get in a lot of fights, and these two have seen me take down men bigger than they are."

Though Maldisi waved her short sword as a distraction, her other hand snatched a throwing star from her belt, and she flung it in a blur. Kenjo reeled, and his jittering hands reached up in an attempt to find the sharp weapon embedded in the middle of his forehead. Blood poured down his face, onto his salvaged Sardaukar uniform, and then his knees buckled. He collapsed lifeless onto the ground.

His terrified henchman turned and bolted, but Maldisi pulled out one of her daggers this time. She let Ritt'n run a few steps, as if considering whether or not he was worth the effort, then flicked the knife. It spun in the air and plunged into his upper spine. The point sprouted from the hollow of his throat. Momentum kept him moving forward a few more steps before he sprawled on the rocks.

"You'll find me acceptable," she said to Zenha, but didn't bother to look back at him as she went to the pair of bodies and casually retrieved her weapons.

The crowd hooted and cheered, as if none of them had felt any loyalty to the Sardaukar poseurs.

"I am impressed," Zenha admitted. "But don't make me regret taking you . . . all of you. If you've survived here, you might have a place in my army." He suddenly realized he needed a name. "My . . . Liberation Fleet."

Several candidates shouted, and more volunteers came forward, men and women.

Now he had enough fighters to fill the additional ships he had commandeered. Enough for a battle engagement—once he figured out what his actual goal was.

A mouth covering can create an effective mask, but we all carry many disguises inside ourselves.

—*The Mirage and the Man*, Fremen wisdom

From an alcove wardrobe, Shadout Mapes found a household servant's uniform for Chani, similar to her own. "Wear this, and you can follow me without being noticed." She yanked down Chani's hood, mussed her cropped hair.

Frowning with questions, Chani removed the assistant's uniform her father had asked her to wear. "What is wrong with my own garments?"

Mapes wrapped the drab covering over the teenager's shoulders and stashed her other clothing inside the wardrobe. "We all wear disguises, and we both share secrets, don't we? The purpose of these clothes is to ensure that no one will look."

The shadout stepped back and inspected Chani's new disguise, then covered her head with another piece of cloth. "Liet wants you to observe."

Chani took a moment to scrutinize the old woman herself: Mapes's dark hair was pulled back and tied tight under her head covering. Her gaze seemed ancient, somehow enduring, yet indefinable. Faint white scars marred the leathery skin on her neck, and Chani saw the hard calluses on her hands, noted tiny tattoo marks on her wrist, a few dots that might be dismissed as moles. "Shadout is an honored Fremen name," she said. "Did you come from a sietch?"

"Long ago, child." A faint smile crept across the wrinkled lips. "A lifetime ago, or maybe two."

"Is that how you know my father?"

"All Fremen know Liet, for he is a great man. He and I have much in common." The housekeeper led Chani through the cool corridors, past large meeting chambers, offices, storage rooms. "We all know the legend, and I try to help in my own small way." Mapes gestured Chani forward. "That is how I fight and serve now, because I am too old to do what I did at your age."

Chani noticed a lump in the housekeeper's bodice, possibly the hilt of a crysknife.

Servants were busy polishing a table, arranging chairs, and setting out basins in a banquet hall. The kitchens were preparing the welcome banquet for Imperial Planetologist Kynes and his "assistant," as well as other invited guests.

Chani wondered if her father intended for her to observe the inner workings of the Arrakeen Residency, or if he just wanted her to meet this Shadout Mapes. The old woman continued to talk, and her voice turned wistful. "I used to be a freedom fighter for our people. I was young and strong, and my blood ran hot. I hated the offworlders, and I felt it was worth any sacrifice to drive them from Arrakis. Ah, I killed so many . . ."

Chani growled under her breath. "Harkonnens."

Mapes raised her eyebrows. "No, in my youth, the planetary governors were House Richese. We despised them. We believed that our lives would be better if we could ruin their spice operations, shame them before the eyes of the Emperor, and drive them out. We were convinced that whoever came afterward would surely be better."

Chani was surprised. She'd been so focused on the Harkonnen persecution that she hadn't considered past history. "But House Richese is gone now."

"Yes, we harassed them for years and years. I lost my lover in the fight, and I lost my son. Oh, how we celebrated when House Richese packed up and left Arrakis. Emperor Shaddam rescinded their governorship—and then the Harkonnens came. First Dmitri, then his son Abulurd . . . and finally the Baron."

On the lower level of the residency, Mapes led her past crowded servants' quarters with stacked bunks, a mess hall, more storerooms. "Now I have a different part of the fight. I serve here in the Residency, waiting and watching. I send whispers back when I learn something important. The time will come, child, when we are saved, when the Mahdi comes, a young man with his mother."

"That legend goes back to the oldest Fremen times," Chani said, quietly scoffing.

Mapes somehow found reason to hope. "And it cannot take forever. Perhaps it will happen in my lifetime, or yours . . . or your children's."

The shadout paused to inspect a busy laundry where workers soaked fabrics and garments in bins of chemicals that dissolved away dirt and rinsed the dust. The clothes were hung to dry, which took only minutes in the air.

Finally, she brought Chani to the upper levels, and they stood outside the door of a large office with an anteroom. "This is where Count Fenring conducts his business. I am one of only four staff members allowed to enter and clean. I am the trusted housekeeper. Before that, the Harkonnens used me in a similar role." She lowered her voice to a whisper. "That is how I learned much valuable intelligence. Count Fenring, however, is . . . much more careful."

"And you serve him willingly?" Chani asked with an edge in her voice.

"I work here. I serve two masters, as does Liet."

Chani felt a twinge of restlessness. "Is this everything my father wanted me to see? How the Residency works, out of view of the nobles?"

"Everything?" The shadout clucked her tongue. "Such an impatient child! I remember those days." Mapes led her away from Fenring's empty office. "One rarely learns 'everything' the first time, but this is a start for you." Her eyes twinkled. "And now you have also met me."

On the way down from the administration levels, they passed a guarded reservoir room where watermasters were distributing water, carrying sealed urns off to the banquet room. Mapes received a report from one of the watermasters, who bowed to her. He said, "My Lord Fenring has been generous, Housekeeper. He has only twenty guests for dinner tonight, but has allocated enough water for thirty."

Chani suspected that thirty city dwellers drank as much as ninety Fremen.

"And enough for the laving basins?" Mapes asked. "Clean towels for their ablutions and more to clean up the splashes?"

"Yes, Housekeeper," the watermaster said. "The beggars are already lining up outside the kitchen doors."

The old woman nodded. "We will make sure none of the water is wasted. Check that the laving basins are quite full."

Chani gave her a curious look. As they walked away from the reservoir room, the old woman said, "The nobles squander water to show off their wealth. Some would let it spill on the floor and simply evaporate into the air. But we wipe it up and sell it to those who come to the back entrance."

"How did the beggars know there would be a banquet tonight?" Chani asked.

"They always wait, and they always hope." Mapes sighed. "It is our way of life. We always hope. Now, come—I must get you back into your regular clothes so you can wear a different disguise. Count Fenring will begin the banquet soon."

CHANI TUCKED HER hair under her hood again and donned the cloak and tool belt with Imperial markings. Quiet as a desert mouse, she sat next to her father in the dining hall. Liet-Kynes did not introduce her to the other guests, and as his mere assistant, she was ignored. She kept her eyes averted and did not make conversation.

Before the dinner, she had watched the spectacle of the nobles washing their hands, splashing their faces, casually wiping off with wet towels, and tossing them on the floor amid the puddles. Servants scurried to clean up and whisk the towels away. Liet watched the ceremony with narrowed eyes and clear disapproval, but he spoke no word. She knew he would like to save the squeezings of moisture from the towels, but in this setting, there was no opportunity to do that.

The various dignitaries and nobles in attendance wore colorful garments, none of them appropriate for being outside in the desert. Here, the cloying aromas of their perfumes and lotions stung Chani's eyes. She viewed them as if they were a different species. The nobles and merchants tittered and talked about inane things, discussing commodities prices or Imperial politics, nothing that was relevant to her life.

Count Fenring was a thin but muscular man with odd features, a weak chin, a narrow nose, and large dark eyes. He wasn't much to look at, yet his presence dominated the hall. He sat next to an empty chair where his wife usually sat, and her absence was plain to all. The Count spoke little at his own banquet, but he listened to the casual conversations, the opinions expressed, the unpopular comments that either went in passing or were challenged. He seemed to be taking mental notes—just as Chani herself did.

As servants brought platter after platter of vegetables, salads, and bowls of tart berries, Chani resented the conspicuous wealth, but was pragmatic enough to eat what she could. The idea of swallowing a bowl full of leaves and greens was foreign to her. She was used to compact dried foods sweetened with honey, laden with melange.

The meats served were two different kinds of fish, very strange to Chani's taste buds, then braised mushrooms and a jellied liver pâté. Her stomach was heavy from the extravagance. She watched her father eat large servings, consciously storing away calories.

She sipped water from a goblet, savoring every drop, and watched the other guests gulping and spilling without paying attention. When servants passed by with pitchers to refill the cups, Chani drank quickly and took a second serving. She wished she could smuggle some of this water back to Sietch Tabr, but in this situation, the best place to store water was in her own body.

Finally, after a round of breads and pastries, Liet-Kynes stood up, drawing attention to himself. As conversation dropped off, he slid the spice-paper book out of the valise that hung from a strap on his chair. He set the report on the tabletop in a formal presentation.

"Count Fenring, Imperial Spice Observer to the Padishah Emperor Shaddam IV—as required, I have compiled my latest observations, meteorological measurements, spice mappings, and a preliminary analysis of present and future melange production on Arrakis. My report has all the necessary ecological footnotes. As always, would you please present it to the Padishah Emperor?"

"Hmmm, ahhh, of course, Planetologist. I shall carry it with me to Kaitain, and hand it to him personally." The volume was passed down the length of the table, person to person, not being opened, until Fenring picked it up, studied the cover, and dismissively flipped through the pages. "Shaddam will, ahhh, read it carefully, as always."

Chani knew that was a lie, as did some of the others in attendance. She sat there, feeling like a caged animal.

"In fact, hmmm, ahhh, your timing is perfect, Planetologist. My Lady Margot has been away for some time, and I am due to return to the Imperial Palace to fetch her. I will take this with me promptly." He held up the report book as if it were a prize.

At the end of the meal—at least Chani hoped it was the end—Shadout

Mapes and servants came around with more water basins and more towels so they could wash their hands and mouths, and again discard the damp rags.

Chani looked around the table, concealing her feelings from the noble guests, and wishing their offworld stink could be washed from Dune.

In making projections and plans, it is important to consider worst-case scenarios. We humans are not always good at that, but we should be, because nightmares come naturally to our imaginations.

—Mentat Planning Committee, contracted to CHOAM

Back on Junction after his disturbing trip to Arrakis, Starguide Serello wanted to feel stable and grounded again, but the implications of the possible Tleilaxu plot kept him unsettled. His enhanced mind was filled with an enormous amount of data from multiple perspectives.

Even so, Serello could not solve, or even adequately consider, this problem by himself. He needed a larger pool of minds. The Guild had to take action.

Outside the concentric rings of cyclopean buildings, beyond the administrative cubes and pyramids, Serello drove a groundcar to the expansive plains of rubbery gray grasses and the cluster of waiting Navigator tanks surrounding the temple of the omniscient Oracle of Time.

He wore a crisp green Guild uniform that sported the infinity symbol as well as Starguide rank markings. His thick, dark hair was neatly combed, and his smooth skin shone with toning oils.

He had dispatched a message to his fellow Starguides on Junction, summoning them to a convocation of the utmost importance, out among the Navigators. Starguides were uniquely qualified to communicate concepts and concerns to the esoteric, mutated beings.

Serello halted his groundcar outside the zone and walked across the strange grasses. He wove his way among the large transparent tanks, some of which were austere and serviceable, others with baroque ornamentation. The air was redolent with melange exhaust from the chambers, a mysterious fog that hid the misshapen bodies inside like a shadow show.

Navigators landed on Junction from their assigned Heighliners so they could commune with others of their kind. More than a hundred tanks were dispersed across the open area in a complex pattern that was comprehensible only to Navigator mathematics.

Many tanks were clustered in reverence around an ancient structure of adamant stone and Corinthian columns. The dwelling of the Oracle of Time resembled a temple, though the Guild eschewed any primitive religious connotations.

As he approached, Serello felt her presence strongly, a psychic thrumming in the air. Within her temple and tank, the Oracle remained silent, as did the gathered Navigators, but they all sensed Serello, and waited.

At the appointed time, eleven groundcars arrived carrying Starguides from the Guild metropolis, all in identical green uniforms. Serello's comrades came together at the site without casual or inane conversation. He could sense their curiosity about his dire news. He knew the Navigators were listening, too, and hoped he had also attracted the Oracle's attention.

Once the audience had gathered, Serello got to the point. "We have a problem. I've gathered disturbing evidence, disparate observations and reports, which are individually concerning but collectively could be disastrous."

A female Starguide spoke up; she had short, steel-gray hair and ageproofed skin that looked more polymer than flesh. "If we have a problem, then the Imperium has a problem."

A shorter man added, "And then all of humanity has a problem."

Serello continued, "It began with the recent funeral for our Navigator . . . my great-grandfather." He wouldn't normally have added that detail, but wanted full disclosure of the personal connection. "We delivered his body to a pre-spice mass on Arrakis, where it should have been obliterated." He paused. "This did not happen as planned."

He told them of the unmarked marauder ship that had seized the body, and the illicit Tleilaxu satellite he had found in orbit around Arrakis. Then, although at first it seemed unrelated, he described his odd meeting with Tleilaxu Master Giblii, and how the man might have taken a cell scraping from his hand.

"Those points have only a nebulous connection," said a Navigator through his throbbing speakerpatch.

Serello turned. "There is still valid reason for suspicion." He revealed the astonishing suggestion the Tleilaxu Master had made to Malina Aru from CHOAM.

Another Navigator boomed out in a distorted voice, "Your suspicions have merit, Starguide."

"But what is the Tleilaxu purpose?" asked a Starguide in the second row behind him.

Others nodded, perplexed. One asked, "Do the Tleilaxu plan to grow their own Navigators? Create gholas in axlotl tanks?"

"They might be able to do it," said the old polymer-faced woman. "They have the ability, provided they obtain the proper cellular samples."

"They would fail," said another Navigator. "Becoming one of us is not merely a matter of genetics and mutations, but of exquisite training to enhance our minds and prescience."

Serello said, "I have considered this long and hard. It does not seem possible, or rational, that the Tleilaxu would try to compete with the Spacing Guild. Would they build their own Heighliners, too? Offer an alternative to our Guild routes? Would they create independent ships, perhaps even offer military vessels to outside buyers?" He shook his head. "That is beyond the abilities of the Bene Tleilax. They do not have sufficient industrial capability."

"It would be folly!" cried one of the younger, more emotional Starguides.

"But why else would they steal a Navigator corpse?" another demanded. "Why else take Starguide Serello's DNA?"

"Perhaps they saw an opportunity and are conducting pure research to assess the potential," said a beautiful female Starguide with long reddish hair. "It is alarming, yes, but what if they have no plan?"

"The Tleilaxu always have a plan," said another Navigator.

"But what commercial purpose might they have in mind?" insisted the strident young Starguide.

Serello felt a crackle on his skin, an electrical charge in the air, and smelled ozone building around him. A chill went down his spine as a glow emanated from the immense chamber surrounded by temple columns. The Oracle of Time had awakened. This being, once known as Norma Cenva, had existed even before the foundation of the Guild, had transformed during Serena Butler's jihad against the Thinking Machines.

All fell silent with awe as the Oracle spoke in an ethereal, angelic voice. "You are thinking within parochial parameters. Navigators do not merely guide ships. Such an assessment limits the scope of their exceptional ability."

After a moment of heavy silence, Serello spoke up. "Pardon me, but what specific ability do you mean, Oracle?"

The lights around the tank rippled, and he saw a silhouetted form drifting in the spice gases, sometimes looking beautiful, other times horrific.

"A Navigator guides ships because of *prescience*. No other being can look along possible timelines to measure causes and effects. A Navigator can choose the path of a Heighliner . . . or the path of history itself." The Oracle fell silent, waiting for the information to sink in.

Serello and his fellow Starguides struggled to grasp what she meant. One Navigator boomed out a conclusion. "And then others can use that prescience!"

"The Tleilaxu could use it," Serello whispered. "For their own repellent purposes."

His Mentat training also kicked in, and dire possibilities unfolded like a black flower before him. No, the Bene Tleilax would not build starships, would not carry passengers, commodities, or military forces. That would be too blatant.

But if they possessed their own captive Navigator clones with expanded prescience, the Tleilaxu could envision changes to markets, to societies. They could manipulate commerce, guide religious prophecies, political movements. Working with subtle hands behind the scenes, they could anticipate events and shape Imperial society.

And no one would know, because the Tleilaxu would leave no fingerprints. A Navigator's predictions would simply help them make countless little decisions across thousands of worlds, which would forge a road to Tleilaxu dominance.

This realization made Serello's fears increase. He saw the alarm on the faces of his fellow Starguides. The Navigator tanks were silent with only a faint background thrumming that led Serello to believe they were communing on their own private frequencies, expressing deep concern.

"This is a far graver danger than I thought," he said. "We must find them."

When reading any report it is essential to know the motives and allegiances of the author, because everything written, and everything said, contains an inherent bias.

—CROWN PRINCE RAFAEL CORRINO,
Contemplations of the Throne

Princess Irulan climbed the uphill path from the largest of four private ponds on the palace grounds. As a diversion, she and her father had been racing old-style model sailboats out on the water. As usual, she allowed him to win, even though there was little at stake. It always put him in a better mood, and the bucolic setting gave them a chance for uninterrupted conversation.

The Emperor remained at the edge of the pond, admiring the model boats as servants unpacked and prepared to launch two new versions. Irulan made her way back to the palace to meet Count and Lady Fenring. The Count had just arrived from Arrakis, while his wife had spent the past two months at court.

Fenring and Margot's marriage had been arranged by the Bene Gesserit decades earlier, according to bloodline possibilities. The Sisterhood had managed Shaddam's first marriage as well, to Anirul, mother of the five Imperial princesses. Unlike Irulan's father and mother, though, the Count and Lady Fenring truly adored each other.

She had recently pondered thoughts of marriage and happiness at breakfast with her concubine, Aron. The quiet briefings about Moko Zenha's mutiny had made her think about the officer's audacious marriage proposal. Irulan had felt no personal attraction for the man, but he wouldn't have been worse than other previous suitors—all of whom her father had found unacceptable for one reason or another.

Irulan wondered about the future match the Emperor would make for her, which would be decided not only by Imperial politics, but by the Sisterhood's manipulations. She was not wistfully romantic like

Chalice—Irulan's own short-term needs were quite acceptably met by the well-trained Aron—but she did want to know her own fate. She was twenty-six!

While Shaddam remained at the pond with his model boats, Irulan encountered a coterie of servants who scurried forward to prepare for the Fenrings' arrival. A groundcar had picked up the Count at the spaceport, and Lady Margot rode with him back to the palace. Sometimes Fenring liked to arrive in secret, drawing no attention to himself. Now, however, he would make a happy show of being reunited with his wife at court. He certainly must be glad to leave harsh Arrakis.

Fenring was a fixture at court, when not off on some shadowy mission for the Emperor. He was a man of intricate layers and contained secrets. Margot was lovely and especially charming, having been impeccably trained by the Sisterhood—as Irulan was. She knew how a skilled Bene Gesserit could disguise her real thoughts.

She pondered the Count and Lady Fenring like a novelist developing complex characters, both hero and antihero. The secretive Count certainly filled both roles, a boon companion to her father since they had been boys together, but also one of the most feared assassins in the Imperium, if rumors were to believed. Someday she might write about him.

Under the clear Kaitain sunshine with barely a cloud in the sky, Irulan waited at the autumn gate by the pond gardens. Fenring and his wife walked toward the Princess across the wide pavers, arm in arm. The Count wore an impeccable jacket with a waistcoat and cuffs, and tucked under his free arm he carried a sealed valise, no doubt with important diplomatic documents. Margot wore an elegant green brocade dress that reached almost to the ground, so only the tips of her ornate boots showed.

Fenring beamed when he saw Irulan and gave her a deep, formal bow. He was not at all an attractive man, with a weasellike face and those large, intense eyes. "I apologize if I still carry the dust of Arrakis, but I, ahhh, hmmm, was in a hurry to get here."

Irulan saw no sign of dirt on his jacket, but Margot plucked at his sleeve. "We shall have to throw these clothes away, my dear, but I have a complete new wardrobe for you in our palace quarters."

Fenring looked past Irulan to the Emperor at the ponds with the little boats. "These garments will be perfectly appropriate for now." He slipped away from his wife and hurried down the path. "Just like Shaddam and I used to do as boys."

The two women shared a glance, acknowledging their common Bene Gesserit bond. "Hasimir is so excitable, but I do love him dearly," Margot said as they strolled down the path. "We should not let them get too distracted."

On the bank of the pond, Shaddam rose to his feet, and Irulan saw genuine joy on her father's face. "Yes, just like we used to do as boys! I have a model boat prepared for you, Hasimir. Irulan let me beat her in the race this morning, but you have no such intentions."

"I, ahhh, intend to keep earning your respect, Sire." Fenring looked around, assessing the grounds. "But your old pond appears to have been covered up and planted over."

"One must always make changes," Shaddam said, "or risk growing stagnant."

Fenring held out his valise. "And one must attend to political duties, or risk a chaotic Imperium. Let us forgo the model boats for now, Sire. A conversation is in order." He glanced at his wife. "In the company of my Lady."

Shifting his mood and plans, Shaddam suggested they meet in the nearby gazebo, and Irulan sent her ladies-in-waiting scurrying off to prepare a course of refreshments. Behind them, servants packed up the model boats, carefully boxing them for storage.

By the time the Emperor brought them to the private structure overlooking the ponds, a pair of servants had delivered tea and hors d'oeuvres. Shaddam didn't even seem to notice them.

Irulan sat next to Lady Margot, while Fenring faced the Emperor across the table. "First things first, Sire." He opened the valise and withdrew a bound volume printed on brownish spice paper. "Your planetologist on Arrakis has delivered his regular report, and I have fulfilled my duty by delivering it to you."

Shaddam frowned at the dusty volume. "Why does the man not use shigawire spools or ridulian crystals, like everyone else? How . . . rustic." He opened the book to reveal pages with tightly written words, scribed by hand with a stylus. "Fascinating reading, I am sure."

Irulan was intrigued enough to speak up. "The facilities on Arrakis are much less civilized than here on Kaitain, Father. The planetologist obviously put a good deal of effort into this report."

Fenring grinned, as if embarrassed. "Dr. Kynes takes his duties seriously, ahhh, Sire, and spends much time in the deep desert, going directly to the source."

"I appreciate his diligence," her father said, without sincerity or interest.

Fenring pulled out a more modern shigawire spool from the valise. "And here is the current report from Baron Harkonnen, with much more thorough data on spice production. Though, ahhh, I may trust the planetologist more."

Shaddam's expression intensified. "Is the Baron cheating us? I presume any errors are within the tolerable allowance, or should I have my Mentat financial advisers dig deeper?"

"No doubt that man slants his own records. Dr. Kynes's data may be useful for comparing with the formal Harkonnen reports."

The Emperor sniffed. "Once again, the fat man must be reined in. Perhaps I should order a major crackdown and a thorough Imperial inspection. Would you like that, Hasimir?"

Fenring's dark eyes shifted. "Hmmm, that would take an extraordinary effort, Sire, and the disruption may not be necessary at this time. Perhaps, ahhh, the mere threat would be sufficient. We can always have the Mentat advisers dig deeper later."

Shaddam placed the spool on top of Kynes's bound report and slid them aside. "Make certain our threat is enough to make the Baron fear the Imperial hammer at any moment." He smiled. "I can always remove House Harkonnen from Arrakis if I am too displeased."

Fenring smiled. "I shall warn him of the possible consequences, Sire. Hmmm, a well-delivered threat can be as effective as an actual audit—and far less arduous and time-consuming."

The Emperor seemed mollified.

As Irulan sipped her tea, she noted the bond of trust between these men. She understood the extent of Count Fenring's power and influence and realized how dangerous he was—and how necessary.

Margot leaned closer to Fenring. "I would rather you stayed here at the palace for a while, husband."

"And I should like to go to Arrakis someday," Irulan mused, noticing how this surprised the others. "It is one of the most important planets in the Imperium, yet I have not yet seen it."

"A visit could certainly be arranged," Margot said. "But do not expect even our Residency to be like the palace here. Arrakis is not a . . . pleasant place."

The Count also seemed skeptical. "You would not like it, my dear

Princess. I, ahhh, strongly suggest that you content yourself with reports such as mine."

Irulan looked at him with a steady, challenging gaze. "It is often through discomfort that important things are learned. If Lady Margot thrives in such an environment, so can I. Yes, one day I shall see Arrakis for myself."

"If that is what you wish," Emperor Shaddam said.

Fenring chuckled. "You display great poise and intelligence, Princess. I see why my royal friend consults with you so closely." He blinked calmly, then shocked them all with an abrupt change of subject. "And what is this I hear about a mutiny in the Imperial military, Sire? A man who killed his superior officer and seized an entire task force?"

"Just a handful of malcontents." The Emperor flushed. "We are taking care of it, while our propaganda ministers and information couriers shift attention away from the matter. We would prefer to keep the incident quiet and not give it undue importance."

"Hmmm-ahh, the threat may be bigger than you suspect. My informants have told me about other incidences of First Officers overthrowing their noble commanders and joining this rebellion. Be careful that it, ahhh, does not become a large-scale outbreak."

Shaddam looked surprised and alarmed. "Your spy network should not exceed mine, Hasimir."

He bowed. "I must serve my Emperor to the best of my abilities. It takes a long time for reports to make their way through proper channels."

Visibly upset, Shaddam rose to his feet. "Get to the bottom of this, Hasimir, and until you do, I want it kept quiet."

Leaving his tea and his companions, as well as the spice reports, the Emperor strode back into the palace by himself.

If all my assassins succeed in reaching their target, the Emperor will be a very, very dead man.

—COMMANDER-GENERAL MOKO ZENHA

Preparing to leave Salusa Secundus, Zenha took aboard fifty new fighter recruits who had already been trained in the harsh environment that created Sardaukar. The fighters included seven women along with Kia Maldisi, who had proved themselves as ruthless as the men from the survival camp.

The recruits were cleaned, fed, and issued new uniforms, then briefed on Zenha's crusade against the dishonorable Emperor. To keep them separated, the newcomers were dispersed to cruisers and destroyers in his motley fleet, while five were assigned to his flagship, including Maldisi. He saw great potential in her.

As his now-united Liberation Fleet moved in formation for an orderly loading into the vast hold of the Guild Heighliner that had come to retrieve them, none the wiser, the Commander-General looked up to see Maldisi standing at his office door. She looked shockingly different and professional. "The uniform suits you," he said.

"Leaving Salusa Secundus suits me," she replied. "I could get used to this."

He heard a low rumble as the dreadnought settled into its docking clamp inside the huge Heighliner. The proper paperwork had been submitted, and the Guild provided any necessary exemptions. Previously, the Guild had delivered these vessels full of loyal Imperial officers, but now that situation had changed. The incompetent superiors had been overthrown, replaced by First Officers, the intransigent crew members purged. Some of the noble commanders remained in the ship brigs, while others had been ejected into space.

His new Salusan recruits would be the most fiercely loyal, since he had given them something the Imperium could not. By spreading them out aboard his freshly indoctrinated ships, the new fighters could keep some of the uneasy mutineers in line.

Now, Maldisi brushed her uniform blouse and smiled. "Fits me quite well, sir. Thanks for the opportunity. I'll do whatever you need."

He sat back in his chair and studied the woman. She was attractive, now that the grime and blood had been scoured away. No longer greasy or tucked into a battered beret, her reddish hair touched her shoulders—longer than regulation length, but he let that go without comment. She had a burn mark on her chin and a small scar at her temple, but the marks gave her character. He could only imagine the ordeals she had faced on the Imperial prison planet.

"After what you've been through, Maldisi, I'm not sure you are cut out for a formal, disciplined military life."

She attempted a salute, grinning in resignation when she knew she hadn't done it quite right. "Probably not, sir. Do you have some other assignment for me that might be suitable?" She leaned against the bulkhead in a relaxed, almost insubordinate pose. Maybe it was meant to be seductive.

Maldisi was not a regular soldier, but she and some of her female companions might work out for what he had in mind.

"In fact, I do. I need you to move among people, listen, manipulate them . . . whatever it takes."

Maldisi sniffed. "I can do all that, if the mission requires it. Depends on where you intend to send me. It can't be any worse than what I've had to do on Salusa."

"You've got the abilities I need, and you're pretty enough, but not so striking that you'd stand out."

"Can't tell if that's a compliment, sir." She crossed her arms and stepped into the office stateroom so she stood closer to him. "I could have been a Sardaukar courtesan to some important officer. When I was first dumped on Salusa, I was willing to do it. But for whatever reason, I didn't make the cut, so I had to survive other ways. I resisted being made a common prostitute for lower-ranking soldiers, or for the prisoners."

She told him she had been a petty criminal and repeat offender at the Imperial capital. Her biggest mistake had been stealing from an influential nobleman, someone who knew the Emperor. Rather than being sentenced to some Kaitain prison, she had been dropped on Salusa, guarded by soldiers, never expected to survive. She was trained as a courtesan, eventually failed, was essentially discarded.

"Bastard Shaddam," she muttered. "I could have been released in a couple of years, if he hadn't twisted the knife . . . as a favor to his friend."

"You survived; that's the important part," Zenha said. "Now you—and your companions, if they pass muster—will have a chance to make up for it. Back to Kaitain and the Imperial Palace. You and a handful of your comrades could win this whole movement for me, if you succeed."

She chuckled. "Now you've got my interest. The survival camp where you found me was a dumping ground for people the Sardaukar didn't consider worth any more of their time. Low security, rarely monitored, no aircraft or ground transportation. Supposedly no escape for any of us."

"I granted you your freedom," he said. "And now I need something in return."

"I'm listening."

"Most people would assume my movement was doomed from the start," Zenha explained. "Indeed, I never intended for any of this to happen, but I was betrayed by Emperor Shaddam. I lost thousands of good men, and I myself shouldn't have survived. Afterward, in disgrace, I was demoted and sent off to serve under another fool—whose incompetent commands would have resulted in even more deaths. So, I said enough!" He slammed a fist down on his desk. "This flagship was Duke Bashar Gorambi's, until I made it mine."

She said with a narrow smile, "You're in big trouble, then."

"Yes, I am, but I do not think small or content myself with some impotent act of defiance. I've sent out trusted emissaries to recruit more disgruntled second-line officers and enlisted men. Look at the ships I just won above Salusa Secundus. The level of antipathy toward the ancient system of nepotism and incompetence runs far deeper than I suspected—but I remain intensely loyal to the Imperium itself. It is *Shaddam* who must be removed."

Maldisi stood at attention, her eyebrows lifted in curiosity, but she did not interrupt.

"Building this Liberation Fleet will take time, and we have to keep moving, draw no attention, keep slipping through the wide net that's out to snare us. Inevitably, we will encounter many battles, many deaths."

He looked long and hard at her, still assessing. "But I can achieve victory much more quickly if my idea succeeds—with your help."

Maldisi's eyes sparkled. "Sounds like an interesting assignment. Especially if it hurts Shaddam Corrino."

"We will send you to Kaitain, complete with financial resources, clothing, and a convincing backstory. You and a handpicked group of companions will be independent, each given great flexibility. I want you to infiltrate the Imperial Palace. There are thousands of servants, civil officials, minor dignitaries, support staff, delivery people, gardeners. Seduce one of the young men or women in the Imperial Court, maybe replace a cleaner or attendant, or find a job as a diplomatic clerk."

"To what purpose, sir?"

Now he smiled back at her. "There is only the smallest chance of success, but the reward would be incredible. It would change everything."

"Sounds impossible."

"It is impossible, but you've done the impossible before. Are you willing to make the attempt?" He paused, looked her in the eye. "One assassination, one huge and shocking victory. If you kill the Emperor, then that corrupt man will be gone—and he has no male heir, no sons, only daughters. His latest Empress, Firenza, is dead. In the immediate turmoil, I can return with my entire Liberation Fleet and force a marriage to Princess Irulan, secure the throne, and ensure that the reign of House Corrino continues. *But without Shaddam.*"

Maldisi blinked at him, then burst out laughing. "Oh? Is that all you want?" She paused, then seriously considered what he was proposing. "What's to stop me and my friends from just vanishing once we reach Kaitain? We could start our lives over there and live comfortably. That's obviously better than a suicide mission."

He continued to stare at her. "Is that what you would do?"

After a tense moment, she shrugged. "Don't worry, this is exactly the kind of demanding assignment I like."

"Good." He brought out briefing materials from a drawer, a ridulian crystal that projected a detailed layout of the sprawling Imperial Palace, each of its levels and wings, the gardens, and the support buildings. He highlighted the separate wings.

"Familiarize yourself with every detail. The Emperor's quarters are here, and he has significant security when he retires behind his privacy walls. His five daughters live in their own quarters, in varying levels of palatial extravagance. The youngest, Rugi, still has tutors, nannies, and minders, and the next one, Josifa, is nineteen years old. Little is known about either of them, as they have been kept out of the public eye. I've heard conflicting reports, but they may have left Kaitain for schooling on Wallach IX."

Maldisi grimaced. "I could dress up in pretty clothes, but I would never be able to infiltrate the Bene Gesserit."

"You won't have to. We'll concentrate on the other daughters as potential weak points. Irulan, Chalice, Wensicia."

She leaned closer to the projection. "Do you want them killed, too?"

He shook his head. "No, they are to be left strictly alone. Since all five daughters are still unwed, any one of them can be used for immediate marriage alliances to cement my new reign."

Maldisi nodded. "I prefer to kill men anyway."

He did not smile. "We'll send you and your companions to Kaitain separately, and I want each of you to look for an opening to get to the Emperor. Redundancy, multipronged attacks to increase the odds of one succeeding."

"I assume we are not to communicate with one another when on Kaitain?"

"Correct. One of my most trusted officers, Staff Captain Dudier Pilwu, is in charge of preparing you. I have many unexpected allies in and around the Imperial Court who will aid and protect you behind the scenes."

Maldisi did not seem intimidated or uneasy about the assignment. In fact, she looked pleased. "You rescued me from a hell-world, Commander-General. I will do as you say, and do it gladly, giving it everything I've got." She snickered. "I can't wait to see the expression on Shaddam's face when he's dying. I'll be the last person he ever sees."

"I couldn't ask for more." He rose to his feet and dismissed her.

The comm gave the signal that all military ships had been loaded aboard the Heighliner and the massive cargo doors were sealed for the voyage. As expected, the Guild had not asked for details or requested verification for moving the Imperial fleet division. After ten thousand years of tradition and treaties, Zenha could count on the momentum of diplomacy.

He remained standing, studied the report from the officers on board his new warships. His revolt had begun less than two months ago, and the vastness of the Imperium meant that rumors and actual facts about what he had done would take far longer than that to propagate. Still, he had to move quickly.

When planning a garden we can choose where to plant seeds, tend the shoots, water and nurture each plant. We can prune unnecessary leaves, even uproot weeds when we see them. In society, we do the same thing with human lives.

—IMPERIAL PLANETOLOGIST PARDOT KYNES,
called Umma by the Fremen, lectures to the sietches

The high canyon walls blocked the direct sun, and Chani worked with her brother in the shade. Under a rough overhang, she and Khouro documented the growing plants in a small alcove garden, a secret island of fertilized soil, chemical nutrients mixed with animal dung and human feces.

Using a stylus and a pad of spice paper, Khouro counted saguaro, mesquite, and sagebrush, then used a measuring guide to note the height of each one. "Two of these plants are struggling. They need more water."

"I'll adjust the catchtrap tubes." Bending low, Chani moved among the equipment.

Thin plastic tendrils extended from catchtraps and color-changing dew collectors tucked into crannies above. Each evening, the equipment condensed a few drops of moisture out of the air as temperatures cooled, then funneled it into the tubes.

She looked at one stunted saguaro no taller than her knee. It seemed to be begging for help. Just another sip of water. She found the moisture tube and shifted it away from a mesquite bush that was thriving.

Khouro frowned. "If you take water from a strong plant to help a weaker one that might die anyway, does that make the best garden?"

Chani countered, "By taking just a bit of water from one that has enough, we could save this cactus and make the entire garden stronger."

Khouro muttered as he moved to the next plantings. The shadowed canyon was not far from Sietch Tabr. The garden produced no food for the tribe, yet it was another small piece in the overall dream. As she toiled among the hardy and defiant plants, she mused about the Arrakeen Residency's tall date palms.

After leaving the dirty, noisy city with her father, she was relieved to be back in the desert, where she belonged. In the familiar sietch at last, she had stripped out of her stillsuit and used clean sand to scrub her skin, removing the unpleasantness of so many people, so many offworlders.

She appreciated the purity of the desert more than ever and was happy to take her turn to work in these plantings, as all sietch members did. Chani was glad to be with her brother, even if he was not talkative. She didn't pry about his mood, knowing he would eventually tell her what was troubling him.

He moved to a taller saguaro and carelessly scratched his hand on the needles. Khouro hissed in surprise more than pain, looked at the dark red line that congealed almost instantly. Fremen metabolism did not waste even the tiniest bit of water. He licked the scratch, and the blood stopped.

Khouro looked at her with hooded eyes and finally spoke. The muscles in his jaw jumped as he struggled to form words. "I should have gone with you to Arrakeen."

"You would not like it there," Chani said.

"Still, I should have gone with you . . . and him. He raised us both to know about planetology, to follow in his footsteps and help build the Fremen future. Yet he took only you, not me."

"I did not want to go," she insisted.

"He keeps reminding us of how his father trained him to follow in his footsteps, ensuring that he could serve as the next Imperial Planetologist."

She saw Khouro's jealous anger, tried to alleviate it. "He thinks I would benefit from training at an Imperial Academy! Ridiculous! He suggested I should become *certified*, whatever that means. Why do I need a paper from some offworld government to prove that I know the science of living in the desert?"

"We both know about that." Khouro scowled as he looked away. "He never turns down a chance to remind me that I am not his son."

Chani was startled by the raw comment. "And you often remind him of that yourself, Liet-Chih." She pointedly used his real name, then quoted a Fremen proverb that Reverend Mother Ramallo had taught her. "Unnecessary conflict waters no plants and gathers no spice."

His expression darkened, as he apparently found no merit in her reasoning.

She softened her voice. "I do not dream of power or influence by gaining the same title my father has. That bureaucratic foolishness is what forces him to split his energy and his work. But I am Fremen in my heart and soul." She touched the center of her chest. "And so are you."

"I am Fremen in my heart, too," Khouro said, "and yes, I know my heart."

FROM A ROCK-RIMMED window opening on the opposite wall of the canyon, Liet-Kynes watched them in the shadows. He had come to this private overlook to contemplate and spotted his daughter and stepson going about their tasks. He was about to work his way down to the canyon floor to join them, but when he heard the buzz of their voices, he thought better of it. Instead, he just watched and listened.

These siblings were like friends holding a casual conversation, but they were more than that, bound by the blood of their mother, although the blood of two different fathers separated them. Seeing them work among the cacti and sagebrush, he recognized familiar mannerisms that were his beloved *Faroula's*, though they probably didn't even know it.

His heart ached for his wife. Faroula had died no more than a weakened husk of who she had once been, yet in his mind she was still just as bright and vibrant as the woman he'd fallen in love with. Now, much too late, Liet wished he had shown his love for her more openly. The Fremen were a passionate people, yet contradictory, because they did not easily reveal their personal emotions. It was not the Fremen way . . . but *he* could have changed it.

Liet's eyes burned as he thought of his lost beloved . . . who was also Warrick's beloved. They had been friends despite their rivalry over Faroula, and they had worked out their differences. The two young men had accepted the challenge of the sandworm race, and Liet had acknowledged his defeat, wishing only the best for Warrick and Faroula as they wed. When baby Liet-Chih had been born, Liet vowed to be the child's guardian. He had never expected—never wanted!—the tragedy that would befall Warrick, not even in the tiniest secret corner of his soul. Later, when Faroula took him as her second husband, he had seen it not as a triumph, but the saddest of victories.

Liet-Chih had been too young to know any of this, but the boy had imagined his own answers and convinced himself they were true. Liet had tried to make peace with him, but the angry young man never showed interest in that. Chani did her best to smooth over the breach, and Liet only hoped that someday his stepson's heart would soften.

Now the pair's words drifted up to him, confined in the canyon walls and amplified by the shape of the cliffs. He had never imagined that Liet-Chih—*Khouro,* he reminded himself—would have had any interest in going to Arrakeen, especially not as the planetologist's assistant.

Liet resolved to make more of an effort to reach out to the young man. He would offer to teach Khouro the formalities of serving as an Imperial Planetologist. Maybe his stepson could help him prepare documents, cover up undesirable data, divert attention from true numbers. Or would the young man simply scoff at that, too?

Liet believed the unsettling story of the mysterious ship the two had seen, a marauder that had stolen the corpse of a Navigator. A secret Tleilaxu project? All Fremen disliked offworlders, but the Tleilaxu were reviled even among citizens of the Imperium. Now the Guild had suggested that the genetic wizards might have a hidden facility here on Arrakis! That offended Liet to his core.

The Spacing Guild wanted to find that facility at all costs, and they had tasked Chani and her friends to accomplish it. But Liet knew this was a much larger errand. It was a crisis that affected all Fremen! Offworlders could not with impunity set up a dangerous genetic laboratory in the Fremen desert. He shuddered to think of the disruptions that might happen to his delicate terraforming work, his careful and precise plantings.

From his alcove, he listened to the conversation dwindle outside. Chani and her brother packed up and moved down the canyon to the next hidden planting. As they left, Liet felt a warmth in his heart, proud of the two of them, proud of his stepson even if the young man kept his distance. He would help both of them.

Concerned about the Tleilaxu, Liet had already sent hundreds of Fremen scouts to look even harder. If the genetic researchers were here on Arrakis, his people would find them.

Then he would be happy to let Chani, Khouro, and their commando friends destroy the place.

Death is a part of life, and life a part of death.

—Bene Gesserit observation

For years, Princess Irulan had thought her pampered life was a pleasant monotony, each day much like the one before it. Even gala palace events and royal court sessions had a familiarity, but she'd been shaken out of her humdrum malaise by the upstart Zenha's audacious proposal. That startling request had triggered a series of dramatic events that no one could have predicted.

Of course it would fail. Over thousands of years of Corrino rule, there had been numerous revolts championing one cause or another, and none had succeeded for more than a brief interim.

Irulan remained dutifully silent, though she agreed with the essence of Zenha's complaint, that the Imperial military was top-heavy with incompetent noblemen. When bad decisions led to the unnecessary deaths of hundreds or thousands of soldiers, was there no imperative to challenge those decisions? In that respect, had Zenha been wrong?

It was logical that the rebel commander would have gone into hiding, taking his outlaws to some obscure planet where they would never be found. Nevertheless, the man had to face the consequences, once he was caught.

Her father shielded her from private discussions of the Zenha matter, but she noticed that he seemed worried and upset every day. The two no longer shared meals and casual conversation as before, no walks together in the garden. More rumors about the rebellious commander trickled in, but the Emperor's intelligence operatives could provide few details. Even under normal circumstances, status updates from across the vast Imperium took months, sometimes as much as a year to arrive.

It was clear that Zenha's task force, seized after the murder of Duke

Bashar Gorambi, had vanished. Other Imperial warships seemed to have gone missing on dispersed missions, and Kaitain waited for them to check in. Irulan had studied the reports of the other missing ships and tried to connect the dots, but saw no pattern yet to prove that an even larger mutinous fleet was converging under Zenha's leadership.

The Padishah Emperor would never admit that his petulant provocation of the ambitious Zenha had instigated the chain of events. Perhaps if Shaddam had made an ally of the man, rather than setting him up for failure and disgrace, maybe offering marriage to Chalice instead. . . .

Her sister Wensicia seemed fascinated by the rebel officer, and she had buried herself in troop movements and fleet deployments. The Spacing Guild delivered ships according to established routes and long-standing treaties, but they did not share their records, even with the Emperor—and certainly not with his third daughter.

Wensicia had, however, offered her insights to Irulan, who listened without being entirely convinced. Irulan did acknowledge gaps in Imperial military reporting, ships with competent second-line officers who served under the worst of the showpiece noble commanders. Those vessels, even entire battle groups, were among those that had failed to report in. Perhaps there was a connection.

For the afternoon, Irulan sat in on an Imperial Court session on the lowest level of the palace, back to the routine daily activities. Here, she watched Wensicia make her case to be named to yet another committee (she was on two already). Even as a child, Wensicia could be demanding and knew how to manipulate others to do what she wanted. Now, CHOAM President Frankos Aru sat in the session, one of the most important people in the Imperium.

Knowing it was better to have her as an ally than a foe, Irulan wanted Wensicia to find a role that would satisfy her ambition. The Princess Royal saw that the lethargic committee members were paying little attention to Wensicia making her case, so she rose to her feet to interrupt the session's discussion. "I vote for my sister for this important committee assignment. Wensicia clearly wants to learn and increase her experiences. As a daughter of the Padishah Emperor, I believe this is unquestionably a good thing. You should allow her to serve."

Wensicia looked at her in surprise, then smiled in appreciation.

Irulan's vote was a highly visible and influential one, and the committee members quickly followed suit.

AS PRINCESS CHALICE Corrino busied herself dressing for that evening's banquet, she heard a disturbance in the corridor outside her apartments. Her three ladies-in-waiting looked up from their tasks—one of them selecting jewelry, another fixing her hair, and a third brushing on her makeup. Two additional attendants had managed to get the new dress on her, while the tailor adjusted the seams.

But Chalice broke away to see what was going on in the hall. She heard shouting, and as she hurried, her attendants followed, clinging to threads, necklaces, pins.

Count Fenring stood outside her door, his expression frightening as he rebuked the liveried palace guard who stood at his post outside her quarters. "Be more alert! Only one guard? For the second daughter of the Emperor? I could have killed you without a thought and been inside the dear Princess's chambers causing havoc! You must always be ready for an assassination attempt against the royal family!"

"I am at my regular post, my Lord. A guard is always assigned to Princess Chalice." The uniformed man squirmed under the Count's obvious ire. "Is something out of the ordinary? We take all necessary precautions."

"Obviously, ahhh, many more precautions are necessary. We have had word of a rebellion brewing, a mutiny among Imperial military ships. One of those criminals could make a move on the Corrino family." The guard paled, and Fenring continued, "You saw what the fanatics did on Otak! And there is a banquet tonight, which is a possible point of vulnerability. I'm going to make certain every guest is searched—for the safety of Princess Chalice and her sisters." He sniffed.

Hearing this alarming news, Chalice let out a small gasp and felt her pulse race. Her attendants stood next to her, aghast.

Fenring's expression instantly changed, grew warm and comforting. "I did not mean to alarm you, ahhh, my dear. But I would not want you in harm's way."

"Fanatics?" She brushed her hand across her forehead, feeling perspiration there. "Like those horrible Navachristians on Otak? Wasn't that officer Zenha sent to Otak? Do you think he's in league with them?"

"Hmmm, an interesting coincidence," Fenring said. "But the Sardaukar have already taken care of every single fanatic on that poor world. You, ahhh, need not worry about them."

"And that treacherous officer Zenha? He wanted to marry Irulan!"

The Count tried to nudge her back into her quarters. "I am certain the outlaw will be captured and brought to justice soon. Do not concern yourself." He flashed a glare at the dithering ceremonial guard. "We will enhance your security without delay."

But Chalice would not be easily calmed. Instead, she hurried in the opposite direction down the corridor.

IN THE MIDST of the dull Imperial Court hearings, after the vote was taken to include Wensicia in an important advisory role, Irulan was startled when Chalice burst into the chamber. She looked disheveled in her long, glittering gown. Typically, her sister prepared early for formal banquets, always wanting to look her best to catch the eye of some eligible nobleman or politician. Now her hair was wild, as were her eyes.

Wensicia was already on her feet, hurrying to intercept the panicked young woman. Irulan also rose, while the rest of the court business ground to an awkward halt. Wensicia took her sister's arm, squeezed hard. "What's the matter? You look terrified."

Chalice could barely get out the words. "Count Fenring says there's a rebel uprising! Ships full of fanatics like the ones that blew up Otak are coming here to kill us!"

Frankos Aru cleared his throat, shaking his head. "Don't be silly, Princess." The President of CHOAM was an infrequent participant at court because of his busy schedule, but Irulan knew he would attend the evening banquet, so he had come to this meeting.

Looking at the distinguished gray-haired man, Chalice drew in a quick breath. Irulan had seen her sister flirt with the CHOAM President before, but Frankos Aru had not reciprocated the young woman's attention. At the moment, Chalice seemed too upset to care about his reaction.

Irulan joined her sisters, added her soothing voice. "I can't recall ever seeing you so upset, dear."

"It's that man who demanded to marry you," Chalice said. "Now he wants his revenge on all of us!" Tears streamed down her face, as if attackers were already here with drawn knives. As the alarm rose in the session chamber, Chalice cried out, "Count Fenring put our Sardaukar on high alert! He warned there could always be assassination attempts against the royal family! Is that why Josifa and Rugi were sent off to the Bene Gesserit school? Maybe I should go, too."

Irulan met Wensicia's eyes, and both shared a common thought. Irulan said, "We need to look into this further, but for now, you're quite safe in the guarded palace. We all are."

"Count Fenring was surely not talking about anything specific," Wensicia said in a soothing voice. "He's just keeping the security force alert, reminding them of their duties. It's for the best."

"I feel quite confident in the security methods in place," Irulan added, loud enough to reassure not only her frightened sister, but the others in attendance. The CHOAM President did not appear unduly concerned.

Wensicia put her arm around Chalice. "Zenha's rebellion is only a minor disturbance. I have looked into it in great detail." She led her sister to the chamber's main doors. "Come, I'll walk you back to your apartments. You need to finish getting ready for the banquet."

KIA MALDISI WORKED angles to get herself ready in the bustling palace. She slept with two workers to get proper recommendations, then secured a position—albeit a lowly one. More than two hundred people worked in the kitchen each day, a series of immense chambers with ovens and heating elements, sinks, counters, prep surfaces. Cook pots simmered, meats and vegetables were cut, and fancy desserts were artfully decorated, then arranged behind the glass of refrigeration units.

As a new worker with unproven skills, Maldisi was given cleanup detail with three others, including one of the young men she'd slept with, and he had fulfilled his promise to find her a place on the kitchen staff. Now as they all worked together, the man watched her constantly, which made her uneasy. She owed him nothing more, and he had done his part. The transaction was complete. She might have to deal with him in another way if he did not accept it, but she could not risk drawing undue attention right now. Her own work had to be done quickly, a lightning strike the moment an opportunity presented itself.

As a new employee, Maldisi's position was so low that few people took notice of her. Her coworkers offered only inane chatter. These people were the bottom tier on Kaitain, but even so they led soft, pampered lives, with plenty to eat and no one trying to kill or rape them each night. . . .

Her gruff immediate supervisor showed her counters and basins that held buckets of kitchen slop and told her to load them onto a cart, then sent her to areas that needed to be swept, or had stoves, hoods, and vents to clean. Much stronger than she looked, Maldisi performed her tasks effortlessly, but not so quickly as to draw resentment from her downtrodden coworkers.

With yet another banquet set for that evening, the kitchens were in full operation, loud and buzzing like a living organism. Each meal served to the Corrino family was rich and sumptuous, so she didn't know how a banquet made any difference to such people, but apparently, this was a special occasion.

Given a brief but unnecessary break, which she took so as not to raise suspicions, Maldisi sat in an alcove with a young cook, sharing a meal of leftover Ecaz beef strips in sweet plum sauce from the previous day. The food was better than any fare she'd eaten on Salusa Secundus, but she was not here for her own enjoyment. Her companion took no notice of her, just kept eating, and Maldisi did the same. They both finished at the same time and went back to work.

The kitchens were a constant clamor as late afternoon moved to early evening, the activity reaching a crescendo before the banquet. From the grand kitchen levels, three doors led to ramps that rose to the dining hall.

With whispered conversations and even ridiculously small bribes, Maldisi switched duties, traded shifts, and maneuvered herself so that she could work by one of the lifts when the guests began to arrive, richly attired people she could observe through clearplaz peepholes in the doors.

She had heard that sometimes the Emperor might visit the kitchens to assure himself that everything was prepared to his liking. If that happened tonight, she was prepared. In deep pockets underneath her work clothes, she had hidden several weapons, ready for any opportunity.

AT THE MAIN table, Irulan's assigned place was closest to the Emperor just down from her father's imposing chair. The secondary chair once reserved for Empress Firenza (on those rare occasions when Shaddam was willing to be seen with her) had been removed to give him extra room at the head of the table.

Irulan watched the dignitaries take seats, noting their names and filing away details, as she had learned at the Bene Gesserit school. Each person was shown to the correct place by nattily dressed men in top hats and tails, in observance of the suggested retro style for the evening's festivities.

Chalice seemed calmer now, having received a mild sedative from the court doctor. Her attendants had heaped even more necklaces and brooches than usual on her sparkly gown. Wensicia sat at her sister's side, occasionally whispering in her ear. Several chairs farther down the table sat the CHOAM President, and Chalice seemed to be trying to get his attention.

Before the initial courses were served, Shaddam strolled among the guests, but he seemed preoccupied. He kept glancing at the time, then toward the kitchens. The first appetizer was due to arrive in only a few minutes, and Irulan could see he intended to inspect the kitchens, as he liked to do. Tonight he seemed tenser than usual. The Emperor left his guests to settle into their assigned seats and marched toward the nearest soundproofed entrance to the kitchens.

Customarily, Irulan did not accompany him in this duty, but tonight she felt a sense of trepidation, perhaps because of Count Fenring's demand for more alert security, and Chalice's hysteria.

As the two of them passed through the doorway, Shaddam frowned down at a servant cleaning up a spilled tray of food. She was scraping the extravagant food from the floor into a bucket. The rest of the kitchen staff fell into an awed hush as they registered their Imperial visitors.

Shaddam walked past the servant, ignoring the dropped food as he strolled into the steamy, aroma-rich chamber. The cooks, servers, and cleaning staff all snapped into respectful poses. Irulan remained close to her father.

Behind them, she still heard the server scraping food into the bucket. Although she wasn't sure why, Irulan felt a general uneasiness, a throbbing sensation from her Bene Gesserit awareness. She looked back.

While the other staff members had their heads bowed in respect, the serving woman had yanked aside her outer household uniform to reveal a garment underneath. She reached for something in a deep pocket.

With a flare of instinctive alarm, Irulan pushed her father down a side aisle, just as two knives whirred past their heads. One blade struck a sous chef in the chest; he cried out in surprise and fell over dishes he had been preparing on a counter, knocking them to the floor as he died.

The kitchen exploded into an uproar. Several people screamed. Pots crashed to the floor. Four cooks and prep workers rushed into the side aisle, throwing themselves in front of the Emperor to shield him from harm.

Princess Irulan assured herself that her father was unharmed, then bounded back into the main aisle of the kitchen.

The attacker fought against a man trying to restrain her, brutally knocked him into a wall. She looked at Irulan with a twisted expression of hatred and determination. In a sudden move, the server dove through the doorway into the dining chamber rather than continuing her hopeless attack against the Emperor.

Irulan yelled over the clamor from the kitchen, "Stop that woman!"

Security had previously been increased in the banquet hall, thanks to Count Fenring, and liveried guards swarmed forward from their sentry positions. Ten of them converged on the fleeing woman, slamming the would-be assassin down on the floor. Many banquet guests lurched from the seats and clustered together like sheep, while some fled the hall entirely. The attacker put up a fierce struggle, but the guards managed to get restraints on her.

"I knew this was going to happen!" Chalice wailed. "No one would listen to me! The fanatics want to kill us all." In the pandemonium, she had been jostled about, and someone had knocked her to the floor. She dabbed at her nose, looked at blood on her fingertips, then let out a shrill cry. The sharp pin of one of her gaudy brooches had stabbed into the pale skin of her shoulder, and she was bleeding there, too.

Wensicia held her sister's forehead, and Irulan saw blood on her fingers. She seemed more seriously injured than Chalice, but Wensicia waved Irulan off, indicating she was all right.

Leaving the guards to secure the attacker, Irulan hurried to Chalice, who had by now discovered the second wound. "I've been stabbed! I've been disfigured! My shoulder!" Her wound did not look serious.

Furious, the Emperor stalked out of the kitchen. He commanded his Sardaukar, not the usual liveried guards, to rush the princesses to their apartments, while Chalice continued to wail for a Suk doctor. Irulan accompanied her, though she would rather have stayed to see the mysterious attacker questioned.

WHILE THE REST of the guests were taken to holding rooms for questioning and given false explanations for the "unfortunate disruption," Shaddam remained, insisting that the room be cleared except for the guards and the struggling captive.

"Where is Count Fenring?" the Emperor shouted, looking around. "Find Hasimir!"

One of his Sardaukar marched off to search for him.

Shaddam strode to the head of the table and lowered himself into his immense banquet chair. Now it looked like the seat of a terrible magistrate. "Bring that woman here to me. Now!"

The attacker was dragged before him, her face bruised, her upper lip split and bloody. He looked at her as if she were an insect, and she glared back at him.

Before he could begin to question her, Count Fenring stormed into the hall, his face ruddy with alarm. "I heard what happened in here," he said, then added, "and it happened to me as well, Sire. There is more than one assassin in the palace! Lady Margot came to the banquet ahead of me, and I was performing a security inspection when another person attacked me! A woman, dressed as a minor courier, walked past me and lashed out at me with a slip-tip! I suspect it was poisoned."

As Shaddam recoiled in shock, Fenring merely stroked his chin. "She, ahhh, would have killed me, except I have a way with such things. I dodged, caught her wrist, turned the knife. I was, hmmm, unfortunately fast and killed her out of reflex before I could think twice."

Uniformed soldiers poured into the chaotic banquet hall, palace guards, the Imperial military, and Sardaukar. Major Bashar Kolona marched forward, and now his normally stony expression roiled with anger; Shaddam had never seen him look so upset.

Kolona stopped in front of the Emperor, saluted, and said, "Sire, Count Fenring killed one assassin—and my men got two more—all women, in various low-level palace positions. We have begun an investigation, but can already see that all of them carried false identity documents."

"And we have this one." Shaddam glowered at the woman who had tried to kill him in the kitchens. "Who are you?"

Not surprisingly, she did not answer, but kept trying to break free of her restraints. Count Fenring placed a dagger against her throat. "She won't remain silent for long, Sire."

"I'm not afraid of you, and you'll never manage to hold me," the woman said, then smiled. "But I want you to know this anyway."

"Know what?" Fenring drew a fine line of blood on her throat with the dagger.

Her eyes flashed. "Commander-General Zenha is coming for you, in such force that you will not be able to stop him."

The woman continued to smile as she was led away for deep interrogation.

Fenring looked concerned, and he leaned close to the Emperor. "This is, ahhh, more than a security matter, Sire. Four different assassins, in one night? One almost got to you, and another nearly killed me. Hmmm, we can be certain we haven't found them all. How many other cells are there?"

Shaddam growled. "The one I want to find is this traitor Zenha!"

"I shall see what I can learn, Sire." Fenring walked away.

I prefer my illusions of paradise to the discouragement of reality. Any Fremen knows how to see through a mirage.

—LIET-KYNES, Imperial Planetologist

After compiling weather reports from sietches across the northern hemisphere, Liet-Kynes planned his trip to the far south. None of this work, however, would appear in any Imperial report.

Two monstrous Coriolis storms swirled across the equator line like battling titans. Kynes had seen such patterns before and knew the pair of storms would wrap together into one mega-hurricane of scouring sand and blown dust. Already, Harkonnen spice-harvesting operations had pulled out of the lower latitudes, hunkering down in armored shelters in Arsunt and Carthag.

Kynes regularly collected data on the storms and exaggerated their severity on the equator, all to bolster the belief that the storm line was impassable, and that Arrakis's southern hemisphere was a hellish place where no one could survive.

After studying these current weather patterns, though, Kynes and his Fremen team planned an alternate course that slipped between the great storms before they converged. With five hardened ornithopters, his expedition flew down to the southern palmaries.

Though he received regular reports of the terraforming projects, he enjoyed observing the extensive plantings himself. Engrossed in the work to the exclusion of all else, Liet's father had never truly comprehended that the desert people saw him as a prophet who would help create their paradise. Liet, however, understood the legend that surrounded him, and he used it to achieve a necessary purpose, just as old Reverend Mother Ramallo invoked vague but hopeful legends to inspire the people.

On the long journey to the southern regions, the drone of 'thopter wings was like a lullaby, but jarring lurches from stray breezes and strong thermals kept him awake. Stilgar piloted the lead 'thopter, staring straight ahead as he gripped the controls; he adjusted the flaps and gained altitude. Liet could see little with so much dust in the air, but the cockpit screens showed the blips of the other aircraft rising clear of the low dust layers.

Despite the danger, the storm offered its own advantages, because the static would disrupt Harkonnen scanners or long-range communications. During this flight, they were free from prying eyes, even from the mysterious Guild search parties. Liet knew that the best way to be rid of the Guild spies would be to find the Tleilaxu facility they wanted, and his numerous searchers were doing their best.

Once Liet and his team passed the equator, the skies cleared again and the 'thopters continued in a tight formation like desert hornets. Now he drew a deep breath, smelled the ubiquitous dust in the cockpit, and let himself relax.

Old Pardot had loved these journeys to the south. The former planetologist would have made a permanent home down in the palmaries, but he could not relinquish his obligations to the Emperor. He had died in a cave-in at one of his hidden garden caverns at Plaster Basin, but his work had not come to an end. After several years of sadness and superstition, Fremen workers had reopened the collapsed caves and established new plantings in Pardot's honor. Liet knew his father would have been proud of everything they had accomplished.

Now the five 'thopters headed to the polar mountains, leaving the open sand behind and crossing over rocky areas. For a long time, the green growths had been kept hidden, covered with camouflage nets. The plants made footholds in fertilized soil; palm trees grew tall enough to be visible for those who knew where to look. Liet smiled in wonder when he spotted them.

The 'thopters landed outside a broad overhang, and their struts settled down on packed gravel. After overhearing Khouro speaking with Chani in the canyon, Kynes had considered bringing his stepson with him this time, but the young man had impetuously departed on another raid, taking Jamis with him. Liet knew that healing the breach with Khouro might require a long-term plan as well.

The planetologist swung out of the cockpit, while Stilgar locked the articulated wings into place and folded the craft low against the ground like a hunching insect. Other Fremen moved about with quiet efficiency, always acting as if they were hunted or observed.

Liet walked under the overhang. This far south, the air had a faint but recognizable moisture, and the temperature was cooler. Water was locked into the soil as permafrost.

Inside the expansive grotto, the ceiling was reinforced with girders and sealed with plaster. Plasteel anchors held loose rock slabs in place, and solar lights filled the shadows. Kynes grinned as he saw progress in every species. One of the Fremen handed him a report, but the evidence of his own eyes was clear enough.

Bees hummed around the blossoms, and small sand pigeons chirped from nests they had made in cracks high in the ceiling. Their guano was delicately harvested and added to the garden soil.

Rows of dwarf citrus trees basked under the lights. The soil around their roots was moist from distributed irrigation. Lemons, limes, and even portyguls—his father's favorite—stood out against the green leaves. Fremen gardeners picked each one with care as if the fruit were sacred. Each seed was saved and stored for a time when resources allowed for expanded plantings.

One of the dedicated gardeners in this redoubt offered him a mottled orange citrus fruit. "A portygul for you, Liet."

He held the treasure in his palm, then handed it back to the young woman. "Slice it into wedges. Enough for each of us to have a taste."

She grinned. "I hoped you would say that, Liet." She looked around, glanced reverently at the ceiling. "Your father's spirit is happy. He watches how we continue the work he created."

"He would indeed be happy about this," Liet said. "So much progress."

The Fremen were no strangers to setbacks, and he continued his father's vision, but with a political spin. Simply turning Arrakis green was not good enough, if the world remained under the thumb of tyrants. Sometimes, he wondered if the fight itself was his reason for existence.

After he had finished his inspection, Kynes enjoyed an evening meal of fresh greens and a boiled pigeon egg, along with spice cakes that were lightly toasted on top. The repast was quintessentially Dune, and he enjoyed it far more than he'd enjoyed Count Fenring's Arrakeen banquet.

Long after sunset, when the first moon had risen high, a scout 'thopter arrived carrying a Fremen patrol, and even more good news for him. A lean, sharp-eyed captain came in from the raging equatorial zone. Liet could tell from the hard glint in his eyes that they had found something.

"We skirted the storms, Liet. Knowing the great Mother Winds would stir up the sands, we wanted to find any new spice beds that we could exploit before the Harkonnens found them."

Kynes nodded. "We always need more spice to bribe the Guild, but very few people venture into that region."

The captain's eyes narrowed. "We found spice . . . and something else. If it is what I suspect, Liet, then perhaps we won't need to pay the Guild for a while."

Liet set aside the hard rind of his portygul, which would be mulched and used for compost. "You found the laboratory?"

"We detected a ship that also skirted the storm, flying low and dangerous-looking. No markings, a configuration we have not seen before. Its hull and emanations baffled our sensors, but we watched it head toward the equatorial ridge."

"No one goes to those mountains," Liet said. "No sietch would be stable there because of the storms." He frowned, recalling old annotations that implied the presence of one or two Imperial botanical testing stations in the area, but they were considered long destroyed.

"The increasing storm drove us off, but we did get close enough to find other indications. We took heat signatures, identified small exhaust ports hidden in the rocks. Something is concealed there." The captain straightened, flashed a hard smile. "I suspect this is the Tleilaxu facility we were asked to locate."

"Perhaps so," Kynes said in a low voice, realizing it would indeed be a clever location that even Fremen would avoid. "We must investigate further, obtain proof and any possible surveillance." He nodded to himself.

And if the evidence bore fruit, then he would let Chani, Liet-Chih, and their commandos have their victory.

Is it cowardly to run, or is it sensible to avoid a known threat? The answer depends upon circumstances.

—SHADDAM CORRINO, to his court chamberlain

Even in the enormous fortress of the Kaitain Palace, each day seemed more perilous than the last. Irulan's life was no longer the calm and mundane existence to which she'd grown accustomed. The multiple assassination attempts had put a paralysis on the Imperial Court. All staff members were interrogated, any dissatisfaction rooted out. Behind the scenes, a handful of low-level employees had vanished under suspicious circumstances.

The Emperor imposed a news blackout to smother word of the assassination attempts, but security was palpably greater than before, and Irulan knew her father could not keep the reason entirely secret. Nevertheless, his propaganda ministers did an admirable job of spreading alternate stories and misinformation. The official explanation for the disruption was that a disgruntled staff member had caused a ruckus.

She and Wensicia quietly discussed the threat, and her sister even presented more possible evidence of Zenha's mutiny gaining momentum, though Shaddam's military aides had not made the same connections.

Chalice was terrified to leave her rooms and imagined assassins behind every flowerpot, but Irulan and Wensicia urged her to join them in one of the smaller courtyards with liveried guards standing prominently at the hedges, the entrances, and the balconies above. Chalice was pale, wearing a bandage over the minor wound on her shoulder; her nose looked bruised.

"I hope they find those fanatics. Execute them all!" She gasped. "What if they bring atomics to Kaitain, like they used on Otak? That terrible

Zenha!" She fluttered a hand in front of her mouth. "Kaitain could be devastated, just like Salusa Secundus thousands of years ago!"

Wensicia tried to reassure her, but her expression was hard. "You realize that Fleet Captain Zenha's gang of mutineers is entirely different from the Otak fanatics, dear sister?"

Irulan patted Chalice on the back, avoiding the injured shoulder. "The Otak debacle was one of the reasons that turned Zenha against us."

Chalice shook her head. "All of our enemies are the same. At least Josifa and Rugi are safely away on Wallach IX. I want to go there—and far away from here."

Irulan realized that her flighty sister had reverted to a weak child, as if she could no longer cope with adult events and worries.

"You're safe here with us," Wensicia said, exchanging a knowing glance with Irulan. "You can be like one of those butterflies you love, without a care in the world."

Prior to this tense outing in the courtyard, Chalice had pinned a number of small fabric butterflies onto her dress. At last she accepted the comfort of her two sisters and brushed at the colorful butterflies. On a whim, she broke away from her companions and began whirling and dancing, talking to herself and humming strange tunes.

Irulan watched her in dismay, also seeing the concern on Wensicia's face. Wensicia whispered, "She's been given sedatives and antidepressants to alter her mood, but deep Suk psychology is what she needs. Rigorous mental health treatment."

"The Sisterhood might also be of assistance," Irulan whispered. "Maybe we should send her to join our little sisters at the Mother School." It seemed an obvious solution.

"A very good idea," Wensicia muttered, then called out, "Would you like to be with Josifa and Rugi at the Mother School?"

Chalice danced closer. "I could be with them? Oh yes, I would be so much safer there! Please, when can I go? Has Father already given permission?" Her puffy eyes shone with hope.

"No, but I'm sure he will, and I'll also talk with Reverend Mother Mohiam," Irulan promised, and she and Wensicia shared a secret agreement to get this done. "It'll be all right. I'm sure the Sisterhood will give you sanctuary for a while."

Chalice flitted away to chase after real butterflies in the courtyard.

Relieved, Irulan nodded to her other sister. "I'll leave her in your good hands now. I must attend an important meeting with Father and his council."

Sharing a mutual concern, the two embraced, though Wensicia was clearly disappointed she hadn't been invited to the meeting. "Be the voice of reason there, Irulan. Remember what I showed you for the military briefing. Zenha's movement has a much wider influence than Father gives him credit for. Don't underestimate him."

"I'll remember." Irulan felt a bond with her sister. "I think you've unraveled more of the true story than the noble officers did."

BY THE TIME she entered the Emperor's staff office, Shaddam was already browbeating his five top military commanders. His commanding Sardaukar, Major Bashar Kolona, stood at attention, watching the events like a looming guardian. Two propaganda ministers in dark suits sat against the wall, listening intently.

"We must prevent word of this violent act from spreading, or it might ignite sympathetic demonstrations!" Shaddam said. "They'll think the Imperial Palace is crawling with assassins!"

"We have already quashed the Otak intransigence, Sire," said Kolona. "Let that be a lesson for all to see. Rebuilding and resettlement efforts are well underway."

One of the propaganda ministers spoke up. "We've contained the situation here in the palace, Sire. The entire kitchen staff has been rounded up and replaced. Any actual witnesses to the event have been interrogated and detained. The banquet guests have been given appropriate bribes and alternative stories, and we've spread our own reports. If we control this, the uproar will die down even before it gets started."

Count Fenring sat on one side of the office, staring at the pompous military officers in their gaudy uniforms in front of the Emperor's massive desk. "Hmmm, ahhh, so long as our Emperor is not *killed* during all these subtle maneuvers. It is clear that we do not have a handle on the extent of this mutiny. Audacious and impudent. Multiple coordinated assassination attempts!"

"We are looking into the matter," said General Xodda, clearing his throat. To Irulan, he inspired no confidence whatsoever. "We are reviewing the status of our task forces around the Imperium, performing a broad station audit to give us a clear picture of their dispersal. As you know, communication lines are slow, and word must travel from Heighliner to Heighliner. By tradition, our ships are deployed in a wide but loose security net as a visible reminder of the Golden Lion Throne. They ensure peace through intimidation rather than actual firepower—unless it is needed. The Landsraad Houses all have their own military forces. Our Imperial military is merely a binding influence."

Shaddam glanced up as Irulan seated herself in the large chair beside his, then looked back at his military officers. "So, you don't exactly know the disposition of our entire fleet."

Lion-Commander Beldin O'Rik, who had once served as superior officer to Moko Zenha, shifted uncomfortably. "We are still in the midst of an inventory, Sire. It appears we have lost contact with a number of squadrons and battle groups. Remember, however, that getting messages out through the Guild networks and receiving responses is a time-consuming process. Please be patient."

"How many of our ships are missing?" Shaddam leaned forward to rest elbows on his massive desk. He clenched his hands so tightly they were shaking.

"Ninety unaccounted for, Sire—an assortment of frigates, corvettes, cruisers, even three dreadnoughts." The Lion-Commander lowered his head. "Enough to constitute a task force . . . or two. Maybe there are—"

General Xodda interrupted. "The troop deployments across thousands of worlds have stood as a prominent peacekeeping force for millennia, Sire." He glared at the liveried captain of palace security. "At present, it seems your greatest concern should be to increase your personal protection here at home. Allow us to assess the status of the entire fleet."

Shaddam's eyes flashed dangerously. "We've been trying to keep a lid on this thing. We cannot let people think the Padishah Emperor is cowering in terror in his own palace!"

Count Fenring made an annoying nasal sound. "Hmmm, ahhh, Sire, we must keep you safe at all costs. I say this as your loyal subject and as your lifetime friend. I recommend immediately taking you into deep protection. I've been monitoring the situation, and I believe it is not safe for you to remain here." He glanced at Irulan, then looked back at the Emperor. "We, ahhh, cannot leave you and your family vulnerable."

"Then how would he appear to rule as normal?" asked Chamberlain Ridondo. "We don't want to start a panic."

"I cannot look afraid of an upstart," Shaddam insisted. "That gives him too much power! What more do you have to add to this discussion, Hasimir?"

The Count removed a small, sharp dagger from his frilly waistcoat, toyed with the blade. "I am still extracting information from problematic witnesses. The one called Maldisi has proved to be remarkably resistant, even to me. She seems to believe there are multiple other assassination attempts underway, and vows that we will never prevent all of them."

The Sardaukar commander spoke up. "Until the situation is under control, the safety of the Emperor is paramount." In Irulan's opinion, Kolona was the only competent officer present. "I will not rely on spotty military intelligence or ineffective palace security. My Sardaukar will ensure that nothing happens to you, Sire."

Irulan recalled what Wensicia had showed her, and her sister's assessment of Zenha's insurrection seemed more dire than the report Lion-Commander O'Rik had delivered. Now she spoke up. "Father, if we take a cautious approach, we should assume that additional sleeper teams of deeply immersed assassins are hidden on Kaitain. Zenha's mutineers are gathering a large attack fleet somewhere out in the Imperium. We don't know where they are or what they intend to do—"

Fenring cut her off. "Their intent is, ahhh, quite obvious."

Irulan calmed herself. "Count Fenring is right, Father. If you continue your daily routine in the palace just to keep up appearances and pretend there is no threat, then you will be vulnerable. Zenha has proved to be unpredictable."

"I have many layers of security around me," Shaddam insisted. "No one can get through."

Even so, Irulan noted slight changes in his demeanor, a paler cast to his skin, faint droplets of perspiration on his brow.

"Hmmm, isn't that what we believed before?" Fenring asked. "And look how close the assassins got to you—and to me. Sire, I strongly recommend that we do something unexpected ourselves. Take you to an offworld place where the mutineers cannot reach you."

The Sardaukar commander looked uneasy, but remained ramrod straight. The noble officers muttered to one another. Looking directly at Fenring, Irulan asked, "Do you mean Arrakis? Your Residency there?"

Fenring smiled at her. "Hmmm, ahhh, Arrakis, yes. Much safer there than here, to be certain."

Irulan stood from her chair, looking at the Emperor but addressing the entire room. "Father, I reviewed the detailed report sent to you by Dr. Kynes. In his executive summary, your own planetologist plainly asks you to see conditions on Arrakis yourself. That would be a perfect excuse."

"Hmmm, ahhh, a good idea," Count Fenring said, "and the sooner we go, the better. We'll tell everyone the Emperor is making a Grand Tour of the Imperium, with the first stop being Arrakis for an indefinite stay." He chuckled. "And, Sire, I can envision you saying, 'Oh, by the way, Baron, as long as I am here, we might as well have a surprise inspection of your spice operations!' The Baron would be most, ahhh, unsettled by that."

Kolona nodded slowly. "It would be totally unannounced, something Zenha or his assassins could not anticipate, and the Sardaukar could keep you safe. I would bring an entire legion as your honor guard."

Irulan had become convinced about the idea. "We would remain on Arrakis until any threats are definitely dealt with."

Her father seemed rattled by how swiftly others took up the idea. "But I can't just vacate the throne. Who would stay here in my stead?" The rising stubbornness was plain on his face. "No, I will remain here, as if nothing has happened."

Fenring pointed to Kolona. "The Sardaukar should escort the Emperor out of here immediately. There is no time to waste."

The Major Bashar stepped close to the Emperor, brisk and formal, and now he almost appeared threatening. "I must insist, Sire, for your own safety." The closed doorway of the staff office opened, and four more Sardaukar guards entered. The captain of the palace guard looked alarmed by the sudden change.

"I'm not going," Shaddam insisted.

Kolona was not moved. "I hereby invoke Rule 77A-4–22Q of the Imperial Charter, in which the Sardaukar are granted the authority to forcibly remove an Emperor from clear and present danger and take him to a place of safety. It is our sworn duty to protect you."

Irulan blinked in amazement. She called to mind her memory of the fine points of the Imperial Charter. "I believe he's correct, Father."

Count Fenring went to stand beside the Sardaukar commander. "We need to take extreme measures to protect the Emperor until we, ahhh, fully understand the extent of the danger. Too much is unknown now."

He gave a broad smile. "My Residency is quite comfortable and well fortified, Sire. You would be with me and Lady Margot."

Shaddam seemed deflated. "Even you turn against me, my oldest and closest friend?"

"It is the opposite, Sire." The Count looked a little hurt. "I would never turn against you."

Shaddam focused his wide eyes on Irulan. "And you concur with this, my daughter?"

"Wholeheartedly, Father."

The other noble officers had not known about this in advance, but none spoke up or intervened in any way. They just watched in stunned silence.

Fenring glided closer to his childhood friend, unperturbed. "Ahhh, you have blinded yourself to the danger, so we are forced to intervene. Arrakis is a harsh world, but ironically, you *will* be safer there than on Kaitain."

Irulan also had to make sure she and her sisters were not targets. She had already filed a request for Chalice to be taken to Wallach IX.

Shaddam nodded reluctantly, then seemed to fix on one particular aspect. "We'll call it a surprise spice inspection. Baron Harkonnen will be quite surprised indeed."

Major Bashar Kolona moved closer. "Until the expedition is put together, Sire, we will keep you under close guard and out of public view. You and your entourage will depart for Arrakis on the next Heighliner."

THE IRATE EMPEROR remained under armed guard in his own apartments. His daily appointments were canceled and appropriate excuses given. Reverend Mother Mohiam agreed to send the flighty Chalice off to the Bene Gesserit school—quietly and under sedation so that she could maintain the appearance of calm dignity.

Irulan, though, insisted on accompanying her father to Arrakis.

The Princess Royal met Wensicia in one of Shaddam's consulting rooms down the corridor from the staff office. She could tell that her sister had made up her mind not to leave Kaitain, and she had a stubborn streak as strong as their father's. Instead, Wensicia presented another provocative idea.

"I'll accept the wisdom of sending Father to Arrakis," she said, "and I certainly agree with dispatching Chalice to the Mother School. Yes, for the sake of the Imperium, we must maintain appearances so that the Imperial Court continues as usual, not troubled by a minor disturbance of malcontents. But someone must remain here, as a proxy for our father. A Corrino on the Golden Lion Throne." Irulan saw a glint of ambition in Wensicia's lavender eyes as she said, "You are missing the obvious solution, dear sister."

Irulan jerked her head back. "You?"

"I am perfectly trained in political matters as well as court functions," Wensicia said. "You are the Princess Royal, but I am also the Emperor's daughter, so I am a perfect figurehead. Everyone on Kaitain will see that all is well in the Imperium."

Irulan considered the idea. "And what if Zenha's task force moves against Kaitain? You would be in danger."

Wensicia let out an icy chuckle. "Some rabble attacking the Imperial capital world? I think not! Even if Father takes most of his Sardaukar with him, we still have strong military defenses here."

Irulan's brows furrowed. "And taking interim charge of the palace would be an unparalleled opportunity for you."

"Yes, it would, but it is for a much greater good than myself." She lowered her voice. "Please support me in this."

Irulan could see that Wensicia intended to put up a strong argument, if necessary, because she was already convinced.

"Very well," Irulan said. "And as Princess Royal, I will stay at the Emperor's side."

As the sisters went their own ways in the palace, Irulan decided to begin a new journal, a chronicle of the rapidly unfolding events.

Even in the harshest negotiations, one must always be courteous. This throws the enemy off balance, because he finds it highly disconcerting.

—COMMANDER-GENERAL ZENHA, war council records

When his Liberation Fleet dropped out of the Heighliner hold, having arrived at the new destination, Commander-General Zenha scrutinized the planet below. *Otak.* He did not need magnification to imagine the scars on the landscape from the last time he was here. He certainly knew the indelible marks it had left on his conscience and his career.

He brought his ships to Otak as a matter of principle. He would face his fear and his shame. The fanatical Navachristian rebels had killed many loyal Imperial soldiers, and the subsequent Sardaukar retaliation had flattened much of the world. Only Emperor Shaddam was satisfied with the results.

Yes, it was the fanatics who had unleashed the forbidden atomics, and yes, it was the Sardaukar who had crushed the remaining populace. But Shaddam Corrino was the one who had sent Zenha's force into a ticking time bomb, and Shaddam Corrino had ordered his Sardaukar to unleash the slaughter against Otak.

Blackened craters dotted the edges of four large cities, and the capital of Lijoh had been entirely obliterated. The Sardaukar's punitive response had erased two more main trading centers and spaceports.

This time, though, Zenha was prepared for the harsh reality, and he was not so naïve as to believe any Imperial dossier filled with misinformation. Not so long ago, his greatest tactical error had been in assuming that the Emperor wanted his own Imperial military to succeed. Instead, Shaddam had been willing to sacrifice so many lives merely for petty revenge.

Moko Zenha would not make that mistake again. He remembered the ruthless expression on the Emperor's face as he used his jewel-handled dagger to slash off the rank insignia, the hard-fought and well-earned medals, in front of the entire Imperial Court. And according to Shaddam Corrino, even that humiliation and disgrace had not been enough for the hapless officer to suffer.

Only gradually had Zenha understood the larger implications, the interconnected schemes in the Emperor's mind. Shaddam had expected a clean sweep on Otak, Zenha's entire force eradicated by the Navachristian fanatics, so he could have his Sardaukar smash the unruly elements on a valuable world, thus getting rid of two troublesome problems at the same time.

On this return visit, though, Zenha was in an entirely different situation, and he was in control. Now he had ten times as many ships as the previous task force—his own dreadnought flagship along with two others, as well as cruisers, corvettes, frigates, and enough fighters to fill several troop carriers.

And this time, he did not intend to lose. His eyes were open, and his Liberation Fleet had a different enemy. This time, *they* would twist the knife and take the resources they needed, right from under Shaddam's nose.

To cure the deadly rot he had identified at the core, he needed to get rid of the Emperor, not the Imperium. Shaddam had made this a *personal* matter.

To set up his return to Otak, the fleet commanders had filed the required paperwork with the Guild for transport across space, while secretly changing the operating numbers and identifiers of the commandeered ships. The counterfeit orders specified that this partial fleet was a peacekeeping force sent to troubled worlds.

As his quiet rebellion spread, Zenha knew he had to be careful. His stolen fleet still had to travel via Heighliner, and the Spacing Guild could simply cut them off at any time. But Zenha was careful not to make unnecessary enemies. There were helpful treaties in place, and bribes paid when necessary. The operation went so smoothly that it looked almost like a matter of routine, transferring twice before eventually reaching Otak.

For the time being, Shaddam didn't know the extent of Zenha's mutiny, nor did he know where to find the Liberation Fleet. The Emperor would never guess the disgraced officer would return to Otak.

When his ships arrived, the Commander-General saw that a swarm of other vessels had come to take advantage of the aftermath: construction haulers to clear debris, mining corporations, agricultural groups, ships carrying merchants and businessmen, along with hardy new colonists who would claim the damaged world. The Emperor's true ambition became more and more obvious here.

Communicating over their private command frequency, Zenha's pilots made several observation orbits to map the damaged cities and choose the best place for their rendezvous. The Commander-General consulted his second-line officers about whether to land in one large force or distribute their points of attack.

Zenha addressed his fellow captains along with the rowdy Salusan mercenaries who were eager for a fight. "Let us be honest with ourselves—this is not a military operation. We are not conquering territory, not punishing the Otak survivors or those new colonists." He allowed himself a smile. "This is a *raid*, pure and simple. As our movement expands, we need resources. Therefore, we will rob the Imperium of any assets we find."

Cheers erupted from his own bridge deck, while similar celebratory sounds crossed the comm.

The commercial space traffic around Otak showed the extent of the vigorous rebuilding activities. Until recently, Otak had been a planet of middling importance whose exports of crystals, rare foodstuffs, and pharmaceuticals had grown less desirable because of the unruly populace. Now, just in the past few months, Otak had been scrubbed clean, ready to be remade. Landsraad families were planting their own flags, pouring resources into establishing new holdings here.

Zenha realized that he had unwittingly been a pawn in the larger plan here.

For the ongoing reconstruction, CHOAM would reap great profits. The commercial conglomerate provided construction materials, architecture consultants, and foodstuffs, as well as cleanup operations. To fund the swift rebirth of Otak, the Imperium had established large treasury houses in the remaining cities, and a Guild Bank had been rebuilt in the new provisional capital.

As Zenha's raiding force orbited the world while taking high-resolution scans of the burgeoning settlements, his subcommanders laid out an operational plan. In a joint conference conducted across the large comm screens on the flagship bridge, Zenha reviewed the surface map.

"We have identified the Imperial treasury houses," said Colonel Sellew, who commanded his own dreadnought now. He highlighted areas on his projected image. "Full of solaris."

Zenha asked, "Presumably they are guarded, and the vaults sealed?"

"Oh, they'll give us no trouble at all," said one of the Salusan mercenaries, a good but outspoken fighter. His grin was twisted by a wormlike scar along his lower lip. "We have all the weapons we need to take care of security and cut through any vault armor."

"Once they see our overwhelming force, maybe they'll just surrender," said Colonel Pilwu.

"Or maybe they won't," said the Salusan mercenary, with a grim, hopeful smile.

Zenha scanned inventory lists and CHOAM warehouses, identifying what his movement would need. For the sake of efficiency, he made a detailed plan of what to take before the full force landed.

"We will strip the Imperial treasury houses down to the last coin and raid CHOAM warehouses for specific materials, though I intend to pay for those items. We don't want to inflame CHOAM against us." He narrowed his gaze, looked around. "Most importantly, we must cause no harm to the Guild Bank. Maintaining the Guild's neutrality is critical. I will go there myself to offer reassurances while you empty out the Imperial treasury."

"Better you than me," said the bloodthirsty Salusan mercenary, who was so skilled a soldier that he knew he could get away with saying more than others. "That leaves me to have more fun." Actually, Zenha rather liked him.

The Liberation Fleet broke into three main attack squadrons with a dreadnought leading each, and headed for the primary population centers with Imperial treasury houses. Cruisers and troop carriers landed like a military storm all across Otak. Zenha's soldiers and the half-trained but enthusiastic Salusan recruits swarmed out in a full assault, taking the partially reconstructed colony towns by surprise. Eager mercenaries overwhelmed the treasury houses, killing any guards that resisted, then unloading bins of solari coins. Other soldiers commandeered required supplies from large CHOAM storage buildings.

Meanwhile, Commander-General Zenha had a different purpose. He went with an honor guard, rather than a military force, to the blocky, newly constructed Guild Bank in the provisional capital. Uniformed

Guild security stood alert in front of the towering arches, their weapons ready; they wore full body shields in a defensive posture.

Dressed in his crisp new uniform without Imperial insignia, Zenha climbed the stairs alone, leaving his honor guard behind. "I wish to speak to the Guild representative. Is there a Starguide present? I want to give reassurance that we intend no threat to the Spacing Guild or the Guild Bank."

The guards remained silent, like statues made of flesh. One touched his temple and nodded. "The Starguide has heard your request. He will be here momentarily."

Zenha remained at attention, showing no impatience even as minutes passed. He remembered the tension of standing in front of the Golden Lion Throne, prepared to submit his proposal. . . .

Heavy mechanical locks shifted in the imposing doors, and with a loud clack and rattle, the portal split open. A tall woman emerged from the shadowy recesses of the immense building. She had a high brow and an ageless demeanor, her skin smooth and thick as if covered with a polymer film.

"I speak for the Guild." The woman's heavy eyebrows drew together. "You are Zenha, who originally failed here at Otak. A notorious officer who was disgraced and stripped of rank."

"Any rank held in service of a corrupt Emperor does not meet the standards I set for myself," Zenha said. "I am now Commander-General of my own Liberation Fleet. My honor and loyalty to the Imperium are intact, which counts for a great deal, but I intend to correct errors caused by House Corrino so that our civilization and the Spacing Guild can remain strong."

The Guild representative, obviously perplexed by these remarks, approached the top of the stone stairs, where she stopped. "And yet you brought a substantial military force to this insignificant planet. At this very moment, your troops are raiding Imperial treasuries and ransacking CHOAM warehouses." A muscle on the side of the woman's face twitched, turning her expression into a grimace. "If you ask me to surrender the funds in this Bank, you will not succeed."

"I have no intention of asking that," Zenha said. "Merely to reassure you that we have no quarrel with the Spacing Guild. We take from the Imperium what they do not deserve. We take from CHOAM to meet our own specific needs, and we keep a careful accounting so that when I have my victory, CHOAM will be adequately compensated."

The Starguide considered this in silence, then spoke. "If you want nothing from the Guild Bank, then why have you come here?"

"I want to explain myself, because some of my Liberation Fleet's actions might be misinterpreted. I consider it mandatory, ethically and morally, to extract payment from Shaddam Corrino. But I *will not* rob the Guild Bank, because I hope to keep doing business with you once the Emperor has been replaced with a more satisfactory and deserving leader."

The muscle in the woman's jaw twitched again. "The Guild is all about business. We recognize the numerous flaws of Shaddam IV, but the Guild also has innumerable treaties and complex connections with House Corrino dating back thousands of years."

"Even so," Zenha said, "surely you recognize the graft, inefficiency, and nepotism that undermines the current Imperium."

"Such things have undermined the Imperium for millennia," said the Guild representative. "But it continues nonetheless, and one day, Shaddam's reign will pass. The Guild and the Imperium will endure, as always."

"The ancient system is corrupt and weak," Zenha said. "It is ripe for a fall—but if done properly, we can turn that fall into a mere course correction."

"The Spacing Guild must continue doing business with House Corrino," the woman said. "We will not join your rebellion."

Zenha just smiled as he recalled his bold initial plan to marry the Princess Royal. A beautiful and intelligent woman, Irulan was also the linchpin to saving the Imperium. "If this gambit turns out as I hope, I will be *a member of* House Corrino, and all will be well. The Imperium will continue as before, and House Corrino will rule, but under new guidance."

The representative considered his words for a long moment. "Until such time, Commander-General Zenha, the Spacing Guild must remain neutral."

Zenha seized on the words. "But you won't stop me. You won't interfere."

"The Spacing Guild is about business," the woman repeated. "Your political squabbles are not our concern." She turned and slipped back into the shadows of the Bank. The Guild guards flanking her had not moved.

On the steps of the great building, Zenha felt satisfied. He and his honor guard marched back to the flagship.

By now, the other assault groups had finished raiding the treasuries. After being loaded, frigates and troop carriers surged into the skies of Otak to rejoin the rest of the task force in orbit. When Zenha returned to his command bridge, he nodded to himself as he listened to report after report and success after success.

Elsewhere, his messages continued to spread across the Imperial military to his old connections, the loyal friends who had celebrated and commiserated with him after his demotion. He expected even more good news before long, as success bred more success.

It was time to consolidate his Liberation Fleet and make their next major move.

We must do more than simply celebrate a victory. We must learn from it as well.

—LIET-KYNES, convocation of the Fremen sietches

The sealed sietch trapped all the smells of humanity. The air was thick with the odor of human bodies, skin oils, dusty hair, dried perspiration. Chani had lived there all her life and could identify the interwoven scents.

In the chamber where her brother and his companions celebrated another successful raid against the Harkonnens, the strongest smell was pungent spice beer. Khouro guffawed at an imaginative insult that Jamis made about Harkonnen genital endowment. The intoxicating liquor apparently made even silly jokes funny.

Chani joined them, welcome among the Fremen commandos, even though she hadn't participated in this most recent raid.

"Two more ornithopters for our sietch!" Khouro sipped on a squeeze bladder, which delivered a squirt of spice beer. He inhaled to enjoy the stinging fumes. "Barely any damage to the craft, nothing our mechanics can't fix."

Jamis chuckled. "And a few fat Harkonnen morsels to whet the appetite of Shai-Hulud!" The commandos raised their drink bladders and took big sips.

"The Baron will blame the losses on a storm in his report to the Emperor," Chani said with a snort. "And the Harkonnens will just buy more 'thopters and send them here, along with spice harvesters and crew workers. Nothing will change."

"Then we will hit them again and again," her brother said. "One 'thopter at a time, one factory at a time, one spice silo at a time, even one person at a time—and we will fill our financial coffers. The sand will be stained with blood, in addition to spice."

Chani had given a great deal of thought to her recent conversation with Shadout Mapes, how the old housekeeper had once fought for the freedom of Arrakis. In her day, Mapes had been victorious, but still ultimately failed to achieve her dream.

"They will fight back," Chani warned. "Harkonnens will strike us wherever they can find us."

"Then we won't *let* them find us." Jamis removed his sheathed crysknife from his waist and toyed with the weapon.

Back home now, the commandos relaxed as they drank liquor. They had removed their stillsuits and now wore loose sietch clothing. They all looked lean, muscular, and hardened with determination.

Chani could not help noticing how the young women looked appraisingly at Khouro and Jamis. None of them would need to be alone this evening. After many conversations, she knew her half brother had no interest in enduring romance, not with so much of the fight left to be won, but he was happy to take brief lovers, and Jamis did the same. Khouro's confidence manifested as cockiness, which some sietch women found alluring.

As a crowd gathered around the returning razzia members in the common room, they told the story again about the recent trap they had laid: Jamis and Khouro had allowed themselves to be spotted out on the sands, alone and vulnerable near Harkonnen spice operations, where scout 'thopters patrolled the perimeter. They'd even waved to attract attention, signaling for help.

A pair of Harkonnen scout 'thopters had circled overhead, closing in with no intention of giving aid. As was painfully predictable, they descended with the intent of toying with the desert men for sport. The 'thopters had landed and soldiers emerged, short swords drawn. . . .

Back in the sietch now, flush and warm with spice beer, Khouro and Jamis boasted that they could have taken care of the enemy themselves. After a belch, her brother even proclaimed he could have defeated them all singlehandedly without any assistance from their Fremen companions, which inspired a raucous round of disbelieving snorts.

Springing the trap, desert fighters had leaped from hiding places, and in swift order, they'd killed all the Harkonnens, seized the 'thopters, and then flown away so swiftly that the rest of the spice-harvesting crew did not know that anything had happened.

The raiders used that to their advantage as they circled back and came in hard, opening fire on an unsuspecting carryall, thus eliminating any chance that the giant factory could be lifted to safety once a sandworm came. Then Khouro and his companions artfully flew their 'thopters past the other scout craft, engaging them in aerial dogfights and drawing them far from the harvesting operations. The factory workers didn't even get an early warning of wormsign . . . which didn't matter, because they were all dead anyway.

Listening to her brother's bravado, Chani tucked her legs under her as she sat on a woven spice-fiber mat. She remembered celebrating similar attacks she'd participated in, each viewed as a Fremen triumph. But now she wondered if the raids were truly milestones toward their freedom or just constant annoyances to be shrugged off by the planetary governors.

Khouro slurred as he made a bold pronouncement. "I say we step up our raids! Hurt the Harkonnens, and hurt them more, until they flee our planet in shame. Dune is *our world*, and they should leave it alone."

Jamis grunted his agreement, and the companions cheered. Another time, Chani would have made the same statements, but now she reconsidered. Her brother's brashness seemed naïve to her. "This world is the only source of spice, and the Imperium depends on it. The Spacing Guild depends on it. Much of the population is addicted to it. They will never just leave us alone."

The Fremen grumbled. Two fawning women who considered themselves seductive glared at Chani for ruining the celebratory mood. Khouro said, "You know nothing, little sister. We'll send the Harkonnens scurrying away!"

She had a heavy heart, realizing that Mapes must have thought the same thing decades ago.

Her brother offered them a hard, appraising look. "Maybe we are thinking too small. Chani has given me an idea. Instead of simply wrecking Harkonnen spice factories and seizing their 'thopters, which can all be replaced, it would be more effective if we cut off the head of the snake. What if we infiltrated Carthag *and assassinated Baron Harkonnen himself?*"

At first, the commandos laughed, but gradually they picked up the call. Adamos raised his sheathed crysknife high in the air. "I could plunge this into the Baron's heart. My blade is long enough to penetrate even his folds of fat!"

The others laughed.

"And what about Count Fenring, the Imperial Spice Observer?" Khouro asked. "That might have an even greater effect. Some say Fenring is a close friend of Emperor Shaddam's."

Two Fremen made rude noises. Khouro jerked his chin in Chani's direction. "My sister infiltrated the Arrakeen Residency. She saw the rooms, the security, the Count's offices. Her father invited her there."

"Liet . . ." one of the commandos muttered.

Khouro frowned.

As if summoned by the name, a man appeared in the chamber doorway. Chani shifted on the floor mat, surprised that her father was back already from his trip to the southern palmaries.

Liet-Kynes stood tall as he looked in at the boisterous group, sniffed the strong smell of spice beer. "That would accomplish nothing, Liet-Chih. If you were to kill Count Fenring or Baron Harkonnen, the Imperium would simply send in another Spice Observer, name another siridar-governor, and they would not rest until they've punished us."

"We are good at hiding," Jamis said, "and we can fight back."

Liet-Kynes looked disappointed and troubled. "But the offworlders don't understand Fremen, don't even know who we are. They would massacre innocent people in the desert villages. They'd kill anyone with dusty clothes and call them Fremen."

A few in the sietch muttered and looked away, because they knew her father's words were true. Chani spoke up, recalling the shadout's story. "Even if we removed Baron Harkonnen, who's to say that his replacement wouldn't be worse? It *has* happened before."

"Killing either of them would not accomplish what you hope," Liet said. "You might feel triumphant for a little while, but then we would all pay the price."

Khouro levered himself to his feet, his face flushed with anger. "And how do we trust your strategic assessment, Stepfather?" He said the term with a sneer. "How do we know you aren't just protecting the Imperials? You send them reports, you collect data on our plantings, on the spice, on our sietches. You play both sides in a chess game. How do we know that your ultimate sympathies aren't really with the Emperor?"

Liet-Kynes looked mortally offended. Chani heard others gasp in the chamber, for they revered her father. He managed to control his anger, struggling to make a tactful response, when a man came running down the corridor. His breathing was loud, and the faint jangle of a cage rattled off the rock walls.

"Liet!" the runner shouted. "A distrans bat flew into the upper alcove. It bears an imprinted message for you." He extended a small collapsible cage that held a tiny bat, its leathery wings furled up close to its mouselike body. "The markings on its wings indicate that it comes from Arrakeen."

Liet turned, his mood broken. With an uneasy snort, Khouro took another sip of spice beer and lounged back. Chani was unsettled by her companions' plans and hoped it was mere braggadocio.

Liet took the cage from the runner and studied the small creature, muttering to himself. "This must be a vital message if the sender chose not to use even our coded comm frequencies." He eased out the flying creature and cradled it in his palms. The bat turned its head upward, opened its mouth to reveal tiny pointed teeth. The creature seemed to be waiting to perform its duty.

Chani knew the old Fremen trick of imprinting secret messages as sound waves on the squeak of a bat, which only a special translating mechanism could unravel. The Harkonnens had never broken the code method. The runner held out a small device no longer than his thumb, which he activated with a button. Liet stroked the bat's chest, and it squeaked several times.

The translation device glowed, then released flat, mechanical words. "Urgent announcement. Imperial party arriving imminently in Arrakeen, including Emperor. Unannounced inspection visit."

Liet blinked in disbelief, and the translation device replayed the message. Khouro, Jamis, and their companions listened in amazement.

Finally, Chani breathed. "The Emperor is coming here? To Arrakeen?"

"The Emperor himself!" Khouro let out a low chuckle. "That changes our plans!" He looked past Chani's father and swept his gaze around the hot-blooded young Fremen as excitement built among them. "Maybe killing Baron Harkonnen or Count Fenring would only be a fruitless exercise."

His gaze narrowed and he set his mouth in a hard line. "But the Emperor is a different matter entirely."

A dazzling spectacle can provide an effective distraction.

—COUNT HASIMIR FENRING, note to Emperor Shaddam IV

As seen from the Imperial frigate in orbit, the desert world looked bleak and mysterious to Princess Irulan, lit by unrelenting sunlight on its day side. Nevertheless, she attempted to see the native beauty of the planet.

Irulan's father and his advisers, along with the Spacing Guild and CHOAM, measured Arrakis only by the melange it provided. But the people who lived down there—the desert tribes of sietch and graben, the merchants, diplomats, and simple townsfolk—saw this as home. How desperate their existence must be if they did not imagine at least some hard beauty on their planet.

The ships in the Emperor's expedition—executive frigates, along with adjunct ships carrying courtiers, protocol ministers, and innumerable attendants—all emerged in a swarm as they dropped out of the chartered Heighliner.

Sitting in her comfortable seat aboard the Imperial frigate, Irulan peered out the windowport, then turned her attention to the high-resolution display screen by her seat. She saw no cities at all down there, just an unbroken ocean of sand. Aron, her loyal consort, sat across the salon in his usual quiet, protective manner, awaiting her needs and instructions.

She studied the stark desert near the terminator line, where the slanting sun cast long shadows that accentuated the texture of the dunes. She increased magnification so she could see the wind-sculpted dunes like endless ocean waves, with tan smudges of dust storms. How horrifying to be stranded out there! Ostensibly, no one could survive, and yet according to her research, Irulan knew that people did live out there in the endless wasteland. Or perhaps they simply had no choice?

As Princess Royal, she tried to imagine the lives of others so she could better understand them. The Emperor and her own Bene Gesserit teacher insisted that this was wise strategic thinking; Irulan considered it astute for her own reasons.

The ships descended, and Irulan saw dark blisters and geometric lines of artificial structures, a sprawling settlement up against black mountains. No doubt this was what qualified as a city on Arrakis. Could it be Carthag or Arrakeen?

Inside the frigate, still not happy about being dragged away from Kaitain, Shaddam sat on an ornate temporary throne, never leaving his role for a moment. He wore crimson-and-gold garments, layer upon layer of brocade and refractive fabric. His hands were covered with rings studded with stones of Imperial and historical significance. He had chosen a more comfortable crown for his travels, but his authority and charisma were innate and apparent to all.

The protective Sardaukar guards, including Major Bashar Kolona, never left the Emperor's side, not even during the passage on the Heighliner. Reverend Mother Mohiam stood beside the temporary throne, not flinching even as atmospheric thermals buffeted the Imperial flotilla. The Truthsayer stared ahead as if assessing every movement, along with every breath she took.

On her screen, Irulan expanded the view to study rows upon rows of prefab buildings in the same monotonous tan with only small, covered windows to protect against blowing dust. She saw no elaborate government buildings, no obelisks or monuments, probably not even statues. Irulan found the very idea of this terribly sad. "Is that Arrakeen, Father? I expected it to be more elaborate. Isn't it the old center of government?"

Her father glanced at her, seemingly amused by her interest in the view, but he did not look at the screen. "What you see is Carthag, the Harkonnen seat of power. We are going there first, as a surprise. Because we are ostensibly on an unannounced Grand Tour, I wanted to impress our visit upon Baron Harkonnen himself." He wore a satisfied smile.

Mohiam spoke up. "For obvious reasons, we do not wish to announce our plans, though word of the Emperor's arrival has already spread down there. To maintain our fiction of a Grand Tour, now that we have arrived, he cannot keep a low profile."

"Our plans are fluid," Shaddam added, "and therefore safer, less predictable."

Ten more Sardaukar marched into the frigate's throne chamber, and Kolona directed them to assume places along the bulkhead, as if the threat increased as the ships approached the Carthag landing fields. Could insurrectionists on the ground open fire on the flotilla? Having now learned of the Imperial visit, Baron Harkonnen would surely have locked down the city.

Even so, a larger and fancier frigate, supposedly the flagship, flew at the front of the flotilla as a decoy, leaving the Emperor's actual frigate in the second position. As much as her father hated to diminish the splendor of his arrival, Irulan had no doubt he would make up for any lack once they landed in Carthag.

Riding with them in the true flagship, Count Fenring wore Imperial finery complete with a spotted whale-fur cape. He strolled into the chamber, smiling and humming. At his side, the beautiful, willowy Lady Margot clung to his arm, and her presence clearly lifted his mood.

"Ahhh, hmmm, I am never quite happy to return to this bleak place, but my wife and I are glad to be home."

Shaddam gave him a slight smile. "The fat Baron must be quaking in his boots and jiggling in the air on his suspensor belt."

"Indeed, Sire. The poor man is no doubt in considerable distress wondering why we have come."

Lady Margot giggled, and even Irulan smiled at the image conjured by the suggestion.

Fenring continued, "After you land in Carthag, however, I will invite you and your entire entourage—including your lovely daughter—to the Residency, which is just as secure, but far more comfortable than anything the Baron can offer."

"He won't like being snubbed," said Mohiam, but her tone did not suggest this was an undesirable result.

Shaddam said, "Let us see what sort of welcome the Baron manages to piece together on short notice."

Over the comm, the frigate's pilot announced in a terse voice, "We are approaching the Carthag spaceport. All local ships, commercial vessels, and Harkonnen operations have been cleared from the area in the name of the Padishah Emperor."

From his throne, Shaddam raised one hand. "Inform my courtiers and staff to prepare for our arrival." He glanced at the nearby Sardaukar officer. "Major Bashar Kolona, before we disembark, you will have the opportunity to survey the area and satisfy yourself as to the security measures."

Fenring stroked a thumb and forefinger along his weak chin. "That will also give the Baron a few additional moments to prepare for whatever you have in mind."

"We all need a few additional moments to prepare," Lady Margot said.

Irulan returned with Aron to her stateroom, using the last moments before arrival to freshen up and select jewelry for the occasion. Courtiers scurried through the corridors, and noble and diplomatic representatives rushed to their staterooms so they could make a proper show.

Only a handful of people aboard the frigate knew the true reason for this surprise trip to Arrakis. Before departure from Kaitain, Imperial propaganda ministers had scoured the palace halls, interviewing courtiers and staff, sweeping up anyone who knew about the multiple attacks. All had been pressed into service for the ostensible Grand Tour, without explanation, where they could be closely watched. No witnesses would be able to spread rumors or share details about the Emperor's surprising vulnerability, nor could they give credence to Zenha's mutinous movement.

A few rumors did start on Kaitain, as they often did—and propaganda ministers sowed confusion where necessary. Very few of the witnesses were so incensed or intractable that Fenring needed to "take care of them," and Irulan heard nothing more about the matter. She was wise enough not to ask.

Most of those reassigned to the Arrakis entourage cooperated, loyal to their Emperor. Others were not pleased about being snatched from the opulent palace, but were mollified with bonuses. The majority, however, had no idea what had triggered this unexpected trip.

When her male companion escorted her back to the frigate's throne chamber, Irulan saw the empty spaceport landing fields outside of Carthag. Ground crews, fueling vehicles, and maintenance equipment had been moved away so swiftly that they looked like toys swept aside by a petulant child. Harkonnen ornithopters streaked in close to the Imperial flotilla to serve as a well-armed escort. More intimidating Sardaukar ships flew next to them, weapons ports glowing in readiness.

Lines of Harkonnen troops streamed out to receive the ships, carrying the Corrino lion banner as well as the griffin of House Harkonnen. The decoy frigate came down first, but moved aside at the last moment, while the true Imperial flagship landed in its place.

Shaddam waited until Major Bashar Kolona gave the all-clear signal, then the Emperor strode out of the processional gangway with slow, dignified steps. Irulan walked at her father's side, followed by his Truthsayer, Count and Lady Fenring, and then a Sardaukar honor guard. Another wave of functionaries and diplomats emerged dressed like peacocks, convinced of their own importance even if no one else was. The parade flowed out onto the armorpave expanse.

The air was so dry that Irulan felt her skin tighten and her eyes burn. The air smelled like flint and exhaust fumes. A tanker vehicle rolled forward, spraying water vapor into the air, a mist that flash-evaporated and made the air hot and muggy, but only for a moment. Across the landing field, Harkonnen-liveried troops faced the fearsome Sardaukar.

Irulan felt no immediate threat, and knew her father did not worry about overt insurrection from the Baron. The real threat lay in the audacious traitor Zenha and his mutinous fleet. She wondered what Wensicia would do if the pesky rebel dared show his face at Kaitain. She smiled to think that her sister might rather enjoy setting a trap for the man.

The hot air was heavy with silence except for the whisper of a desert breeze. The Harkonnen troops remained at attention, along with more rigid Sardaukar. A crier bellowed out, "His Majesty, Shaddam Corrino IV, Padishah Emperor of a Million Worlds, blesses Arrakis with his presence and commands an immediate and thorough Imperial inspection of all spice operations run by House Harkonnen."

The Harkonnen honor guard raised banners high and parted to allow passage for a corpulent man draped in finery, buoyed by his suspensor belt. The Baron spread his hands and bowed in an obsequious gesture. "Sire, you had only to summon me! A surprise inspection of spice operations? I would have come to Kaitain with fully documented assessments. Have my monthly reports been unclear?"

Shaddam stared him down. "So, you are not ready for me now?"

"Of course, of course, Sire! We are always ready for your presence, and you honor us with this visit, but we were not expecting you. Welcoming preparations are being made as swiftly as possible. We greatly respect your patience."

Fenring spoke up. "The point of an inspection tour on short notice, ahhh, my dear Baron, is that you do not know in advance when it will occur."

The Baron was flushed, embarrassed, nervous. Irulan studied his mannerisms, the flickers of his facial muscles, and noted how terrified he was. That led her to conclude that he must indeed be hiding some operations or skimming melange from his regular reports. Her father would play on that and keep the fat man guessing.

"How long has House Harkonnen governed here?" Shaddam asked, though he knew the answer well enough.

The Baron looked away, as if considering, "Three-quarters of a century, Sire. And under my administration, I have increased spice production to your satisfaction."

"I will determine my own level of satisfaction," Shaddam snapped. "We will spend a week, perhaps several, learning all there is to know about melange and Arrakis . . . and how you manage things around here."

The Baron tried to cover his uneasiness. "I shall have an entire wing of the Carthag headquarters prepared for you."

"Not necessary, Baron." The Emperor raised a finger, flashing a large aquamarine ring in the sunlight. "We will establish our base of operations on neutral ground. Count Fenring has agreed to host us in the Arrakeen Residency, where the security is unparalleled. He and the lovely Lady Margot will be our hosts." Shaddam skewered the Baron with his gaze. "Meanwhile, be prepared to open all of your records. I brought Mentats as well as my own industrial experts."

Shaddam gestured, and a small army of specialists strode forward, men and women dressed in formal business attire. "My analysts will accompany you now. Take them straight to your books of account, so they can begin the examination of your records without delay."

The Baron paled even under the hot sun. "Immediately?"

"*Immediately*, and we shall see what we shall see."

Shaddam strolled across the landing field, while Count Fenring hurried ahead of him. "We will ferry you and your closest servants to Arrakeen in my luxury ornithopters, Sire," Fenring said. "I always keep several in reserve at Carthag. The rest of your entourage can set up operations here at the spaceport."

An impossible plan is not always an exercise in futility. It can instead be a rallying point for hopes and dreams.

—IMPERIAL PLANETOLOGIST PARDOT KYNES,
address to the Fremen tribes

Even though she now had a mission that might accomplish something, Chani still hated the crowded and smelly Arrakeen. She didn't know if all cities on Dune were as dirty and dismal as this one; in fact, some townspeople muttered that Carthag was even worse, more oppressive, and with a stronger odor.

But Arrakeen was where she needed to lay her plans, make her contacts, and open doors for her friends. Arrakeen was where the Emperor would stay.

After hearing the news from the distrans bat, Khouro and his razzia companions became obsessed with the outrageous idea of a dramatic strike against the Imperial leader. They schemed, argued, and shouted. Liet-Kynes was deeply troubled by the suggestion, and he sternly tried to convince them otherwise, but Khouro ignored him and took his own friends to a private chamber, where they could talk alone.

That evening, Chani had stayed with her father a little longer, her pulse racing. Liet-Kynes and Shadout Mapes had both made her doubt that targeting the Baron or Count Fenring would accomplish much, but the stakes were infinitely higher with the Padishah Emperor.

"You could never accomplish it, daughter." Liet shook his head. "Emperor Shaddam has an entire Sardaukar army to protect him, and the Arrakeen Residency will be locked down. This is just drunken foolishness."

Chani frowned. "I admit this scheme began with spice beer, but the idea is sound, and when my brother sleeps it off, his determination will remain. We must develop and perfect a plan. We know what Fremen can do."

"I hope you will see common sense—all of you." Liet looked resigned. "I can speak no more of the matter. Liet-Chih will say that I sound like an Imperial puppet." He drew in a sharp breath. "I cannot let my standing among the tribes be damaged. My important work for this world will last far longer than the reign of any Emperor or any of our lives."

Her father retreated to his sietch offices to bury himself in planetology work. Watching him go, Chani whispered under her breath, "We must at least consider it."

As expected, her half brother did not let go of the idea. The following day, even though they all suffered from pounding heads and queasy stomachs, Khouro, Jamis, Adamos, and the others consumed melange powder to clear their heads. They went outside the sietch to a quiet place in the open desert rocks to talk further.

Chani felt hurt when she realized they were avoiding her, closing her out. Khouro had never kept secrets from her before, and when she understood why he was doing so now, she confronted him directly. "You think I will side with my father—that I'll reveal your plans and ruin your chances!" She placed her hands on her narrow hips, assessing him, wondering if she could defeat him in combat. Her brother wouldn't expect her to be physically aggressive, and she just might be able to slam him to the floor and make him yield.

"He is an Imperial," Khouro said with a snort.

"He is also a Fremen, born among us and living among us. Where do you think his loyalties lie?" Chani responded.

"I also know he took an oath to the Emperor." Her brother's dark eyebrows knitted together. "And he is Fremen enough to take any such oath seriously. It is not wise for us to let him know anything about our plans."

"But why cut *me* out?" Chani demanded. "You need me if your wild plan has any chance of success."

The other razzia raiders watched as he gave her a condescending look. "And why would we need you? You're only fourteen."

"My age never bothered you in previous raids. And I've been to Arrakeen! I have a connection inside the Residency where the Emperor is staying. I know the layout of the place." Khouro hesitated, showing that he clearly hadn't thought of this, and Chani pressed on. "How did you think you were going to get close to Shaddam? Just barge in with a band of dirty young Fremen and demand to see the Emperor?"

He looked away with a darkening expression. "You are right, sister. I should have thought it through." He made a welcoming gesture. "Come help us make our plans."

It soon became apparent that the ambitious plotters had a lot of work to do, more than just outlining the broad strokes of a nearly impossible scheme. They would have to reconnoiter, share information, and modify their plans accordingly. But that would take time, and no one knew how long Emperor Shaddam would remain on Arrakis. The group stayed away from the sietch, drawing no attention and raising no suspicions. Chani noticed that Liet-Kynes intentionally avoided them, as if he didn't want to know.

Several days after sending out word, Jamis uttered a mysterious promise that at least twenty additional Fremen from other sietches were making their way to Arrakeen. They would spread out, whisper questions, and gather intelligence about how they might infiltrate the Emperor's entourage, how they could station themselves with weapons or explosives along any parade path, how they might sabotage an Imperial ornithopter before it flew out on an inspection tour of the spice fields. Perhaps they would even find a way to poison Shaddam's food or kill him in his bedchamber. The possibilities were unfocused, but endless.

The more Chani heard, the more she realized how raw and undeveloped the plan was.

Leaving Sietch Tabr, the group traveled across the desert to outlying villages along the base of the Shield Wall, communities that eked out a living through a little mining, hand-gathering windblown melange from the rocks, or sending workers into Arrakeen. Chani and her friends knew that these settlements had no love for the Harkonnens, and the people did not ask questions when Khouro surreptitiously asked for help.

Best of all, Jamis learned the name of someone in charge of hiring heavy laborers in the spice silo farms at the Arrakeen spaceport. The village elder, who had done similar work in his younger years, shook his head in scorn when he saw the excitement in his guests' eyes. "A terrible job, hard and dirty for pitiful pay, all while you're under the close scrutiny of the Harkonnens. Better off joining a spice-harvester crew. At least you'd be out in the desert."

"We need to be in Arrakeen," Jamis growled.

Together, they left the village at sunrise when the shadows of the Shield Wall extended like a dark lake across the city, but Chani could still see the glows of numerous late-night businesses. The heat of smelters, repair yards, and shuttle-fueling facilities simmered like evil fires. One of the spaceport fields was illuminated with a constellation of lights, and she could make out shining Imperial ships, giant ornate frigates and Corrino military vessels. Prefab barracks stood around the perimeter, and even in the early dawn Sardaukar patrols marched as if ready for an invasion.

Chani studied the details from afar as other weary desert villagers trudged into the city for their daily work. Following her gaze, Khouro nodded, neither of them speaking.

Despite the obvious security in the city, Chani knew that Emperor Shaddam and his inner circle lived in the Residency fortress with all the comforts and protection Count Fenring could provide.

By the time they arrived in dusty Arrakeen, it had awakened into its sullen daily activities. The villagers went to regular work assignments, and several commandos followed them. Their village contacts had assured them that the only time Harkonnen crew leaders scrutinized worker IDs was when they came to collect their pay.

Armed with the name of their contact at the spice silo fields, Jamis and Khouro said goodbye to Chani, then headed off to the noisy industrial complex, where dust and exhaust smoke curled into the tan sky.

Chani made her way alone through the crowded streets, weaving among preoccupied pedestrians, water sellers, pickpockets, street preachers and street walkers, and servants going about their errands. One man tried to snatch her bound water rings, or perhaps he was attempting to fondle her; Chani broke his hand and walked away without a backward glance as he shrieked in pain.

At the side door of the Residency, she asked for the Shadout Mapes and waited for many minutes until the old housekeeper arrived. Mapes recognized the young woman immediately, and her dark eyes widened in surprise. "You've come back, child—and this time without your father."

"This time my purpose is different from his."

"So, you still come to learn?" Mapes asked.

"I come to observe and collect information."

The housekeeper gestured her inside. "And what is that but learning?"

After the insulated door closed behind them, Chani said, "I need to stay here for a while. Can you find me a position among the household staff? I must be able to move freely and watch."

The old woman scoffed. "Not an easy request to fulfill, child! The Emperor and his entourage are here in the Residency, so security has increased tenfold! Armed Sardaukar march down every hall, and Imperial observers lurk in the kitchens. Poison snoopers test every morsel of food. Even I must be escorted as I change the linens."

Exactly as Chani had expected. "With so much extra work, then surely you need additional help, and I am in desperate need of a job."

"I do need help, but it is not so easy to get you in now. Beggars are turned away from the doors. New hires are vetted carefully and then observed for an endless probationary period."

Chani's heart sank. She had promised Khouro that she could get inside, although even she wasn't sure what she could accomplish.

Noticing her disappointed reaction, Mapes pursed her wrinkled lips. "Still, I am the Residency's chief housekeeper, and I can vouch for a new serving girl. I know how to get the proper approvals and the appropriate paperwork. No one will think twice about a young desert girl, though we will have to clean you up—just a little, but not so much that anyone notices. If you're too beautiful, then you are no longer invisible." The shadout gave her a wry smile. "My mother taught me long ago that one of the greatest weapons a woman possesses is to be silent, unnoticed—and underestimated."

Chani could understand that philosophy, though she was never one to be silent.

Mapes introduced her to the staff, none of whom congratulated her on the new job. Instead, they seemed to pity her. But they asked no questions, and they gave no support.

The old woman issued her household garments, and Chani fitted herself into a drab shawl, cinching the waistband, prepping the folds and scarf so that her face was half-hidden, but not in a furtive way.

Mapes adjusted the fabric, then gave a nod of satisfaction. "You're not afraid to work, are you?"

"I'm not afraid of anything," Chani said, which drew a skeptical snort from the housekeeper.

"A proud answer, though foolish. I will assign you to the kitchen, cleansing cookware and dishes. Then in the laundry. Afterward, you can sweep floors, first in the common rooms and the banquet area."

Chani averted her eyes so the housekeeper could not see her excitement. She felt that if she became more familiar to Sardaukar eyes, she might gain access to the living quarters.

She did as she was told without complaint, asking little and speaking only in response to direct questions. Sardaukar were everywhere. Some of the household workers chattered with gossip, which consisted mainly of whispered suspicions. They all worried that Count Fenring had eyes everywhere, not just in the Residency, but throughout Arrakeen. Everyone was afraid of him.

Lady Margot was treated with greater respect than her husband, and Chani guessed that was because the noblewoman knew how to put on a kind face. But Lady Fenring was reported to be a Bene Gesserit, so Chani did not trust the woman's altruism. Nevertheless, she listened to the gossip and filed away any tidbit that might be useful.

After Chani had spent two days cleaning dishes and cookware, Mapes allowed her to join the servers who brought platters of food for a luncheon, though only a few nobles and courtiers attended. Emperor Shaddam, Count Fenring, and the inner circle were off on some sojourn. As Chani served the meal, head down, she remembered when she herself had sat at the same table next to her father, a guest of the Count. Back then, she had noticed the silent and unobtrusive servers. She acted the same now.

That afternoon with the Emperor and his party still off on their own business, Shadout Mapes rushed up to Chani, her eyes lit with excitement. "Come, child! There's a special assignment, and I need your help."

Three uniformed Sardaukar joined the two women on their errand, one on each side and one leading the way, as if three of the Emperor's terror troops might be needed to fight off an old housekeeper and a young serving girl. Instead of guiding them to the separate wing that held the Emperor's sleeping quarters, though, they went instead to the watermaster's offices, where Mapes added her thumbprint to a document, then received a pair of sealed jugs, each holding three liters of water.

She carried one and gave the other to Chani. The Sardaukar escort did not offer to help. "What is this for?" Chani asked.

"You will see," said Mapes, with an undertone of wonder.

The group moved along winding inner corridors lit by glowglobes. Chani could feel the cool shadows. The housekeeper whispered, "Lady Fenring built a water-sealed greenhouse chamber for her own pleasure. It is a room filled with flowers and shrubbery, fresh fruits, butterflies, and water mist in the air."

The Sardaukar pretended not to hear her talk.

"Like the date palms out front," Chani said.

"More than that." Mapes paused. "You will see."

At the end of an unmarked corridor, they stopped before the hatch of a guarded room. Chani held the water jug close to her chest.

The shadout continued to explain. "Lady Margot intends to show her botanical garden to Princess Irulan this evening. She wants the plants watered and freshened up, any dead leaves pruned. She trusts me with this." The old woman shot her a quick sidelong glance. "You'd better do well."

"Under guard." The Sardaukar worked the secure door seal and opened the hatch into a room full of greenery and misty air.

Chani caught her breath in wonder. She had seen images of offworld jungles before, forests with trees and underbrush so dense that the root systems surely strangled each other. How could there be enough water for so much?

Shadout Mapes moved forward, cradling her container, and Chani followed her. Yes, she had been to the palmaries in the south, which were the most vibrant Fremen plantings on all of Arrakis, and she had seen the enclosed terrariums in her father's botanical testing stations—but none of those examples were like . . . this. Chani absorbed the details so she could tell her friends and describe them to her father.

"We are watching you," said one of the Sardaukar.

Chani nodded, letting the man think she was intimidated by him.

"I will show you what to water, child. There is an established routine." Chani wondered how the plants would know about routines, but she followed instructions. She observed the housekeeper for the first few waterings, pouring a carefully measured sip into the soil at the base of the stems and trunks, and then she was dispatched to tend part of the greenhouse chamber on her own.

When they emptied their jugs, exactly per the measurements, they hurried to their other duties. The Sardaukar guards glanced at their chronometers. The old housekeeper whispered with a hint of urgency, "We are only allotted a certain time here. Lady Margot knows exactly how long it takes for me to complete my assigned tasks."

The two inspected each plant, brushed the leaves to find any dried stems or withered blossoms. Chani's fingertips were tough with calluses from the work she had done in the sietch, but she enjoyed the soft, fleshy feel of the plants.

Mapes snipped off any debris, and Chani collected the plant material in a mulch bag. When finished, she had to surrender it to one of the guards.

Finally, the Sardaukar hurried them out and sealed the door hatch behind them, and Shadout Mapes led Chani on to more work. The young woman felt uplifted. Even though the greenhouse vault had given her no useful reconnaissance information, she did have a greater appreciation for her father's sacred work as planetologist.

All spice belongs to the Padishah Emperor. We harvest it in his name and use it with only the greatest respect.

—BARON VLADIMIR HARKONNEN, periodic report on spice operations

The Baron offered every assistance to facilitate the Imperial inspection team—of course, he had no choice. Knowing how vindictive Shaddam IV could be, he did not want to raise the powerful man's suspicions.

Outwardly, he was calm and cooperative, all smiles, as he offered staff to help with the bureaucratic work and delivered his best factory managers for interviews. He opened his spice silos and Carthag warehouses for inspection.

He insisted he had nothing to hide, but the Baron's own suspicions drove him to near panic, and he desperately tried to guess what alleged wrongdoing might have attracted the Emperor's attention. He feared he had left a loose end dangling somewhere. What were the Imperial Mentats going to find?

It annoyed him that Count Fenring had slipped him no forewarning of this Imperial invasion. What was the real reason? From his Carthag headquarters, the Baron pored over his own records, reviewed all spice-production reports and the numbers that had been submitted, then he called in Piter de Vries.

His lean Mentat entered with mincing steps and feline grace. Piter's large eyes darted from side to side as he absorbed details in the office. His lips were stained red like sloppy bruises from the sapho juice that increased his mental acuity. "You summoned me, my Baron?"

"I need my Mentat for an analysis and a worst-case scenario. Apply your skills to every record, every bit of data." His voice boomed louder as his anger increased. "Root out any irregularities before the Emperor does. We've been clever and have not shown them everything yet."

"We have always been careful to operate within an acceptable margin of error, my Baron. Considering the scale of our operations, there will always be measurement variations, equipment losses, reporting errors, a general . . . sloppiness." He waved a thin-fingered hand. "Even the best manager cannot account for every grain of spice."

"But *we* must, Piter! The Emperor wants something. Why else is he here?"

Rabban strutted into the Carthag office wearing a pseudo-military desert uniform. The Baron's thick nephew would often stride through city streets with a troop escort, flaunting his power and watching people tremble. The man was a bludgeon without finesse, but sometimes a bludgeon was the most effective tool for a necessary task. The Baron didn't compliment his nephew even when he did something right, because that would dull his edge, and Rabban already blundered too much. Still, the Baron knew how to use him under the proper circumstances.

Now Rabban wiped a thick-fingered hand down the side of his face, acting as if he had been summoned here as well. "At least the Emperor and his main entourage are staying in Arrakeen, Uncle. If they had accepted your invitation to reside here, we would face many more problems."

"Their eyes are still here," de Vries said. "We cannot let down our guard."

The Baron let his frustration come to a boil. "But what should we guard against? What mistakes have we made? Why did the Emperor come here?"

The Grand Tour and this surprise spice inspection had been a complete shock to him. The forceful Imperial occupation had nearly a thousand in the party, from attendants to diplomats, hairdressers to seamstresses. And Sardaukar! Rabban was correct, in his own way; if the Emperor had commandeered the Harkonnen residence and headquarters in Carthag, the Baron's daily life would have become intolerable.

The enormity of the expedition, however, called into question the idea that it was merely an inspection tour. The planning, equipment, and expense of such a trip would have been significant, not something even the capricious Shaddam would do on a whim. There must be some reason! Why had there been no word from his spies?

The Baron conducted regular business on Kaitain, and had operatives at the Imperial Court, but none of them had heard any plans for the Emperor to travel to Arrakis. It had been a last-minute decision. A reaction to something?

There must be some reason!

"I will run projections, my Baron," Piter said. "The stated purpose of this visit is not necessarily the true reason."

Rabban snorted. "If the Emperor is here for something else, then Count Fenring knows what it is." A sneer crossed his face. "I wish we could lock him in a room and interrogate him."

"I'm sure the Count could thwart even your best torture methods, Rabban," the Baron said in a dismissive voice. Fenring was so deadly, in fact, that in such a situation, his nephew would probably end up injured or dead on the floor.

"Then how are we supposed to learn the answer?" Rabban asked.

"We ask questions. Of everyone." His nephew's eyes hooded with concentration, and he nodded. "At the same time, Rabban, push the spice harvesters hard. I want increased production, but also contact the smugglers, obtain some extra spice for our private use, but keep no record of it."

Rabban looked confused. "But why, Uncle?"

"Because we may need to pad the stockpiles if there should happen to be a deficit. After his thorough audit, the Emperor needs to see that our inventory is slightly more, not less, than expected."

With his marching orders in hand, Rabban stalked off.

The Baron tapped his large fingers on the black ovoid desk, looked down at his jeweled rings, then up at his Mentat. "Meanwhile, Piter, I want you to comb over every record. If anything is amiss, we must fix it."

Piter said, "The Emperor has his own Mentat accountants already at work on what we have shown them, but I have more files, and I will be more thorough than they are."

"Good. Devote yourself entirely to this problem." The Baron looked at a wall chronometer and sighed. "I need to go to Arrakeen and once again smooth the Emperor's feathers. I offered to take him out to the spice fields so he could observe our work, but he declined."

The Baron felt genuine relief at that. He racked his brain for a real explanation and hoped Piter de Vries would find answers.

ODDLY ENOUGH, IT was Rabban who discovered the true reason, two days later.

While the twisted Mentat sifted through every entry in the complex account books, Rabban's men worked their way into the backstreets, sending feelers into the marketplaces and street businesses of Arrakeen as well as Carthag, especially near the Residency, where they might hear some whispers from the Emperor's party. Count Fenring had his own guards in the old city, but House Harkonnen governed Arrakis, so their security forces kept the peace everywhere, arresting suspects and paying bribes.

When a grinning Rabban strode into the Baron's office to present his report, he walked with a childlike excitement. "It has nothing to do with us, Uncle! The Emperor came to Arrakis because *he's afraid*."

"Afraid of what?" the Baron demanded, while pressing a button to summon his Mentat. If Rabban thought he had an answer, Piter de Vries should also analyze it.

"Shaddam came here for safety, because there was an assassination attempt at the Imperial Palace."

The Mentat scurried into the office just in time to hear those words. "Assassination attempt? There has been no report of that."

"*Multiple* assassination attempts," Rabban said. He raised his square chin.

The Baron leaned onto the polished black surface of his desk. His suspensor chair supported his bulk. "I think you've been duped. What is the source of this information?"

Rabban crossed his meaty arms over his chest. "A disgruntled member of the Imperial entourage. Hundreds of people joined the Emperor's expedition. They packed up in a great rush and left Kaitain to come directly here, with no advance warning and no preparations."

"We know all that," de Vries said in his nasal voice. "It's part of Shaddam's Grand Tour."

Rabban sighed. "There were multiple attacks at the palace. The Emperor survived in each instance. Count Fenring thwarted one, as did Princess Irulan. But they locked down all reporting and covered it up—or tried to. The Emperor is either embarrassed or frightened. That's why he's taking refuge here with his Sardaukar—they want to keep him safe from further attacks."

The Baron leaned back, bobbing on his suspensor chair. "Because Arrakis is such a safe and comfortable world?"

Piter de Vries stroked his lower lip. "It's true that outside assassins would have a harder time striking the Emperor here. The Arrakeen Residency is practically a fortress."

"But what assassins struck the palace?" the Baron asked. "Who?"

"Members of a mutinous fleet." Rabban flushed. "I know it sounds ridiculous, but a disgraced military officer murdered his commander and gathered rebellious troops, stole Imperial warships, and now means to overthrow House Corrino."

The Baron laughed at the idea. "How is that possible? We would have heard!"

"It's what my contacts said! Multiple sources," Rabban insisted. "The Emperor is not on any Grand Tour, just stopping over here on Arrakis until it is considered safe enough for him to return to Kaitain."

"I suspected as much," Piter said.

The Baron half smiled at Rabban. "Sometimes you are not so stupid as you seem to be."

Rabban scowled, then continued, "So many courtiers and serving staff were uprooted from the Imperial palace, given no choice—because they were near the assassination attempts, and the Emperor did not want them to talk! But some are very unhappy about it. So far from Kaitain, the restrictions are loosening now, and some of them do spread gossip in the Arrakeen marketplace. One of my people overheard them."

Rabban seemed pleased, as if he expected his uncle to give him a reward.

"We need to verify this." The Baron glanced at Piter. "And you uncovered nothing about this plot?"

"My Baron, I have been studying the account books, as you commanded."

The Baron's pudgy lips frowned. "Indeed I did." He turned back to Rabban, thought of Feyd-Rautha, his other nephew who remained on Giedi Prime, studying House Harkonnen affairs. Though intelligent and talented, Feyd was only thirteen and still untested. The Baron had already given Rabban offhanded credit for what he had discovered, and Piter would continue to sort through the account books.

The Baron said, "We will appear to cooperate with Shaddam's supposed inspection, and we will maintain the ruse, but we must also keep our eyes and ears open. Perhaps further assassination attempts will follow the Emperor here to Arrakis . . ."

The Baron smiled. He could only hope.

Life is full of second chances, but they must be recognized and acted upon.

—A teaching of the Imperial War College

In his new uniform, Zenha took special pride that he no longer wore the old, meaningless medals he had received for exemplary service—service to a broken system that led to the deaths of too many soldiers, corruption, dishonesty, and petulant arrogance. His Liberation Fleet was not like that. His soldiers all recognized him as their Commander-General.

After finishing breakfast, he marched down the corridor on the lowest level of his flagship. His mission here at Otak was done, and he had arranged to take his fleet to a succession of other systems, other hiding places. His commandeered ships had all been reconfigured, their duty numbers and vessel IDs altered, and their mission documents and deployments registered as classified. After his discussion with the Guild Bank representative, he knew the Guild would remain neutral. Away from Otak, his other ships dispersed to undisclosed locations. Even if Emperor Shaddam sent out widespread alarms, he could never find and identify the Liberation Fleet.

As he walked down the passageway, Zenha nodded to crew members who saluted him, some regarding him with awe. Bright light from Otak's sun streamed through the windowports, illuminating the corridor better than the artificial glowpanels. Another Heighliner would arrive within hours, and he expected even more warships and fighters to join his movement. And then they would depart for their next destination.

But the most important person had already rejoined the battle group at Otak. Zenha had been waiting to hear Kia Maldisi's full report, and already it seemed unbelievable.

He entered the infirmary as the door slid aside. He smelled the cool, sterile chamber, the undertone of medical chemicals. More than a dozen fighters had been injured during the recent raid on Otak, several through their own carelessness, but no fatalities. The soldiers had been treated and released for duty. The infirmary would be quiet until their next active engagement.

For now, Kia Maldisi had the medical ward all to herself.

She had arrived on the previous Heighliner, stowed aboard a diplomatic ship and merchant courier from Kaitain. A doctor tended her now, using wound sealants and bone-knitters, but without the grim urgency he would have shown a patient who needed intensive care.

Zenha spoke as soon as he entered. "How is she? What is the extent of her injuries?"

"She will live," the doctor said. "She's extraordinarily tough and resilient—but she's been through hell."

Maldisi stirred on the bed, ignored the wound dressings, and barely flinched from the pain. She even managed a smile. "Takes more than some Imperial pummeling and torturous interrogation to kill me, sir." She drew in a wheezing breath, then lay back, still smiling. Her upper lip had a red, healing cut where she had been injured during her capture. The previous day, when she'd been smuggled aboard on a suspensor platform, Maldisi had been incoherent, but now she seemed ready to talk. "Escaping from the palace guard and their holding cell was a little harder than the interrogation, but once Count Fenring left Kaitain with the Emperor, his underlings were . . . lax."

Zenha leaned closer, his brows knitted. "The Emperor is not on Kaitain?" Thoughts began turning in his mind. If the throne was vacant, that offered unexpected opportunities. "We need a full debriefing from you. Everything. Then maybe you can help us plan our next move."

The doctor adjusted the patient on the bed, and she grunted, then demanded a stimulant from him. "I need to be clearheaded for this!"

The same Heighliner that had smuggled Maldisi also brought a cruiser and two corvettes flaunting Imperial military insignia—but their crews had overthrown their officers, marooned them in a disabled troop carrier, and traveled here to join the Liberation Fleet. Zenha's movement grew with every encounter, and they would be ready to converge on the Imperial capital soon.

When she was ready, Maldisi described the assassination attempts that had taken place in the palace. "We made multiple independent strikes, but each of us failed, sir. Surely the others are dead by now. I doubt anyone else broke free from interrogation."

Zenha gave a grim nod, shifting his expectations. "We all knew it was an impossible challenge. Likely a suicide mission."

"I kept my mouth shut, even when they tried their worst," she insisted, then let out a scoffing laugh. "I've been through enough pain on Salusa that I could withstand whatever they threw at me. I don't know how well the others fared."

Zenha's thoughts became darker. "None of you had any information that I didn't want the Emperor to learn. I don't care if he knows we're coming for him." She had known to travel to Otak to find them, but even if the interrogators extracted that information, Zenha already planned to take this task force away on the next Heighliner. They would be gone before the Imperials could track them down.

"Why did the Emperor leave the palace? That changes our plans."

A wide grin crossed Maldisi's battered face. "Oh, we scared the hell out of him, sir, with all those attempts to kill him. His propaganda ministers frantically tried to cover up the news, embarrassed by the very idea that so many of us got close to him." Her chuckle sounded like a wet rattle. The doctor bent over to check on her, but she brushed him away. "Shaddam has taken his Sardaukar, Count Fenring, and even your darling Princess Irulan and gone into hiding." Her sarcasm was thick. "They're all hunkered down on Arrakis. That's why I was able to break away on Kaitain. All of them disorganized and incompetent! The Emperor left one of his other daughters behind as a figurehead."

Frowning, Zenha sat on the bed next to her. Maldisi raised an injured hand, seemingly unconcerned that the torturers had torn off her nails, one by one. She mused at the mangled fingers. "Good thing I was never one to lacquer my nails."

Zenha grimaced at her wounds, but knew the doctor's regrowth pads would help her heal swiftly. "You'll be back on duty for the next fight. The scars will give you character." He was impressed with her, found beauty in her hardened features, her outgoing and determined personality.

"I already have plenty of character, sir." She sat up straighter. "In another few days, the doctor will release me to return to combat training. Gotta get ready, sir. Do you have any ideas on how we can strike the Emperor on Arrakis?"

"Oh, we're not going to Arrakis." He smiled as the thoughts filled his head. Her debriefing had given him another option, a perfectly acceptable way to do an end run and accomplish his mission. It was as audacious as anything else he had done so far. "If the Emperor took his Sardaukar and a large entourage into hiding, then he left the Golden Lion Throne more vulnerable than it's been in a long time. With the assassination attempts, he thinks *he* is our only target. But that is not my main goal at all. I wouldn't think so small."

Maldisi's shadowed eyes lit up as he rose from the infirmary bed, ready to issue orders and send word across his Liberation Fleet. On the next Heighliner, he would dispatch an urgent call wherever his loyal ships had gone.

"We are going to use all our might to take the Imperial capital."

The difference between schemes and dreams depends on the perspective of the participant.

—Old Earth saying

Though he wanted to know every detail about the ecology of Arrakis, Liet-Kynes turned a blind eye to other things. Especially now. He heard dangerous gossip, but when it concerned the outrageous plans of his daughter and stepson, he did not want to know. He refused to ask any details of their plans, because though his heart and passion belonged to the Fremen, he had also sworn a formal oath to serve the Imperium.

And he knew the Emperor had brought his Truthsayer to Arrakis. Better that Liet did not know.

He moved through Sietch Tabr now, noting the Fremen workers who churned spice substrates to make fabrics. Others in the tribe assembled equipment, repaired ornithopters, tended beehives. Chani and Liet-Chih had already been gone for days, but if asked, he could honestly say that those two often went on desert journeys, just exploring the wasteland. How could he know where they were?

He rubbed his temples, hung his head. Naïve and audacious, the band of restless youths couldn't possibly harm the Emperor, and they would be fools to try. Surely they would realize the truth of it, once they blew off steam. Maybe his daughter would talk some sense into her companions. Chani was an intelligent and well-grounded young woman. She often managed to control her hotheaded brother.

Spice raids or the sabotage of Harkonnen equipment did not bother him, because the Baron and his ilk had inflicted enough damage here already—not just on the Fremen, but on the planet itself. Yet attempting to assassinate the Padishah Emperor was another matter entirely. It had to be just talk. Had to be.

Still, he was sick with dread and waited for news. Chani, Khouro, and the others had been gone for so long. . . .

AFTER WEEKS OF shadowing the old housekeeper as her apprentice, Chani had learned how to be invisible in the Residency. She achieved the optimal balance between when people noted her presence and when they simply paid no attention to her at all.

But *she* paid attention all the time—to every room, calendar event, meeting, and change of guard. She did not dare smuggle an imager or find some way to record the things she witnessed, but she kept clear pictures of everything in her mind. The importance of her mission sharpened her thoughts.

Four times now, she had accompanied household workers on errands into the city to purchase items from the bazaar or to deliver documents to city administration offices. Now she arranged to go on a household errand of her own, unaccompanied. This was her chance. She needed to be by herself for a prearranged meeting with her fellow conspirators.

Wearing her stillsuit and household garments, she hurried through the Arrakeen streets, pulling the hood down to shadow her face. Most people she passed also looked at their feet, rather than around them.

Chani made her way down a narrow backstreet to the unmarked tavern in a shaded cul-de-sac. The place was a well-known drinking establishment for spice crews and shipyard workers.

After steeling herself, she unsealed the corroded hatch and pulled it open to enter the dim, busy tavern. Though she was only fourteen, no one gave her a second glance. The noise inside was loud and droning, but furtive. People talked in low voices, complaining, expressing their misery, or just sitting in sullen weariness.

As soon as Chani entered, Khouro caught her eye. Chani hurried to the table he shared with Jamis and five others in dirty, patched uniforms from the silo farm. The men hunched their shoulders and pressed their heads close, as if whispering about some sort of romantic assignation. They clutched small drinks, milky gray or brightly colored liquids. The bar held dusty bottles of imported liquors, far too expensive for average crew workers. Most people drank raw spice beer; some just spent their water rations.

Khouro slid a glass over to her when she sat down. "We've been waiting, Chani."

She furrowed her brow. "I needed to leave without drawing attention, and now I am here."

Khouro tapped the glass he extended to her. "Specialty of the house. It's water, but flavored with an offworld fruit."

She frowned down at the glass and leaned closer to sniff. "Why would they do that?" She took a sip, rolled the tart flavor around on her tongue. The water seemed polluted.

"Because offworld dilettantes have so much water they find it dull and boring, so they try to create variety."

Chani took another sip, refusing to waste it. Even with the bad taste, it was still water.

Jamis rubbed his shoulder against Khouro's. "We work all day under the sun around the spice silos. Factory groundtrucks come in and deliver new loads from spice tankers. Other vehicles load shuttles and CHOAM ships for delivery to Guild Heighliners." He ground his teeth together. "It's miserable work."

Her brother placed his elbows on the table and drank his spice beer. "But we have many crew workers, and they know many others, all of whom are connected to the desert societies of Dune." He smiled at her. "And all hate the Harkonnens! We have allies here, and places to hide once we take action."

"It is no surprise they hate the Harkonnens," Chani said. "But what about the Emperor?"

"They understand the importance of what we propose," Khouro said. "Cut off the head, and the rest of the serpent will wither. Now . . ." His eyes grew harder. "Tell us what you've learned."

Chani took out a blank sheet of spice paper and used a stylus to sketch out a careful interior layout of the Residency: the floors, workers' quarters, banquet halls, briefing rooms, offices, and noble living quarters. She talked while she drew, and used two more sheets of paper to detail other floors, especially the wing that housed the Emperor and his staff.

"Sardaukar guards fill the halls, and Count Fenring has spies throughout the Residency," she said. "I know some items from the Emperor's personal calendar, but his movements are kept closely guarded."

"Can you slip into his quarters?" Jamis asked. "So we can kill him as he sleeps?"

Chani shook her head. "I've not gone into the Imperial quarters, never even got a glimpse of him or his daughter, the Princess Irulan. The doors are constantly monitored by guards. Shaddam has a satellite throne room where he conducts the business of the Imperium, and he never holds open court. Even Count Fenring rarely appears with him."

"It sounds like the Emperor is a coward in hiding," Khouro said.

Chani took another sip of the fruity water to contemplate this, then nodded. "That may be so. He seems concerned about assassination attempts."

One of the other conspirators, Adamos, sucked in a breath. "Do you think he suspects what we're planning?"

Khouro grimaced. "We haven't done anything yet!"

Chani tapped the spice-paper sketches. "The Residency is well fortified. You may have a band of Fremen on the outside, but it would require a sizable army to take down the Emperor."

Her brother sniffed. "Only if we did it as an outright frontal attack, but you said you work in the kitchens. Can you put something deadly in his food?"

She shook her head. "They test each dish with poison snoopers before putting anything in front of him, and everything he drinks, too."

"Maybe put some ground glass in his meal," Jamis suggested. "That would appear on no tester."

Chani knew it was fruitless. "I've tried to think of a way. I watch every day, but I simply have no access to the Emperor. We may have to give up on our plan. It was a wild idea in the first place."

"What if he goes on a procession through the streets? Or a spice field inspection?" Khouro asked. "Surely he travels to his other ships at the spaceport."

"Maybe he goes to meet with Baron Harkonnen in Carthag," Jamis added. "If we could get the Emperor, the Princess Royal, and the Baron all together—one large explosion!" He raised his hands and grinned with delight.

Chani snorted. "Yes, and maybe a sandworm will break through the Shield Wall, come to the Residency, and swallow them all up. You are fools."

"We are ambitious," Khouro replied with amused patience. "The possibilities are numerous. We must consider all of them." He looked around at his companions. "Even our crysknives are a viable option, if we get close enough."

"You have all the reconnaissance I can give you." Chani looked down at her half-empty glass of water, then drank it all, because she would not waste it, then waited to finish a few last drops that had settled to the bottom of the glass. "I will deliver any ideas that occur to me, but your plan does not seem possible. It is doomed from the start."

But Khouro and his companions refused to relent. "Our odds improve greatly if we are willing to give our lives for the cause—and I am!"

The others nodded, which did not surprise Chani. With a heavy heart, she rose from her chair and slipped out of the smelly drinking establishment, remembering all of Mapes's advice on how to be invisible, unnoticed. As a Fremen, Chani already knew how to do that in desert regions, but here in the city it was different, and the shadout had been very helpful.

Even so, she felt many eyes on her as she opened the moisture-seal door and went back outside.

What works for one Emperor or Empress will not necessarily work for others. Each situation is different, and so is each ruler.

—PRINCESS IRULAN CORRINO, *Perspectives on Leadership*

Serving as figurehead in the Imperial Palace, Wensicia Corrino arrived in the throne room early in the morning, as she liked to do, giving her time to organize her thoughts and daily activities. She took her new role seriously, and right now she wanted to review her schedule.

Her father and his entourage had been gone for two weeks, and already her routine seemed familiar, comfortable . . . and right. She was pleased with what she had accomplished so far by invoking her position and her father's name. Only nine times in the history of the Imperium had a woman served as the lone, powerful Empress. The thought made Wensicia smile.

For years, she had imagined herself as the Princess Royal, sitting at the Emperor's side instead of Irulan. And whenever she looked over at the massive Golden Lion Throne, she could imagine so much more.

Even though Shaddam was gone from Kaitain, he remained the Padishah Emperor. Still, Wensicia took her proxy role seriously. She would not squander this opportunity, because as the third daughter, she had few chances to prove her skills and prepare. The entire court would be impressed with what she achieved.

She did not want to ruffle the feathers of the influential Chamberlain Ridondo or cause any muttering or scandal, so she did not take Irulan's designated chair. Instead, Wensicia had a different throne brought in from the archive warehouse as her own ceremonial seat. Now, an elderly serving woman dusted off the temporary throne, which had been placed next to the slightly larger chair that Irulan used when she sat at court.

Wensicia dismissed the servant. "Enough. You've done a good job, and the people will notice." The old woman bowed and retreated, beaming from the compliment. Wensicia knew her father would never have done that, and now the servant would remember her personal kindness. . . .

This ceremonial throne had been used by one of her ancestors, the Empress Bertl Corrino. It was not a pretentious seat of state, but rather quite ordinary, made of common stone, but it was solid and suited Wensicia's purposes perfectly. She had allowed the blemishes and scuffs to remain on the front, a subtle message of humility.

After Zenha's little rebellion was ended and the Emperor came back to Kaitain, Wensicia hoped she might accompany their father on some of his future military parades or inspections, especially if she did well here. Even more than Irulan—or even Shaddam himself—Wensicia had learned intricate details of the Imperial military, including attending classified briefings. She knew about the inner workings of the officer corps as well as standard recruits, even Sardaukar training routines on Salusa Secundus. She knew inner, highly compartmentalized secrets and backdoor access codes for Imperial warships. Content in the power and stability of his military, Shaddam had never bothered to learn esoteric details, relying on his upper-echelon officers—who were mostly fools. On that, Wensicia and Irulan agreed. . . .

As usual, Wensicia would hold scheduled audiences in the morning, but the day's primary event would be her speech to the Imperial Court.

When the Emperor's party had rushed off on such short notice, they'd left a large hole in the palace staff. In only a few weeks, Wensicia had shifted assignments and granted minor court positions to her own people. Because her father had taken so many courtiers abruptly away, there were numerous interim openings. She took advantage of that.

She had also been busy streamlining various defense projects that had grown bloated and inefficient from years of nepotism and neglect. She couldn't blame all the malaise on her father, but during his reign, he had appointed too many showpiece officers, granting ranks and command positions on a whim. Now, Wensicia doled out rewards of a different sort, to strengthen what remained of the rank structure.

In the wake of the multiple assassination attempts, she needed increased protection wherever she was on Kaitain. No one could argue with that. As the Corrino proxy on the throne, Wensicia created her own new division of the Imperial Guard, an enhanced police force with a deep interrogation arm to replace the previous interrogators, whom she had executed for letting one of the main assassins escape!

She had been busy. Given her limited mandate from her father, much of it was a matter of negotiation.

For the public eye, Wensicia had taken it upon herself to be prominent and reassuring. Every citizen of the Imperium must see her appear daily in the throne room, to know that House Corrino had not abandoned the palace. Wensicia held regular audiences to keep the business of the Imperium going—and she considered it much more than a pro forma exercise.

On schedule, Chamberlain Ridondo entered the chamber with spidery movements, adhering to the busy schedule. The sallow-skinned man gave her a proper greeting as he placed a sheet of parchment on the ornate table to Wensicia's right, then adjusted a ridulian crystal player next to it. "Your calendar of today's events and duties, Royal Highness."

He stepped back, and she appreciated the dignity and respect he showed her. "Will there be anything else?" The chamberlain had never seemed to notice Wensicia before, not until the Emperor and Irulan left.

"That will be all, thank you."

Alone again, Wensicia studied her daily schedule, the noble dignitaries and businessmen who would appear before her. She wanted to make each meeting memorable and efficient.

Wensicia had already gotten herself onto various committees. At first, it had seemed like a triumph, but that work bogged down in administrative complexities, bureaucratic momentum, and apathy. Now, acting in her father's stead, she made small but incontrovertible decisions, accomplishing things that the slow committees would never have gotten done.

Yes, she was a good proxy empress. She secretly hoped the Emperor and his party would remain away for quite some time.

Now she set aside the parchment, and it rolled itself back up on the side table. She activated the ridulian crystal player and skimmed down the projected treasury report she had ordered, including shortfalls in important military projects. She would leave her mark by finding the best way to reallocate available funds.

Throughout the morning, she held court from her stone seat, thinking of ancient Empress Bertl as nobles approached her, one by one, Earls and Duchesses and Baronesses and Viscounts, all paying homage to her.

Wensicia could tell they were using the opportunity to curry some favor, though she was only a caretaker. For now.

She understood them. She, too, had done similar things, just in the past few days.

Near the end of the morning session, a young noblewoman came forward, Lirenda Obison. The woman bowed before the proxy throne, trying to keep her composure, but then the tears came as she explained how her noble house had fallen on hard times due to climate shifts on their agricultural world and poor decisions about which crops to plant. Wensicia had already reviewed the woman's story in preparation for meeting her. Due to the significant loss in standing, her family had been removed as a House Minor from the rolls of the prestigious Landsraad, and the stress and shame of that decline had resulted in the death of her father.

Wensicia listened as the shaky woman finally made her request. "I ask for assistance from the Imperial throne, Your Highness. House Obison still holds valuable patents, including the design for improved drop boxes used for hauling grains and produce to and from orbit."

Wensicia narrowed her eyes. "What kind of assistance? Exactly?"

Lirenda Obison snapped to attention, strengthened by hope. Wensicia was impressed as the woman presented a specific plan and a detailed request. To get her House back on its feet, Obison needed to modernize her agricultural and manufacturing operations. After summarizing her plan, she bowed. "In return for assistance, Your Highness, I am prepared to offer House Corrino twenty percent of our profits for the next ten years."

Wensicia pursed her lips, considering. She glanced at Chamberlain Ridondo, who wore an indecisive frown. On the side of the throne room, the Imperial Mentats stood, considering and nodding.

"Your offer has merit," she said. "Out of compassion for you, until my father returns from his Grand Tour, I will grant you enough to get started, along with a continuing stipend, until such time as the Emperor decides otherwise." She knew that Shaddam would probably never review the matter, but at least she had acted without overstepping her bounds, and it would change the future prospects of House Obison. It felt satisfying.

This woman and the noble observers would remember what Wensicia had done. As she considered it more, 30 percent of the profits seemed more reasonable to her. Perhaps renegotiations would be in order, eventually.

AFTER A PRIVATE lunch to prepare her thoughts, Wensicia went to deliver a speech to the Imperial Court. As a princess of House Corrino, even just the third daughter, she had often been present at small diplomatic ceremonies where she'd given minor talks or announcements.

Today would be different, because she would truly be the center of attention, carrying the weight of the crown. Now, as she stood before the crowd and gazed out at the gathered dignitaries, nobles, and CHOAM representatives, she felt confident, and her words flowed easily.

She spoke of the Imperial history she had so closely researched, how its enduring strength and stability had saved billions of lives and wrapped so many planets in the warm safety net of House Corrino.

Wensicia took great care never to criticize her father or Irulan. Even with Shaddam away from Kaitain, Wensicia could not help but notice the genuine respect they held for him, even for her sister. Now she wanted the same measure of respect for herself. . . .

Her days were long, but she would not have had it any other way. That evening, in the privacy of her apartments, Wensicia continued to study internal military records, including classified files about the command structure and fallback systems in the fleet ships.

She remained fascinated by what the mutinous officer Zenha had managed to achieve, not only with his own task force, but with his growing number of followers. There were definitely flaws and weaknesses in the Imperial military, overconfidence and incompetence. The second-line officers seemed to know far more about the workings of their own ships than the noble commanders did.

Wensicia smiled with delight when she found a centuries-old deeply classified file documenting a set of fail-safe systems that had been installed in all capital ships. Such measures had been taken by her great-great-grandfather Emperor Horuk IV, when he feared a military coup among his inner-circle officers. It was a "self-destruct/shutdown" command to be used as a last resort by a betrayed Emperor if his own military ships turned against him. In Horuk's time, the command apparatus had secretly been installed in all Imperial vessels. Wensicia wondered if it was still in effect.

She doubted her father even knew about the system, because Shaddam never bothered to dig for such details, keeping himself occupied with the business of the Imperium, not military details.

But she found the information useful. Wensicia had to develop her own preparedness, no matter how long the Padishah Emperor and his entourage remained away.

A key element of strategy is to understand your enemy's motivations.

—Sardaukar command lectures, political section

The cushions on the portable Imperial throne were plush crimson and purple, and the lingering perfume reminded Irulan of the palace. Her father pretended that this satellite throne room in Count Fenring's Residency was as lavish as the one on Kaitain. With a great flurry, this substitute had been decorated by his courtiers with trappings, tapestries, pennants, and expensive furniture the Emperor needed to keep up appearances on his Grand Tour. He could not seem to be hiding.

Shaddam's secondary throne had been transported from the Imperial frigate and placed on a raised platform in these temporary quarters. Irulan sat in an ornate chair, erect and alert, utilizing observational skills from her Bene Gesserit training. Reverend Mother Mohiam also had her traditional place beside the dais.

Count Fenring entered the spacious room, casually taking a seat in one of the guest chairs. Irulan wasn't surprised at his lack of formality in private, as the two men had a close friendship that went back many years. The Count had helped her father solve problems that went outside of normal diplomatic or administrative channels.

"Your safety is paramount, Sire," Fenring said, fidgeting with his fingers. "And we can be confident that Princess Wensicia is quite safe in the palace."

"I would have been safe there as well," Shaddam grumbled. "Maybe I should worry more about what institutions my own daughter will knock down while I'm away." His expression was pinched with frustration. "How much longer do I need to stay here in exile? How many secret assassins can there be?" Irulan watched him slump on his throne in resignation.

Normally he would sit erect and imposing. "And the Princess Royal is safe as well. My Sardaukar should be hunting down that traitorous rebel, but with my forces already divided, I don't want to fragment them further." He shook his head. "I humiliated the man for his failure, but I should have executed him instead."

Shaddam tapped his fingers on the thick, jewel-embedded arm of his portable throne. He continued his grumbling. "Even if the man managed to seize several Imperial ships and recruit mutineers, their entire crews can't be traitors to me! Why don't *they* mutiny against Zenha and bring his head to me?" He gave an impatient sigh. "Perhaps I should have remained on Kaitain as bait, luring him into a trap." With a manicured fingernail he picked something out of his teeth. "But I'm perfectly safe here!" He said it as a curse.

Irulan asked, "Count Fenring, have you heard of any specific plot here on Arrakis?" Even with the loyal Sardaukar and the Residency defenses, no security was perfect. "I have heard grumblings about dangers in Arrakeen and Carthag, too."

"Local unrest, hmmm," Fenring muttered. "A few instances of sabotage by desert Fremen, disruption of daily activities in Arrakeen. Nothing to worry about."

Shaddam did not take the comment seriously. "Wherever I go and whatever I do, the street rabble will complain that I don't do enough, or that I do too much for a certain group of people. Some hate me for simply living as an Emperor should." He gestured to the transplanted opulence in his satellite throne room.

Fenring was his usual calm self. "Sire, I, ahhh, receive regular reports on any local unrest from my sources. I will keep you and Major Bashar Kolona apprised of developments. My operatives know who the Fremen desert rats are and where they hide."

Irulan tried to wrap her mind around the totality of the situation. "What are the local grievances you mentioned, Count Fenring? We'd like to understand."

Fenring raised his eyebrows. "Well, ahhh, the Harkonnens are at the heart of the misery and objections, Princess. As both of you know, the Baron imposes a harsh rule, and the people suffer greatly because of it. It is no wonder they get riled up from time to time."

"As I recall, they made similar complaints to my father about House Richese," Shaddam said. "They will whine regardless."

Irulan did not like the fat, rude Baron, and had heard that Harkonnen troops ground the poor people under their bootheels, especially Glossu Rabban, the Baron's nephew. "Should we ask the Harkonnens to employ a more humane set of rules?"

Fenring and Shaddam chuckled at the idea.

Her father said, "The Baron governs with an iron grip because the desert people will not stay in line otherwise. We have imposed large quotas, and the flow of spice must continue. You understand the matter well enough, Irulan. Or did the Mother School on Wallach IX teach you nothing?"

"I understand, Father," she said quietly. She applied the Sisterhood's training now to study the Emperor's mood and to analyze Fenring's words.

The Count continued, "There is unrest among the city people, yes. Also among the Fremen tribes in the desert—they are few, but dangerous. They are backward people and religious fanatics, and that is why the Baron employs Rabban to control them. Fremen won't be satisfied no matter what changes you make." He offered a withering, sarcastic grin. "Unless, Sire, you abdicate the Golden Lion Throne and withdraw all spice operations and remove every offworlder from the planet." He snickered. "Then, ahhh, perhaps they would be satisfied."

Shaddam chuckled along with him. "Oh, they would still find reasons to complain, Hasimir."

The two men laughed, and the Emperor gave a casual gesture. "Order your operatives to find out what they can about this rabble. Arrest whomever you need and make an example of them. Otherwise, it is not a matter of concern."

Soldier contingents, body armor, blades, shields, attack ships—those are obvious defenses. But one must never underestimate the destructive quality of a rumor.

—COUNT HASIMIR FENRING, Arrakeen defense assessment

Hearing a scuffle accompanied by groans of pain in the corridor, the Baron looked up from the polished black surface of his desk.

Grunting with effort, Rabban lurched through the door, hauling a shattered man. The squirming victim was covered with blood. The head lolled, and red drool streamed from the open mouth. Both arms flopped; one was bent in three places from broken bones. Rabban breathed hard, but he was grinning.

Kept awake by repeated pain as Rabban jostled his injuries, the victim exhaled a wet rattle, then went unconscious. The Baron sat back in his suspensor chair, keeping the desk surface between him and his nephew.

"I obtained the information you wanted, Uncle." Without a care, Rabban tumbled the tortured body onto the immense desk surface. "I had to do some convincing, but I think the information is valid."

The Baron frowned in distaste at the mess, saw the victim awaken, his glassy eyes rolling. His teeth had been broken. When Piter de Vries used extreme methods to interrogate a subject, he caused less obvious damage but inflicted more pain, deeper pain. His nephew was no Mentat—a laughable idea, that!—but he was still effective enough, under certain circumstances.

The Baron rose from his chair and walked around the desk, light on his feet from the suspensor belt around his enormous waist, as if he were walking on a low-gravity world. "This is one of the conspirators? He schemes to assassinate Shaddam?" He nodded to himself. "Good that you kept him alive. The Emperor and Count Fenring will want their time with him."

Rabban blinked, not comprehending. "A conspirator? No, Uncle—this is a witness. One of my contacts suspected he might have seen or heard something, so we asked him politely." His thick lips formed a grin. "We had to refresh his memory."

The man on the desk stirred, groaned.

Rabban nudged him and pressed into a broken rib, which made the man yelp. "He runs a drinking establishment in Arrakeen, frequented by spice-yard workers, cargo loaders, mechanics. He pours drinks, looks at the customers, listens in on conversations."

When the man gurgled, the Baron looked down at him, then at Rabban. "And what did he hear that you found interesting?"

"He's observed two meetings of a secret rebel cell," Rabban said. "Desert people, filthy Fremen, he said. He overheard parts of their conversation."

The Baron tapped his ring fingers together, considering. "Did he record what they said? If he's to be our informant, perhaps we should install listening devices in his establishment, put an implant in his ear."

Through his fog of pain, the tortured bartender squirmed on the desktop, gasped. "No . . ."

"It was a group of furtive plotters, and he was able to identify some. He gathered names of their associates and listed them all for me. I passed those names to my men, and they are going through the city right now to locate all the rats' nests."

"And what plans have they made against Shaddam?" the Baron asked. "How do they intend to kill the Padishah Emperor? Do they have weapons, explosives? Have they infiltrated assassins into the Residency?"

"I'm still investigating that, Uncle."

The bartender coughed blood and managed to say, "All . . . talk."

"Talk leads to action," the Baron snapped. "And seditious talk itself is a crime. If there is a violent rebel cell in Arrakeen, we must be the ones to uncover it and report to the Emperor."

He pondered possibilities. Shaddam IV had five daughters, no sons. If he were to be assassinated—perhaps by some convenient local rabble here—the Imperium would be rocked to the core. House Harkonnen was already powerful in the Landsraad, and the fact that they were governors of Arrakis, the source of melange, gave them significant status. If Shaddam were to die, someone would have to marry Princess Irulan and take the Golden Lion Throne. The Baron would never marry her, of course, but his protégé Feyd-Rautha might be an excellent possibility.

But that thought seemed viable for only a moment before he dismissed it. These Fremen malcontents were all bluster, and he doubted they had any resources to pull off an attack on that level. They would be up against armed Sardaukar and all of Fenring's household security. Even if their malcontent network had spread throughout the city, they were fools to think they could overthrow an Emperor. Their plans would surely fail. It would be embarrassing.

Therefore, Baron Harkonnen realized that his greatest advantage would come from exposing the plot. Even if the desert rabble had no possible chance of succeeding, Shaddam would certainly reward the Baron for thwarting them. His star would rise, and the Imperial inspectors would set aside any suspicions regarding Harkonnen melange production. He would no longer need to worry about the alleged spice inspection.

Nodding, the fat man said, "Rabban, we must round up these conspirators ourselves and deliver them to Arrakeen. You have the names from this . . ." He frowned at the bloody, broken body staining his desktop. "This informant."

"I have several names from him, Uncle."

"Get more. Unravel the network as far as it goes. Can this man be an effective informant from now on?"

Rabban studied the groaning bartender and grunted. "No, he is too damaged. The customers would know what was done to him."

The Baron agreed. "Dump him in the desert and cultivate someone else. Spread your men into the city of Arrakeen. Listen and track down the main names. We will thwart this widespread conspiracy and claim victory."

Rabban dragged the body off the desktop, let it crash to the floor. Bending down, he reached under the man's broken arms and lifted him, a clumsy burden of limbs. The victim barely had the energy to struggle.

"I'll root them out, Uncle. I'll hunt down the Fremen rats and crush them." He grinned as he left. "Thank you for this opportunity."

Soft societies fantasize about a life of comfort, with no toil. Fremen do not dream of such things, for they do not understand relaxation or decadence. And through their strength, they live for victory and independence.

—LIET-KYNES, *Desert Aspirations*

In the Arrakeen bazaar, stalls were crowded close together: metal tables, rickety stools balanced on the broken flagstones. Awnings were stretched overhead, some drab and brown, others flashy with colored dyes. In the open air, vendors all wore stillsuits; some kept nose plugs inserted and face masks in place, while others left their faces uncovered so they could call out their wares.

A water seller in traditional costume strolled along carrying a large bladder on his back and nozzles with measuring gauges. He jingled water rings, flashed a bright sash and scarf to draw attention. He yelled out the familiar song, "Soo-soo-soooook! Fresh water. Clean water!" He lowered his voice to an awed whisper. "*Cool* water."

Wearing housekeeper's garb, Chani hurried past the stalls. One man offered oversize roast crickets on a skewer, insects he had caught in the alleys of Arrakeen; another sold honey and biscuits. A broad tent-covered area held low tables where groups drank spice coffee while discussing business or friendship. One man sold painted pots; another held strange-looking birds in a cage, said to have armored bodies that made them capable of carrying messages through storms. Two men sat together playing balisets and singing mournful songs.

Chani moved from vendor to vendor in search of a familiar face. Finally, she spotted a seller of sandpearls, where she was supposed to meet Khouro and his companions. She touched a pocket at her side, where she still heard the crackle of spice paper. Her detailed map.

She had taken the time to draw every door in the Residency, from which she could guess at some of the rooms she had not actually been in, the possible quarters of the Emperor, the Princess, and important members of their entourage. Another sheet held meticulous records of the Emperor's appointments, noting the rare times when he might leave Count Fenring's fortress and venture back to the spaceport, where his Imperial ships had landed.

It was precisely the data her brother wanted.

Four men conversed in low voices outside the sandpearl booth, ostensibly haggling over prices. A bearded old man stood behind a tray of his wares, glowering as if convinced everyone was trying to cheat him. Chani knew it was all an act. The vendor was also part of their plot.

Sandpearls were fused nuggets of silica created by lightning strikes out in the desert. Sometimes, Fremen found and treasured the oddities, and Khouro had a large one he had found as a boy. Often, sandpearls were recovered in the exhaust bins of spice factories, left in catchtraps after the centrifuges sifted out the melange. Factory operators and Harkonnen governors paid little attention to the debris, and the crew workers smuggled them out to sell to desert merchants like this.

Behind the table the bearded man held a greenish nugget between thumb and forefinger. "A fine and rare jewel. Use it to romance a desert princess."

One of the hooded men scoffed. "Maybe I could sell it to a noble lady from Kaitain. Sandpearls are worth much more offworld."

Chani knew the hooded man was Khouro playing his role.

The merchant said, "And how would you ever get offworld, friend? If you buy the pearl, make use of it here."

She realized that the assistant was Jamis, dressed in a gray robe with green stripes. Eight others were gathered around the table, most of them familiar faces.

The water seller strolled past again, yelling out, "Soo-soo-soooook! Fresh water. Clean water. *Cool* water." They all fell silent as the man passed by, afraid he might be eavesdropping.

Khouro noticed his half sister and gave a slight nod. When she pretended to be a potential customer and bent close to look at the sandpearls, Jamis whispered, "We are all here. It is time to make our plans."

They slipped into a room behind the booth, leaving one person outside to deal with any customers. Chani followed them. Khouro looked at his sister. "Do you have more information for us?"

Chani removed the sketches, unfolding the spice paper and tracing her fingers across the detailed blueprint. "There may be ways you could infiltrate the household. Deliveries, couriers, workers who haul trash and sell it to businesses in the city."

"The Emperor would never let such a lowly person get anywhere near him," Khouro said. He pored over the blueprint sketch, noting the Imperial quarters.

Jamis said, "If Chani opened one of the side doors late at night, we could infiltrate. We have fifteen, maybe twenty fighters—good fighters who know Fremen ways."

Chani felt a chill at the possibility. Or impossibility.

"We'd sweep in, quick and silent," Khouro said in a hushed tone. It was obvious that he and Jamis had already discussed this plan. "Look here." He touched the drawing. "We enter through this door, pass through these rooms and galleries, not making a sound."

"There will be guards," Chani warned. "Sardaukar."

"So we kill them," Jamis said, "and keep running."

Chani rolled her eyes, while Khouro was breathing harder. "If we get to the restricted wing, we fight our way in, break down the doors. Kill Count Fenring if we see him, eliminate the fancy Princess. Most importantly, we find Shaddam and slit his throat!"

This was growing more absurd by the minute. Chani shook her head. "You would all be killed."

"But the Emperor would also be dead," Khouro said. "My blood is Fremen, and I am willing to pay a price in Fremen blood. Ten of us, even twenty of us lost in the fight—but if we succeed in killing Shaddam IV, we change the course of history and the future of Arrakis."

Chani heard the water seller outside, calling, "Soo-soo-soooook! Soo-soo-soooook!" But then he raised his voice and whistled out. "*Sekah! Sekah! Sekah!*"

Chani knew it was the Chakobsa word for *alarm*. Jamis backed away from the table. Khouro and Chani spun. The rest put hands to their hidden crysknives. Jamis opened the door a little, and they saw troops flooding into the market square. Harkonnen troops! They did not march in formation, but rather lunged in like wolves. They bowled over the cricket vendor's stall. They smashed the pottery maker's wares.

The soldiers had long knives drawn, their faces twisted with anger. They weren't searching, Chani saw. They already knew their target—and they were running toward the sandpearl stall.

"We've been discovered—run!" Khouro jammed the spice-paper drawings into his robes.

The conspirators bolted outside through a side exit, running through fabric sellers and ducking into a coffee tent to emerge from the opposite side. Chani grabbed her brother's arm and dragged him with her. He looked furious, wanting to kill the Harkonnens, but she kept him moving. "We have a safe house," he said with a hiss.

Jamis flung himself on the first soldier, stabbing him deep in the kidneys. The Harkonnen reacted with astonishment before he felt the pain and crashed to the ground. Jamis upended the metal table and smashed it into the soldiers, bowling them onto their backs before he sprinted away.

More Harkonnens rushed up to the bearded vendor, who flung a faceful of sandpearls at them. The soldiers cut him to pieces with their swords.

A thick man in uniform with a flushed face and square shoulders charged along with his troops, waving a short sword in one hand and a dagger in the other. Both blades were already stained with blood. His face was tight with the intensity of the hunt. Chani recognized him from images she had seen, knowing him for all the torments he'd inflicted upon her people. Rabban—the man the Fremen called "Beast."

The potter tried to protect the rest of his wares from being smashed, throwing curses at the marauding Harkonnens. As Rabban stomped past, he hacked the man's head off. "They're all conspirators! Capture them, so we can peel the truth out of them."

Chani wore drab servant's garb, but she did have her crysknife tucked into her bodice. She drew it now, but kept it hidden in the fabric, remembering what Shadout Mapes had said about staying invisible. Khouro yanked out a plasteel dagger, probably because he kept his crysknife secured when he worked among the spice silo crew.

One of the soldiers pointed at Chani and Khouro. "Those are the ringleaders! They are the ones to get."

They darted between stalls, ducked under awnings, but the soldiers lumbered after them among the wares, coming from different directions. Her brother turned to face the Harkonnens, raising his blade, and the enemy closed in, fixed on him and ignoring Chani. She stabbed the first soldier in the side, deftly sliding her milky blade into his liver. She withdrew the knife and stung again like a serpent, this time severing his spinal cord. Like the one before, he was dead when she pulled the blade free.

Khouro killed another Harkonnen. "Do we have a rendezvous point?"

Chani called out in Chakobsa. "Someplace the others will know to find us?"

"We have to get ourselves away," Khouro said. "Each fighter for himself. All know the way."

Yelling a mixture of laughter and rage, Rabban faced off with Jamis. The Beast was blustering and overconfident. Jamis fought like a dervish, and slashed a gash down Rabban's left arm, which made his opponent bellow in astonishment. Jamis tried to close in for the kill, but three Harkonnen soldiers swept in to protect their commander. Jamis fought hard and killed two of them and injured the third, before bolting away, smashing through awnings, scattering the tools and fabrics of a stillsuit maker.

Making her own escape with her brother, Chani ducked between hanging dyed scarves that blew in the breeze.

They reached the other side of the bazaar as even more pandemonium erupted. The Harkonnen soldiers were smashing vendor stalls, attacking any desert person as a possible suspect. She watched one of her companions fight a pair of soldiers, who were obviously trying to capture him alive. The wound in the Fremen's side bled heavily, and he realized he was losing. When he knew the Harkonnens had him, he plunged his dagger beneath his own chin, into his throat.

Seen through fractured glimpses, she counted at least seven Harkonnens dead and two of their own. But the conspirators had scattered, and now the rest of them had to get away.

She was panting hard. Khouro remained silent, his expression grim as he ran beside her. She saw blood spattered across his face. They ducked into an alley in the old town souks, and he led her through crossways and convoluted passages. Khouro knew his way, and Chani followed him, turning left, running straight, ducking under an arch, then right again.

Here, the shadows were deep and the dwellings close together, the doors low and unmarked. Khouro stopped before one door that looked no different from any other. He rapped hard against the smooth wall, and an access port opened. He inserted his finger to press a hidden latch. The door opened, but it was so low that Chani had to duck as he pushed her inside. "Our safe house."

In the dusty shadows, she heard rustling, saw low hangings, cushions crowded together. Only a single dim glowglobe shed light.

"Ah, three of us are already here," Khouro said. "We'll stay until the soldiers go away."

Chani slumped down onto one of the cushions, feeling a prickle of perspiration on her skin that was absorbed by the sandwich layers of her stillsuit. Adrenaline throbbed through her bloodstream. Her muscles were shaking.

All business, Khouro removed the spice-paper drawings he had retrieved and set them on the low table. "We'll finish our planning here when the others arrive."

"We lost Tokta," said one of the men.

"I saw," Khouro said. "It could not be helped."

"We killed many of them," said another rebel.

A few minutes later, the door opened again, and everyone grew tense, touching their weapons.

Jamis entered, his eyes dark. "How did they find us?" He sealed the hatch behind him.

"Rabban has spies in Arrakeen. Someone must have overheard or seen something," Khouro said. "We knew it would be dangerous. We'll have to be more careful from now on." He spread out the blueprints as if this were the only way to quell his panic. "But we are almost ready, we know what we're going to do."

The hatch opened again, and they turned to see who else had made it to safety. A ruthless uniformed Sardaukar crashed through the low door, followed by several others, all with weapons extended. They boiled inside, shouting.

The Fremen rebels were in too confined a space. They pulled out their bloody weapons, but the Sardaukar were on them like a shockingly sudden sandstorm. They flooded the chamber, firing a blur of stunners at everyone crowded there. Struck by the projectiles, Jamis and Khouro dropped.

Chani dove behind a side table, hoping for just one more moment.

A rebel lunged at the Sardaukar, but the grim commander struck the man with the flat of his blade, rendering him senseless. The Sardaukar seized two other fighters who tried to defend themselves. There was no other escape. The attackers blocked the only door.

Behind them, one more man entered, slipping smoothly through the low entryway. "Ahhh, hmmm, we found a nest of vipers." Chani's skin crawled when she saw Count Fenring. "Rabban was an embarrassing interference, but we knew where to find you anyway." He noticed the spice-paper drawings and picked them up. "Hmmm, interesting. I wanted the details of your plans. Hmmm-ahhh, you might have succeeded, but not any longer."

Chani looked at her brother, who lay twitching on the floor, his eyes half-open but showing only the whites. Beside him, Jamis lay stunned. A Sardaukar grabbed her arm in a tight grip, as if he didn't consider the girl worth stunning.

Fenring's gaze skated over her, then returned. His brow furrowed as he tried to place her, but failed. He shrugged. "We will learn all about you, and I'll convey the plot to the Padishah Emperor." He nodded to himself as the Sardaukar mopped up the scene, binding the prisoners, preparing to move them out. "Ahhh, it is a good day for Arrakeen."

A victory is often in one's own mind, while a failure is for all to see.

—Political annals of EMPEROR FONDIL III, the Hunter

In the Residency, Princess Irulan sat off to the side of Shaddam's satellite throne in a formal chair, while Reverend Mother Mohiam stood nearby.

Her father had never been pleased enough with any of his wives to have them hold court as a full Empress at his side, sharing power. Irulan had been young when her own mother died. Then for political reasons, her father had married again and again, always hoping for sons. She realized that he hadn't been overly fond of Anirul either, but the later ones were even less to his liking.

Nearby, the old Truthsayer gave her a knowing look.

Irulan knew the Bene Gesserit wanted one thing from their precious and well-trained Princess Royal, while the Emperor saw his eldest daughter as a valuable tidbit to dangle as a marriage alliance, but he was as reluctant as a miser to spend his bargaining chip. Regardless, Irulan vowed to learn from every opportunity, to prepare for her own eventual role.

At the guarded doorway to the satellite throne room, the Sardaukar stepped aside as a bald crier entered in garish red-and-gold garments. The man lifted his chin haughtily and called in a thin, high voice, "The Baron Vladimir Harkonnen, siridar-governor of Arrakis! And his nephew Glossu Rabban, the Count of Lankiveil."

Shaddam feigned boredom as he raised his ringed hand and gestured for the visitors to enter. He said to his daughter, "They claim to have something important to say, but we shall see."

Irulan had closely observed her father all morning. He seemed to be in a good mood, pleased about something. He glanced at Count Fenring, who stood next to a gold-embroidered hanging. Fenring seemed to share the secret, whatever it was, because he was actually grinning as he watched the Baron and his nephew.

The enormously fat Baron wore a purple cloak with fur-lined cuffs and collar. Gold chains and pseudo-military medals of rank adorned his chest. When he walked, his toes barely touched the floor, buoyed as he was by a humming belt. Next to him strode a man with similar features but a blockier appearance. The Baron's second-in-command on Arrakis wore similar finery, but it looked like an awkward costume on him. When the Baron made a formal bow, Rabban clumsily copied him.

With her sharp observation skills, Irulan noted that the nephew's arm was stiff and rigid, as if he had been injured.

Her father leaned forward on the throne, pursed his lips. "Baron, have you come to provide updated data on your spice operations? My Mentat accountants continue to scour the numbers. Is there something else you wish to tell me? Or explain?"

The Baron hesitated, as if his self-importance had been deflated. "This has nothing to do with spice operations, Sire. We have grave news regarding your personal safety, an impending threat against your life!"

The Sardaukar stiffened. The courtiers in the throne room began muttering. Irulan glanced at Reverend Mother Mohiam, both of them paying close attention.

Shaddam, though, lounged back and merely raised his eyebrows. "I feel quite safe here, Baron. The Residency is secure, and my Sardaukar are invincible, never defeated."

"You are not quite safe, Your Imperial Majesty," the Baron said. "Because House Harkonnen is in charge of planetary security, our own operatives constantly gather intelligence information. Our spies listen for whispered plots." He paused, lowering his voice. "And we have just identified an insidious terrorist group of Fremen. They've been conspiring to assassinate you while you are here on Arrakis."

"Interesting," Shaddam said, not sounding frightened at all.

"My nephew Rabban has a report," the Baron said.

Put off by the Emperor's aloofness, Rabban stood shoulder to shoulder with his taller and more rotund uncle, as if they were equals. "Sire, my operatives tracked down a group of plotters in the Arrakeen market. I took my best troops, intending to surround and capture them inside the bazaar."

He pressed his thick lips together. "When my troops moved in to seize them, they fought and scattered. They killed several of my soldiers, and we struck down two of them, though the rest remain fugitives." Rabban's voice became a deep growl. "We will find them. My men are now combing the streets, crashing through doors, conducting searches. We've already uncovered many sympathizers, who will be interrogated." He stopped abruptly as if he had run out of things to say.

The Baron added, "You are not safe even here on Arrakis, Sire. Rest assured that our Harkonnen security net is rounding up the rabble in the streets. We will find these assassins and bring them to justice. For the time being, however, we recommend that you remain here under full guard. Do not leave the Residency to conduct further spice field inspections."

The Emperor tapped his fingers on the arm of his portable throne. "Assassins, eh? A dire threat to my life? I appreciate your concern and diligence, Baron, but there's really nothing to worry about."

The Baron blinked. Irulan studied every flicker of the fat man's expression, recognized genuine surprise and bafflement. Mohiam was staring at him with a gaze intense enough to drill a hole through rock, picking up even more details than the Princess Royal could ascertain.

Baron Harkonnen continued to stress the urgency. "We believe they might even have infiltrators here at the Residency. These are *Fremen*, Sire. They've destroyed many factory crawlers and scout 'thopters out in the desert."

"Yes, yes, I'm sure you have lost equipment and men to these desert rabble, but there is nothing for me to worry about," the Emperor repeated. After a pause he added, "Because you see, we've already taken care of the problem that you couldn't solve."

Rabban let out a surprised grunt, and now Count Fenring rose to his feet. "Ahhh, hmmm, I'm sure you did your best, Baron, and your nephew is ruthless and ambitious. But, as the Emperor says, we have taken care of the problem." He flicked a finger in the air. "I, ahhh, have my own network of listeners in Arrakeen, working in the shops, taverns, spice fields, and spaceport. They whisper, they bribe, and are quite effective."

"But . . . we already uncovered the nest of scorpions!" the Baron said. "My interrogation efforts produced a list of names! We know who the lead conspirators are."

Fenring's brow wrinkled. "Yes, ahhh, but just knowing their identities is not sufficient to protect the Emperor's life, is it? Not when they're still on the loose! My operatives located their safe houses, their hiding places. With the assistance of a few Sardaukar, we arrested them. Perhaps, hmmm, the rabble fought and defeated Rabban's troops, but we cleaned up the mess."

The Baron and Rabban were both speechless.

Shaddam said, "Twenty-eight are in custody. Believe me, they will be planning no more assassinations, but they were never any true threat. Just some angry young malcontents complaining about local conditions. Insignificant, really." Now his eyes flashed with real anger. "And they wouldn't have expressed such discontent if you had done your job, Baron."

Irulan's curiosity was piqued about these militants currently being held. What drove them to such desperation? She needed to learn more about them.

"You found them and caught them all?" Rabban blurted out, and the Baron nudged him with an elbow.

Bowing, the Baron eased a step back from the temporary throne. "Sire, we are relieved to hear that any danger to your person has been minimized. May we have control of the prisoners to question them? They might reveal further information about conspiracies against House Harkonnen."

The Emperor's expression darkened. "No, they are Imperial prisoners, held in a Sardaukar brig. They never planned much of anything and put no assassination attempt in motion. Under normal circumstances, the entire matter would be beneath my notice. They will all be executed, of course." He gestured with his other hand. "The mere fact of their plot against me makes such punishment mandatory, but there is no need for you to interfere, Baron." His voice grew harder. "You have other concerns."

The Baron fumbled for something to say. "Sire, I insist. Justice on Arrakis is a matter for the governor."

"You have, ahhh, already proved your inability to handle it, Baron," Fenring said. "This is no longer your concern."

The Baron's round face reddened, and Shaddam dismissed them. "I'm sorry your nephew got a black eye for his efforts. He was well intentioned,

I'm sure. Now, in light of this turn of events, I will take several ornithopters and part of my entourage, to have a look at the Shield Wall and spice operations out in the desert." He smiled with renewed determination. "Since the threat has been eliminated, I may as well get down to business."

Knowing and accepting imminent death promotes clarity of thought.

—*The Azhar Book*, Bene Gesserit manual

The prison chambers in the Arrakeen barracks were dark and hot, filled with close-pressed bodies. Chani was perspiring, and so were her companions, none of them able to completely prevent it. Precious water was being wasted in this cell! So far, they had been given nothing to drink.

The four sealed chambers, converted from Sardaukar barracks, held twenty-eight captives, including her brother. Chani had counted the prisoners in the dim light of two small glowglobes. There were no windows.

She and her comrades had been captured in the safe house, not one of them slain in the fight—which, in some ways, was worse. More prisoners had been rounded up in the streets, "suspicious-looking" characters who had the misfortune of being in the wrong place.

Most of Khouro's coconspirators were here with them. The few missing ones might have escaped or were more likely killed. She had seen two dead in the bazaar, and could hope that a few remained free. In her own situation, she knew her outside comrades would never mount a rescue. It was impossible that someone could break them out of a Sardaukar brig.

And now the Emperor would deal with them. Baron Harkonnen was violent and ruthless, as were all Harkonnens, but she expected no mercy from Shaddam IV or Count Fenring either.

Wrapped in her own thoughts, she whispered a prayer that Reverend Mother Ramallo had taught her, one that Chani had spoken at her mother's deathbed. The words comforted her, though she expected no miracles, not from God or from their friends.

Her brother sat next to her on the hard metal bench, and she reached out to take his hand. It was like gripping a slightly moist stone. Khouro just stared ahead, his eyes boring into the opposite wall. Over in the adjacent holding rooms, more prisoners wailed and pleaded. They demanded representation, protested their innocence. No one was listening.

Throughout the first day, Chani had grieved for the unfortunate bystanders swept up in Fenring's wide net, sympathizing with their plight. Now, though, she found the caterwauling and whining pleas a distraction, and she tried to focus her concentration on nothing at all.

A few captives had already been dragged away by guards, never to be seen again. The others muttered in fear, some even whispering an absurd rumor that those prisoners had been set free, yet Chani knew that would never happen. They were just the first few taken away to undergo aggressive interrogation and mortal injuries, while the tense waiting softened up the others. Count Fenring still needed to understand the framework of the conspiracy. By the time the captors realized that the first interrogation subjects truly knew nothing, any surviving victims would be too broken ever to return to normal lives.

Jamis hunched over, squeezing his hands together, strangling imaginary enemies. The handful of Fremen sat around Chani in sullen silence, trying to convince themselves that they could withstand Fenring's worst interrogation techniques. She felt the waste from her own sweating in this confined, hot place and wished she could stop it somehow, though she wondered if it made any difference if they were all going to be killed.

"I will find a way to die by my own hand before I tell them anything," Jamis vowed.

"We will all resist," Chani said, though she didn't know what she meant by that. It sounded brave.

Jamis looked at Khouro with reddened eyes. "You could kill all of us right now."

Her brother looked up at the angry young man. "They have taken all of our weapons."

"You can kill with your bare hands." Jamis's voice sounded like a scoff. "Break my neck. Strangle Adamos here, and Chani, too. All of us, by Shai-Hulud!"

The other prisoners muttered, some of them terrified, some inspired.

Khouro began to nod slowly. "An honorable death by Fremen hands, rather than being tortured and polluted by offworlders."

Chani swallowed hard; her stomach felt heavy. When her brother looked at her, she saw the love in his eyes, and the sadness that they might have to part in the worst way possible. She did not fear death, nor did he—yet now she realized that she herself was his weakness, and he was hers.

Khouro sighed, and his shoulders slumped. "Even if they question and torture us, what could we tell them that they don't already know? We had not put any plans in motion, so there's nothing they can stop. Our information has no real value."

"We are all dead anyway," Jamis said.

Chani could see, though, that Khouro did not want to kill her. "That is an option," he admitted, "but we'll wait. Something is not right here."

Chani found it curious that they had all been taken to Imperial barracks guarded by Sardaukar, rather than to the giant Arrakeen prison run by Harkonnens, where malcontents were usually held before execution. Shadout Mapes had described how her first love, the father of her child, had been imprisoned in Arrakeen, then executed in a horrible public spectacle by the Harkonnens.

She was sure the same fate waited for them all.

"A simple blow to my neck would feel merciful, brother." She squeezed his hard, cold hand again.

"I don't feel merciful right now," he muttered. "I just wish we could have killed more of them, even a few Sardaukar."

"We must make our peace with what is about to happen now," Chani said. "Our spirits remain pure, no matter what our bodies suffer."

Her companions muttered, hung their heads. Over in the adjacent cells, the wailing, pleading, and begging for mercy rose even louder, but Chani closed her ears and drowned out the sounds.

She spoke just loudly enough for her brother and Jamis to hear: "At this point, we are most valuable as martyrs."

A battle won by diplomacy requires a different kind of bravery than surging into the fray with an onslaught of weaponry. It is a matter of choosing how to fight, where, and when.

—Imperial military class instruction

Once Zenha spread the word among his Liberation Fleet, his scattered ships coalesced at the predetermined deep-space rendezvous point. Word continued to flow among other rebellious and incensed second-line officers, exasperated with the weakness and incompetence of their noble commanding officers. Sometimes the arriving ship was nothing more than a solo frigate or dreadnought on patrol, whose disgusted crew had overthrown their pompous commanders. Sometimes, the indignant frenzy swept across the ships in an entire battle group.

Open skirmishes had occurred when the newly rebellious commanders turned against the crews of ships that remained staunchly loyal to Emperor Shaddam. Many solid vessels had been damaged or destroyed on both sides, many more soldiers lost. Zenha heard reports from mutinous officers who managed to make it to the rendezvous point. How many other would-be allies had lost their flashpoint battles and now lay in wreckage in space?

Verified information would be spotty, with the Spacing Guild maintaining its historic neutrality. No doubt the Guild, and CHOAM, delivered reports to Kaitain—but Emperor Shaddam was not on his capital world, so that could delay the rest of the Imperium discovering the extent of Zenha's movement. The information would only be exacerbated by the Emperor's propaganda ministers censoring news about what was really happening. It was like a slow-burning fire in underbrush, and the Imperium was just starting to notice the smoke. . . .

Zenha could use that to his advantage.

More and more ships arrived at the rendezvous, and the Liberation

Fleet had become a formidable force. The Commander-General would make his move, while he knew that Kaitain was vulnerable.

Moko Zenha had survived his tests and ordeals, and he had changed. Shaddam's betrayal had begun the process, and Duke Bashar Gorambi had completed the transformation, like a fever that surged through him and so many other wronged secondary officers. And that fever spread, with so many other fighters breaking free of their clumsy, doomed service in favor of justice and integrity—like going from prison to freedom.

On the bridge of his dreadnought, he received a report from a bright-eyed, recovered Kia Maldisi. "With the arrival of the most recent Heighliner, sir, we have three additional battle groups, ten more frigates, nine cruisers, and three fast corvettes, though one is pretty banged up. Weapons still work, though."

Zenha added the numbers to his mental inventory, then took a moment to give her a smile. "You're looking well, Kia."

She touched one of the lingering scars on her face. "I'm back to my fighting condition, according to the doctor, sir, but I'd prefer to be addressed as Lieutenant Maldisi on the bridge. I worked hard for this rank."

Zenha's smile didn't fade. "Of course, Lieutenant . . . but I'd like to institute another change. Let's make it *Captain* Maldisi. Call this a battlefield promotion, after what you accomplished."

She covered her flush with sarcasm. "Soon enough, you're going to make me into one of those swollen-ego noble commanders."

"You? Never." He lowered his voice. "And after we've taken Kaitain and I marry into House Corrino to seal a new rule, I'll work on restructuring the ranks to reward competence. Imagine how efficient the Imperial military could be." He smiled grimly. "I've never lost my allegiance to the Imperium—the Emperor just doesn't realize it. Ironically, the only way I can prove my loyalty is to defeat him."

"We have a long road before that happens, sir." Though she tried to remain formal, her eyes gleamed with anticipation.

"A road that leads to Kaitain," he said.

"We won't get there unless we rally the fleet and move out." Maldisi raised her eyebrows. "Sir."

After the debacle on Otak, Zenha had searched his own conscience, weighing his guilt to gauge how much of the failure had been his own fault—overconfidence, trusting the briefing at face value, covering for foolish commanders. He now realized he had been naïve and gullible. His own culpability gnawed at him, but he had to set that aside to have confidence in himself and function properly. It was better to be driven by hatred than guilt.

He had done the *right* thing back at the flare-star cluster against Gorambi's suicidally foolish orders. And he continued to do the right thing with his movement. He had to see it through to Kaitain, and beyond, if necessary.

This required the removal of one key piece from the figurative chessboard: Emperor Shaddam IV. And he would do so with great satisfaction. He had never considered himself a vindictive person, but the petulant punishment the man had inflicted on him, and so many innocent soldiers, warranted all the vindictiveness Zenha could bring.

He was pleasantly surprised with the Spacing Guild cooperation, or at least how they turned a blind eye. The Guild had allegiance to the Imperium as a whole, not to any particular Emperor. Shaddam was responsible for the consequences of his own incompetence and corruption. Judging from his recent conversation with their representative on Otak, the Guild seemed curious about how much he and his Liberation Fleet could actually accomplish. They preferred to let business competitors fight it out among themselves.

But the Spacing Guild might not be averse to replacing the troublesome Shaddam, reforming the graft and noble nepotism that undermined the Imperium. If Zenha did succeed in capturing the Imperial palace and marrying Irulan, he would bind himself to House Corrino, and the dynasty would continue, as it had for ten thousand years. The Guild would be content with that.

Finally, the growing Liberation Fleet was ready, the officers briefed, the tough Salusan conscripts eager for a real fight. And, after the many messages he had dispersed, he had a few other surprises up his sleeve.

Now, to Kaitain.

COUNTLESS HEIGHLINER ROUTES crisscrossed the galaxy, but Kaitain was a nexus point, the center of business and politics. After paying the Starguide and the Guild Bank another significant bribe—mostly stolen from the Otak Imperial treasury houses—and activating the Guild's formal obligation to transport military ships, the Liberation Fleet made its way to Kaitain.

The fleet traveled on what was, officially, a "classified business matter." Zenha suspected the Guild knew full well what was happening.

Arriving in the capital system, the Heighliner disgorged the usual load of commercial ships, diplomatic transports, passenger liners, and cargo haulers from its hold. Waiting to the last, Commander-General Zenha's military force flowed out and dispersed in Kaitain orbit with enough ships now for ten full task forces, with additional squadrons of dreadnoughts, frigates, cruisers, corvettes, and associated fighter craft. The deadly swarm of battleships filled space above the Imperial world.

And the Emperor and his Sardaukar were not here.

Zenha smiled. *His* fleet operated efficiently. *His* officers were well trained and competent, and *his* ships moved like an immense, well-coordinated machine.

He issued orders over the inter-ship comm. The Liberation Fleet commanders had already been briefed and drilled. Each leader and crew knew what they were expected to do. One after another, the major warships went into formation behind his dreadnought, along with armed escort craft. Following them came the squadrons of frigates and corvettes, along with troop carriers ready to deploy and storm the palace once ground operations began.

A portion of the intimidating force dropped down over the skies of Kaitain, descending first over vast farmlands north of the capital city of Corinth. It was a cautious course, a tactical ploy that allowed the commanders to watch the scramble of Imperial defenses in the Palace District. As a prudent leader, Zenha also had to consider the possibility that a trap might have been set for him, though he doubted the Emperor would ever guess the mutiny would strike directly at the heart of the Imperium.

Keeping the bulk of the fleet in high orbit, Zenha amassed his interdiction ships over the farmlands in battle formation at different altitudes, with his flagship highest. All of his ships shimmered with the protection of Holtzman shields. In the short time he had already been here, he could have annihilated the capital and palace, but he didn't want his legacy to be that of a destroyer. Once he succeeded, Moko Zenha wanted to be remembered as the rebuilder of the Imperium, as the man who saved the empire of a million worlds.

Even though Shaddam was away with his elite Sardaukar, the defenses left behind to guard Kaitain were impressive. The normal Imperial fleet stationed at Kaitain had ships in the air, sounding the alarm and scrambling. Huge battle cruisers rose from Palace District air bases to meet the largest rebel warships. Over the palace, more than a hundred armored vessels entered formation to counter Zenha's threat.

Maldisi's eyes flicked back and forth on the tactical screens, the orbital projections, the scrolling data of fleet assessments. "We look evenly matched."

Zenha drank it all in, wished he had a Mentat Commander to help him strategize, but he had already developed a good plan. His opponents were showing enough strength that he didn't see them feigning weakness to draw him into a trap. He had been through all the same tactical training they had. "Yes, more defenders than I expected," he admitted. "But I trust the talent of our officers and the determination of our fighters more. We have the winning hand here."

In the crowded skies, the Imperial defense ships began to advance toward the Liberation Fleet. Watching carefully, Zenha issued orders to his helmsman, which were spread among the rest of his ships. "Withdraw at a steady pace, maintaining standard separation, but be ready. Be on high alert." He smiled.

"According to plan, sir," said his First Officer, LeftMajor Astop.

At the comm station, Pilwu touched the pickup on his temple. "Waiting for you to give the word, sir."

Overconfident despite the rebel ships arrayed against them, the Imperial defense fleet closed in on Zenha's largest battle cruisers. To counter them, the Liberation ships took up a defensive posture in the sky, just as ready to fight.

From the flagship bridge, the Commander-General stared at the growing force of Imperial warships rising up, in defense of the Palace District and the city of Corinth.

Zenha counted down the seconds until he finally nodded to Pilwu. "Send the coded message. Now is the time for our allies to act."

He had to trust his gut, had to believe the secret reassurances he had received from his steadfast contact, Leftenant Bosh, who had been working behind the scenes. Zenha had faith in integrity, honor, and justice, and knew his cause was right. This signal was as important as when he'd dispatched Kia Maldisi and others in an attempt to remove the Emperor and stop him from doing further damage.

This was even bigger.

"Signal sent and acknowledged, Commander-General," Pilwu said.

Now Zenha regarded the Imperial ships in the sky, standing erect and facing the screen. At the highest altitude, battleships hung ready to blast one another into molten debris, but Zenha had even greater reinforcements in orbit above.

"All forward, approach the Palace District," he said to his helmsman, making a knife-edge gesture with one hand to point the way. The looming Imperial military fleet hung there in front of them, ready to open fire. It seemed like a game of chicken.

Zenha smiled, waiting for the second part of the plan to click into place.

"It's beginning, sir," one of the bridge officers said.

On the screens Zenha watched the Imperial defense formation start to break apart. One by one, the major warships facing his Liberation Fleet simply withdrew from their companion vessels. They shut off their shields and separated from the menacing cluster, leaving the battle zone.

"Nearly a third of them, sir!" said LeftMajor Astop, cheering.

Zenha smiled in wonder. "I expected maybe a quarter of them," he said under his breath. "Now, forward—full ahead!"

New images appeared on his screens, frantic transmissions from the bridges of the Imperial ships. He watched the carnage as quiet second officers, secretly in league with him, rose and dispatched their noble commanders in a well-planned move. It was a quick decapitation of a significant part of the Imperial protective fleet.

Blood ran on the decks as mutineers took command and turned the Imperial defense ships against themselves. Even those warships not immediately overthrown were in complete turmoil. Their tight battle formations scattered in the sky. The newly commandeered vessels fell into formation behind Zenha's flagship, shifting the balance of power in the air.

Standing in front of his command chair, the Commander-General announced, "Now we just have to finish what we started." His bridge crew cheered.

The Imperial Guard flagship accelerated toward the core of the airborne Liberation Fleet, aiming for Zenha's dreadnought. The enemy flagship was accompanied by a cluster of corvettes and cruisers, warships that had not been overthrown by mutineers.

"Evasive action!" Zenha said. "Transmit to our fleet. We need to block their advance, throttle them."

His dreadnought veered to starboard, followed by his own escort craft. Maybe he could lure these aggressive defenders away from the rest of the Liberation Fleet. Escort corvettes on each side fired weapons, and the exploding projectiles caused damage that even shields could not entirely stop. Deeply ingrained in any military commander's mind was a strict prohibition that forbade using lasguns against shields. No one would trigger pseudo-atomic explosions so close to the Imperial Palace.

Standing on his bridge, Zenha sent a message to the opposing commander. "You are outnumbered and cannot hope to win. You just lost a third of your ships when your own officers turned on their incompetent leaders." He drew a breath. "Stand down, and you and your crews will be treated well."

The response blared across the dreadnought's command bridge: "I will not surrender to a disgraced underling!"

The corpulent face of Lion-Commander Beldin O'Rik appeared on his screens. Early in Zenha's career, the man had been his noble-born superior officer. "I am surprised to see you at the front lines, Lion-Commander . . . as opposed to enjoying a banquet or a charity gala."

The enemy leader did not respond. He cut off the channel, and his core defenders closed in tight formation around the Imperial flagship, their weapons active as they surged toward the Liberation Fleet dreadnought.

Zenha recognized what O'Rik intended to do, and knew how he had to respond. He opened a channel to all of his own ships in the air at the perimeter of the Palace District—frigates, cruisers, corvettes, and a swarm of smaller fighter craft. "That ship holds their Lion-Commander. It is our most important target."

He watched the comms light up with acknowledgments from more than a hundred of his rebel warships. He said, "Destroy it."

WHEN HE PLANNED his overwhelming attack, Zenha had been adamant that the Imperial capital and the Palace District must remain intact. Thankfully, he had succeeded in his goal by luring the Imperial defense forces out into the agricultural landscape, where the devastating battle had taken place.

O'Rik's flagship was destroyed, along with dozens of other defense vessels that remained loyal to the Emperor even in the face of the surprise turnabout. Flaming wreckage was strewn across many square kilometers of grain fields. One battered corvette had spiraled out of control and smashed into the outskirts of the Palace District, ruining a park and a small Corrino museum.

Thirteen of Zenha's ships were damaged, two severely, but overall, his casualties were acceptable. For the most part, the Imperial defenders arrayed against him were commanded by arrogant, incompetent officers, noble fools who simply couldn't conceive that anyone might disobey their orders. Those pompous commanders did not imagine their mission could fail—and they had indeed failed miserably.

But Zenha was proud that he had kept the destruction away from the immense and historic palace itself. He wanted the capital as a prize, not a bloody example.

As his dreadnought left the battlefield behind and ascended to the main fleet in orbit, he did not give a second glance to the crashed ships that smoldered on the plains like game pieces knocked over in a particularly ruthless chess match. He left a powerful Liberation Fleet siege force to patrol the airspace around the Palace District. Massive, heavily armed vessels loomed over the capital city, enormous battle cruisers with weapons trained down on the metropolitan area. In orbit, the rest of his ships formed a tight fist around Kaitain.

On the bridge, Kia Maldisi gave him an admiring look. "Time to claim your victory, sir. Are you going to ask the palace to surrender?"

Zenha sat back in his command chair and remembered when Duke Bashar Gorambi had issued pompous, foolish orders from the same seat. "It won't be that easy." He gave a nod to his comm officer. "LeftMajor Pilwu, we know the Emperor left one of his daughters here as a minor proxy. I wonder if she has the authority to surrender . . ."

"Let's find out, sir," Pilwu said.

The initial communication was met with bluster and defiance from an Imperial delegate, and Zenha threatened to blow up a few buildings to make his point. He had already identified a list of prominent, but inconsequential, targets. He hoped they wouldn't force him to prove his resolve.

After an hour of excuses, he was finally piped through to Court Chamberlain Ridondo. "Fleet Captain Zenha, or whatever your self-declared rank is now—your insolence will be punished, and all of your traitors executed. Your name and reputation will be burned through the history books. Your—"

"My will and resolve have been demonstrated," Zenha said. "Now let me speak with the Princess . . . Wensicia, I believe her name is?"

"A mutinous highwayman does not speak with Her Royal Highness. Your audacity is unbelievable, sir!"

Zenha sniffed. "I've already had the audacity to ask the Princess Royal to marry me. Now I ask whichever princess is in residence to face the reality of her situation and meet me, to discuss terms."

The chamberlain spluttered, but on the screen, he was shouldered out of the way, and a young woman took his place. She had dark auburn hair, piercing lavender eyes, and a shrewd expression on her heart-shaped face. She met his gaze. "So, Officer Zenha, you seem to covet the Imperial Palace. I'm glad you haven't damaged it in your escapade."

"Not yet," he said. "But as you can see, your city and planet are under interdiction. I control everything here. Since the Emperor has fled Kaitain, I shall deal with you instead. Come to my flagship and sign a document of unconditional surrender."

Wensicia seemed amused. "We have barely met, Officer Zenha! I suggest a more formal setting. Come here to my palace with whatever honor guard you deem necessary, and we will have a banquet in your honor. That should give us private time for our discussion."

His bridge crew muttered with dissatisfaction. "She's setting a trap," said Pilwu. Maldisi's eyes flashed with suspicion.

"Why should I trust you?" Zenha asked.

Wensicia said, "If it's a trap, then you could easily level the Imperial Palace with your overwhelming military might. I'm not that much of a fool! Come and join me for dinner, Officer Zenha." Her lips quirked in a razor-edged smile. "I will speak with you, face-to-face."

The goal of punishing a crime goes beyond the mere administration of justice. It provides a warning and an example to others who might break the law. It provides satisfaction to those who were wronged. Most of all, and most underrated, it provides an opportunity to demonstrate mercy, a valuable coin for any Emperor.

—*Annals of Imperial Justice*, codified by CROWN PRINCE RAPHAEL CORRINO

The dreaded news reached Liet-Kynes as he worked in his primary botanical testing station.

Analytical equipment hummed around him under bright glowglobes. His sample terrariums contained insects that pollinated plant species being tested for desert adaptations. His cup of spice coffee sat beside a meal of energy-rich honey wafers.

A Fremen man hurried into his office, still covered with the grit and dust of a long, hard journey. Nose plugs dangled at the sides of his face. "Liet, the Imperials arrested a group of Fremen in Arrakeen! They claim our people are traitors and will execute them!"

Unspoken dismay filled Kynes. "The Harkonnens always do this. With trumped-up charges, they mean to keep the populace in fear, but Fremen do not back down. They hunt us for sport in the desert, but out there, at least we have a fighting chance."

"This time it's the Emperor, and his Sardaukar," said the messenger. "Our people are in an Arrakeen prison, guarded by Sardaukar . . ." The man's face was a mask of misery. "Chani and Khouro are among the captives, charged with plotting to assassinate the Emperor!"

Liet lurched up from his chair, leaving his spice coffee unfinished, his food untouched. "Fools . . ." He had dreaded this might happen. "Does the Emperor really fear a handful of dissatisfied desert youths?" He scoffed, but knew how grave the matter was. He would have to change into his formal planetologist outfit, clean himself up, and use every skill he had learned in his offworld training. "I depart immediately for Arrakeen."

"Shall I summon a worm, Liet?"

He shook his head. "No, I'll take a 'thopter and fly directly to the city. Alone." He glanced at his botanical experiments and records, but decided they were unimportant. By now he had hoped his operatives would know more about the secret Tleilaxu research lab in the storm zone. He could use that target to deflect Liet-Chih's angry energy, sending him and Chani off on a more useful raid. Now he had to make sure they stayed alive.

As he hurried down the corridor to the hangar, the dusty courier followed him. Liet called over his shoulder, "Has the date of execution been set?"

"Two days hence. I don't believe the Emperor will attend, nor will they make it a grand spectacle, so as not to give the matter any importance."

"But the prisoners will still be dead." Liet had only a little time to stop it.

HE FLEW HIS ornithopter through the night. The throb of wings and whir of engines rattled him rather than lulled him. The light from the two moons cast split shadows on the desert, reminding him of the blasted landscape he had seen on Salusa Secundus as a young man. He felt like a smuggler with no flight plan filed.

When he saw the glow of Arrakeen against the Shield Wall, he activated his transponder so his aircraft would show up on the traffic-control grids. He identified himself, requested and received landing clearance, and flew in over the crowded mass of buildings. Given the urgency, he sent a message to the Imperial Protocol Ministers and Count Fenring's office to request an immediate meeting. He did not specify the subject; that would wait for direct conversation.

After landing, he secured the articulated wings and shut down the engines. He still hadn't received an answer from the Residency, but he made his way directly there regardless.

Some Fremen, including his own stepson, felt he was too tainted by offworlder thinking and Imperial obligations. Now, though, Liet-Kynes had to be more Imperial than ever. He wore a clean desert uniform with Imperial insignia; he had trimmed his hair and beard, wiped himself clean with mild solvents. He carried his credentials.

On his way across the city he sent another request for a meeting, which remained unanswered. Finally, he presented himself at the imposing doors of the Residency and formally requested entry. The Shadout Mapes might have let him in the side door, but he could not be furtive now. In fact, he had to be bold.

Two Sardaukar guards blocked his way. He stepped up to them. "I am Imperial Planetologist Liet-Kynes. I must speak with the Emperor immediately."

"We received your message," said the Sardaukar captain in a monotone. "The Emperor is not at the Residency."

"I must speak with him," Liet insisted. "It is a matter of great urgency."

"On what subject?"

Kynes felt reluctant. "It is a personal matter, but with dangerous implications."

"The Emperor is not present," the Sardaukar repeated. His companion remained stony and silent.

Another line of uniformed guards appeared, as if Kynes himself might try to crash through and assault the Residency guests. The Sardaukar captain said, "He is with Baron Harkonnen at a welcome gala in Carthag, to be followed by a two-day inspection tour of spice operations."

Liet's pulse raced. "What about Count Fenring, then? Perhaps I can speak with him."

"The Count is with the Emperor."

Liet's heart fell. He could race off to Carthag and attempt to find them, but the hour was growing late, so he wouldn't be able to speak with them until the following morning. He feared the execution would occur before he could get to the right people.

And there was no one else here he could talk to.

Then a thought occurred to him. It was a long shot, but he had to attempt it.

RETIRED IN HER cool, private chamber, Princess Irulan listened to music from one of the greatest performers on Chusuk. Before dinner, at the suggestion of Reverend Mother Mohiam, she had spent hours reviewing a Bene Gesserit manual and practicing her skills.

Her male concubine also relaxed in her chambers, not disturbing her, but she felt content just to have Aron's presence. He had adapted well to the rushed Arrakis trip and remained alert, calm, and unflappable. He comforted her just by being there, a skill the Bene Gesserit had taught him, which Irulan often found more important than his sexual prowess.

When her father had flown off to Carthag with much of his entourage, she remained behind, deciding not to spend time with Count Fenring or Baron Harkonnen. Here in the Residency, she wrote down observations in her journal, even a few lines of poetry she had composed. She intended to chronicle every aspect of the Emperor's Grand Tour and his visit to Arrakis.

At a message signal from her chamber door, Aron glided to the entrance and received a note that had been rushed to her from the household staff. He handed the note to Irulan. She scanned the lines and looked up, puzzled by the news. "The Imperial Planetologist is here?"

She glanced over at Dr. Kynes's roughly bound report that she had left on her side table. Irulan had read portions of it in the evenings, absorbing the data and details the planetologist so meticulously recorded. She knew her father would probably never read it. However, since she was sequestered on Arrakis for an unknown time, Irulan wanted to familiarize herself with the ways of the desert, the details of spice production, even the culture of the people here. She found it fascinating.

And now the man himself was here.

Aron looked at her, showing no emotion. "The Sardaukar denied him entry, but he refuses to leave, saying it is a matter of utmost importance to the entire planet. What would you like to do, Princess?" He raised his eyebrows.

Irulan smiled and rose, thinking of the opportunity this presented for her. "Send word that he is not to leave."

Aron departed after the drab housekeeper. Meanwhile, Irulan took a moment to review her appearance in the mirror. Because she had expected to retire for the evening, she wore less formal clothes now, but they were still gaudier and more ornamented than the gowns worn by other noble ladies. Aron had complimented her on her appearance, as he always did. Now, she added jeweled pins and a comb to hold up her blond braids, then selected a soostone necklace to highlight the teal of her dress.

Customarily, she would have been dressed by a flurry of retainers to make sure every thread, every fold, every strand of hair was in place, but having read the planetologist's no-nonsense report, she doubted the desert man would notice.

Irulan made her way to the receiving hall and sent word that Dr. Kynes was to be shown directly to her. Normally, this large chamber was under the purview of Lady Fenring, who was presently at her husband's side in Carthag. Due to her own rank as Princess Royal, Irulan served as lady of the Residency now, and no one would question her orders in the household.

While studying the planetologist's writings about Arrakis, Irulan had constructed a mental picture of him. When the tanned and weathered man strode in, flanked by Sardaukar guards, Liet-Kynes met her expectations. As she stood there looking at him, she could envision the rugged man standing out on the dunes, facing an oncoming sandstorm, all the while planting meteorological devices to take measurements.

He stared at her for a moment before making a formal bow. She acknowledged with a nod. "Planetologist Kynes, I am Princess Irulan, eldest daughter of Emperor Shaddam IV. My father is away and cannot meet with you." She softened her tone. "But I am here to listen, if I will do?"

He raised his head and she could tell he was assessing her, absorbing details, while she did the same with him, each with their own methods. As a planetologist on such a difficult planet, Liet-Kynes would have had to learn to react and adapt. "Your Majesty, I am honored. I come here to discuss a political matter with potentially serious repercussions for the stability of society, not just here in the city but across all of Arrakis. It is somewhat urgent."

"A grandiose claim." Irulan led him toward a corner that held two lavish chairs. With a slight movement of her hand, she signaled the Sardaukar to remain out of earshot. Kynes awkwardly took a seat, while she continued, "I know you are a man with large-scale plans and a long-term view."

His brow furrowed. "And how do you know that, Princess?"

"I've read your planetology reports, and I've studied you, as well as summaries from your eminent father. Much of what we know about modern Arrakis comes from the two of you. The Imperium, the Spacing Guild, CHOAM all owe you a great debt."

Kynes could not keep the surprise from his face. After a moment's hesitation, he pressed forward, taking a gamble. "Then I hope I can call on that debt, because this is a matter of great personal importance to me."

"And to all of Arrakis, you said," she added.

He shifted on the opulent chair. She found it refreshing that he didn't fall into obsequious formalities.

"Recently, Highness, mass arrests were made in the Arrakeen market. Count Rabban's troops marched through the bazaar, attacking and arresting anyone who caught their eye. Great damage was done, and several people were killed, including some of Rabban's troops."

"Yes, I read the report," Irulan said. "Quite disturbing. And Count Fenring's infiltrators arrested an entire cell of treacherous assassins."

Liet let out a pained chuckle. "Treacherous assassins? The prisoners are fabric merchants, food vendors, a pottery seller, a Zensunni poet, and some boisterous youths." He swallowed visibly. His deep gaze met hers, and she sensed that this was what he really wanted to say. "I have discovered—to my great dismay—that those youths include my own son and daughter."

Irulan froze, but did not show any emotion. So that was it!

"I assure you, Highness, they are not ruthless assassins. Chani is only fourteen and has barely even noticed young men. My son is a year older, and like all brash young men his age, he says stupid things. Some of his friends might have made foolish statements, but it was only drunken bravado."

Kynes sat straight again in the ornate chair, pressing his point. "These rough arrests have outraged the Fremen tribes. Rabban's ham-handed raid left dead citizens and a great deal of property damage. The people of Arrakeen are terrified and indignant, after they've already been so greatly oppressed." He leaned forward, uncomfortably close to her. "The Harkonnen rule breeds discontent, Princess. This clumsy action is like a stick stirring up a nest of fire ants, and it is all unnecessary."

She assumed a cold demeanor. "It is necessary to maintain the rule of law, Dr. Kynes."

"I am aware that Imperial law is balanced and merciful. Harkonnen implementation of it, however, is harsh and bloody, and does not reflect well on Emperor Shaddam IV."

"My father has nothing to do with Harkonnen overreach," Irulan said.

Liet clasped his hands on his lap. "And yet the Emperor is here now on Arrakis. Surely he can see the suffering people and their harsh lives."

"I have seen it with my own eyes." Irulan lowered her gaze. "And I feel sorry for them."

"My son and daughter are being held in a military brig in the Sardaukar barracks. You will find that more than half of the prisoners are simple citizens and shopkeepers from the bazaar. Some of the youths might be impetuous, but if you study the report, you'll see that they never really did anything, made no concrete plans to do harm, just voiced empty complaints. I assure you it was all talk."

"But talk can lead to violence," Irulan said.

"There are ways to avert that," Kynes said, "and a small act of generosity would have great impact here, like a tiny pebble thrown into a pond."

"Do you have ponds on Arrakis?" Irulan mused.

"I have been to Kaitain," he said. "I ask for a simple gesture of mercy, Princess. Those prisoners pose no threat. If you could commute their sentence, grant them a pardon, all of Arrakeen would be relieved. They will see the Emperor's benevolence—in stark contrast to the ruthlessness of House Harkonnen. Your father would look like a hero." He lowered his voice. "And if the people of Arrakeen see the real benevolence of the Padishah Emperor, it may avert a great deal of bloodshed later on. The rule of law is easier to maintain in an atmosphere of peace and justice. And justice would not be served by prosecuting these people."

Irulan listened to the man make his case. With her Bene Gesserit training, she spun out possibilities, assessing advantages and disadvantages. She knew her father didn't care one way or another. Irulan, though, had to look at the matter as a princess of the Imperium, and also as a Bene Gesserit.

She made her voice warm and sincere. "You have done much for all of us, Dr. Kynes." Irulan rose again, and he took his cue that the meeting was over. "I will consider your request."

So many opportunities have been denied to me. I do not intend to miss this one, because I might not see another.

—WENSICIA CORRINO, third daughter of Emperor Shaddam IV

Princess Chalice had not done well during her brief sojourn on Wallach IX, and at the height of her frustration there, she had asked to be sent home to Kaitain. The fear of mysterious assassins was supplanted by exasperation at the austere drabness of the Mother School. She wanted to be back at her beloved palace!

In the past two days since he'd come home, a pair of Suk doctors had helped ease her moods and irrational fears, and Chalice did indeed feel much safer back in her familiar environment. She had been reassured that all the assassins had been caught and dealt with. Emperor Shaddam had been the real target anyway, not she or her sisters. And he was away with Irulan and most of his Sardaukar to Arrakis—such a horrible place! She shuddered to think of being sent there.

Two Bene Gesserit Sisters accompanied her from Wallach IX when she returned to Kaitain, but they merely watched and didn't participate in any of the entertainments that Chalice found so enjoyable.

In the meantime, Wensicia had thrived in her role as proxy Empress, relishing her chance to serve as the figurehead for the entire Imperium to see. Chalice, though, remained in her private suites much of the time, surrounded by her ladies-in-waiting and occupying herself with butterflies and music and sumptuous meals. She had truly begun to relax, feeling content again.

She barely had time to settle in, though, before another disaster happened.

The terrible invasion force arrived, led by the monstrous Commander-

General Zenha! She hurriedly retreated to her chambers and refused to come out.

NOT LONG AGO, Moko Zenha had been content to follow orders and excel in his military career. He worked hard at it, rising to become a Fleet Captain at a young age, earning the respect of his soldiers and fellow officers.

Knowing that no reward ever came without a risk, he had taken a wild chance by humbly presenting himself at the Imperial Court. The Princess Royal remained unmarried at the age of twenty-six, seemingly being reserved by Shaddam for some purpose. Why not him? He had expected his offer would be declined but, if nothing else, it would have brought him to the attention of influential nobles. No matter what, his request would have demonstrated panache.

He realized now that he'd been too full of himself, and he had greatly underestimated the vindictive backlash from the Emperor. It had been cruel and maliciously personal, and it demonstrated that Shaddam Corrino IV was not fit to lead humanity.

Now Zenha had turned the situation around.

Heading down to Kaitain in a troop carrier filled with handpicked officers and uniformed bodyguards, all of whom would fight to the death on his behalf, Zenha prepared to arrive at the Imperial Palace for his meeting with Wensicia, third daughter of Shaddam. He looked around as the troop carrier landed in an open paved area surrounded by fountains. Kia Maldisi was with him, and she sat tense and ready for treachery. Zenha hoped there would not be any outright violence, and he would do his part to avoid it, not wishing to imperil the capital city or the Imperial Palace in a battle.

Wensicia had stated the obvious in her communication, but with all of his battleships looming in orbit over Kaitain and filling the skies above the capital city, the retribution would be severe if any harm came to him.

He was the first to disembark from the vessel, walking with renewed pride and confidence—even more than when he'd asked for Irulan's hand. He turned to his entourage. "Let's go to our first Imperial banquet, shall we?"

The honor guard flowed behind him, weapons held ready, alert for snipers or other surprises. But Zenha thought the greatest danger he faced might be from Wensicia herself.

Earlier, while preparing for the meeting, the banquet, and unconditional surrender, Zenha had scoured the flagship's library for any information about Wensicia. He had already done his research on Irulan, but the Emperor's third daughter did not seem inconsequential. According to information Maldisi had delivered after her escape, the other Corrino princesses, Chalice, Josifa, and Rugi, had apparently been sent away to the Bene Gesserit school, but Wensicia remained behind in the Emperor's place.

Why would Shaddam give her such an important role now? At first, Zenha had expected her to be an empty figurehead, yet her accomplishments at court and in committee appointments seemed moderately impressive, if barely acknowledged. Maybe Wensicia was more than he expected. Even if she had little authority in the Emperor's absence, her bloodline alone made her important.

A dozen Sardaukar guards marched out to meet them, stone-faced but threatening. Zenha knew these were deadly fighters, but he didn't think they would harm him. Kia Maldisi gave the hardened soldiers a hungry look, as if wanting to test her skills against real Sardaukar. Zenha gave her a quick signal to stand down.

"These men are here to escort us to the banquet," he said, eyeing the hard, blank expression of the Sardaukar commander. Shaddam had taken a significant portion of his elite troops with him when he evacuated Kaitain, but Zenha wondered how many remained behind. "Come, I am eager to meet this Princess Wensicia."

He paid little attention to the opulence of the court, the fabulous galleries and the statuary, the crystal fountains and arched ceilings. "Would be a shame if we had to turn all this to rubble," Maldisi muttered loudly enough for all to hear. Two of her companions snickered, but were scolded by their companions.

When the Commander-General strode into the banquet hall in his uniform, decked with medals and ribbons he had created strictly for the effect, he saw the auburn-haired woman sitting in an oversize stone chair. She waited for him at the head of the longest table, though the secondary chair available to him was far less impressive, as if to demonstrate his subordinate role.

Zenha did not concern himself with such petty little games. For all he cared, this middle Corrino princess could have her imposing chair in a dining hall. He had an imposing fleet looming overhead.

He stepped up to her chair, formal, but without undue deference. She did not rise to greet him, never breaking eye contact as she looked up at him. "Officer Zenha, we meet under unfortunate circumstances."

"They can be fortunate circumstances, if we understand the opportunities and possibilities available to us."

She extended her hand, obviously expecting him to kiss it in a gesture of deference. He weighed his options, then did as expected, reminding himself of his respect for the Imperium itself, and for the long-standing bloodline of House Corrino. "Princess Wensicia," he said. She smiled defiantly, showing no fear of him.

Maldisi, LeftMajor Astop, and the rest of his honor guard stood close by, shifting uncomfortably, but Zenha remained relaxed and confident, facing the Emperor's proxy. The Princess was not as perfectly beautiful as her sister Irulan, but still had Imperial bearing, fine noble features, and a sharp intelligence in her eyes. By contrast, he had read that Princess Chalice was flighty and bland, even insipid, but Wensicia was obviously much more than that.

Shining with perhaps more importance than she actually possessed in her role, Wensicia wore an elegant gown that draped onto the floor around her chair. Her hair was coiffed and studded with glittering gems, and she wore a priceless necklace, all of which framed her heart-shaped face.

"So, Officer Zenha, you arrive with a great deal of storm and fury, and you destroyed numerous Imperial defense ships. Many people are impressed and intimidated. Others are indignant." When she rose from the stone chair, her gown shimmered around her with a scaly, serpentine effect.

A servant brought forth a carafe with two glasses on a serving tray, then poured a thick red liquid. Wensicia took the glasses and offered both to Zenha, letting him choose. "This excellent imported liqueur is said to be among the finest in the Imperium. You've never had anything like it."

Zenha chose a glass, while Astop hurried forward with his own poison snooper, scanned the liqueur, and nodded. Wensicia seemed offended by the action. "You suspect chaumurky from me? I am a much more gracious hostess than that. Under these circumstances, it would be foolish for me to attempt something so inept." She paused to drink her liqueur. "And I am not a clumsy fool."

He sipped. It was indeed one of the finest he had ever tasted, but he only nodded.

Wensicia lowered her voice. "Shall we delay our farce of a celebratory banquet long enough to speak privately?" She resumed her seat without taking her eyes from him. "If you are willing to send your eavesdroppers away."

Zenha ran possibilities through his mind. "Perhaps a straightforward conversation can iron out details more easily than a full-fledged military engagement. My Liberation Fleet officers are fully capable of taking command if anything should happen to me." Behind him, Maldisi and Astop were both clearly angry and uncomfortable, but he gestured back at them. "Withdraw to the hall outside. Princess Wensicia is fully aware of the consequences she and the entire Palace District will suffer if she tries any treachery."

He put on his most determined, threatening expression, but it was largely bluster. He reveled being in the midst of all this Imperial splendor and finery, longed for it to be accessible to him—as a consort of House Corrino, where he had the power and influence to fix the many things that were wrong with the Imperial military.

Maldisi glared daggers at Wensicia—did he detect a hint of jealousy there?—but she backed away with the rest of his honor guard, leaving him alone with his adversary in the immense banquet hall.

Zenha accepted the subordinate seat next to Wensicia's stone chair. As if he didn't have a concern in the world, he sipped the liqueur again. "Now let us take the measure of each other."

She chuckled. "So you can assess whether I might make a more appropriate marriage candidate than my sister? Will you demand to marry me like some ancient barbarian?" She paused. "Am I what you expected?"

He couldn't believe she spoke so casually with the capital world under siege, a rebel military force overhead just waiting for his command to begin bombardment. "My proposal to your sister didn't go very well."

"A pity my father reacted so sourly. You are handsome enough, and I've read your dossier. A most impressive career, many accomplishments, despite being hindered by incompetent senior officers."

"I'm glad you recognize that."

She sniffed. "Anyone can see the situation that affects our entire Imperial military, but the noble officers themselves don't seem to be aware of it. If nothing else, Officer Zenha, you have uncovered mortal weaknesses in our command structure. Perhaps long after you have fallen to dust, a few histories might even acknowledge what you have brought to light."

"That depends on who writes the histories." He met her gaze and got down to business. "To avoid any unpleasant violence, Princess Wensicia, I require your formal surrender. I give you my word that you will be treated with respect, allowed to live comfortably in the palace."

Her laughter sounded like breaking glass. "You mean for a week or so, until my father's punitive fleet comes here to crush you? His Sardaukar have never been defeated. I represent House Corrino, and I carry all of the weight and political power of the Imperium. You will *never* receive a surrender from me."

He raised his eyebrows. "That power isn't much evident right now." He shifted in the seat. "I will lock down control of the Imperial Palace long before your father even learns what happened here. In standard military and political tactics, I should have you imprisoned, if not executed."

Wensicia looked at him steadily, fearlessly. Her mouth was a tight line. "And why would you think of wasting me like that?"

Life-saving mercy granted for calculated political reasons is still mercy. Motivations are not important to those who receive such an unexpected blessing.

—*The Azhar Book*, Bene Gesserit manual

Cool moisture hung heavily in the air, and the hiss of the timed humidity-misters made a soothing sound inside Lady Margot's sealed greenhouse chamber. Here, Irulan could almost imagine she was having a relaxing tea with Reverend Mother Mohiam in the palace gardens. It was so quiet in here, and sheltered.

Irulan had asked her father's Truthsayer to meet her here. They had grave matters to discuss, and the Princess had a very weighty decision to make.

Shaddam, along with the Count and Lady Fenring, was in Carthag with most of the Sardaukar. Following the arrest of the subversive suspects, the Emperor wanted to flaunt the fact that he now felt perfectly safe on Arrakis. Irulan knew that she and Mohiam could be entirely alone in this chamber.

Irulan's invitation to meet seemed casual, but she harbored no pretenses; the Reverend Mother would not be fooled by her dissembling.

The two of them took seats at a small table that Margot used for contemplation. The drooping leaves of jungle plants hung over them. Water trickled into a tiny pool adjacent to a flowering bush. At another, less complicated time, Irulan would have found it a nice place to write in her journal.

The lush environment felt refreshing after weeks on the desert planet, but more importantly, the greenhouse chamber could be privacy sealed; Margot Fenring had ensured that no listening devices were present in her sanctuary.

Mohiam did not relax, nor did she treat the Princess Royal with any deference, but rather as a Bene Gesserit proctor to her former student. "Now then, Irulan, you and I need not waste time on empty pleasantries. It is early morning, and we should be at breakfast. What is so urgent?"

Even with all of the etiquette training she had undergone at court, as she faced the old woman, she reacted like the young acolyte who had spent years being shaped and molded by the Sisterhood.

"I face a difficult decision, Reverend Mother," Irulan said. "It would normally fall to my father—or, failing that, Count Fenring or even to Baron Harkonnen."

Mohiam considered. "So it is a local matter, then. Why would you get involved?"

"Because I am here, and I could make a difference."

"You can guess how your father would rule, then? You intend to show your prominence by acting in Shaddam's stead."

"I know exactly how my father would rule," Irulan said, "and I know what Count Fenring and the Baron would do. But I have a different thought, quite opposite from what any of them would do."

This surprised the Reverend Mother. "So you would go against your father?"

Irulan didn't blink. "I would simply prevent him from making an error. Once I announce the proper decision—a pardon for all of them—my father would find it too awkward to overrule me."

The quiet hiss of the timed misters stopped, leaving only the sounds of water dripping and leaves stirring from the air filters and circulators.

Mohiam pursed her wrinkled lips. "Explain."

Irulan paused to consider how she would phrase this. Then, in an efficient report that was reminiscent of those she had presented to her school proctors, she summarized Dr. Kynes's visit, his perspective on the arrested prisoners, and his personal plea on behalf of his son and daughter.

Mohiam put her hands palms-down on the table. "The Imperial Planetologist rarely gets involved in political matters. From what I understand, he is virtually a ghost working out in the desert, even living among the Fremen tribes."

"He works for *us*," Irulan emphasized. "I have read his reports. He's a very useful man, dedicated to his grand scientific purpose. Our understanding of Arrakis is largely due to his work."

Mohiam snorted. "What little we know."

"We do know that Harkonnen reports of civil unrest here and

crackdowns against citizens are assuredly sanitized. You have seen as well as I that these people are hurt, angry, and hunted. All due to the Harkonnens."

"The new prisoners spoke of a plot to assassinate the Emperor." The old woman's frown deepened. "It had nothing to do with Harkonnens."

"The locals wanted to make a grandiose statement out of a feeling of helplessness," Irulan said. "Dr. Kynes said it was some sort of demonstration, perhaps, but no one was hurt. Ultimately it was all talk. They never put plans into motion, never posed any threat to my father."

The Reverend Mother's face remained full of doubt. "But what is the advantage of pardoning them? Would it not merely encourage others to act out, maybe even commit terrorist acts? You are correct in asserting that Emperor Shaddam would never show leniency to such people. It would give entirely the wrong impression."

"Maybe we need to give a different impression," Irulan said. "I reviewed the records. The Baron conducts ruthless executions at regular times. The people are forced to watch in horror as 'terrible criminals' meet horrifically creative, violent deaths. I hear that Rabban is particularly inventive."

Mohiam nodded. "That is true."

"But the citizens never see trials, never assess evidence laid against the accused. They are not given an opportunity to air their grievances, to ask for injustices to be redressed."

Mohiam chuckled. "You sound so naïve, child. Have we taught you nothing?"

"Their grievances are real, Reverend Mother, and their reactions are predictable. We have an opportunity to adjust the trajectory."

"In what fashion?"

"I am worried that there was a genuine plot to assassinate my father, but there will be more threats to his safety if we let the unrest reach a flash point. The people must love their Emperor and know how diligently House Corrino works for every citizen of the Imperium. But I was shocked to see the clear hatred for him here—a hatred generated by the harshness of Harkonnen rule. Those brutal methods increase the danger of a violent attack against us."

"Then we must tighten security even further," Mohiam said. A butterfly flitted close to the old woman's face, but her eyes did not flicker.

Irulan tapped her fingers against the tabletop. "A gesture of unexpected and harmless mercy would shift the conversation and make the people think that my father is kinder and more just than Baron Harkonnen. Then, if the people continue to express their unrest, the hatred would not be aimed at the Emperor."

"To the Baron's detriment." Mohiam sounded amused.

"That is not my concern."

The Truthsayer smiled broadly. "Nor mine. I have loathed the Baron for a long time, and he feels the same toward me." She laughed in a way that Irulan thought was painful, but did not explain further. The old woman stood and paced slowly around the greenhouse chamber. Irulan joined her.

Mohiam paused to smell a bright orange flower. "This reminds me of our greenhouse gardens at the Mother School . . ." She turned back to Irulan. "Recall your instruction. You know that the Sisterhood has a philosophy of 'calculated benevolence.' I don't know if this small gesture you have in mind will change the attitude of the Arrakeen people, if it will warm their hearts toward the Emperor and make them forget the daily oppression they endure. But that is of no matter. If you do this, it will create a different paradigm that we or your father might use."

Irulan bent over to smell the same flower. "And what is that?"

"It would soften the heart of Planetologist Kynes. We know he lives among the desert tribes, and he's probably indoctrinated to some of their beliefs. His connection to the Imperium is tenuous, and therefore, his loyalty to Emperor Shaddam might be tenuous as well. But if you stop these relatively minor executions—minor to us, but not to Kynes—it would certainly reinforce his allegiance to the Golden Lion Throne. And out of gratitude, he might spread a differently nuanced opinion of your father among the desert tribes. That would surely benefit all of us."

Irulan caught her breath. "So you agree with me, then?"

The Reverend Mother was cagey. "I agree that if left to themselves, the Harkonnens would crack down with an iron hand and increase the misery of your father's subjects. Your idea, however, has a chance to alter the course and mood of society here."

Irulan raised her chin and felt the responsibility of being the Princess Royal. "Then I will take action and make my mark before Father returns."

WITH THE EXECUTION spectacle set for later that morning, the time passed with the swift imminence of a sandstorm.

Her decision having been made, Irulan summoned court scribes and lawtechs to a private room to formalize the matter, but she knew her writing skills were as good as theirs, so she decided to spell out the proclamation herself. Appalled, the scribes insisted that they must do the work, but Irulan brushed them aside. The lawtechs read her draft and pronounced it technically accurate.

Through a window, she saw a troop of Sardaukar standing by a Residency wall, and knew more were guarding the barracks that held the doomed prisoners. Since she planned to speak the words herself, she made the document short, clear, and to the point—the way all legal and Imperial documents should be, but rarely were.

Her first idea was to stand before the Sardaukar in front of the barracks, so she could observe—and be seen—when she pardoned the rabble and released them into the streets. Mohiam had reacted to that naïve suggestion with horror, as did the courtiers, and a Sardaukar officer.

The officer, along with a succession of minor nobles and functionaries, assistant secretaries, and puffed-up diplomats, begged her to wait for Shaddam to return from Carthag, or at least send a message to request his permission for what she intended to do. Irulan refused. "If I don't act now, the executions will be over and the point moot." She narrowed her gaze. "Do you doubt this is within my own power?"

They quailed and backed away, afraid to challenge the Princess Royal. Mohiam watched from the sidelines, looking proud and almost amused. One dignitary suggested a compromise. "You also have the authority, Majesty, to postpone the execution, and then let the Emperor make the final decision, with your wise counsel."

"The decision is mine, and I will deliver my proclamation from the Residency steps." She glanced at the Sardaukar officer. "I assume that will be safe enough?"

He nodded.

Two hours remained until the scheduled execution. The public dais had been cleaned and prepared in the main Arrakeen square. Irulan still had time, and she needed to do this properly.

With Aron's assistance, she changed into court finery so that when she emerged into the hot sunlight, barely able to breathe in the dry air, she was the epitome of a regal Imperial princess. Her consort complimented her, quietly gave her confidence. Harsh sunlight refracted off countless jewels in her gown, in her rings, in her necklace. Criers around the city called out that there would be an important announcement, and a crowd gathered in front of the Residency, not knowing what to expect.

As she waited for masses to fall silent, Irulan gazed out upon the people—*her* people in a very real sense—and considered their lives, understood their desperation. This kind gesture from her would give them hope and make them think well of her father. That would accomplish a great victory with a small amount of effort.

Reverend Mother Mohiam remained inside the Residency entrance, a dark-robed form within the shadows, observing but not noticed.

Honor guards around the square bellowed Irulan's formal name and titles, and the crowd fell into a hush. Standing before them, she unrolled the proclamation, but was nearly blinded by the intense daylight. However, she didn't need to see the written words because she had memorized them.

"To the people of Arrakeen," Irulan enunciated clearly. "It has come to my attention that a group of innocents were rounded up in the marketplace, falsely accused, and imprisoned. Other brash youths have been sentenced to death merely for complaining about the difficulties in their lives." She paused to let the import grow. "I will have it known that this is not the way of House Corrino."

She lowered the proclamation and swept her gaze around the crowd. Showing surprise at her words, the townspeople shuffled uneasily, not quite understanding what she was going to say next.

Irulan repeated, "This is not the way of Emperor Shaddam IV! In his mercy and in his name, I, Princess Irulan, hereby commute the sentences of the marketplace prisoners who were detained under false pretenses, and I grant Imperial pardons to all of them. Furthermore, I will personally review the grievances they have expressed. My father and I will take up the matter with Baron Harkonnen to consider possible reforms."

The protocol ministers had strenuously objected to her adding that part, but Mohiam pointed out that it was not a legally binding promise, merely dangling a bit of optimism.

"They are officially pardoned!" Irulan shouted. "I hereby command their immediate release, and they are not to be harassed further." She rolled up the proclamation and waited.

A stunned silence ensued, until a few let out joyous cheers. The sound rose to a loud cacophony of shouts and applause. She had already directed the Sardaukar commander to go to the brig and fling the cell doors open. The officer was clearly reluctant to do so, but did not question Irulan's instruction.

She imagined the prisoners would fall to their knees at the news, sobbing with relief. Some would want to express their deep gratitude to her and throw themselves at her feet, but Irulan would not give them the opportunity to do that. She had already ordered the Sardaukar not to allow the prisoners near the Residency—which they undoubtedly would not have done anyway.

Instead, she took satisfaction in knowing that as soon as they left the prison barracks, the Fremen youths, abused Arrakeen vendors, and shopkeepers would simply scatter into the hot, dusty shadows.

Even the most adept observer can spend a lifetime studying human motivations, but in the end such things are not always understandable.

—Missionaria Protectiva training manual

Now Chani knew what a desert beetle felt like when a rock was flipped over, exposed and scurrying for some other dark crevice. As she and her fellow captives were unceremoniously rousted from the brig, she kept her head down, certain they were all doomed. But instead, they were set free!

Exhausted from days of fear, lack of water and food, she stayed close to her brother as they darted out into bright sunlight burning down on Arrakeen. She paused to blink, but Khouro's instinct was to keep moving and she kept up with him.

Chani couldn't fathom why they were all being released. "It must be a trap," she muttered in Chakobsa. "This could be a ruse, and they'll kill us all for trying to escape."

Khouro glanced at her as they hurried into the cheering, milling crowd. He replied in the same ancient tongue, "Take nothing at face value when it comes to offworlders. But we were dead before anyway. Now at least we have a chance."

At the barracks doors, the Sardaukar guards ignored the stunned prisoners, who began to stagger past them. An Imperial crier recited an announcement from House Corrino that Emperor Shaddam's daughter had commuted their sentences. None of them would face execution after all.

The crowd cheered at the unexpected Imperial benevolence. Some hailed the Emperor, and a few brave voices rose to curse Baron Harkonnen, the voices not identifiable in the mass of bodies.

Some prisoners, mostly shopkeepers and hapless bystanders swept up in the purge, stopped and spread their arms high and wide, offering prayers to the sky. Some wailed or groaned; others dropped to their knees weeping. A bearded man wrapped his arms around the legs of an indifferent Sardaukar guard, but the soldier kicked him aside.

Jamis, Adamos, and other core conspirators were wary among the prisoners. They wore a variety of clothes, since some had pretended to be merchants in the bazaar, others spice-yard workers, some ragged beggars. Chani was still wrapped in her household garb from the Residency. She was sure ruthless interrogators had already questioned the entire staff, and she feared Shadout Mapes had been singled out and tortured, but the old housekeeper had endured a great deal in her life. If anyone could manipulate answers or avoid suspicion, it was Mapes.

Chani, though, could never go back there. Her time in Arrakeen was done. The ill-conceived plan to assassinate the Padishah Emperor would go no further.

Scattering like windblown sand, they slipped into the Arrakeen crowds. Jamis ran beside her, jostled her shoulder. He whispered an address to her, then said, "We meet there—it's safe."

Khouro heard as well, gave a quick nod. Without glancing at his sister, he bolted to the left down a side street. Ahead, four women carrying literjons of water on their shoulders were dressed in garments similar to hers. She blended in with them, as if she were part of their group.

After the water carriers moved on, she ducked into a narrow alley and stripped out of her soiled and wrinkled outer garments, turned her headscarf inside out and wrapped it around her head in a new fashion, so that when she emerged from the shadows, she looked entirely different. Behind her, many of the truly innocent captives were being welcomed into the crowd and hailed loudly, but Chani tried not to draw any attention to herself.

She still couldn't believe they had been turned loose without conditions or questions, and no explanations other than the unexpected proclamation. An Imperial princess had granted them clemency—a pale blond beauty so delicate that the desert would ruin her quickly. The two of them lived in different universes.

Was it a spoiled woman playing a sort of make-believe altruistic game? A naïve princess showing mercy for poor unwashed masses? It made little sense, but most offworlders from soft Kaitain made no sense either. Chani realized she didn't have to understand; she just needed to avoid being recaptured in case the proclamation was found to be a mistake.

She worked her way through the streets alone, knowing that her comrades would take care of themselves. Word of the rendezvous address would spread, and Chani planned to make her way there, but not right away. Her throat was parched, and the dry air sapped the moisture from her body. She, Khouro, Jamis, and the others would need new stillsuits, but they had no money, no possessions, no place to go.

Yes, the Princess's apparent benevolence had set them free, but a penniless beggar in the streets of Arrakeen, with no stillsuit and no water, wouldn't survive long.

Inside the barracks cells, they had morbidly discussed the various cruel and agonizing ways that Beast Rabban or Count Fenring might execute them. No one expected Emperor Shaddam's family to be kinder or gentler. The condemned had resigned themselves, muttered their prayers, gathered their courage, or wallowed in fear. Chani had regretted not being able to say farewell to her father.

She'd never expected to be set free.

She passed the sealed door to an unmarked tavern like the one where she had previously met her companions. Several men in stained spaceport uniforms stood outside, grumbling to one another. She couldn't understand why anyone would remain *outside* in the dry heat rather than sheltering in the shade of the tavern. The men had an evil look to them, perhaps mercenaries or cutthroats. They perked up when she walked by, but her stance and her sharp glare took them aback. Chani hurried on.

Over the next several hours she made her way to the rendezvous Jamis had whispered to her. Her main goal now was to find a way out of this horrible city and return to where she belonged. Chani wanted nothing more than to go home to the deep desert, to her sietch.

She found herself in a large warehouse area that held construction materials, synthetic stone slabs, and plasteel girders. The roof was sloped and low to the ground in a huddled defense against storms. Finding a mound of stacked tiles made of fused sand, she crouched in shadows to wait.

Before she could relax, Khouro came from behind, taking her by surprise. "I watched you enter the area. Come with me. We made a hiding place."

"Are we safe now?"

"Never completely safe, but we can let down our guard for a little bit."

Her brother led her through a maze of girders and blocks of stone, a labyrinth of narrow gaps between stacked materials. The positioning of the piles looked random, but Khouro took her to a surprising open area in the middle, entirely out of view. Jamis and two others already sat together; they glanced up at her and looked relieved.

Jamis moved aside so she had a place to sit. She realized how thirsty she was. "Is there water?" As Fremen, they would share and meet one another's needs, but if there was nothing to share . . .

Adamos slid aside a synthetic stone slab to reveal a hidden cache. He pulled out a dented literjon container. "We have a reserve supply. Take what you need."

Chani sipped the warm water, sloshed it in her mouth, used her tongue to wet her lips. *Take what you need.* Some greedy offworlders would have gulped their fill, but she took only a few carefully rationed sips, then screwed the top back on, clicked down the seals, and handed the literjon back to Adamos, who returned it to the hiding place and covered it with the rock slab.

Khouro said, "We sent out runners to obtain stillsuits for us." He looked resigned. "The suits might not be of Fremen manufacture, but our people will have to take what we can find, and afford."

"We only need to survive long enough to get back to the sietch," Chani said. "A day or two. I won't like it, but even a cheap stillsuit might last that long."

"Why did the Imperials set us free?" Jamis shook his head from side to side. "Was it truly the whim of some princess trying to show off?"

Khouro pressed his back against the stacked stone. "Maybe they are tracking us to learn where our sietch is, and what connections we have."

For herself, Chani felt certain she had eluded pursuit, and all the others had similar training, so they should have gotten away cleanly as well.

"Did Count Fenring somehow plant trackers on us?" asked Adamos. "They could watch where we go."

After running through possibilities in her mind, Chani shook her head. "What trackers? We've been together the whole time. How could anything have been planted on us?"

"Maybe tiny Ixian devices in our food or water," Jamis suggested.

Khouro scoffed. "What food or water? They gave us nothing while we were in the brig." He looked at his companions. "I want to understand, but I don't *need* to. What I know is that we are no longer prisoners, and it is a blessing from Shai-Hulud."

The others lowered their heads, murmuring in reverence.

As darkness set in, two more of the scattered conspirators reached the rendezvous point. Three of the group were still missing, but they had to hope everyone would make their own way back to the sietch.

Long after midnight, their city contacts met them outside of the construction warehouse, bringing a selection of stillsuits. Chani and her companions donned them in the shadows, checked one another's fittings, looked over the seams, and shook their heads at the quality. They knew they would have to make do.

BY THE TIME the first moon had set, they slipped away from the outskirts of Arrakeen, leaving the crowded squalor. Avoiding the smaller peripheral settlements, they worked their way up the rugged Shield Wall, noting subtle chips and marks, barely perceptible cairns of pebbles that guided them on a safe but invisible path.

Once they reached the top of the great wall and stared across the starlit expanse of dunes, Chani admired the raw, harsh beauty of her native land. She turned her back on the dusty ugliness of Arrakeen, which had been contaminated by offworld influence. The others wanted to rest, but Chani set off, picking her way along the rocky ridge, anxious to be on the open sand again.

Khouro hurried after her, and the others followed. He gave his sister a knowing nod. "You are anxious to get back to our sietch—and safety."

Chani paused to look at him. "Our sietch has always felt safe, but now I don't think it will ever seem the same again."

She would have to tell her father what they had tried to do, and how badly it had gone. Despite the failure, she would be home. She kept her thoughts to herself and trudged on with a determined pace.

An hour before dawn, they reached the open sands and made their way out to the dunes, where they began to walk with uneven steps. As soon as they were a few kilometers away, they could summon a sandworm and be far from this community of devils.

Life is often a fine line between love and war, a balancing act between pleasure and death.

—Observation by PRINCESS WENSICIA

Despite the tremendous threat to Kaitain, Wensicia smiled inwardly at her small victory after she'd sent Zenha away. The mutinous Commander-General was certainly caught off guard by her bold demeanor. When she was done, he would have much to consider.

Her father, thinking only of himself, had taken much of the Imperial defense fleet with him to Arrakis, along with most of his Sardaukar. The Emperor was certainly well protected against assassins . . . so Zenha had logically come here, mounting a threat against *her*.

As a Corrino princess and proxy on the Golden Lion Throne, Wensicia had twenty elite Sardaukar soldiers stationed around her at the palace, and they would take every necessary action to ensure her personal safety. One Sardaukar was supposedly worth ten ordinary fighters, but that would not help if the mutinous fleet bombarded the capital city and left the beautiful palace in smoking ruins.

She had to find another way to tip the balance.

I am Wensicia Corrino, not so helpless as Zenha might think.

When the mutinous commander called his honor guard back into the echoing banquet hall, Wensicia summoned her staff, the anxious-looking chamberlain, and the fearsome Sardaukar guards. She smiled sweetly as she watched Zenha. "Now we can relax and enjoy our banquet."

He was not impressed. "But we have resolved nothing, Princess. There is still the matter of your immediate surrender."

She called for servants to bring the first course, and a small army rushed in carrying plates and platters. "Then you will be disappointed."

She found the rebel commander attractive, and he was certainly intelligent, ambitious, and able to accomplish seemingly impossible tasks. If their father had kept an open mind, Zenha might not have been such an unacceptable match for her sister. As successors to the throne, he and Irulan could have been remarkable rulers.

Or, under other circumstances, Moko Zenha might have been an acceptable consort for Wensicia instead. Now, of course, that was out of the question.

The mutinous officer looked down at his roast fowl garnished with edible flowers. Most of Zenha's honor guard stared dubiously down at their food, although one tough-looking woman devoured the fare with great gusto, even if she never let her wary gaze lapse.

The commander said in a no-nonsense voice, "We have Kaitain under siege, Princess. My warships are overhead. I have interdicted all commerce and communication with the Imperial capital. You have no choice but to submit, before I level the entire Palace District."

How wrong he was! She began eating her own course, thinking of the secret weapon she could turn loose against him at any time, to make her point. "I will consider your suggestion, Officer Zenha. Meanwhile, let us enjoy our banquet."

No one, in fact, enjoyed the banquet.

Finally ending the charade, she rose from her great stone chair at the head of the long table, leaving most of her food untouched. She had her own plans to implement. "You have given me much to consider. Please await my response." She extended her hand to him for a second time so he could kiss the back of it. He gave her a steely look, but performed the gesture.

He turned his attention to the large, ornate seat that she'd had carried into the hall for the event. "That is an impressive chair, though hardly an Imperial throne."

"It is a priceless antique, used by the former Empress Bertl Corrino." She stepped away in her flowing gown, rested a hand on the carved back. Concealing an impish smile, she said, "You look like a man who appreciates such things, but you can see that it doesn't belong here in the dining hall. Would you kindly instruct your guards to move it to the largest salon in the palace, just inside the main entrance? I know you will take great care with it."

Zenha's honor guard stood from their seats, watchful and confused.

Obviously indignant, the rebel commander clearly didn't understand why she made her request either, but he controlled his reaction. "I am happy to do a small courtesy for the youthful *proxy* Empress." He gestured for several of his men to approach the heavy chair. "And I will await your answer on the much larger question."

Moving with great care, the rebels lifted the enormous seat and carried it out of the hall, followed by a Sardaukar escort. Wensicia found it amusing to watch them do her bidding.

Once Zenha and his followers departed, Wensicia decided to put more of her research into practice, so she could keep this officer off balance.

He departed, unsatisfied, still not realizing that she had the upper hand.

THE IMPERIAL WAR Room was her father's command center, but now Wensicia was in charge of it. As she stood in the midst of recon screens and sweating officers, she pondered how much destruction to unleash. And which to do first.

Commander-General Zenha needed to learn a harsh lesson.

She had decided not to give the mutinous fleet any warning whatsoever—not this time. Normally, she would have called in Lion-Commander O'Rik and other senior generals, but those inept failures had created this debacle in the first place, and now they were all dead. Instead, she relied on her close contingent of Sardaukar. Even though Emperor Shaddam had left her with only twenty elite troops as her personal bodyguard, they were *Sardaukar.* She trusted them.

The darkened War Room projected a three-dimensional map that marked the positions of every ship in the "Liberation Fleet." Looming battle cruisers filled the skies above the Palace District and the capital city. In high geosynchronous orbit, the dreadnought flagship, a dozen huge carriers, and well over a hundred warships had their weapons aimed directly at the Imperial Palace.

But they were not so invincible as they thought.

Another portion of Zenha's forces were deployed farther out in the system, where they could drive off commercial and diplomatic ships that arrived by Heighliner. They enforced the cordon, keeping the capital planet under siege.

The previous day, Wensicia had watched closely when the first scheduled Heighliner arrived. The ships were allowed to disembark from the vast carrier vessel, but none could land on the planet, stonewalled. Guild representatives aboard the Heighliner offered the departing ship commanders a choice, either remain in space above Kaitain in hopes that the situation would be resolved and the blockade removed, or be loaded back aboard the vast ship and taken elsewhere.

None of Zenha's rebel warships took any hostile actions against the Spacing Guild.

Wensicia used the opportunity to transmit an emergency record of their dire situation, how she, acting in the name of Shaddam IV, stood firm and awaited Imperial reinforcements. She had no doubt the Liberation Fleet would intercept the message, but she left the most important parts out. Wensicia might well have the situation resolved before the message ever reached her father on Arrakis.

Now, looking with cold calculation at the hologram projection of the rebel fleet, she studied the warships orbiting near Zenha's flagship. Instinctively, she wanted to clear the skies right above her, but destroying those large ships would rain down wreckage on the capital city. Wensicia would make her point elsewhere.

She glanced at the Sardaukar guard who was in charge of her protection squadron. "Kefka Rumico, prepare to transmit the coded burst to this vessel." She pointed to a large troop carrier not far from the dreadnought in orbit. "This one."

The Sardaukar officer began working the shielded comm controls. Wensicia admired the man's efficiency.

"Signal sent, Highness. Command sequence received."

She smiled as she imagined what would start happening aboard the first carrier she had targeted. How she wished she could see inside their command bridge, their engineering decks!

"It's best to make a point first and then emphasize it in no uncertain terms. Wait five minutes," she said, "then send the same signal command to that ship." She indicated another glowing dot, a destroyer. "And that one . . . that one . . . and that one." She selected three other targets at random, then smiled as the Kefka acknowledged and sent the activation signal.

The die was cast.

After receiving the penetrating override signal, the carrier's core reactors would start going wild with a power surge, followed by a cooling system shutdown. Inexorably, over the course of fifteen minutes, all shielding would fail, and the ship would self-destruct.

Wensicia rolled her tongue around in her mouth. It would have been more delicious if she could have drawn out their doom for an hour or two, letting the traitors wallow in panic as they realized they could do nothing to prevent the inexorable self-destruct routine. But that would risk a destructive attack on her, and Wensicia would make her point in a manner that would startle and frighten the rebels.

In the holographic image of the orbiting enemy cordon, she watched the first target—the troop carrier—swell, brighten, and then wink out in an explosion.

"Success, Your Highness," reported Kefka Rumico.

With a smile, she crossed her arms over her chest. "When Officer Zenha sends his expected transmission, pipe it directly here." She wondered if he would wait until the remaining four ships also detonated before his very eyes.

Two minutes later, the Commander-General's image appeared on the screen, his expression harried and outraged. She heard frantic shouting in the background as the bridge crew issued urgent reports. He glared at her, but before he could speak, she interrupted, "Good evening, Officer Zenha. Did you miss me?"

Distress calls blared in the background. The rebel officer leaned closer. "What have you done?"

"Oh, are you experiencing difficulties? Imperial military ships may be powerful and intimidating, but also notoriously unstable—especially in instances of mutiny."

She watched five more bright flares appear on the orbital map, then wink out—more Liberation Fleet ships annihilated, at random. They couldn't guess which ones would be next.

At a bridge station, one of his crew yelled, "Four more lost, Commander-General!"

Another officer cried out, "Nothing we can do, Commander-General! They're . . . damn, they're gone!"

"How are you doing this?" Zenha demanded of her.

Wensicia glanced casually over her shoulder. "Kefka, select five more targets at random—no, make it ten this time. These traitors have far too many ships up there. It must be crowded in orbit."

"Yes, Your Highness," said the Sardaukar.

"I command you to stop!" Zenha said.

Wensicia raised her eyebrows. Her voice was icy. "Oh? Is that more of your invincible leverage? You see, Officer Zenha, I am intimately familiar with the workings of the Imperial military. I studied all ship designs, including classified reports meant for the eyes of the Emperor alone.

"Centuries ago, my great-great-grandfather Horuk IV faced a mutiny of his own when his upper command echelons tried to overthrow him. That insurrection failed, as yours will. Following the unfortunate incident, Horuk instituted a fail-safe sequence deep inside every Imperial ship's propulsion and reactor controls. After so many generations of peace, it has been all but forgotten—I'm quite certain that even my father was unaware of it—but anyone with Imperial authority, such as myself, can target and trigger the destruction of any rebellious ship. As you've seen."

"Ten more isolated, Your Highness," Kefka said. "Command destruct signal successfully sent."

"Good." Wensicia turned back to Zenha on the screen. Behind him, she saw the continuing uproar around him on his bridge deck. "If you doubt me, Commander-General, you'll see more proof soon enough. How many more ships and crew would you like to lose?"

Zenha went pale as the information sank in. "This fleet's weapons are targeted on the palace and the surrounding capital city. Cease your actions, or I open fire!"

Wensicia countered, "I already have the command signal loaded into our transmitters. Yes, if you fire upon the palace, you will indeed cause tremendous damage and likely kill me—but minutes later, your *entire* fleet will be obliterated, including your flagship. Once the signal is sent, it cannot be rescinded and no one can escape it."

She heard shouting rise to a crescendo on the rebel flagship. Now Zenha's men had identified the ten additional doomed ships, and they could only watch as the destruct routines went through their unstoppable sequences.

"There's nothing you can do." She smiled sweetly at him. "So you see, we are at a stalemate. Quite frankly, your bluster was getting dull." She let that sink in. "I suggest we search for a different solution. Mutual annihilation is too easy."

She already had certain ideas in mind.

Zenha cut the transmission, and the comm screen went blank.

Corrino family history is long and complicated, encompassing thousands of years of critically important decisions. But few decisions proved to be more significant than those of Emperor Shaddam IV and two of his daughters, Irulan and Wensicia.

—*Retrospective on a Fallen Imperium*, Muad'Dib commentaries

After discovering the ludicrously unlikely Arrakeen plot to murder the Emperor, Irulan thought her father had reacted with too little concern. Though that scheme would never have succeeded, Shaddam was never entirely free from threats—as the multiple assassination attempts had shown. Even then, he had gone to safety on Arrakis only under duress, and he still did not believe he could be at risk.

Considering how little they knew about Moko Zenha's mutiny and how widely it had spread, Irulan feared that the rebellious officer might pose a more realistic danger, even here on the desert planet. He had already infiltrated several dedicated killers into the Imperial Court; could he not plan the same on Arrakis?

Yet Shaddam acted aloof and flew off with Count Fenring and the Baron, confident that every precaution had been taken for his protection. He and his entourage had just returned from the receptions in Carthag and a tour of spice-harvesting operations. He happily continued the fiction of the Grand Tour.

Still, she knew the Residency was almost a fortress, and it would take an army of Sardaukar to break through the layers of security. Alarmingly, one of the arrested young Fremen had worked in the household itself. The remaining staff had been thoroughly questioned by the Truthsayer, and replacements had been made.

Security had been redoubled, and the Emperor insisted that he was perfectly safe. He seemed preoccupied when Irulan had informed him about her decision to pardon the prisoners; though he didn't approve, he indulged his eldest daughter. Count Fenring had reacted with a sour expression, but he did not argue with her.

Several days later, as their life got back to normal in the Residency, Irulan finished a pleasant lunch in a bistro room, glancing out a heat-shielded window. Aron had joined her, listened to her troubled thoughts, then left her to her business. Now she watched the Sardaukar outside, patrolling the Residency perimeter in sealed, armored vehicles. Count Fenring, always an alert, wary man, conducted regular scans and searches of his own. Ornithopters flew overhead, flapping their wings smoothly and surveying the property.

Suppressing her unease, Irulan went in search of her father, finding him in his commandeered quarters in the main wing. When Sardaukar guards let her through, she saw Shaddam standing in an open doorway that led to an outer terrace where he could gaze at the dusty city. The view was blurred by thrumming house shields, but Irulan didn't like the open exterior door.

Seeing her, he closed the door. "Ah, daughter, I was considering the whole situation and resenting my lack of freedom. I should be able to stand on that terrace, because *I am the Emperor*, but my wiser self prevailed." He gave her an indulgent smile. "Even if your brash action of freeing that rabble endears the populace to me, I still believe there may be real threats against me after all."

"Unfortunately, yes, there are." She was glad to see his shifted attitude. "The house shields provide protection, but better if you remain inside, behind armored walls and plaz."

Shaddam patted her on the shoulder, as if she were a child. "Don't worry about me, daughter. I insisted I would have been fine back on Kaitain as well, but I was dragged off here . . . for my own good, it seems."

Count Fenring hurried into the apartments, looking alarmed at first, then relieved to see the two Corrinos standing inside the reception room. "Hmmm, ahhh, Sire, an open door to your terrace triggered an alarm, but I am pleased to see you safe."

The Emperor looked frustrated and impatient. "You know I am perfectly safe here, Hasimir. Just as I would be safe back on Kaitain. I fear we have left Wensicia there too long already. Isn't it time to end this farce and return to the palace?"

A breathless female servant appeared, blurting out, "S-Sire! H-he insists on s-seeing you! A G-Guild messenger! I ran as f-fast as I could!"

Behind her came a clatter in the hall, brisk marching footsteps as guards escorted a rangy Guildsman, who loped along with them in a rolling gait. At their head, Major Bashar Kolona announced, "We have searched and cleared him, Sire."

The Guildsman's face was offset at a most peculiar angle, and his brow seemed overly large, too bulky and heavy. He carried a sealed, embossed message cylinder. "I bear a message for the Padishah Emperor, vetted by the Guild and dispatched from Kaitain, with all possible speed."

Fenring intercepted the man and took the cylinder. Irulan felt her pulse racing when she saw a marking on the outer shell. "From Wensicia?"

"This is rather dramatic," Shaddam said with a frown. "Whatever it is, she could have included it in her regular report. Open it, Hasimir, and read it to me."

Shaddam dismissed the Guild messenger at the threshold, but the man did not leave. "I already know the contents of that message, Sire. I have been instructed to discuss the matter with you, should you desire my input."

The Emperor seemed annoyed rather than alarmed. "What is it? Has the mutineer finally been captured?" He reached for an ornate tray on a side table and popped a concentrated melange tablet into his mouth.

Fenring broke the seal and removed a sheet of instroy paper inside. His face turned ashen as he read the message. "Sire, that madman Zenha has interdicted Kaitain with a gigantic fleet and laid siege to the palace!" He handed the sheet to a disbelieving Shaddam, then reached inside the cylinder to find a ridulian crystal. "Mmmm, here is your daughter's recorded message."

Irulan retrieved a crystal player from the credenza, and together they watched Wensicia's defiant message outlining the situation. Her father reddened, unable to articulate words. Without being asked, Irulan replayed the transmission so she could study it more carefully, focusing on her sister's tone of voice. This was no trick.

The Guildsman stepped fully into the room, and the Sardaukar did not try to stop him. "That was two standard days ago, Sire. A Heighliner countermanded regular routes to rush here directly."

"I never should have let you take me away from the palace," the Emperor snapped at Fenring and Major Bashar Kolona. "What has Wensicia done? I would not have allowed this nonsense!" Indignant, he took another melange tablet.

"Sire, then, ahhh, you would be the hostage instead of Wensicia," Fenring said. "If the treasonous commander has such a massive military force, it is fortunate that you were not on Kaitain. Thanks to our foresight, your rule can continue uninterrupted from here, while we find a way to deal with this insurrection."

Irulan agreed with the Count, but was also worried about her sister. "Father, we must help Wensicia immediately, by sending reinforcements."

"We must defend the Imperium!" Shaddam said. "Chase the traitors away from my capital world!"

The Guildsman interrupted, "The palace and the capital city remain under grave threat, but Commander-General Zenha has not unleashed a campaign of destruction, though he is capable of doing so. He issued an ultimatum of surrender, which the proxy Empress is defying."

Shaddam scowled. "Wensicia doesn't have the backbone to stand up to that man."

Fenring paced as he considered. "Hmmm, we brought a significant force of Sardaukar and defense ships with us here to ensure the Emperor's safety, but we did not leave Kaitain entirely undefended. What is the status of the protective fleet stationed at the capital world? Surely this mutinous fleet cannot stand against the Imperial military?"

The Guildsman's strange eyes focused elsewhere, as if retrieving data. "A large portion of the Imperial defense ships have been compromised. Their own officers rose up and dispatched the noble commanders, then joined the insurrection. The turnabout was swift and unexpected."

Feeling her knees go weak, Irulan sat down. She had known the dissatisfaction among the ranks of competent officers, had repeatedly brought it to her father's attention, but Zenha must have inflamed them, organized them. What an astonishing, coordinated reversal to overthrow the noble fools.

And now he had a large enough fleet to threaten Kaitain itself! Irulan had studied Zenha's character, and she knew his motivations. He was not power mad, nor was he a wild anarchist. Somehow she couldn't believe he would simply lay waste to the glorious capital planet out of petty revenge.

But he was an intelligent, driven man. What did he really want? She had to assume this was no bluff. When she exchanged glances with her father and Fenring, she knew they were thinking about the same thing.

What would Wensicia do when backed into a corner like this?

"My sister has studied military history," Irulan said, "but she has no direct experience in combat or crisis. This is very bad."

Fenring offered her a melange tablet from the tray, and she gratefully accepted, needing her thoughts sharp and clear.

Shaddam glared at the Guildsman. "But how did the rebel fleet get to Kaitain in the first place? They must have traveled on board Guild Heighliners. How could you transport a traitor and his ships to Kaitain?"

The Guildsman remained cool and neutral. "In our original charter, on terms demanded by one of the first Emperors, Roderick Corrino, the Guild *must*, without exception and without inquiry, carry Imperial military ships to their destinations."

"Those are no longer Imperial military ships if they've been stolen by a treacherous renegade!" Shaddam roared. "We issued a warning as soon as we learned he had killed his commanding officer and taken a battle group into hiding."

"By long-standing tradition, Sire, the Guild does not ask the business of Imperial military ships. We transported no ships matching the ID numbers of the vessels you identified. If an Imperial officer claimed to be on a classified military mission, we would not have been able to inquire."

The explanation seemed too neat. As her father searched for a counterargument, Irulan spoke up. "It is in the Guild's interest for the Imperium to remain stable, and for a strong member of House Corrino to rule. I remind you of thousands of years of cooperation between the Spacing Guild and the throne."

The Guildsman held fast. "With all due respect, individual Emperors come and go. The Guild supports a stable Imperium, but not any particular man. We will not take sides in a war, if the Golden Lion Throne isn't strong enough to hold on to itself."

Visibly angry now, Fenring reached into his garment, as if for a hidden weapon.

The Emperor put up an arm to restrain the Count. Shaddam said, exasperated, "But Zenha is just an upstart! And this is no more than a . . . kerfuffle!"

Irulan lowered her voice and spoke urgently, for his ears only. "Father, we must not lose the support of the Guild. Perhaps we can make them see it is in their best interests to help House Corrino now."

He turned to her and wrinkled his brow. "What do you mean?"

They withdrew to the other side of the room, away from the Guildsman. As Fenring and Shaddam listened closely, she whispered several suggestions that came to mind. They looked at her in surprise, but she remained firm. "Yes, it will hurt, Father, but we must resolve this immediately."

A calculating look replaced his indignant anger. He looked up and now raised his voice so the Guildsman could hear. "Take a message to the highest levels of the Guild hierarchy. In exchange for your cooperation in putting a swift end to this unpleasant situation, I will reduce tariffs to benefit the Guild. Now more than ever, the Imperium must stand united."

The representative bowed and backed away. "By your leave. I will bring word as soon as I receive a decision from my superiors."

Kolona remained behind as the Guildsman left, and he stood at attention, awaiting further orders.

Emperor Shaddam said angrily, "We cannot just wait here for the Guild to decide whether or not to help us!" He glared over at his Sardaukar commander. "We must send a large force to Kaitain and oust the traitors before they destroy my palace."

Irulan felt a rush of alarm. "And we must protect my sister."

"Perhaps he is merely bluffing," said a dry, raspy voice from the doorway. Reverend Mother Mohiam glided past Sardaukar guards and made her way toward the Emperor. Her gray hair looked windblown, as if she had rushed across one of the courtyards. She appeared to be uncharacteristically energized. "I bring interesting news, Sire. I have just received information from Sisterhood intelligence sources that I am authorized to share with you. An oral message—it seems that Commander-General Zenha has an Achilles' heel."

Irulan raised her eyebrows. This was most unusual.

The Emperor was clearly interested. "You mean beyond the fact that he is foolish and impetuous?"

Mohiam's dark eyes glittered. "The Sisters have performed a deep analysis on his record and his personality. We believe he does not want to go down in history as the man who laid waste to the capital world, as Salusa Secundus was annihilated so long ago. Our assessment suggests he would do anything to avoid a destructive battle on Kaitain."

Irulan's thoughts spun. "I would agree with that, and Sisterhood sources are very reliable."

Mohiam continued, "Zenha wants to simply get rid of you, Sire, along with the military command structure. He despises Imperial systems that rely on cronyism instead of advancement by merit. He thinks of himself as heroic and patriotic."

"Bizarre," Shaddam muttered. "This traitor thinks he is a hero."

Fenring pursed his lips. "Ahhh, be most careful, Sire. What if this dramatic siege is intended to lure you back to Kaitain? We already know the man is clever."

Irulan said, "Count Fenring is right. Father, you must remain here under absolute protection. Surely, Zenha would like nothing more than for you to be vulnerable. He would find a way to capture you, use you as a spectacle, and publicly execute you."

Fenring said, "Then afterward, he could *force* Irulan to marry him and cement his claim to the throne."

Shaddam looked nauseated by the whole scenario. "I could not stomach that man marrying my daughter. It was his foolish and impetuous demand that triggered this mess in the first place." He paced the room, stopped, and faced the others with his arms crossed over his chest. "Very well, I will remain here, if you insist, but I'm sending Major Bashar Kolona and the Sardaukar. They'll attack with massive force and eliminate the bastards—just as they took care of the upstarts on Otak."

"Ahhh, hmmm, Sire, Otak was entirely laid to waste. Beautiful Kaitain—"

Irulan cut him off. "And Wensicia could be killed in the chaos of battle."

"I've got *five* daughters." He was coldly dismissive. "And Wensicia got us into this situation by not properly defending my capital."

Irulan felt a chill. "She's not expendable, Father, and we need to protect her. Remember, Wensicia was determined to stay on Kaitain and prove herself. She could have run off to safety on Wallach IX with my other sisters."

"What a Grand Tour this has been so far," Shaddam grumbled bitterly.

While Mohiam watched, Irulan suggested another idea. "I agree we should send the bulk of these forces back to Kaitain and retake the palace. But with a modification." She looked hard at her father. "*I should go with them.*" Before he could angrily dismiss the idea, she insisted, "You cannot go yourself, Father—you must remain protected here. Zenha has already shown that he wants me. My presence will throw him off balance, and that will present opportunities. You taught me well . . . and so did the

Bene Gesserit. After assessing the situation on-site, I'm sure I can find a solution. If he really is bluffing, that knowledge serves to our advantage—especially if he does not realize we are aware of it."

Shaddam shook his head. "But if you go there, then both you and Wensicia are at risk. Two of my daughters."

Two of my bargaining chips, Irulan knew he was thinking. And she said, "Kaitain is already at risk—the capital of the Imperium, site of the palace and your Golden Lion Throne. You would never keep your rule, Father, if all that is lost."

Count Fenring swallowed another melange tablet, pondering deeply.

Mohiam said, "In a perverse way, Zenha considers himself patriotic and wants to seal his role in the Imperium. When he asked to marry Irulan, it was not romance but naked ambition." She stared hard at Irulan. "Perhaps the Princess Royal could make him listen to a peaceful resolution of the crisis."

Shaddam flushed. "I won't come to terms with that man."

Irulan straightened. She could feel the melange coursing through her now, and she understood the possibilities. Nodding slightly, she said, "If his insurrection fleet is as powerful as the Guild report says, we could be faced with a long, bloody civil war. He has the means to level the palace and all of Corinth right now. What he wants is legitimacy. Let me parley with him, and also help save Wensicia. Together we might make him stand down."

She was not anxious to throw herself into the hostilities, but saw no real alternative. If she failed, then the full might of the Imperial fleet would be unleashed against the mutinous ships—bluff or no bluff on his part.

Mohiam said in a reassuring voice, "It's a gamble, but it might indeed give us a way in, and perhaps we can see how to hamstring him. By her training and position, Irulan has many tools and resources at her disposal."

Shaddam pursed his lips, deep in thought. "I know you are competent, daughter. Very well, I will send Major Bashar Kolona with enough of my fleet to make an impressive show. And to protect you, of course."

He reached for another melange tablet, obviously anxious, but was slow to swallow it, as he stared at it in his hand, then looked up and said, "The Baron has substantial forces here to protect me while you are gone. Do not worry about me. I will be safe."

Little did I know what entangled circumstances would ensue after my meeting with the rebel commander. He is talented and clever, but I am better.

—PRINCESS WENSICIA CORRINO, private journals

It was an impasse, a stalemate—and Princess Wensicia intended to take advantage of it. Zenha's mutinous ships could bombard the Palace District, but if he did, she would activate the self-destruct routine throughout his fleet. And that meant she could force the Commander-General into another parley.

The man was still reeling from the ships she had coldly and indiscriminately destroyed, but since he and his mutineers had slaughtered so many noble military commanders and seized so many Imperial battleships, his angry indignation rang hollow. She expected he had teams of engineers scouring every system aboard his fleet, looking for ways to neutralize her destruct command, but she knew how fully integrated it was into the core systems. He could not make his ships safe.

Most importantly, he had learned not to trifle with her; Wensicia was not some wilting figurehead princess. Pressing her advantage, she demanded that they meet and negotiate again, but not at some polite banquet in the Imperial Palace. This time, it would be on neutral ground, with heavy guard escorts. The stakes could not have been higher.

After mutual discussions, they agreed to meet on board a CHOAM vessel in high orbit, away from the Liberation Fleet. The détente ship had been emptied and prepared, inspected by both sides, and pronounced acceptable for the discussion. CHOAM President Frankos Aru himself would host, which emphasized the importance of the meeting and the security of the venue.

Zenha and his top commanders arrived on time and took their places. As befitted her rank, Wensicia came in last, stepping off a shuttle with two Imperial advisers from the Ministry of Defense and her twenty assigned Sardaukar, led by Kefka Rumico. The agreement allowed Zenha to bring the same number of officers and guards, but they could not match Sardaukar if a fight broke out here.

Yet she did not want violence. In fact, she would propose a way to avoid conflict, on a small or large scale.

Clearplaz walkways encircled the CHOAM ship on all decks, providing spectacular magnaviews of the glittering world below. Even though the vessel was in high orbit, the viewing system showed expansive parks, opulent palaces, elegant villas, and country estates in some detail.

It was a reminder to Wensicia of everything that would be destroyed if the Liberation Fleet unleashed its vengeful bombardment. But she knew the Commander-General would not forget the annihilation she could cause as well.

The CHOAM conference chamber took up most of the top deck. Her Sardaukar marched ahead to announce her presence. When she stepped through the entrance, Zenha and his fellow officers rose to their feet in a show of respect, standing until she was seated. Her Sardaukar filed in, taking positions along the walls. The bulkheads displayed images of major CHOAM projects, including precious mineral mines, deep-sea excavations, vast domed farmlands and cities on desolate worlds, as well as fleets of merchant ships.

In his own spot, Zenha wore a pale blue uniform with black trim and epaulets, festooned with a new set of medals she did not recognize. His own guards stood at attention by the bulkhead behind him, five of whom were women, looking as fierce as Sardaukar. They wore uniforms in reverse colors to his own, black with pale blue trim, as if they belonged to a special unit.

Two officers sat on either side of Zenha at the far end of the long table, including the redheaded woman who had glowered at Wensicia during their initial meeting in the palace banquet hall. This time, the Princess stared her down.

Alongside the conference table, the CHOAM President stood at a formal podium and bowed to both Wensicia and the rebel commander. "Commerce cannot continue in the Imperium unless peace returns. I provide this venue in hopes that you can negotiate a satisfactory resolution and end these hostilities."

Frankos Aru departed the chamber and sealed the entrance door behind him. Wensicia felt as if she and Zenha were Salusan wolves thrown into a fighting pit. She took charge and spoke first. "I've done additional research on you, Moko Zenha, and—"

"My rank in the Liberation Fleet is Commander-General," he interrupted.

"I do not recognize your Liberation Fleet," she said, then continued to recite facts. "Born to a failed noble house, you left home at a young age to enlist in the Imperial military. I found altered data in your biography, such as the fact that you were not of proper age for service." She smiled. "You were really only sixteen?"

He smiled in return, said proudly, "*Fifteen*."

"Such dedication to the Imperium. It shows your ambition . . . Moko. May I call you by your given name?"

"Of course." He had the good sense not to call her *Wensicia*.

The exchange put her in a superior position, like master to servant. He seemed a little off balance as he waited for her to finish talking.

"I know about your military accomplishments. Originally you rose to serve under Lion-Commander Beldin O'Rik, where you became a Fleet Captain. Under other circumstances, you might well have been a viable marriage candidate for a Corrino daughter, but not for the Princess Royal. My father would never tolerate that."

She saw the sting on his face, even though he certainly knew the truth of this.

"However, I also know that the failure on Otak was not entirely your fault. I've seen the incomplete briefings you received, vital information intentionally edited out. We both know you were set up to fail."

His gaze was as sharp as two knives. "Your father wanted a convenient yet disgraceful way to get rid of me. But when I survived and came back, I was made to suffer yet more humiliation and outrageous incompetence. I was expected to shrug and do nothing while my ignorant commanding officer placed thousands more troops in mortal danger." The anger was clear in his voice. "You understand why I feel no allegiance to such a corrupt system—though I remain loyal to the Imperium itself. Your own words justify my actions."

Wensicia glared. "Even so, do not make the mistake of assuming I would ever betray my father. You, on the other hand, betrayed the Imperium, committing outright mutiny and treason."

"That depends on your definition of the Imperium. In the face of blatant corruption and treachery, I vowed to *save* the Imperium. That is why I have taken this course of action to rebuild the command structure of the Imperial military forces. The entire rotting system can only be changed from the top."

She let out a mocking laugh. "And you thought you could accomplish that by marrying the Princess Royal?"

He surprised her with his counter. "I've done research on you as well, Princess Wensicia. I suspect that you envy and resent your sister Irulan's position."

She wondered what he was getting at. "It is a matter of happenstance that she was born first and I was born third. I have accepted this."

"Have you really?"

Suddenly, the CHOAM ship shuddered, and the deck tilted noticeably. The Sardaukar guards tensed and reached for their blades. Zenha's escort closed in to protect him, but he raised a hand to signal his people. "Hold, until we know what's going on."

Wensicia gave a small nod to Kefka Rumico, who stood ready.

Frankos Aru burst in from the outer corridor, looking unsettled. "My apologies! We had to divert this vessel away from unexpected orbital debris left from the recent skirmish. I should have warned you this could happen." The CHOAM President raised his hands to settle the near-explosive tension in the air. "Everything is fine!"

The agitated parties settled back into their seats and awkwardly resumed the meeting. Wensicia noticed a sheen of sweat on Zenha's brow.

The Commander-General assumed a gruff, businesslike posture. "Clearly, Princess, you and I have established mutual-assured destruction." His expression softened. "How do we resolve this standoff? We need a way that is quick and permanent. I have no intention of letting you stall for time until Imperial reinforcements arrive."

She smiled pleasantly, as if at a garden party. "Mutual destruction accomplishes nothing, whereas mutual benefit—you and me, Moko—might allow us a unique avenue."

He steepled his fingers, seeing only her and ignoring everyone else in the room. "Exactly what do you mean by that?"

"I have ambitions not unlike yours. I understand honor as well, and I would never harm anyone in my family. Even so, you are correct that I would like to improve my position. I may be only the third princess, but I am still the Emperor's daughter, and that is no small thing."

She let a pause drag out before bringing up her bold, surprising suggestion. "If the two of us were to marry, legally and formally, then you would be bound to House Corrino, and House Corrino would be bound to you. By association, the Imperium would be bound to you as well."

Zenha looked astounded, as did the officers with him. "After all that has occurred, all that I have done—you offer your hand? All is forgiven?"

"We have propaganda ministers to rewrite what happened. A marriage between us will unite the Imperium, without further bloodshed or destruction." She narrowed her gaze. "And it can be done quickly."

The red-haired woman grimaced, then leaned close to whisper in Zenha's ear. She kept glaring at Wensicia as she spoke. Zenha listened to her with his full attention, then nodded. He said, "You make an intriguing suggestion, Princess Wensicia Corrino. I shall consider this as a possible swift and effective solution, but I cannot make a rash decision. Let me consult with my officers." He rose from his seat, ending the discussion. "In the meantime, our weapons are still trained on the Imperial Palace. Just in case."

"And I have potent weapons as well," she countered.

Zenha and his party exited the conference room, while Wensicia remained behind, thinking. Her Sardaukar guards regarded her with barely concealed surprise, and she knew that if the rebellious commander did agree to her proposal, then *her* greatest battle would be in convincing her father after the ceremony.

Anger is a powerful force. If turned inward and held too long, it can destroy a man's soul. But if directed outward *at a carefully chosen target, anger can be an effective, even decisive, weapon.*

—Teachings of the Swordmasters of Ginaz

When she and her companions made their way back into the sietch after the ordeal in Arrakeen, Chani could not relax. She felt more disoriented than ever.

The returning group stripped off their dusty cloaks and peeled out of cheap stillsuits. Chani let out a sigh of relief as she undid the bindings, loosened the straps. She'd been having a hard time breathing.

Jamis shucked out of his stillsuit, tearing some of the poorly sewn seams in his haste. He looked down in disgust. "I am glad to be done with this piece of garbage. Poor craftsmanship! The moisture loss was embarrassing."

"At least the suits got us home," Chani said.

Khouro tossed his stillsuit on the floor, kicked it into a corner. "Maybe they can be sold back to fools in an Arrakeen market."

"I won't be going back there again," Jamis said.

"Nor will I," Chani agreed. She felt the watchful eyes of her people and appreciated the thick stone walls that had hidden the tribe for generations. But now she viewed the place differently.

The tribe members gathered around, rejoicing, wanting to hear their stories. Rumors already buzzed like gnats in the air. Others might have been eager to exaggerate the dire circumstances they had faced, but no embellishment was needed. Chani and her companions would have been executed in horrific ways, if not for the baffling miracle, the act of *an Imperial princess*!

As food was passed around, ancient Reverend Mother Ramallo was carried on a litter into the gathering hall. She rasped, "The universe allows many injustices, but sometimes they are too great for even God to bear. A person is made to see the correct and righteous choice, even if they themselves do not understand it. That is why you were freed."

Other Fremen intoned their own prayers in response. Khouro raised his glass of spice beer to make a loud toast.

Despite the happy mood, Chani felt too unsettled to enjoy the welcome. When her father had taken her into Arrakeen disguised as his assistant, she had not liked the experience and had only let her brother talk her into the fool's errand because she believed in him. She still loved Khouro, but she would not be so easily swayed again. He was too impulsive, imperiling the lives of other Fremen.

Even by the age of fourteen, Chani had experienced many dangers, but she had never so clearly faced her own mortality, and now she didn't feel safe even inside the sietch, not even with all these familiar people.

Her brother and his companions showed the opposite response. They laughed and shouted across tables to one another as if they were immortal. They told stories, sneered at the dangers they'd faced, bragged about what they thought they had accomplished. Jamis let out a loud cheer, echoed by others in the chamber.

"Emperor Shaddam will never sleep quietly again!" Khouro crowed. "He ran to hide on Arrakis because he feared assassins at the Imperial Court, but we showed him he's not safe anywhere in the galaxy. Where will he flee to now?"

Then a stir of whispers rattled through the crowd, and heads turned toward the entrance, where a man in desert robes entered. He shrugged back his dusty hood and shook his sandy hair.

"Liet," someone muttered.

"Liet," someone else said. "Liet!"

Chani rose to her feet, smiling toward her father.

The planetologist swept his gaze across the faces, and seeing her, his expression softened. "You are safe," he said quietly, then raised his voice. "You are all safe! I spoke to Princess Irulan myself, pleaded for mercy, asked her to intervene. I see some of my words got through to her." Then his expression darkened. "That was a foolish ploy, and you almost died!"

Confusion spun through Chani's mind.

Khouro snorted. "So you *bought* our freedom?"

"I didn't say I paid anything for it."

"You must truly be in the Emperor's pocket, then."

"My service to the Imperium is what saved your lives," Liet snapped back. "Do not disparage what you do not understand."

The conversation dropped to a low undertone. Even with the joy of having the group returned home, this air of tension with the revered Liet-Kynes made the people uncomfortable.

Khouro sat back on the stone bench and took a gulp of spice beer. "We'll try again, and we'll succeed next time. The Emperor is still here—and until he flees again, he is vulnerable to us."

Liet frowned with disappointment so deep it looked like disgust. "I thought you would have been cowed by your failure, not made more arrogant."

"You don't understand," Jamis said. "We fight for Arrakis."

"Oh, I understand, and I fight for Arrakis, too, but not in such a blundering way that it will surely cost you your lives."

"We have different perspectives." Khouro got up and departed the crowded chamber. Jamis and several others followed him.

Chani went to her father instead. Awkwardly, he put his arm around her, and she could tell he was shaken. "In the future, be more careful, child," he said. "Only months ago, I lost my beautiful Faroula. I have no more capacity for grief."

CHANI SAT WITH Khouro in a high cave that overlooked the desert, talking little, when one of the sietch children trotted in with a note written on spice paper. Chani scanned the handwritten words—her father asking her to join him in his office chamber. "And bring Liet-Chih with you," he wrote. "He will not want to see me, but please make him come with you."

After the child scurried away, Khouro regarded her with playful interest. "Who is sending you secret messages, little sister? Love notes, perhaps?"

"It's from Father." She extended the scrap of spice paper. "He wants to see both of us."

With a tight expression, he crumpled the paper and tossed it out of the high overhang window, where it drifted to the rocks far below. "I don't want to hear anything he has to say."

She took his hand. "He is a great, important man."

Khouro only grunted a response.

"You might not agree with him," Chani continued, "but out of respect you have an obligation to listen. He saved our lives." She withdrew her hand and crossed her arms over her chest. "At least give him a few minutes."

"If Shai-Hulud wanted us to live, He would have found a way for us to be rescued, with or without that man's meddling."

Chani shot a fierce look at him. "Then be respectful to him because *I ask*, and because I am your sister! How often do I request anything of you?" Though the young man remained haughty and defiant, his expression grew troubled. She lowered her voice. "If you love me, come with me now. He would not make such a request if he didn't feel it was important."

Khouro let out a long sigh. "I do this for you, then."

Liet-Kynes sat at his desk surrounded by ecological equipment, weather devices, and record books. He was busy making notations.

Chani gave a pleasant, formal bow. "You summoned us, Father."

"I did." He looked up, seemed relieved to see both of them; Khouro remained at the threshold, not speaking a word. "Thank you for coming." He gave a sincere look to her brother. "I said brash things last night, in front of others. My joy of seeing you home safe was overshadowed by my frustration at what you tried to do." Liet held the silence for a moment as if expecting his stepson to apologize.

"I am proud of what we attempted to do," Khouro retorted. "Even if we didn't succeed, at least we tried."

"Indeed, you tried," Liet-Kynes said, "though you let anger guide you."

The young man's nostrils flared, but he said nothing, waiting.

Chani stepped closer to the desk. "We learned our hard lesson, Father. We should have made more realistic plans."

Her father, having calmed himself, sat back. "I admire your angry drive, even though it causes pain and problems. It simply needs to be directed against a proper target. It is a weapon to be aimed, not fired in a haphazard fashion."

"Anger is the fuel our people need to accomplish great things," Khouro said.

"Good." Liet smiled. "Because we have a use for yours now." He shifted the papers in front of him. "I have news. I finally received surveillance reports I've been awaiting." He pulled out observation images, a map of the equatorial regions, highlighting a line of rocks in the storm belt.

"The Spacing Guild tasked you with finding the secret Tleilaxu lab complex, if it existed. My network is widespread among all the Fremen tribes and sietches, and at last, my searchers discovered this." He tapped the chart, on the equatorial region. "An unknown facility right here, where storms and static make most observation devices useless."

Chani drew a quick gasp. "The Tleilaxu lab?"

Khouro was interested now. "We shall destroy it."

"I intended to send my own commando troop out, but now that you are free again . . ." Liet narrowed his eyes. "Can we direct your anger against these offworlder trespassers?"

Khouro had never calmed down, but now his shoulders drooped in submission. "My anger can be turned against many enemies."

Excited by the news, Chani said, "If we destroy this Tleilaxu facility, the Guild will owe us a debt. We'll be free from a year of spice bribes."

Liet said, "I already dispatched a detailed communiqué to Starguide Serello of the Guild, giving him the information my scouts gathered, but now you and your companions can take care of the matter here."

Khouro looked down at the markings, then said, "I'll call Jamis right now to bring our razzia band together. We shall set off immediately."

Liet was about to say something, but Chani interrupted him, giving her brother a stern look. "*No*, this time, we will not rush out. This isn't a little raid against Harkonnen operations. We have a different target. *This time we plan.*" She nodded toward her father, and he seemed satisfied.

Khouro responded with a tight, painful smile.

When I journeyed to the war zone, it never occurred to me that I might fail in my mission, or that I might not even survive.

—Interview with PRINCESS IRULAN

Detained and rerouted by Imperial command, the Guild Heighliner remained above Arrakis, while half of Shaddam's escort fleet prepared to depart for Kaitain. Irulan remembered the flurry of their initial arrival here, the heavily armed vessels, the Imperial frigate, the decoy ship, and the sprawling entourage.

As the imposing vessels rose into orbit, this operation felt different. This time, Irulan knew they were going off to war. Unless she managed to avoid it.

As Princess Royal, she thought she could get the rebel commander to listen to her. Zenha had so impetuously appeared in court and asked to marry her as a ploy to increase his own standing. His actions, and all the details in his service record, gave her the key to understanding the man's psyche, and she could use that. It was plain what Moko Zenha had wanted. She could offer him something he would not be able to refuse, even if it did make her father furious. And she had the Sisterhood intelligence report on him as well, which reinforced her own instincts.

She sat in her father's secondary throne in the Imperial frigate's command center, with the Sardaukar commander standing near her, alert to everything. Officers spoke over the comms, while crew members kept busy at their duty stations. Through the deck, she felt the barely perceptible hum of engines as her ship settled into its docking clamp within the cavernous Heighliner.

Although designed for ceremonial purposes, the ostentatious Corrino frigate was an imposing warship in its own right, with concealed weaponry, projectiles, and energy transmitters. She had seen the vessel perform in practice maneuvers, and knew that it was the equivalent of a powerful Imperial battleship.

Five years ago, when Irulan was only twenty-one, her father had permitted her to join him in the new frigate's christening ceremony—halcyon days when the Imperium seemed glorious, untroubled, and eternal. She used to hear the term *Pax Imperium* in those days, but not for some time now, not with so much to worry about.

As the large battle group loaded into the Heighliner for immediate transport to Kaitain, Irulan felt out of place on the ornate throne . . . yet it also felt right for this purpose. This would be her command center and war room. She was the Princess Royal, Shaddam's firstborn, and she would fill that role. This fleet, in all of its aspects, would provide every bit of the grandeur and dread Imperial power she would need against Zenha and his mutineers.

Kolona said, "Are you ready for this, Your Highness?"

Irulan paused to give the matter due consideration. "Yes, Major Bashar, I am." She lowered her voice. "But I'm hoping Zenha is not."

THE HEIGHLINER EMERGED from foldspace well beyond Kaitain orbit. Princess Irulan was with Major Bashar Kolona when he received an immediate situation report. Her concubine also joined her in the command center, though he observed without speaking. She allowed him to be there because he could offer valuable insights to her upon request.

"Let's take our time and assess this," Irulan said.

The projection showed the numerous threatening ships of the Liberation Fleet, the blockaded commercial and diplomatic vessels waiting in high orbit and unable to land—even the drifting wreckage of numerous destroyed vessels, indicating that space battles had already occurred.

"What about the planetary surface?" she asked. "Scans of the Palace District? Is the palace still intact? Is . . . is my sister still alive?"

"No damage to the Imperial Palace that we can determine, Your Highness," Kolona said. "It looks like a siege and a standoff."

Feeling some relief about the lack of damage below, she glanced at the Sardaukar commander, whose gaze flicked back and forth, absorbing details of intelligence scans. In his gray uniform and cap, he looked more intent than she'd ever seen him.

Irulan reviewed Wensicia's last message, knew her sister was a strong person, but this deadlock had gone on for days. How had Wensicia been able to withstand the threat from such an overwhelming enemy force? Perhaps the proxy Empress was even more skilled at negotiation than she had imagined.

For her first step, Irulan would contact Zenha and find a way to neutralize him and resolve this mutiny. She sat upright on the throne. "Major Bashar, we'll deploy the Imperial frigate and all of our military escort ships from the Heighliner's hold. Zenha has to know exactly whom he's facing. If he expects any end to these hostilities, he will have to deal with *me*. I want to find out how he's threatened Wensicia."

The Sardaukar formally nodded. "As you command."

The Heighliner disgorged the Imperial guardian fleet that had traveled from Arrakis, each vessel shrouded by shields. Irulan let Kolona handle the operation, while she prepared for her own part. Down there, her sister was caught in a maelstrom of politics, pinned down and trying to survive.

She said, "Open a comm channel and notify Zenha that the Princess Royal wishes to speak to him. That should get his attention."

Until she knew more about Wensicia, she was certain that mere weaponry would not defeat this insurrection and restore stability to the Imperium. It would take political finesse, intelligence, and a willingness to do what had to be done, requiring her political skills as well as her Bene Gesserit training. A plan had been forming in her mind, beyond what her father had sent her here to do. She would certainly get his attention.

All her life, Irulan had been a cat's paw, a bargaining chip for the Emperor and House Corrino, pushed and pulled by simultaneous obligations to the Sisterhood. She intended to use all her talents now and take her destiny into her own hands.

The Sardaukar commander showed only a faint satisfied smile at how quickly Zenha responded. "The rebel officer is ready to speak with you, Your Highness. He has blocked our communication with the palace, so we can speak only to him." Kolona flicked his gaze over the reports streaming in. "He is also moving many of his warships into defensive positions, both in orbit and in the skies below."

Irulan made certain that her image on the comm showed her sitting on the formal Imperial throne. "Put him on."

The man on the screen looked much different from the fresh-faced young officer who had presented himself before the throne dais. In only a matter of months, Moko Zenha had aged visibly, and the scars had hardened his appearance.

He offered a formal greeting on the screen, but before he could make any attempt to take control of the conversation, Irulan raised a hand to halt his words. "I am here with my father's warships and Sardaukar . . . but most importantly, I am here in his name. If you behave, I have certain leeway to parley with you. Before we speak of any other matters, however, I demand assurance that my sister is safe. If you have harmed Wensicia, then there will be no negotiations."

The man's eyebrows rose. "Your Highness, I would never harm an Imperial princess. I am a man of high moral principles, and I revere the long-standing rule of House Corrino and the traditions of the Imperium. Recall that I came before you and your father to humbly request your hand in marriage."

"*Humbly?*"

Zenha let the comment slide. "I regret the unfortunate actions your father forced me to take. I have nothing but the greatest respect for your sister, and for you. In fact, I have had the opportunity to discuss terms with Princess Wensicia, and we may have already found a way to resolve this situation that keeps both sides satisfied, while strengthening the Imperium."

Out of the comm frame, Kolona looked agitated and unconvinced.

Irulan made a sound of disbelief. "Before any further discussions with you, I must speak with my sister in person. Your ships will grant me immediate safe passage to the palace."

On the screen, Zenha offered a thin smile. "With respect, Highness, I am not under your command."

She didn't miss a beat. "Make it my *official request*, then."

He let out a soft chuckle. "You are a formidable one, aren't you! Very well, go to your dear Wensicia. Take a shuttle down to the palace with as many Sardaukar guards as you like. I personally guarantee your safety, and hers." His expression held a secretive smile. "I have not yet given her my answer, but I will let Wensicia make the case herself."

"The case for what?"

He didn't answer, turned off the comm link.

Science is determined to find answers, but the consequences of curiosity can be deadly.

—Suk medical school teaching

Sand hissed as the pair of worms churned toward the equator. The great beasts struggled against their territorial instincts to fight each other, but Jamis and Khouro forced them to comply. With one wormmaster atop each beast, they used goads and spreaders to open the sensitive inner flesh between rings, forcing the creatures to go where they did not wish to go—to the location of the secret Tleilaxu lab.

Chani rode on Khouro's sandworm, settled into a sturdy rope sling just behind her brother. She hunched down against stinging windblown sand near other fighters. A rising storm whipped around them, and the air crackled with static electricity.

Under normal circumstances, no Fremen would venture into this zone where weather patterns were capricious and dangerous. On the standard charts compiled by generations of Fremen, the line of rocks near the equator held nothing of interest. Perhaps that was why the insidious Tleilaxu had established their hidden lab here.

Dust blurred the early-morning horizon, and knotted clouds darkened the skies overhead. Chani was tense, instinctively wanting to find shelter upon seeing conditions like this, yet still Jamis and Khouro drove their worms onward. The Fremen fighters tightened their ropes, huddled close against the rough rings. Chani could hear her brother's voice even over the loud wind. "This brings to mind the storm that trapped my father and Liet."

She thought of the two men stranded and without shelter, how they had thrown gambling sticks to decide their fates. "We aren't going to die today," Chani said. "We must be almost there."

Jamis shouted from his sandworm, "Rocks ahead! This is it."

Chani leaned forward, calling to her brother. "The storm will hide us from any Tleilaxu sentries. We should dismount early and make our way across the sands."

"Shai-Hulud will not mind," Khouro said. Holding his ropes, he raised himself into a crouch and commanded his team to prepare. Jamis drove the other worm to the north to give extra room for the running commandos. If they were lucky, the exhausted creatures would simply burrow deep under the sands, but if the beasts had too much energy, they might turn and attack each other.

Either way, Chani and her companions would have to run.

Through the veil of blowing dust, she made out the blur of a rocky ridge a kilometer away. It would be a hard sprint across the soft sand, but she could do it.

She took her equipment, checked two crysknives at her belt, a maula pistol, and a long worm hook, which could also serve as a spear. Every team member was similarly armed for when they took the Tleilaxu by surprise.

Crouching, choosing her moment, Chani sprang off the worm as it began to plow back under the sand. She rolled onto the ground, bounded to her feet, and jogged away to gain distance.

Khouro was the last to dismount, holding his ropes and pressing down on the spreader until every member of his team was off. He let out a final shout that was swallowed up in the winds, then dove off and ran toward them. In the near distance, Chani could see Jamis's great worm lumbering away. The rest of the Fremen raiders bolted across the sands.

Instinctively, they ran with stutter steps across the sand. Chani's thighs ached, her calves burned. The exhausted worms were not likely to turn and attack, but sometimes they could be spiteful.

Through blowing dust, Chani focused on the low line of rocks that reportedly sheltered the lab. She was panting hard by the time her companions all huddled in a windbreak of rocks, preparing for their next move.

Khouro glanced at his team. "Scouts spotted unmarked ships flying in and out of this facility. Through long-distance oil-lens binoculars, they saw what appear to be camouflaged entrances."

"We'll see for ourselves," Jamis said, impatient.

Blown sand hissed against the rocks, and the murky sky was a tan fog. Chani prepared her weapons. Moving together, the twenty Fremen climbed the ridge and worked their way over loose boulders until they found stone pathways and an overhang that Chani could tell hid an entrance.

Jamis ran forward, eager to be first, though he'd been warned about booby traps and security locks. He held a pair of crysknives, as if the worm-tooth blades could crack through any lock. As he approached the camouflaged entrance, however, the shadows shifted and the rock changed. Two burly armored figures melted away from the wall, bulky men in camouflage gear that made them blend into the rock. Chani wondered how long these invisible sentries had been watching the Fremen approach.

Jamis sprang backward, a blade in each hand, ready to fight.

The burly guards were human, but physically altered. As powerfully built as Sardaukar, their skin was mottled and lumpy, obvious genetic alterations to resemble rocks in a chameleonlike defense. The Tleilaxu sentries made no noise, spoke no words—simply drew blades and activated thrumming body shields. Chani saw the shimmering movement of air.

The sentries lunged, powerful and swift. Wearing a broad grin, Jamis blocked their blows with his crysknives. He spun, ducked, and struck at the guards, but his blade slid away from unfamiliar body shields.

As Khouro, Chani, and their companions prepared to defend themselves, four more camouflaged guards emerged from the rock shadows.

The chameleon men fought like machines. Jamis grunted with the effort, and even though he was one of the best Fremen fighters, he was not well practiced in fighting against shields. Finally, he pushed his crysknife through the shimmering field and drove it hard into the kidney of his opponent. The sentry flailed and fought even as he died, and still he made no sound.

Chani faced one of the other opponents, using her best skills to dodge and block, but the enemy shields caused her great consternation. The sentry's lumpy stone face showed no fury or hatred, simply a bland expression.

She thought of all the times she had practiced knife fighting with Jamis, learning his moves, and dueling with Khouro as well. This guard had a different style, more brute force, but she could defeat him. She darted in like a swift desert mouse. In her left hand, the crysknife slipped through the shield behind his body, and she used its edge to slash the back of his leg, hamstringing him. As the mottled Tleilaxu collapsed, he kept stabbing at her with his other hand. Then she drove the crysknife into his throat.

Khouro fought like his namesake desert whirlwind, but his arm was slashed. In the battle, the stone-colored guards managed to kill one of the commandos, but the rest of the Fremen finished the job, until all the strange sentries lay dead.

As Chani looked solemnly at their fallen comrade, a young man who had been known for his quiet personality, Khouro straightened and addressed the rest of the group. "Take heart—this means we did find the facility that was hidden from the Spacing Guild."

"It's time to destroy it," Adamos said.

"It would be my pleasure," Jamis added.

They took ten more minutes to breach the door seal, then broke into the warren of the hidden facility. Foul vapors stung Chani's senses—evil-smelling chemical odors with an undertone of rotting flesh. Deathstills had an odor like this, which Chani disliked intensely.

Brash and ready to destroy whatever they found, the razzia team ran into the tunnels. Khouro led the way, though his wounded arm bled heavily. He ignored the gash, but Chani could see he needed medical attention. He paused only long enough to receive a quick field wrap, then ran on.

The first chamber they encountered was lined with metal and plaz. It contained racks of biological samples, tables with analytical instruments. Two panicked Tleilaxu scientists scurried about, trying to lock up their precious samples. The offworlders were unusual gray-skinned humans, thin and sallow, almost corpse-like. Their body frames were small, their movements fidgety. They shouted at each other in a strange guttural language.

Chani flashed her brother a sharp grin. These Tleilaxu seemed to think the raid was a matter of espionage, that someone wanted to *steal* their vile research.

"Just kill them!" Khouro shouted as the team began to ransack the room. "The Guild's orders are to turn this place into rubble."

Jamis grunted as he pulled one of the sample racks off the wall. It smashed to the floor, scattering slides and plaz containers. Malodorous fumes bubbled up from chemical stations. The Tleilaxu scientists wailed until two Fremen struck them down with crysknives.

"This is just the outer section," Chani said. "There could be a lot more in this place." A part of her dreaded finding out.

Two fighters remained behind to continue wrecking the first chamber, but Chani saw more of the complex ahead, presumably more laboratories. She wanted to understand what these evil researchers were doing, why they had so enraged the Guild.

She had seen the Tleilaxu snatch the Navigator's body. What were they doing with it? How had they made use of the dead cells? Surely to create something abominable.

This laboratory itself might be valuable to the Spacing Guild, but Chani was not obligated to save anything for them. Her father had already transmitted a basic report containing everything he knew. Thanks to Liet's teachings, she respected science, but her skin crawled with revulsion at what she had already seen in the facility. She didn't want to understand what these researchers had been doing.

"Here!" Jamis shouted from the main passage.

Chani and Khouro ran out to see two more of the mottled guards in the tunnels, both wearing body shields. They threw themselves on Jamis, but by now, the Fremen were learning to fight against them. With efficient movements and strokes, they killed both camouflaged guards.

With the additional sentries, Chani guessed they were stationed there to protect a particularly sensitive part of the facility.

Stepping over the bodies, the team passed through another sealed entrance into the main Tleilaxu laboratory. There, what they saw was far worse than what they had seen before.

Gray-skinned Tleilaxu rushed about grabbing makeshift weapons, calling for guards to defend them. But Chani stared in disbelief at the grotto, and nausea welled up inside. Yes, this all must be destroyed.

Bubbling fleshy tanks were connected to recirculating apparatus, each one larger than a coffin—translucent biological wombs filled with an orange-tinted liquid. Each tank held a hideous growing lump like a giant fetus with an enlarged head, withered arms and legs, a distorted face, and enormous eyes. They looked unfinished, like figures made of soft wax.

"Abominations!" Jamis lunged toward the nearest womb tank and slashed with his crysknife to cut open the rubbery walls. Three frantic Tleilaxu threw themselves on him, desperate to pull him away, but Jamis stabbed them to death.

More blotched guards marched into the laboratory, ready to fight—and the Fremen were just as ready to kill them. Chani stabbed one of the guards with her worm hook and pushed closer to the nearest womb tank. Sickened, she stared at the twisted and tortured giant embryo that squirmed like a larva in spice-saturated amniotic fluid.

With lips curled back in disgust, she shoved the sharp prod through the wall and speared the undeveloped monstrosity. Melange-rich liquid spewed onto the floor, along with blood. Other Fremen splashed around, butchering Tleilaxu, slaying the chameleon guards, and wrecking the horrific tanks.

In the chaos, Chani realized that the heaviest fighting was concentrated around the far end of the chamber—by another secure door. Anger flared within, and she nodded to Khouro. "There! Something more!"

Smeared with blood and fluids, her brother's grimace was like a death mask. Together, the two of them defeated another mottled guard, then reached the back chamber. Chani worked the door controls while Khouro defended her from more desperate attacks, despite the wound on his arm.

The last few Tleilaxu wailed, their voices high-pitched and terrified—and that gave Chani all the incentive she needed. She had to see what loathsome secret they were protecting.

When the Fremen broke into the securest inner chamber, Chani was even more aghast. Khouro clutched his stomach, driving back the desire to vomit.

Four more fleshy translucent tanks hung against the wall, considerably larger than the others. The forms they contained were bigger, more developed, more complete. And the creatures' eyes were open and aware.

Their mouths gaped in constant, wordless screams.

Chani remembered the misshapen corpse the Guild had reverently deposited on top of the brewing spice blow, a mutated and enhanced human. But these were horrifically worse. "They're growing Navigators here!" she whispered.

She'd heard of the Tleilaxu process of creating gholas, growing new creatures from the cells of dead bodies. Now she saw clearly what the awful offworlders had done with the stolen corpse. The Tleilaxu had made warped genetic clones from the cells of the Guild Navigator—and now they had four ghola Navigators, whose enhanced minds possessed the prescience to see into millions of paths of the future.

In the main laboratory chamber, these enslaved Navigator clones howled in agony from their tank prisons, their appalled voices rumbling through amniotic fluid. Bubbles escaped their screaming mouths. Their emaciated limbs twitched as they tried to break free, but the womb tanks trapped them. Their starry eyes were filled with terrors they could not express.

If these creatures could indeed see into all possible futures, Chani wondered if they had foreseen the Fremen raid, and if they had known of their impending deaths this day, did they welcome them?

Jamis charged into the back chamber, joined by a small group of fighters. Seeing the tanks, he stumbled to a halt and let out a loud Chakobsa curse.

Tleilaxu researchers tried to defend themselves with lab equipment, glass tubes, sharpened probes. Khouro ignored the trivial men as he attacked the nearest womb tank, using his good arm. The freakish Navigator inside looked out at him with a sad, pitiful expression, totally apart from any fear—a creature just wanting its wretched existence to end.

Her brother ripped open the fleshy wall, spilled out the distorted form that twitched even as the foul-smelling fluid poured onto the floor. Khouro stabbed the monstrosity in the back of its head with his crysknife.

Jamis offhandedly killed two frantic Tleilaxu researchers while the other terrified scientists hid behind a metal table, huddled in their loose robes and hiding their hands in their sleeves.

Chani stared at the dying ghola Navigator in front of her. Its huge eyes held the universe and immense misery, as if its prescience revealed only the most appalling paths. She felt a flicker of sympathy, knowing that the creature had not chosen this existence for itself. It had been created from the dead cells of a stolen body.

The Tleilaxu were to blame. This thing was just a victim.

Yet it still had to be destroyed.

Khouro and Jamis felt no such pity. They hacked and smashed open the womb tanks, butchered the remaining three creatures inside. Her brother's face was a merciless mask.

One of the last Tleilaxu men scuttled from his meager shelter and let out an accusatory shriek. Khouro turned just as the researcher flicked his arms. His loose gray sleeves flopped, revealing dart projectors—a flurry of bright needles sprayed out like a cloud of hornets. The tiny darts peppered Khouro's face, neck, chest, and arms.

The Tleilaxu man cackled and screamed out in Galach, "Die, vermin!"

"Khouro!" Chani slashed the researcher's throat so deeply that she nearly beheaded him. She paid no attention as the hated man fell, instead running to her brother.

He looked mystified at the dozens of tiny needles that poked like spines out of his skin. "What is this?" he asked, as if they were little more than gnats.

Then a little flash came from the first one in his chest, and another and another. The needles flared into sparks, and each tiny detonation left a pockmarked crater in his skin. Khouro's face suddenly became a moonscape of little red wounds, while other needles burrowed deeper into him.

He screamed in agony and terror. Chani grabbed him, eased him onto the floor, but the needles weren't done. He screamed out that he was burning up in pain, as acid-like poison fed into his bloodstream. More needles tunneled into his chest and exploded inside, one after another. With each tiny spark and explosion, Khouro howled more.

She yelled his name, cradled his head. Jamis bounded over to them, waving his crysknives dripping with blood and fluid. Helpless, he stood beside Chani.

She frantically tried to pluck out any remaining needles she saw, while her brother jerked and twisted in his horrific death throes. Some of the needles held fast-acting toxins that made his skin bloat and blacken, while tiny internal detonations kept shredding his body, piece by piece.

"Khouro, Khouro!" she moaned.

Finally, almost mercifully, two darts in his neck exploded, leaving his throat a gaping wound, and he went limp. Chani wept as she rocked her dead brother, but there was nothing she could do for him.

Shocked and grieving Fremen gathered around. For the moment, she just held on to Khouro and the memories they shared. But as a Fremen, she forged that sorrow into hot iron. She glanced around the horrific laboratory and knew there were more chambers in this complex.

She nodded, remembering the Guild's specific instructions. Her voice was hoarse. "Destroy it," she said. "Destroy it all."

When dealing with an opportunist such as Moko Zenha, it may seem easy to predict his actions, but that could be by design. With such a personality it is easy to be deceived.

—Filmbook lesson commentary

Irulan's armored shuttle departed the ornate Imperial frigate in orbit and descended toward the palace.

Zenha's Liberation Fleet escorted the shuttle down with an impressive show of force, no doubt attempting to intimidate her, but Irulan made no comment. She knew the rebel commander would grant her safe passage. He had far too much to lose if he broke the uneasy truce now. Irulan thought she might be able to reach a bargain with him, if she could only figure out how he intended to achieve his aims. It would be a bargain that Zenha ultimately would not like, but perhaps she could fool him.

After the shuttle landed on the pavement outside the palace proper, Wensicia rushed out to greet Irulan. In a flash, Irulan assessed little details of her sister's appearance and immediately felt relieved. She had imagined that Wensicia might be ready to break under pressure, but instead, the younger princess looked defiant, even confident. She was lovely in a sapphire gown with a ruffled collar and magnificent, sparkling jewels.

They first clasped hands, then embraced. Irulan's pulse raced. "I'm glad to see you unharmed, sister! When we withdrew to Arrakis, I never expected you would be in such danger here." She gazed up at the sky, saw ominous enemy battle cruisers hanging there like gigantic armored thunderheads.

Wensicia lifted her chin. "We're in no danger right now. Those are all for show—"

"I am convinced Zenha does not intend to destroy Kaitain," Irulan interrupted, "but he is still a threat." She quickly summarized the Sisterhood intelligence report on the rebel commander's personality profile.

"That is very interesting, and I agree," Wensicia said. "But he doesn't dare begin an attack, because I have found a very big hammer to hold over *their* heads." She gave a dismissive gesture toward the threatening ships and chuckled. "I found a way to emasculate them all. With a snap of my fingers, I can destroy every one of Zenha's warships." A frown crossed her face like a shadow. "But he could still rain down fire in his last minutes. So, we are at a standoff."

Irulan's brow furrowed. "What do you mean? What defenses do we have?"

Wensicia took her arm as the Sardaukar escort followed, out of earshot and alert for any threat. "You know I study obscure classified military details. In old records, I found a way to neutralize the Liberation Fleet, a back door into all their control systems. I have Commander-General Zenha wrapped around my finger."

As they entered the Imperial Palace and walked along the polished hall, tense emptiness echoed around them. Irulan wondered where all the courtiers had gone; perhaps they huddled in hiding somewhere.

"Poor Chalice would love to see you as well," Wensicia said, then lowered her voice. "I'm afraid she hasn't been very social since the invasion. She made a poor choice in coming home when she did."

Irulan blinked. "Chalice returned? But she went to Wallach IX for her own safety!"

"That didn't last long." Wensicia clucked her tongue. "She found the Mother School too austere for her tastes. Josifa and Rugi are doing well as acolytes, but when the Bene Gesserit wanted Chalice to participate in rigorous studies, she came running back to the Imperial Court instead. She arrived just in time for the siege. She is tended by the court Suk doctor for outbreaks of hysteria, and is rather heavily medicated."

Irulan imagined the consternation and terror her flighty sister must feel, but didn't think she could face Chalice just yet. There was too much at stake. "It is best if you and I talk privately now, Wensicia."

Her sister nodded, but she seemed energized, not overwhelmed. "I have much to tell you—and I even worked out a way that we could control a formidable opponent like Zenha, but keep him to our advantage. As his actions have proved, he is much more competent than the noble fools who held superior command positions. We shouldn't waste such a man."

Irulan frowned as she walked beside Wensicia. "*Keep* him? The man launched an insurrection and murdered countless noble officers. He's now attempting to overthrow the Imperial throne!"

Wensicia just gave a satisfied smile. "Even so, we might rein him in and make him useful to us—on a tight leash."

Wensicia took great pride in explaining how she had proved her mettle by blowing up fifteen of Zenha's vessels, rendering him almost impotent and backing him into a corner. "So, despite all his bluster, he won't launch a massive attack on the palace. Empty threats! You and I are perfectly safe here, Irulan. I know he wants a resolution, and I've offered him one." She arched her eyebrows. "He wants peace, he wants a way out . . . and he wants *me*."

Irulan was surprised. "What do you mean he *wants* you?"

"To marry me, of course, which would bind him to an Imperial princess, and thus to the Golden Lion Throne." She flashed her lavender eyes, looking both scheming and satisfied. "I suggested that he could resolve the military standoff with a marriage alliance, and he seemed pleased by my suggestion."

Irulan's thoughts raced. "So he accepted?"

"Not yet, but he will. What's to think about? We can arrange a quick ceremony here at the palace to instantly seal the peace. We'd avert this war and remove any threat of further destruction. All neatly wrapped up." She sniffed. "I intend to hold the ceremony in the next day or two." Wensicia seemed impatient. "We didn't expect you to come here. I would have had it all resolved."

Irulan was taken aback. "Zenha's intentions were obvious months ago when he asked for *my* hand. You and I both know how ambitious he is. You think Father would accept him, just because he's wed to one of his daughters?"

"Oh, he would probably want to execute him in a public spectacle, but it would be better if we put the man to good use instead. Legal and security guarantees would be made. I already have lawtechs drawing up suggested language," Wensicia said. "And once Zenha marries me, I can control him. *The leash*." She leaned closer to Irulan. "You know as well as I that eliminating all those useless noble officers was no great loss. A necessary purge that will now allow us to rebuild the Imperial military and make it stronger. Why waste a truly visionary commander like Moko Zenha? We're not fools."

Irulan felt all her muscles tighten, even if she did agree with her sister's assessment. "Because he's a traitor!"

Wensicia gave a dismissive wave of her hand. "After all is said and done, we can spread whatever stories we like and rewrite history as we wish. It can all be resolved. Over the history of the Imperium, a great deal has been swept under the rug."

Irulan felt her anger rising. Her sister had always been ambitious, and no doubt Wensicia saw this as a way to increase her own standing. Irulan could see how she was planning to mold Zenha as her husband and work with him as her partner. That thought brought a greater chill. Zenha and Wensicia working together, shoring each other up and scheming . . . they would be a formidable power couple.

And with their merged ambitions, they might prove to be even more dangerous to the Imperium than this rebellion ever was.

"I have a better idea," Irulan said impulsively as the pieces fit into place. She needed to control her sister, too, and subtly put her in her place—and even more importantly, make Zenha pay. "Your reasoning is sound, but he came to Kaitain first to ask for *my* hand. Being wed to the Princess Royal, the Emperor's firstborn daughter, is a much more tempting bait to dangle in front of him."

Wensicia's mouth was agape.

"And he hasn't said yes to you yet, has he?"

"No, but—"

Irulan gave her sister a cold smile. "You must step back from this. I will take it from here." Plans were already turning in her mind—with an added twist from her Bene Gesserit training. "Yes, I think that is what we shall do."

Wensicia's eyes flew open in surprise and rage. "No! I won't let you steal my role again. This is my solution, not yours to hijack."

"I have made my decision, and I speak with the authority of Shaddam IV," Irulan replied. "I'll have the Sardaukar commander relay a message to Zenha. I'll make him an offer that is exactly what he wanted in the first place." She knew her sister was furious, but Wensicia would understand once it was all over. "Assuming he agrees, we will host a swift and decisive Imperial wedding here in the palace. That will put an end to this." She turned away so as not to see Wensicia's furious face, and added, "How could he refuse?"

AS SOON AS Princess Chalice learned that her eldest sister had returned with a rescue force from the Emperor, she took a stimulant and bustled out of her suites, excited to see Irulan. Finally, this nightmare would be over!

Her ladies-in-waiting scurried after her, followed by the Bene Gesserit watchers. The stern Sisters insisted she was taking a foolish risk outside of her protected rooms, but Chalice felt nervous and fidgety from the Suk medications. She longed to see Irulan, to be reassured that the Princess Royal and the Padishah Emperor would eliminate the threat from the traitor!

She found her eldest sister at the front portico, preparing to leave again with her Sardaukar escort. Her shuttle was ready, waiting by the misty fountains. Chalice caught her breath in dismay. Irulan was going to depart without even speaking with her! Wensicia stood at a distance watching their regal older sister stride toward the craft, and she seemed upset with Irulan, but the two sisters had been in spats before, and Chalice brushed the matter aside.

"Wait!" Her voice was like a thrown stone that shattered the tension in the air. She ran forward. "Irulan, dear sister, take me with you to the Imperial ships! I am trapped in the palace—I never should have returned from Wallach IX!"

The Bene Gesserit attendants caught Chalice's arms to hold her back, but medications made her pulse race and her breathing come fast. She felt dizzy with desperation.

Startled, Irulan turned, but she seemed preoccupied. Both she and Wensicia dealt with so many weighty matters, but Chalice couldn't let them forget about her own personal plight. "I don't want to be here!" She looked up into the sky at the looming ships like weapon-studded asteroids ready to crash down and destroy everything. "We're all going to die here!"

While ladies-in-waiting fussed over Chalice, one of the Bene Gesserit Sisters grew sterner. "It is time for your sedative, Princess. The Suk doctor warned that the stimulants could induce paranoia."

"Paranoia? Can you not see the enemy ships ready to destroy us?" She sucked in a breath. "Irulan!"

Wensicia had reached the limit of her patience. "Secure her before she hurts herself!" She approached Irulan and said in a low voice, "She must be heavily sedated for her own good. She tries to break away at every opportunity."

Chalice knew her sisters only wanted what was best for her, but they didn't listen! "I know who betrayed us, and I'm going to get them, every one of them! There could still be assassins at court."

Irulan gave her a calm and reassuring smile. She was Chalice's favorite sister sometimes, and other times it was Wensicia. Her opinion changed with circumstances.

While Wensicia simmered about whatever was troubling her, Irulan gave Chalice a brief smile. "You'll be safe here at home. Wensicia and I have figured out a way to stop Commander-General Zenha from threatening us."

Chalice let out a sigh of relief. "Oh, that's wonderful! What can I do?" She looked at Wensicia. "How can I help?"

A Bene Gesserit Sister addressed Irulan. "Princess Chalice was highly agitated on Wallach IX, and the Mother Superior was happy to return her here, where she could be attended by the Emperor's Suk physicians. We were concerned that she might harm herself."

"I would not!" Chalice insisted. "And I take my medication. But I want to hear this good news. Right now." Her eyes flicked from side to side.

Irulan straightened, looking powerful and noble. "Provided Commander-General Zenha agrees, we will soon have a grand Imperial wedding."

"A wedding?" Chalice gasped and looked over at Wensicia, imagining her sparkling romance with the rebel general. Oddly, though, Wensicia glowered, looking like a statue made of thorns.

"Yes," Irulan said, "I will accept his offer of marriage and seal a peace at last."

Her mouth agape, Chalice watched as the Sardaukar led Irulan to the armored shuttle.

IT WAS TIME for Irulan to throw caution to the wind and trust in her abilities to put an end to Zenha's rebellion. She would offer him what he would see as the lifeline he needed, and considering his obvious ambitions, he would naturally choose the Princess Royal rather than Shaddam's third daughter. Love was never a factor under consideration.

She transmitted her flight plan ahead and directed the shuttle commander to set course for the orbiting flagship of the Liberation Fleet. Zenha was willing, even pleased, to receive her.

Led by a uniformed officer who introduced herself as Kia Maldisi, the Princess Royal walked from the shuttle landing deck to the bridge of the battle-scarred dreadnought. Maldisi wore a military cap, with her hair tucked under it, and Irulan gave her barely a glance, because she was interested in the attention of only one person on this ship.

Irulan arrived with Major Bashar Kolona and three other Sardaukar, who stood like loaded weapons. She had walked straight into a lion's den, either a lamb for the slaughter . . . or someone who might tame the fearsome beast.

Moko Zenha was sitting in his command chair as if it were a throne, but he rose to greet her formally. He looked relieved, but cautious. "Coming directly to my flagship is an enormous gesture of good faith, Princess." He bowed, then reached out to take her hand.

His grasp was warm and firm, but his touch made her skin crawl. She said, "We must trust each other if we are to put an end to this matter. If either side chooses to make this an outright military battle, then we both have lost—all would be destroyed, your fleet and my capital city. Wensicia told me how she has already made her point with you." She withdrew her hand and stepped back from him. "I know how valuable I would be as a hostage, but I think you will choose a neater solution before my father returns."

Irulan's eyes bored into his, and he stared right back, waiting to hear her suggestion. He sat back down in the command chair and said, "Wensicia has already suggested a way to end this, with a royal wedding." His brows knitted together. "I will admit that marrying the Emperor's third daughter would provide protection and satisfaction. Wensicia is quite beautiful, and I think she'd be an engaging intellectual companion. Together, we could achieve my primary goal of strengthening and reshaping the flawed Imperium."

"I'm sure you could," Irulan said. "But you originally requested my hand, not my sister's."

The Commander-General looked away. "I never wanted it to come to this. Surely you understand that?"

"Yes, but wishes cannot change the past. My father did not anticipate the consequences of the . . . way he declined your offer of marriage. It is a regrettable thing."

She looked around the bridge, noted the old markings of the Imperial fleet to which this man had previously sworn allegiance. She saw the riding crop of Duke Bashar Gorambi mounted on the bulkhead wall. Had Zenha plotted all along to overthrow his commander? Had he seized an opportunity . . . or had he truly been forced into a desperate situation where he saw no other way out?

Irulan narrowed her eyes. "It's good that you did not accept Wensicia's offer yet, Commander-General, because I have a better one for you."

Zenha straightened in the command chair.

"Marriage into the royal family would bind you to House Corrino and force the Emperor to patch this horrendous breach." She gave him a cool smile. "But would Wensicia's status really be sufficient to accomplish your aims?"

A calculating look crossed Zenha's face. Nearby, the officer Maldisi seemed to bristle. She looked very tough, and . . . familiar? Irulan wasn't certain, but sensed something about her she did not like.

The Commander-General said, "As you recall, I originally aimed higher."

Irulan smiled. "And now I accept your offer, Commander-General Zenha."

A gasp rippled around the flagship's bridge.

She continued, "We will arrange a wedding ceremony down at the Imperial Palace. A formal gala with appropriate priests and dignitaries—and it will be legally binding. The lawtechs already drew up appropriate language for Wensicia, which can be easily modified. Afterward, once my father returns to Kaitain, I will convince him to bless the union as a way to end civil war and bloodshed. Marriages have been used to end wars throughout history. Provided your ships and crew swear allegiance to the Imperium again, you'll become an important member of House Corrino, bound by marriage if not blood, and our children will be Corrino heirs."

Zenha's face illuminated with surprise and hope, then tightened into suspicion. "And what does Wensicia think about your bold and unexpected offer?"

"She understands politics, and knows her role in the Imperial family, as well as mine. She will accept it."

As his crew murmured behind him, Zenha squared his shoulders and dictated his own terms. "Our wedding must take place immediately. I cannot wait for messages to be dispatched across the Imperium or for

Shaddam to return from his hiding place. We will seal our union and make our vows before the palace and the court, witnessed by my representatives and yours. Time is of the essence, Princess."

Irulan had suspected he would say this, had in fact counted on it. "Indeed it is. We shall arrange the event at the palace within the next day so we can end this standoff. You will come down with your escort party, and all will go smoothly. Your ships are stationed above to ensure there will be no treachery from us . . . and you know we can destroy all of them with a single code, should you try something of your own."

Zenha chuckled, but seemed relieved. "Now that sounds like the start of a great romance, my dear Irulan!"

From his expression and demeanor, she thought he might try to kiss her. She stepped back.

"Yes, a great romance," she said, keeping her tone neutral. Then she turned and gestured for her Sardaukar to take her back to the shuttle. "I have a lot to prepare."

The true purpose of righteous punishment is not to inspire contrition, but to establish a proper hierarchy of power.

—Spacing Guild administrative memo on Junction

The report from the planetologist on Arrakis caused great consternation among the Guild, and Starguide Serello made immediate plans for retaliation. In a very real sense, the future of the Bene Tleilax lay in his hands. He had been instructed by his superiors to manage this operation, and they had authorized an enormous amount of funds to take care of the problem. It was that serious.

The situation was grave, far worse than he could have imagined months ago when he received his first inkling of insidious Tleilaxu schemes. If the biological wizards succeeded in growing their own Navigators, it would change the very order of not only the Spacing Guild but the hierarchy of the entire Imperium. It could not be allowed to continue.

Sending the native Fremen to find the hidden lab had been an excellent idea. The desert people had been poking into lost corners of the wasteland, and had indeed discovered what the best Guild searchers could not locate. The Fremen had once again proved to be a useful resource.

Now in his high geometric office overlooking the Junction skyline, Serello ran his fingertips over the virtual report as if he could absorb data through his skin. Dr. Kynes's operatives would eradicate the Tleilaxu research facility, leaving no evidence behind—for which they would receive significant compensation.

Under other circumstances, Guild scientists might have seized the research data to study what the demented genetic scientists had done with the dead Navigator. *My great-grandfather!* No, that knowledge should be destroyed and mixed into the sands of Arrakis. He was confident the Fremen would complete their task.

But that penalty was not sufficient. For the next step, Starguide Serello would impose a righteous punishment on their entire race. The Tleilaxu would never forget this lesson.

He called up Heighliner routes and ship availabilities, then rescheduled the great vessels, revised their cargo obligations, and adjusted their priorities. His enhanced mind scanned over second- and third-order repercussions as he diverted Heighliners, changed delivery schedules, imposed delays on certain routes, and doubled up the frigates and cargo ships to be transferred at the main hubs.

He needed the ships for his own purpose. Without leaving his polished office, Serello separated out a hundred massive Guild ships and pulled them into a huge and imposing interdiction fleet filled with mercenary warships and fighters. It took many days to assemble all the vessels at Junction, but his manipulations were subtle, and the Tleilaxu would suspect nothing amiss. They would have no warning.

When it was time, the Starguide shuttled up to the primary Heighliner and assumed his position on the navigation deck. In silence, he stood next to the ominous tank and looked out at the vast field of stars. The misshapen form of this ship's prescient Navigator hung suspended, staring through the tendrils of orange mist. Bitter exhaust vapors wafted out of the vents, and Serello inhaled deeply.

He spoke to the great tank in front of him. "Have you foreseen the success of our mission?" Despite the fact that Serello was an enhanced Starguide, the superior Navigators still considered him little more than a child.

The misshapen form shifted in its swirling bath of melange, then said in a distorted voice through the speakerpatch, "I see many possible successes."

"And failures?" Serello asked.

"I see infinite possibilities of each."

Serello looked out through the starry window. "Then let us choose the correct path to a favorable result. Prepare to depart."

ONE HUNDRED GUILD Heighliners emerged from foldspace, dropping one after the other like bludgeons, ready to hammer the Tleilaxu homeworld. The sudden blockade was imposing enough, but mercenary ships also dropped out of the Heighliner holds, adding more visible firepower.

Starguide Serello felt a warmth of success as he saw the enormous ships crowding space above the mysterious planet. Although the necessities of commerce required business and political representatives to meet with the Tleilaxu, almost no powindah foreigner was allowed down to the surface. Instead, they conducted business aboard orbiting quarantine stations so that offworlders did not set foot on the sacred soil.

The Starguide had no personal interest in visiting the capital city of Bandalong. His only intent was to break the Tleilaxu scheme with such force that they never attempted such a thing again. He could do that from orbit.

The planetary observation systems had set off alarms the moment the Guild interdiction fleet arrived. Dozens of commercial ships were docked at the quarantine stations high above the planet. Shuttles moved up and down through the atmosphere, carrying Tleilaxu Masters. Satellites patrolled the high orbital lanes.

Even after the Guild ships arrived, the Navigator remained silent in his tank, having guided all these Heighliners to the proper place. The other Guild vessels maintained communications blackout, but the operation was perfectly coordinated as they followed the pattern of the plan.

The ominous Guild fleet loomed, waiting. Serello bided his time. Sensors showed panic spreading throughout the orbital quarantine stations. Numerous Tleilaxu shuttles immediately returned to the surface. Tleilaxu security ships rose up in formation, an impotent show of strength, but they did not dare open fire. A flurry of coded communications crossed the standard frequencies, but the enormous interdiction ships remained silent. Threatening.

Serello gave them fifteen minutes to understand the hopelessness of their situation.

Finally, he asked his comm officer to open a channel and send a message superimposed on a battering-ram carrier wave so that it could break through any blocks or dampening fields. He did not show his image, though. Not yet.

"People of Tleilax, you have been found guilty of crimes against the Spacing Guild and the Imperium. We have placed this planetary system under total quarantine, and the Guild will no longer provide any transportation or commercial needs. No ships will be allowed to arrive at or depart from the Thalim system. Effective immediately, you are entirely cut off from the rest of the Imperium."

In a burst of images that took a moment to coalesce, the sour, elongated face of a Master appeared on the screen. "This is outrageous. You have presented no evidence! We will appeal to the Emperor and the Landsraad Court, and file a formal grievance with CHOAM."

Serello recognized the oily man—Master Giblii, a person of great importance in the Tleilaxu sphere of influence . . . and the Tleilaxu who had once brushed Serello's palm and surreptitiously collected cell scrapings for illicit research.

"How can you file your grievance?" asked Serello. "You have no ships capable of carrying you to any destination beyond your own star system, and it will take years for any transmitted message to reach the nearest inhabited constellation. You are cut off from Guild services."

Now he showed his own image on the comm screen. "I am Starguide Serello. You will remember me." When the man didn't respond, Serello let anger seep into his voice. "Your pretense is foolish, Master Giblii. You do remember me. You stole from me." Serello held up his hand, palm out. "You scraped my cells under the guise of a handshake. And you stole the body of a Guild Navigator from its sacred burial place on Arrakis."

The Tleilaxu Master trembled with rage. His jaw worked, and he was about to blurt denials, but Serello cut him off.

"If you refuse to admit what we both know to be true, then the Guild will extend the quarantine for centuries, until your entire race is no more than a withered husk."

Giblii's demeanor changed. "What is it you want?" His defiant tone did not mask his clear sense of defeat.

Serello squared his shoulders. "Choose one of your orbital stations, and meet me there by yourself to discuss the terms of your punishment."

Giblii squirmed, then sent coordinates for one of the quarantine hubs before he signed off.

STARGUIDE SERELLO DID not fear for his safety when he went to the orbital station. With his interdiction fleet, he had every possible weapon at his disposal. He could reduce the planet to a charred ball, if the situation required it. The Tleilaxu would not dare try anything.

A Guild shuttle docked at the designated station, and he entered the tomb-like facility, where the metal decks and walls smelled like cleaning solvents and disinfecting solutions. The recycled air had a metallic tang. He located the appointed conference chamber and sat alone in the sterile environment, waiting. He felt strong.

When the Tleilaxu Master finally appeared, he walked with an agitated gait that made his robes swish. Seeing that he was accompanied by an escort of robed minions, Serello shot to his feet, angry and annoyed. He gestured for the others to go away. "This is a private conversation. Master Giblii can pass along my words once he learns the fate of his people. For now, leave."

The sour Master shuffled his feet, swallowed visibly, and dispatched his companions. They sealed the door shut behind them. The ugly man took a seat at the metal table far from Starguide Serello, and in an apparent attempt to avoid contamination, he turned up vents in his portion of the room, causing his long, thin hair to blow. He looked like a nervous, beaten pet.

Once the unwanted eavesdroppers had scuttled back out into the corridors, Serello used a scanner to assure himself that no one was listening electronically, then brought forth a solido-hologram projector. Without further word, he displayed the damning surveillance of the secret desert laboratory facility that Dr. Kynes had sent. Next, he showed records of the illegal Tleilaxu spy satellite he had blasted out of Arrakis's orbit. Finally, he revealed what he knew about the Navigator body that Tleilaxu marauders had stolen.

In an icy voice, Serello said, "I also know you stole cell samples from me. From *me*! Perhaps it was because you knew that persons in my bloodline have the potential to become Navigators."

Giblii feigned indignation. "We meant no such—"

The Starguide raised his hand, cutting him off. "The Guild *knows*. Any one of these sacrilegious things is grounds for extreme sanctions, and your denials or absurd rationalizations will only increase your punishment." He pointed toward the documents and the hologram projector. "This is merely the surface. If necessary, we intend to share much more in Landsraad Court, or directly with the Emperor on Kaitain."

The Master's shoulders drooped in defeat. He placed his thin, grayish hands on the tabletop. "How can we make amends, Starguide?"

"You will provide me with a complete, detailed report of your illicit research on Arrakis. By now, the entire facility has been destroyed. Our operatives have wiped it out along with all of your research data."

Giblii sagged but didn't argue.

Serello continued, "Gather any laboratory records that have been transmitted from Arrakis and surrender them to us. You had best find them, because I will not believe you if you claim they don't exist."

The Master raised his head, showing alarm. "It was a rogue group of researchers! They saw an opportunity and acted without sanction. So far we have received only a few scant reports along with requests for financing, which we did not provide. I learned after the fact that they financed the work solely through one of our wealthiest—" He paused, added, "I—we didn't condone this work."

"That is a good enough story for now," Serello said, his curiosity piqued but not enough to dig. He did not soften his voice. "You understand that the Spacing Guild will retaliate with a massive response if we ever find that your words are untrue."

Giblii spoke in a rush. "The research program existed only on Arrakis! I have few records, but will provide all of them to you—if you lift the quarantine."

"You are not one to lay out terms, Master Giblii."

"It is a plea, then," the Tleilaxu man said.

"You *know* how the Guild can retaliate."

The Tleilaxu hung his head. "Yes, we understand."

"All right. We will increase your tariffs for a period of fifty years. We will inspect any Tleilaxu cargo that we find suspicious in any way. We will sever some of your connections with CHOAM and reassign your business channels to less profitable planets."

Giblii shuddered. Each of Serello's words was like a blow.

"But your people will survive. That much was not assured at the beginning of our conversation, so you have made progress." He let the words sink in. "As long as you accept and agree, and as long as I find your records acceptable."

After a long hesitation, the Master heaved a deep sigh. "Yes, we accept your terms. You give us no alternative."

Then, because Serello knew the Tleilaxu loathed touching other human beings, he strode to the other end of the table and reached out to grasp Giblii's sweaty, soft hand. The Master recoiled but conquered his disgust and accepted the Starguide's grip. This time Serello squeezed hard, stopping just short of breaking bones.

"We have an ironclad agreement," the Guildsman said.

Even the most intelligent and aware person never would have expected violence from such a source.

—*A Chronicle of Corrino Weddings*

Princess Irulan had studied the history of extravagant weddings that had been performed in the Royal Chapel, spectacles almost as grand as a coronation, followed by gala receptions and entertainments on the manicured palace lawns or in specialty sections of the sprawling gardens.

But such impressive events took months or even years to plan. Both Zenha and Irulan knew their wedding had to take place formally, legally—and *swiftly*. But she did not want this politically necessary ceremony to take place in the chapel. Rather, she announced they would hold the event in the grand throne room, within view of the Hagal quartz throne, the primary symbol of Imperial power. Zenha would appreciate that, and she felt it might make him lower his guard.

In Irulan's mind, today's event was about demonstrating the power of House Corrino and restoring stability to the Imperium—much like so many other historical weddings. She intended to do that with an exclamation point, in her own unique and memorable way.

Zenha would anticipate the same goal himself, a resolution to his uprising, and he would already imagine how to reform the Imperial military. No matter what he had told his followers, deep down he must have believed his mutiny was a hopeless cause, even if it did expose the weaknesses in the corrupt system. Now, by marrying the Princess Royal, he might be in a position to save the armed forces.

As the rushed wedding preparations were underway, Wensicia fumed in an anteroom as her ladies-in-waiting tended to final details on her bridesmaid dress. When Irulan came to see her, her sister was icy. "This should have been *my* triumph, not yours. The Emperor's third daughter traditionally marries a military officer, you know that. You have taken unfair advantage. Father will be furious that his firstborn daughter is wasted on an upstart traitor!"

Irulan remained calm and confident. "I grant you, the situation is not ideal, but our father has had many years to marry me off to whomever he chooses, yet he decided not to do so. When he dispatched me from Arrakis, he gave me instructions to resolve the crisis. And I found a solution."

"But *I* found the solution first, dear sister!" Wensicia spun away so that Irulan could not see her expression.

"Perhaps we don't have the same solution in mind," Irulan said in a low voice, but did not explain further. "The day is not yet over."

Additional ladies tended to the Princess Royal's makeup, hair, and jewelry. She wore a spectacular white dress encrusted with tiny gems, an exquisite garment tailored to fit her figure perfectly. One attendant adjusted the priceless rubine necklace she wore.

Her male concubine entered and gave her a quick bow. Aron was as elegantly dressed as a young nobleman, presenting himself with the faultless poise he had learned from his Bene Gesserit training. "Is there any other way I may assist you, Your Highness?" He looked as if he expected to be dismissed.

She gave him a penetrating look. She had enjoyed his company and conversation over the years. Irulan wondered if Zenha would allow her to keep him, the way so many noblemen maintained their own courtesans. Shaddam IV had a long list of concubines ready to serve him at his whim, so why not the same for her? She did not intend to get rid of him.

"Do not think you are obsolete, Aron. Attend and remain unobtrusive, as always. Stand ready." She couldn't tell if he was upset, or disappointed, or simply accepting. "Meet me in my chambers in a few moments. I need your assistance in one last thing."

"I would serve in any manner necessary, Your Highness." With a flowing bow, Aron retreated from the preparation room.

Wensicia looked after him, her eyes sharp. "Maybe I will take him for my own purposes once you no longer have any use for him." She snorted. "Or maybe we should give him to Chalice."

Using the careful techniques she had learned at the Mother School, Irulan modulated her voice, tried to soothe her sister. "I have only the kindest thoughts toward you, Wensicia. Don't be bitter. We stand together, both of us Corrino princesses, and we will make the Imperium strong, whatever the price. Today, I pay one such price, but I promise you that with this wedding, we'll end Zenha's insurrection."

"It must end, by any means," Wensicia said in a low voice.

Irulan insisted on giving her sister the proper credit. "I am impressed by how you managed to hold off the Liberation Fleet. No one expected you to be thrown into such a crucible, and you handled it very well. It shows you are a true leader, even under duress. Father will be proud, and I'm sure he'll reconsider your role here in the palace. Discovering that destruct override code was genius! Without it, Kaitain would have been overrun before word ever reached Arrakis. When the Emperor returns, I will make certain he knows how much you contributed. With this wedding ceremony, we put an end to the rebellion. You'll see. Stand with me."

Her sister remained silent while the ladies-in-waiting retreated, and Irulan could see the thoughts churning in her mind. Finally, Wensicia nodded, still angry but resigned. "Very well. I'll do my duty today and for all my life—as a loyal Corrino princess."

Irulan extended her hand, and Wensicia took it, rising to her feet. Her sister's grip was warm, but Irulan felt cold inside. When she released her hand, Irulan looked at her own palm and steeled herself for what lay ahead. She reviewed her deepest Bene Gesserit training. "Now, I must return to my chambers before the ceremony begins."

She had one last, vital preparation to make.

WAITING IN THE anteroom of the vast throne room, Irulan inhaled deeply, exhaled, concentrated on her pulse. Commander-General Moko Zenha had arrived with his entourage of mutineers and prepared for his grand ceremonial entrance.

She had her father's orders to follow, but she also had her own end game. The definition of "happily ever after" changed with the circumstances.

Not surprisingly, her stomach was queasy, but she pushed the uneasiness away. She flexed her hand, imagined her skin tingling, burning. Her attendants had turned her into a sculpture of what a Princess Royal was expected to be—her dress, jewels, makeup, hair—all to perfection.

Beside her, waiting for the wedding procession to begin, Wensicia looked nearly as beautiful in her crimson dress, a House Corrino color. Wearing a similar gown, Chalice was giddy, as if attending her own wedding. She had been brought out of monitored isolation in her private chambers, reassured that Zenha and his rebels would keep the peace, if only to ensure that their Commander-General got what he wanted. Chalice's attending Suk doctor had given her a strong calming drug so that she would be cooperative but blissfully unaware of deep thoughts.

Outside, the large chamber had been swiftly decorated with the ostentatious trappings expected of an Imperial wedding, though the Emperor's throne room was already so lavish, it could not accommodate much more. Courtiers from across the capital city crowded the vast diamondwood and kabuzu-shell floor. The people were fascinated—frightened by the violent siege they had just witnessed, but eager for the show, sure that this would mark an important turning point in history.

With spectacular fanfare to announce his presence, Moko Zenha marched into the throne room accompanied by guards in fine uniforms. His tough female officer removed her military cap for a moment, adjusted the band, and then replaced the cap, tucking her hair under it again. Irulan suddenly recognized her as the would-be assassin who had attacked Shaddam in the kitchens! Kia Maldisi! She was striding just behind him, like his personal bodyguard.

The crowd had been cleared to create a long passage. Zenha's suit was flashy blue and black, tailored specifically for the occasion, but not in the best of taste. Irulan wondered if he had culled his wardrobe from the staterooms of the gaudy, overthrown noble officers. His shoulders were squared and his head held high, as he basked in his moment of supreme glory.

At the opposite end of the hall, Irulan's Sardaukar marched into position with a thunder of boots, followed by a contingent of palace guards in crimson-and-gold uniforms, much more impressive than Zenha's party. Loyal soldiers were stationed throughout the palace as well.

The rebel battleships in the sky kept their ominous weapons trained down at the Palace District, but would not open fire while Zenha was in the throne room for the wedding ceremony. With the large fleet Irulan had brought back from Arrakis, the forces were roughly even, a military impasse in the skies, no one making a move.

A ceremonial wedding dais had been erected opposite the immense Golden Lion Throne, which stood empty and foreboding, as if its normal occupant could not bear to witness this sacrilegious event. As the Princess

Royal prepared to step out with her own formal party, she glimpsed Aron standing in the front of the crowd. She had asked him to stand close to the dais, though few outside of her inner circle knew who he was. He seemed invisible among the throng of people.

After the fanfare faded, Irulan paused long enough to emphasize her importance, then emerged into the large chamber, gliding forward with grace and poise. An even louder fanfare sounded the moment she came into view. Despite the closeness of so many people, she took great care not to touch anyone.

Wensicia and Chalice followed close behind her, also proud princesses. Wensicia kept a close eye on her flighty sister, who wore a dreamy smile and seemed to be drifting through her role. Behind them came six bridesmaids, noblewomen who had been recruited from the courtiers for the rushed wedding, including two visiting Bene Gesserit. The robed, secretive Sisters, as well as Aron, had helped Irulan prepare for this.

The Grand Priest of the Imperium, wearing a layered silvery robe and the medallion of office, stood at his post on the wedding dais, gazing out on the assemblage. The priest's broad face was serene, as if he had taken the same sedative as Chalice. In front of his chest, he clasped an ornate copy of the Orange Catholic Bible.

Commander-General Zenha waited on one side of the dais before a set of wide steps, and Irulan stopped her slow procession across from him. Well timed, even though they'd had no opportunity to rehearse, the bride and groom ascended the steps to meet at the top of the platform. They faced each other, but by tradition did not hold hands until the priest offered his ceremonial signal. Irulan gave the mutinous leader a firm stare, careful not to show defeat or subservience.

The priest reveled in his own position even if the circumstances were tense. He had presided over Emperor Shaddam's last two weddings, and would no doubt officiate for the next one, whenever her father decided to marry again. The court had been waiting a long time, however, for the marriage of an Imperial princess.

The crowd murmured, some pretending happiness and joy, others muttering in uncertainty, a strangely unpleasant combination of sounds. As the priest opened his Orange Catholic Bible for the ceremony, Zenha violated protocol by whispering across to her, "I'm glad we found a way to resolve this without further bloodshed."

Further bloodshed . . . She did not acknowledge him.

A flicker of annoyance crossed the priest's face to hear the quiet disruption, but he lifted the holy book and intoned, "Now, you may hold hands."

Irulan reached out, and Zenha took her offered hand, as if seizing her the way he had attempted to seize Kaitain. She gripped back, demonstrating her strength, pressing her palm against his. She felt perspiration on his skin.

Behind her, Wensicia let out a quiet, exasperated sigh.

"We shall begin," the priest said, raising his voice.

Oh, it has already begun, Irulan thought with a dark smile. Right now, on cue, she knew the palace would have activated powerful jamming signals to prevent any images transmitted to the enemy ships above.

She met Zenha's gaze, and her green eyes flashed in what she knew must be a strange way. Suddenly wary, he blinked, as if unsettled.

As the priest began to read his passage, Zenha turned oddly pale and grayish. He blinked again, shook his head as if to drive away a buzzing sound. Then he began to tremble, a little at first, then with increasing violence. Spasming, he squeezed Irulan's hand, clutching her, but she calmly used her other hand to pry loose his grip.

The priest's voice faltered, and he stopped reading. The crowd sensed something was happening, and a hush rippled through them, then gasps.

Irulan stepped back and let Zenha collapse onto the dais, writhing in agony. Calmly, she joined her two sisters. Wensicia looked hungry and pleased.

Chalice asked, "Oh, is he sick?"

The priest called for a doctor, but Irulan knew that would do no good. The Bene Gesserit contact poison she had used was swift and deadly. Her stomach remained unsettled from the potent antidote she had taken, but she herself felt no effects from the poison.

Zenha's honor guard rushed forward, drawing their ceremonial weapons, but Major Bashar Kolona and his Sardaukar intercepted them, blocking the dais. Front ranks of palace guards joined them. They all drew their swords, activated their shields.

On the floor, Zenha twisted and spasmed in pain. Irulan did not feel sorry for him in the least. From the side of the dais, she glimpsed Aron among the milling crowd, watching everything. He gave her a calm nod, though she had told him nothing in advance.

Moaning, the priest bent over and vomited on the polished tiles. He dropped the heavy Bible from his trembling hands.

With a chorus of screams, the audience scrambled for the exits, nearly trampling one another in their panic. Chalice finally grasped what was happening, and she screamed.

Somehow, Zenha managed to crawl toward the princess he had tried so hard to win. Major Bashar Kolona stepped closer to protect her, but Irulan told him to stand aside. "He can't hurt me now." She gazed down contemptuously at her ruthless suitor.

Zenha slumped, his entire body twitching as he looked up at her in disbelief. "Princess . . ."

"My father was right. You are not a fitting consort for the Emperor's daughter."

He spasmed so violently that Irulan could hear tendons ripping, bones cracking. Then he finally died.

On the dais, Chalice turned and fled, stumbling in her fine crimson gown. She ran screaming into the milling crowd.

As the throng churned in shock, the Sardaukar moved forward and ruthlessly fell upon Zenha's honor guard—traitors who had mutinied against their commanding officers. Now fighting in real combat against the Emperor's deadliest warriors, they were slaughtered.

Irulan glanced back at Wensicia, who watched with grim self-composure, but she did not see Chalice nearby. She barked orders to the Sardaukar commander: "Major Bashar, make certain my family is protected. Find Chalice." As Kolona hurried off, Irulan moved with great formality to pull on a pair of white gloves that would cover any remaining trace of the contact poison. As the Princess Royal, she stepped down the wide stairs.

The crowd was in too much chaos to notice her exit, but she refused to flee in terror. With a hard smile, she met her waiting concubine, who stood strong and ready. "A marvelous turnabout, Your Highness," Aron said. "The Mother School will be proud of you."

With a gloved hand, she took Aron's arm. "I've always had a bit of poison in me. You just didn't see it."

Before they could make their way to safety, the crowd in front of them parted as two bystanders were killed in a flurry of blades. One of the staunch Sardaukar fell back, bleeding from a wide wound in his side. He wore a look of astonishment on his face as he stumbled.

The redheaded woman—Kia Maldisi—lunged forward, snarling. She let the dying Sardaukar drop to the floor as she raised two bloody short swords to run at Irulan.

The Princess tensed and fell into a fighting stance, but her gown and embellishments were like a stiff straitjacket, inhibiting her flexibility to dodge or counterstrike.

But as the murderous woman attacked, Aron darted in to block her. His arms were a blur as he snapped up a tight fist, knocking Maldisi's left arm aside, though she still held one of the short swords in her other hand. He followed through with a sharp punch to her inner arm, hitting hard enough to deaden the nerves in her bicep. Maldisi's fingers twitched, as if suddenly liquid, and the red blade slipped out of her hand.

Aron caught the hilt of it as it dropped, while simultaneously sweeping with his right foot to catch her behind the ankle. Irulan watched everything in a frozen instant, knowing the precise and careful moves of the Bene Gesserit weirding way of fighting taught by the Mother School. Aron had been well trained in all things before he'd been sent to join Irulan as her concubine.

As Maldisi snarled, she turned her remaining sword on him, but Aron was too fast. He turned the blade and drove it into her chest, stopping her cold, then thrust harder, all the way through, before withdrawing the blade. Maldisi fell back, spurting blood.

Major Bashar Kolona reached Irulan, but she focused a withering gaze on the fallen woman on the floor.

The elegant Princess Royal, without a drop of blood on her, took Aron's arm again and strolled toward the main doors, while the onlookers opened a path for them.

"Most impressive, Aron," she said. "It seems we are both deadly."

The storms of the desert eventually erase all marks of a Fremen life, so we must keep that person forever in our hearts and memories.

—REVEREND MOTHER RAMALLO, Sietch Tabr

As she looked at her brother's mangled body in the Tleilaxu lab, Chani felt grief and outrage. She had been on many razzia raids with Khouro, and on each of them they had flouted danger, fearing nothing while exposing themselves to mortal harm. They had been fools to think of themselves as invincible.

"Khouro, Khouro . . ." Tenderly, she cradled his head. He looked like a man ravaged by a horrific sandstorm—like the stories of his real father, Warrick.

Chaos continued in the lab chamber as furious Fremen toppled sample tanks, smashed records and files, stabbed the corpses of Tleilaxu researchers and guards, though they were already dead. The twisted bodies of the ghola Navigators sprawled like humanoid stillbirths outside their fleshy tanks. Their star-filled eyes had gone dull with a gray film. Had they foreseen their own deaths? Had they envisioned Khouro's?

Jamis stepped up to Chani, his head down in grief and respect. "We have finished our mission, but at great cost. Our people killed the last few Tleilaxu, as well as their guards, who were good fighters." He glanced around the ruined facility. "Do we keep any of this? Take it back to your father?"

Chani was surprised to realize he was looking to her as a leader. Some Fremen considered her little more than a girl, but she was strong—and she was the daughter of Liet-Kynes. That gave her respect.

Awash with emotions, lamenting Khouro, she tried to think like her father, the scientist, the planetologist. Tleilaxu Masters had conducted forbidden research here. Ridulian crystal sheets were scattered throughout the rooms, and she suspected that the Spacing Guild would pay dearly for the information. Maybe she could give them the laboratory data to further reduce the spice bribe the Fremen were forced to pay. But the idea of negotiating over all this disgusted her.

She looked down at her brother's mangled face, the swollen and purple contaminated skin, the craters from tiny needle explosions.

Jamis spoke in a low, husky voice. "We cannot take him back and give his water to the tribe."

Chani clutched her brother. "His body belongs to the tribe."

"No, his water is contaminated by Tleilaxu poisons."

She knew Jamis was right. The biological researchers played with too many vile substances. They grew sickly abominations in tanks, added mutagenic chemicals. She could not guess what cursed substances they had implanted in her brother's flesh.

Her shoulders slumped, as if she carried a heavy boulder on her back. "We must leave him here."

Jamis was solemn. "We can only hope his shade is pure and free."

"I hope he haunts the Tleilaxu," Chani said.

Gently easing her brother to the floor, she stood up and brushed herself off, yet bloodstains remained. Without hesitation, she took Khouro's crysknife and sheath, fastened them to her hip. "The Spacing Guild hired us to find this place and destroy it. We will do exactly that." She hardened her voice. "And we will be thorough about it."

Stilgar might scold her about wasting the leverage this material might have given them over the Guild, but there were more important things to consider. Stilgar was a Naib, and he was Fremen. He would understand.

The raiders went from room to room, smashing equipment, destroying records, emptying tanks. They set fire to anything flammable, and the evil, toxic fumes made her eyes burn and her throat sting, so she covered her mouth and inserted nose plugs. There was nothing here she wanted to take.

They found one last Tleilaxu man barricaded inside a storage container. When the Fremen hauled him out, struggling and spitting curses, Chani killed him herself, though it gave her little pleasure.

On the lower levels, they found a small hangar built into a rock grotto, holding two of the unmarked ships, like the one that had stolen the dead Navigator from the pre-spice mass. Chani pushed her anger back into rationality. "We will take those ships. Our tribe can use them." Two members of their team were skilled pilots, and now they climbed into the cockpits and familiarized themselves with the controls.

In a daze, she walked through the ruins of the facility, passing dead guards with mottled skin and strange offworld weapons, as well as protective shield belts that no Fremen would use out in the desert.

The destruction was not enough to suit her purposes, though. Chani had an idea.

She kicked one of the dead Tleilaxu guards and bent down to unclip his shield belt, holding it far from her body, as if it were a snake. She shouted new orders to her Fremen. "Search the bodies. Collect all of these devices."

Jamis scoffed. "But why? How can we use them back in the sietch?"

"We will use them here," Chani said. "Shai-Hulud will finish the job for us."

OUTSIDE, THE EQUATORIAL storms had increased, whipping and lashing curtains of dust. Sand pelted the rocky ridge that hid the Tleilaxu facility. Chani emerged from the entrance tunnel and faced the wind, feeling the power of the desert around her.

She intended to bring a bigger storm to this place.

Adamos, whose face was covered with blood and grit, stepped up to her. "Daughter of Liet, their airships are strange, but simple enough to understand. We can pilot them out. The two craft will take all our remaining people." He lowered his voice. "But perhaps we should wait? If we leave now, our course would take us directly into the storm wind."

"We have flown into storms before," Chani said, "and this is the equatorial zone. The winds will not diminish."

Adamos gave a brisk nod. "I will prepare the craft."

Chani gazed out on the dust-blurred sea of dunes where she had dispatched several runners. "They will return in half an hour, and then we must be away from here. Without delay."

Jamis and four companions had gone out onto the open sands, heading in different directions. They each carried a thumper and salvaged shield belts.

Now she used oil-lens binoculars to search for the tiny figures. The blowing dust obscured them intermittently, but she could still tell what they were doing. The most distant silhouette was Jamis. He loped along, still using an uneven gait even though the need for speed outweighed their method of walking without rhythm. When he reached the rise of a high dune, Jamis thrust his thumper into the sand. He set the clockwork mechanism, raised the trip hammer, and let it begin pounding vibrations into the depths—summoning a monster worm.

But instead of the Fremen tradition of crouching and waiting with worm hooks, ropes, spreaders, and goads, Jamis activated one of the shield belts and dropped it on the sand.

Then he began to run flat out.

Sand kicked up beneath his boots as fear-infused adrenaline gave him speed. When he had gone a third of the way back, he activated a second shield belt and dropped it on the dune face without pausing.

Out on their own different paths, the other Fremen did the same, planting thumpers and dropping the confiscated shield belts. They all raced toward the low ridge that held the Tleilaxu lab.

The Holtzman fields would not only summon the great worms, but would also drive them into a destructive frenzy. The throbbing shield belts were like breadcrumbs drawing the worms to the target.

When she saw the others running back to her, Chani transmitted a signal for all the raiders to meet in the hangar grotto. Adamos and the second pilot had already activated the engines and were ready to fly away in the unmarked craft. While the rest of her crew boarded the ships below, ready to escape, Chani watched Jamis and his companions return. At the entrance to the research facility, she held more shield belts.

Normally these rocks would have been safe from any worm, but the shield belts were like screaming, taunting voices, infuriating the great worms. Jamis began climbing the rocks to reach her, the others not far behind. Now Chani activated one of the last shield belts, felt it throb in her hand, and flung it out away from the entrance. The device tumbled down the slope and landed in rocks near the sand's edge. She activated and tossed two more belts closer along the rocks, then left one pulsing right at the doorstep.

Jamis reached her, panting. The other exhausted Fremen were scrambling up the path. She nodded, grateful for what they had done, then touched the hilt of Khouro's crysknife for reassurance. "Now let's get out of here."

They ducked inside the laboratory complex and ran down the main passageways, taking the ramp until they reached the lower hangar bay, with its camouflaged doors now open to the winds. The two offworld aircraft stood ready, loaded with Fremen fighters. As her companions climbed aboard, Chani stared around the wrecked facility.

The Fremen would call this mission a victory. They had accomplished what they'd been tasked to do, and the Spacing Guild would pay them well. Their losses had been "minimal" in human terms . . . but nothing about her half brother was minimal to her.

"Goodbye, Khouro," she whispered, then climbed aboard one of the strange Tleilaxu craft.

Adamos activated the engines and pulled the controls. The ship lifted off the dusty stone floor and moved forward to the open hangar door. The other flyer exited first, racing out into the storm, and Chani's craft followed. Immediately, they were buffeted by powerful winds, but the pilots steadied their course, gaining altitude to circle around the crags that sheltered the Tleilaxu laboratory.

"There!" Jamis tapped his finger on the side windowport. "Worm sign!"

"Three!" said another commando who looked out the opposite window.

Coming from separate directions, the behemoths hurtled toward the vibrations of the shields, churning up mountains of sand. The first one broke the surface where Jamis had planted his thumper and shield belt. It lunged upward, scattering sand in all directions and engulfing the offending object, then it churned toward the second shield belt, gaining fury and speed.

From a different direction, another sandworm was driven into a frenzy powerful enough that it ignored its territorial instincts. It smashed and devoured the shield belts in its way and kept coming toward the line of rocks.

Chani watched the enormous beasts fling themselves wildly onto the uplift beyond the sand, maddened by the throbbing Holtzman fields. She'd never seen such a length of exposed worm before, the armored rings repeating on and on like an enormous whip.

The first beast crashed onto the rocks, pulverizing boulders. The second worm lurched even higher, rolling, creating an avalanche. All three crashed and pummeled in a mad attack, slamming onto the buttress where the Tleilaxu had thought they would be safe. But this place was safe neither from the Fremen nor from the worms.

Chani closed her eyes for a moment, thought of Khouro's handsome face, before the Tleilaxu mangled it, and she whispered, "Bless the Maker and His water. Bless the coming and going of Him. May His passage cleanse the world. May He keep the world for His people."

Inside the aircraft, the Fremen whispered in awe, uttered their own prayers. Some even cheered.

"This was a battle for Dune itself," Chani said. "It is fitting that Shai-Hulud helped us win it."

The Fremen pilots flew the unmarked ships into the storm and headed home.

Sometimes there is too much excitement, and too much blood.

—KASEK, minstrel to the court of
Crown Prince Raphael Corrino

Irulan heard the clamor of alarms in the palace, and outside came the zinging, percussive noises of explosions, along with weapons fire and the hum of distant but powerful shields.

Though they still didn't know what had occurred, the Liberation Fleet finally retaliated, and a fierce battle erupted in the skies over the Imperial Palace and up in orbit. To the north, Imperial warships, including the Sardaukar vessels her father had sent from Arrakis, faced off against the rebel forces, who still didn't exactly know what was happening.

Less than half an hour ago when she and Moko Zenha stood on the wedding dais and the ceremony reached its high point with the two of them clasping hands, the palace's powerful jammer net had blinded the rebel ships. She knew that across the insurrection fleet, the screens went blank, so they did not see what was happening in the throne room.

While making her urgent plans, Irulan had known this would buy her only a few minutes, but the commanders of the Imperial military fleet mobilized as soon as the jammers activated. They swept in and opened fire on Zenha's ships, attacking in the momentary confusion before the rebels knew their Commander-General had met a horrible death in front of the wedding crowd.

Now, however, Irulan could hear the air battle as she and her concubine made their way to shelter. She had no doubt that the competent officers serving in the Liberation Fleet would not give up easily. The clash in the skies was fierce, and she knew the space battle up in orbit was ferocious as well. She had to get to shelter.

As Sardaukar guards tried to keep the Imperial family and other nobles safe in the frantic crowds, Irulan spotted Wensicia. Her sister's face was flushed, but determined. Irulan now nodded to her. "Time to finish this, and I need your help. Send a priority communication and demand the immediate surrender of all ships in the mutinous fleet. If they refuse, then identify them—and use your self-destruct command."

Wensicia smiled, wrapped up in her new role. "With great pleasure, dear sister." In her crimson gown, she rushed off, looking like a predator.

The Sardaukar tried to control the milling crowd, but the booming violence in the sky increased the panic. Alarms continued to resound through the palace, and Aron whisked Irulan out of the throne room. "The armored catacombs are the safest place for you, Highness."

She agreed, hurrying after him, but then one of the palace guards ran toward her with Chamberlain Ridondo in tow. "Princess, no one can find Chalice!"

Irulan felt a wash of alarm, recalling that she had seen her flighty sister dash away as the uproar rose. The Sardaukar and the guards had been busy fighting Zenha's soldiers, and somehow Chalice had slipped away in the pandemonium.

Ridondo looked sickened. "I will help organize the search! Your sister is not well, and the medications make her unstable. I fear she will come to harm!"

Irulan looked at Aron. His neat garments were stained with blood, but he seemed ready to do anything she asked. She came to a decision. "You and I need to help find her."

The chamberlain and the palace guard raised their voices in disagreement. Ridondo said, "No, we must keep you safe, Highness! Wait in the reinforced catacombs while the search is conducted."

"We will find her," the guard insisted. "Princess Chalice is probably just lost in the crowds."

But Irulan shook her head. "I know the places my sister likes to go. She is likely to run somewhere familiar to her. I know this palace as well as anyone, and I know her habits better than you do."

Seeing her determination, Aron stepped closer and addressed the chamberlain. "By command of the Princess Royal, I guard her with my life, so I go with her." He glanced at the blood on his garment. "I won't let anything happen to her while we search."

Through the shielded windows along the perimeter, Irulan saw the sky light up with weapons fire and explosions. Beyond the city, wrecked vessels crashed to the ground, erupting in fireballs. She heard a whistling roar overhead as a dying cruiser smashed into a tall ministry building.

Flinching, Ridondo pointed down the hall. "Your sister was seen on this level, darting into a preparation room, but she is gone now. Two servants saw her huddled in a corner, sobbing and praying, but when they tried to help her, she ran away."

Irulan considered for a moment. "She must have gone somewhere she thinks she's safe. When Chalice was eight or nine, she had nooks and crannies around the palace where she liked to hide." Thinking of several possibilities, she dispatched the chamberlain and servants to check them, while she and Aron raced to other locations, hoping to locate the young woman before she came to harm.

Palace guards and Sardaukar flashed by, pulling defenses together, trying to organize the evacuation. An Imperial captain gave Irulan a rushed summary of the space battle in orbit, adding to the visible aerial combat taking place in the skies overhead.

Aron was deeply concerned. "My priority is your well-being, Irulan." He used her given name, which emphasized his seriousness. "Let me take you to the underground shelters. We cannot find your sister in time."

Irulan looked at a stairway that led to the tiered highest levels of the palace, the observation decks and rooftop gardens. "Chalice had hiding places up there, one in a shelter by a ceremonial flag, and another in the open among the parapets."

"It's unwise for her to be up there, with a battle taking place overhead," he said. "And I shouldn't risk you either."

Irulan tugged her white protective gloves higher up her forearms. "She isn't thinking rationally, and in her panic she might even stumble off a parapet. Follow me." Aron offered to go search by himself, but she was adamant. "Chalice is my sister! I have to do everything I can to help her!"

Running as fast as she could manage in her ornate gown and fine shoes, she climbed stairs, past observation galleries, and finally emerged on the top level, which was surrounded by carved parapets inset with rare stones.

There, palace guards were manning defensive positions, operating shield projectors and artillery, blasting and deflecting debris that fell from damaged war vessels. Smoking hulks tumbled out of the sky, engines whining, but only minor pieces of debris made it through the safety net.

When Irulan and Aron emerged onto the rooftop, a tall officer waved them back down into the building, his face flushed with alarm. "Highness, it is not safe up here! You should be in a shelter. I'll summon the Sardaukar to escort you!"

"Princess Chalice has fled, and we must find her!" Irulan looked around. "Have you seen her?"

He shook his head. "No, Highness. But you must—"

Aron stood between them, blocking any move by the agitated guard.

"She used to come up here as a child." Irulan looked around. "I need to check everywhere."

The officer relented and barked into his comm, passing along the news, then turned back to her. "I can spare a few men to spread out in the search."

To the north, the battle was drawing closer. A squadron of Sardaukar-led cruisers formed a defensive line in the air, keeping the dreadnought flagship and rebel battleships away from the palace. One of the Imperial corvettes was hit, engines erupting into flames, and it spun out of control, crashing just outside the Palace District.

Transfixed, Irulan watched a squadron of small Imperial fighters race into the battle to assist the Sardaukar ships. They closed in on the flagship dreadnought. Even with Zenha now dead, his main vessel was the most powerful enemy warship. The knot of airborne rebel fighters was being forced back, while the rooftop defenders manned their guns and shield projectors, continuing to deflect fallout from the raging battle in the skies.

Running, Irulan led Aron along a walkway on the edge of the parapet. At the end of the exposed path stood a stone obelisk flying a small ceremonial flag, marking the spot where a young Corrino prince had fallen to his death centuries ago. There was no breeze, even with the explosions and smoke in the air, and the banner hung limply.

Ducking her head, Irulan worked her way around the monument, then slipped under a platform that was used for Corrino family ceremonies. She crouched as she entered the dimly lit interior, and her eyes took a moment to adjust. She knew this place.

Aron gripped Irulan's shoulder and pointed. "There she is! Back in the corner."

Even in her ornate crimson dress, Chalice had crammed herself into the confines of an alcove, trying to hide under the ceremonial platform. Crouching under the low ceiling, Irulan moved forward.

Her sister was irrational with panic. The sedatives had worn off, making her sharp and reactionary. Heavy doses of stimulants and mood-altering drugs had left her paranoid. Now, like a frightened animal, Chalice darted to one side, tearing the side of her gown, squirming and thrashing in a desperate attempt to get away.

But Aron moved faster. He grabbed Chalice's arm, holding tight as she tried to pull herself free. "Forgive me, Princess." He refused to let go.

Irulan rushed to her sister. "We've been worried about you, Chalice! Come with us to safety."

As if to emphasize the danger, a loud explosion erupted in the sky, and they heard the rumble of another crashing vessel.

"Don't come near me!" Chalice shrieked, looking at her sister in horror. "You're a killer! You murdered your own husband! I saw it."

Irulan backed away to give her space, but Aron did not relinquish his grip. Though Chalice struggled, he kept her from scratching his face as he forcibly removed her from the alcove, taking her outside into the sunlight.

Seeing blood spattered on Aron's fine shirt and jacket, Chalice screamed again.

Two palace guards came running, part of the search. Irulan waved them closer.

Just then, she heard a horrendous shuddering screech and the percussive zings and thumps of artillery fire. In the sky, Sardaukar ships and Imperial forces pressed hard against the rebel ships. Under a concentrated barrage, some of the enemy vessels were hit, but the mutinous flagship and a powerful escort of large cruisers backed away, all of them shifting course and accelerating up toward orbit.

But Irulan's attention was wrenched back to the high, exposed rooftop as a smoldering chunk of debris whistled down through the sky, trailing a ribbon of black smoke. It plowed through a gap in the defensive net and smashed like a meteor onto the palace roof, sending a tremor through the deck.

IN THE DISTANT Thalim system, the Guild's tremendous show of force easily drove the Tleilaxu into submission. Starguide Serello had not needed to use the Guild interdiction fleet or his numerous mercenary warships to bombard the planet, though he could have done so if he'd wanted. The drastic threat of quarantining the entire star system, cutting off the Bene Tleilax from all space travel, commerce, and business interactions with the Imperium, had been enough to secure immediate concessions.

Serello watched Master Giblii and the entire Tleilaxu council surrender while scrambling to control the damage. The Starguide and the other Guildsmen in the large fleet let them squirm for more than a day.

The victory was swift enough that no one outside the star system even needed to know the conflict had occurred at all. After only a slight delay, the Guild reopened the blocked spacing routes again. The Tleilaxu paid handsomely, which satisfied the Guild. Peace was reestablished.

Now, except for two Heighliners to remain in orbit over Tleilax, his entire interdiction force could fulfill another obligation, following long-standing treaties that ensured the stability of the Imperium. It was a duty he had to perform.

Standing on the Navigator deck he communicated with the other Heighliners, all hundred ships in this operation. "It is time for a show of force again," he said. "Our next destination is Kaitain."

He looked out at the planet below and the stars that extended in all directions. All the Navigators in the interdiction force silently conferred, then obeyed the Starguide's instructions.

The Holtzman engines powered up. The Navigators inhaled their spice, used prescience to gaze into countless possible paths. Then almost all of the gigantic vessels folded space in a simultaneous operation.

And then reappeared near the Imperial capital world.

A space battle was already taking place in orbit over Kaitain, and scan viewers reported evidence of an aerial conflict in the vicinity of the Palace District as well. In high orbit, Imperial ships of similar designs fired on one another, equally matched—some of them loyal to the Padishah Emperor, and some who followed the cause of Commander-General Zenha.

The unexpected arrival of so many Guild Heighliners triggered a flurry of panicked transmissions. Starguide Serello listened for a moment, then announced to all the ships in orbit that the Spacing Guild stood with Kaitain and Emperor Shaddam IV.

Ninety-eight Heighliners alone should have been enough to make the rebels stand down and surrender, but Serello saw another squadron rising up from the capital city below, a dreadnought and several cruisers moving at full acceleration. The Imperial battleships sent out warning signals, threatening the Heighliners.

The Starguide quickly realized that he needed to increase this show of force, so he instructed the Heighliners to unleash their own Guild warships. Serello watched the stream of new armored vessels drop out of the cavernous holds.

"You will all surrender," he announced.

INSIDE THE IMPERIAL War Room, Wensicia felt alert and ready to do what she needed to do. The tension in the air invigorated her, and she also felt a steely satisfaction with what Irulan had done, even if it had wasted a man who would have been a valuable military resource.

She knew the panic in the palace itself, could see battlefield reports from the skies overhead as well as the clash in orbit. She saw how to control the outcome of the conflict. She drew a breath and calmed herself, focusing her thoughts. Wensicia had prepared for this. No one had expected much from the third daughter of Emperor Shaddam, but she would prove them wrong. Again.

She glanced at the Sardaukar officer who had accompanied her into the War Room. "Kefka Rumico, prepare to send the self-destruct override to the rebel ships, just as we did before. We have the bridge command controls—including their flagship. Let's target the dreadnought first." Her voice hardened. "They will all fall unless they submit."

Rumico worked the comms to activate the command.

Wensicia stepped into the projection zone, terrible in her wrath as she made her announcement over the military channels. "To all rebel officers, this is Wensicia, Princess of House Corrino. The leader of your mutiny, Moko Zenha, is dead, and members of his honor guard have been executed when they tried to kill the Princess Royal. Your ships are outnumbered and outgunned. I demand your immediate surrender, or your ships will self-destruct." She paused just a moment. "You already know I can do it."

She received an overlapping flurry of curses, insults, and defiance, as she had expected, so she spoke again. "I have the self-destruct code for each of your ships. I address whoever remains in command of this rebellion, if you even have a leader now." She sneered. "Tell your ship captains to stand down and cease fire immediately."

Wensicia waited, tracking the movement of the ships as they followed the flagship and cruisers into the sky and heading toward orbit.

Suddenly, she was astonished to see a large force of Guild Heighliners arrive, nearly a hundred unexpected reinforcements. Their Starguide broadcast his own demand for surrender, reaffirming the Guild's allegiance to House Corrino.

She felt a surge of hope, but tried to keep the smugness from her face.

Now the screen flickered and a harried-looking officer appeared, his face drawn. "I am LeftMajor Astop, second-in-command, named by Commander-General Zenha. I now make the decisions for this fleet . . . and we will fight until the end. Our cause is just, so we will destroy the corrupt Imperial military. We will make House Corrino reel."

Wensicia folded her arms over her chest. "Then you will all die."

Astop raised his chin in stubborn defiance. "But we will make our point."

The Sardaukar officer issued a crisp report. "Your Highness, nineteen rebel ships have surrendered. They've drawn down and stopped firing."

"LeftMajor Astop, I swear I will send the destruct override signal to your flagship. Once triggered, you can do nothing to avert the chain reaction." Her voice was hard as steel. "This is your final warning."

On the screen, she watched the dreadnought and its accompanying cruisers in high orbit as they altered course and charged toward the cluster of Heighliners. Did they expect to simply book passage and fly away?

She realized that Astop would never concede. On the comm screen, he turned toward her. "There is nothing more to say, Princess Wensicia. If an objective history of us is ever written, all will know that the Corrinos were the real traitors."

The screen winked off, and Wensicia paused a moment, then nodded to Rumico. "Send the destruct signal."

ON THE PALACE rooftop, Irulan pulled Chalice back after the smoldering chunk of debris hit the parapet, and they fell against the stone wall after the explosion. Smoke filled the air, and the floor beneath them continued to shudder. Her sister sobbed.

The sky was filled with streaks of sparks and flames as wreckage continued to rain down. More large pieces bombarded the area around the palace. Irulan heard one thunderous impact after another.

When the dust cleared, Irulan saw that the nearby strike had torn into the stairway that she and Aron had just climbed. Now they were blocked by ruined stone and girders.

"We'll never get away!" Chalice moaned. Seeing the body of a crushed palace guard, she whimpered again.

Aron indicated an emergency ladder connected to the outside of a parapet. "We can climb down that way."

Chalice thrashed and struggled. Fire blazed in her eyes. "I hate you! I hate you!"

Irulan knew they would never get her down the ladder, unless . . . She hated to do what she had in mind, but there seemed to be no alternative. In a sudden Bene Gesserit combat move, she struck Chalice on the side of her neck and rendered her unconscious. Chalice went limp in Aron's arms.

"I'll carry her on the ladder," he said.

Aron slung Chalice on one of his broad shoulders and climbed over the parapet and onto the ladder. Even with his burden, as well as the fires and wreckage around him, he was athletic and nimble as he negotiated the rungs.

Overhead, the sky was filled with streaks of smoke, but the fighting had diminished and most of the enemy warships withdrawn. Wensicia must have done her part. Irulan looked up, knowing she could get through her own ordeal here. She hoped the battle was won.

WITH CALM SATISFACTION, Starguide Serello watched the orbital battles dwindle. Many rebel warships stopped firing and stood down, transmitting their surrender. Dozens of cruisers had been damaged or destroyed. The Guild would have great concerns about the obstacle hazards from so much space debris, but CHOAM and the Guild had services to sweep the orbital lanes clean.

Once this unnecessary battle was over and the mutinous fleet mopped up, Emperor Shaddam would return to his Golden Lion Throne and rule as before. Serello was certain that news transmissions and witness reports would be modified and censored, the story reshaped to the way Shaddam wanted the events remembered.

The Imperium would continue. The Spacing Guild would continue. The universe would continue.

His massive fleet of Heighliners loomed in orbit, their cargo bays open, the defender ships streaming out. But then the Navigator made a burbling sound of alarm in his tank. Signals were sent across the Guild interdiction fleet.

The rebel flagship and its accompanying cruisers shot directly toward the great vessel next to Serello's. They were like a group of ravenous sharks, picking up speed, showing no sign that they would change course or avoid impact.

Serello insisted that a communication line be opened to the rebel dreadnought, and the projection in front of him showed panic on the flagship's bridge. A commanding officer—LeftMajor Astop, according to transmissions—looked grim-faced and sweating. Alarms rang out across the bridge.

"Reactors breached, sir! We can't stop the buildup!"

"Detonation imminent, LeftMajor! We have about two minutes!"

"We know," Astop said, then he faced forward, staring at Starguide Serello on the screen. "Princess Wensicia has triggered the self-destruct on all these ships." His resigned smile contained no humor whatsoever. "There's nothing we can do to stop it . . . but we will still make our deaths count. I'll do my best to make good use of whatever time there is. This would not have happened, Starguide, if the Spacing Guild had honored its word and remained neutral."

The dreadnought and cruisers headed straight for the open maw of the adjacent Heighliner. Serello sounded the alarm, but on-duty Guildsman had already seen the peril. The Guild defenses opened fire on the suicide force and managed to damage and eliminate one of the cruisers, but the others flew into the open cargo bay of the enormous Heighliner.

The self-destruct sequence occurred simultaneously in all of the renegade ships. The dreadnought and cruisers erupted into a nova of light and fire, spraying debris into the Heighliner's gullet.

Serello watched in horror as the internal shock waves blasted the hull plates away, twisted and broke the structural ribs. The contained destruction roared through the interior of the Guild vessel.

Beside him, the Navigator screamed in sympathetic connection to the other Navigators, who amplified the pain and anguish of their comrade who was dying. Grief and dismay wailed out of the speakerpatch. The Navigator beside Serello floated in his spice gases, thrashing and writhing.

Serello stared wide-eyed through the windowport as the adjacent Heighliner cracked and burned, hanging in space like a bloated corpse, with pieces of debris floating around it.

"This would not have happened, Starguide, if the Spacing Guild had honored its word and remained neutral."

Serello tried to control his thundering emotions as he stared at the devastation.

Life is not so much about happy endings, as it is about endings.

—COUNT HASIMIR FENRING, departing on a mission

Dressed in Imperial finery, though decidedly not for a wedding, the Princess Royal stood with her sisters outside the Imperial Palace's main entrance. Repairs continued, but most of the structural damage had been cleared and covered up. Any signs of fire or smoke had been scoured clean for the triumphant return of the Padishah Emperor Shaddam IV. After visiting only Arrakis, he had declared his Grand Tour over.

Someday, Irulan intended to write about Zenha's uprising and put it into historical context. She would document the entire incident, especially the events leading up to her showdown and staged wedding, and her justification for dealing with the rebel leader in such a deadly manner. She was a keen observer, and her insights were valuable.

But that would only come after she'd had time for research and contemplation. Right now, she had to welcome their father back to his throne.

The three princesses' gowns were a spectrum of pale pastel tones from Wensicia's orange to Chalice's green to Irulan's blue. It was late morning, and bright sunlight bathed the women, highlighting them.

The three elegant gowns had been Chalice's concept, demonstrating that she was finally thinking clearly. Chalice had undergone extensive medical treatment and counseling, and now seemed much calmer, more at peace with herself, and not entirely because of the drugs from the Suk doctors.

Hoping to pull her sister out of her mental funk, Irulan had put her ideas into action. The Imperial tailors had worked swiftly and expertly, and the gowns had turned out well, even with transitional hues on the edges that led from one sister to the next. Chalice was cheered by the compliments.

Hundreds of palace guards and Sardaukar stood at attention around a landing area as the Emperor's shuttle set down, its suspensor engines humming smoothly. The oldest daughters of Shaddam stood together as sisters, bound by blood. They had survived. Soon their little sisters, Josifa and Rugi, would return from Wallach IX, when Imperial security declared the palace ready for them.

Irulan and Wensicia had resolved their differences, and both knew the other had played a vital role in quelling the rebellion. They had worked together, and now they stood proudly, understanding each other, and ready to greet their father.

Chalice exclaimed and pointed excitedly as Shaddam emerged from the Imperial shuttle. "Oh, look! Father is wearing royal purple! Just like I hoped."

An hour ago, to keep her from being disappointed, Irulan had sent a message to her father when the Heighliner had arrived in orbit, requesting that he wear the expected color, and now she was glad to see the delight on her fragile sister's face.

Aron had helped Irulan prepare, and then had vanished into the background. He would be there at the palace when she needed him.

The Sardaukar saluted as the Emperor marched away from the shuttle as if ready to head straight for his throne and begin making long-overdue decisions and pronouncements. Behind him, his Truthsayer followed like a shadow. More members of the Imperial entourage disembarked from the shuttle.

The princesses waited to receive their father at the arched entryway. Irulan noted that he was not smiling as he ran his gaze along the main roof, which had been heavily damaged by falling debris. On the parapets high above, workers had fallen silent in respect, watching the Emperor's return.

The three princesses curtsied in their formal gowns, and finally Shaddam did smile. "I am pleased you are all safe. I understand you worked together to defeat the traitor and his forces. A neat solution."

Irulan felt a rush of pride and saw that Wensicia also flushed. Chalice beamed, as if he had complimented her as well.

The three let their father pass, and he paused to affectionately touch each of their faces. Irulan was surprised to see unusual emotion in his eyes.

In sharp contrast, Reverend Mother Mohiam swept by them like an icy breeze, sparing hardly a glance for Irulan.

SHADDAM WASTED NO time calling an inner-council meeting with a cadre of Imperial advisers and propaganda ministers. Irulan was invited to attend, but Wensicia was sent off to watch over Chalice. Wensicia was clearly disappointed at not being included, but the Emperor didn't seem to notice the snub he had given. Even after what she had done to keep Kaitain from falling, Shaddam never saw her as more than the third daughter. Irulan decided to look for an opportunity to speak with him about it.

Now that they were behind closed doors, the Emperor allowed his anger to show. "The Spacing Guild is conducting a complete investigation of the debacle. They have never lost a Heighliner in battle before." He shook his head. "The self-destruct sequence Wensicia triggered caused a great deal of damage."

Before Irulan could defend her sister's actions, Major Bashar Kolona spoke up. "Wensicia's use of the secret signal forced the rest of the rebel fleet to surrender at the most crucial time, Sire. And the Guild's records show that the rebel flagship and attendant cruisers were on a suicide run, regardless."

Scowling, Shaddam shook his head. "We need to convince Starguide Serello of that so he conveys it to his Guild superiors. We can't have them blaming House Corrino for the loss of their Heighliner." He sighed. "How did Wensicia ever learn about the self-destruct command? And why didn't *I* know about it?" He sniffed. "If I had known, I would have just destroyed them from the outset, every single mutinous ship."

Kolona bowed his head. "Much of the Liberation Fleet surrendered because of the command, Sire. We saved countless military ships that had been commandeered, and now they can be returned to service in the Imperial military."

"Still, far too much damage," Shaddam said. "And those debris impacts on my palace!" He turned to the Sardaukar commander. "Round up the mutinous subcommanders who surrendered to Wensicia's ultimatum. We must have them under arrest!"

"Yes, sir," said the Major Bashar. "Where would you like them taken?"

The Emperor lashed out. "To unheated holding cells, awaiting execution! I will impose my official sentence upon them within the day."

Kolona looked shocked. "Every one of them, Sire? But they surrendered."

"Every last one. No forgiveness for traitors."

One of the propaganda ministers, a stuffed shirt named Sanders Dreed, said, "Despite the destruction and damage that occurred here, Sire, this insurrection could have been much worse. Ultimately, the pirate Zenha proved to be only a minor annoyance, and his movement is easily erased by counterpropaganda. You see how easily he was tricked and neutralized by the brave Princess Irulan."

Hearing this, Shaddam nodded, but he still looked upset.

"I would not say the solution was so simple," Irulan said to the propaganda minister.

"Be that as it may," Dreed said, ignoring her, "we will distribute our own version of events so that the rest of the Imperium believes whatever you want them to believe, Sire. I suggest we minimize this group of malcontents and stick to the story that you went to Arrakis as part of your Grand Tour. No need to let the masses think their Emperor is weak or easily threatened."

Hearing this convinced Irulan more firmly that she would write her own historical chronicle, even if it remained in her private journals.

Shaddam seemed uncertain where to direct his ire. "I will consider that." He dismissed the advisers and ministers, leaving only Irulan and the Sardaukar commander.

After motioning them to sit in the large chairs in front of his desk, Shaddam looked to his daughter. "Irulan, I commend you for your handling of the matter—your quick thinking and willingness to throw yourself into the fray. It was quite innovative." He chuckled. "I wish I could have watched him writhe on the wedding dais from your poison."

Irulan felt grim about what she'd done. "I killed a man, Father. It was a necessary act, but still difficult." She paused, then added, "Do not overlook Wensicia's contributions, beyond discovering the self-destruct commands. She was the first to suggest marrying that dangerous man as a way to neutralize the threat."

Shaddam pursed his lips, nodded reluctantly. "Remind me to thank her later." He turned to Kolona and said, "Major Bashar, once again you performed with extraordinary skill and valor." He beamed with pride, as if Kolona were his son. "I hereby promote you to the rank of *Colonel* Bashar."

Obviously uncomfortable in his seat, the Sardaukar officer adjusted the cap he held on his lap, then rose to his feet and bowed. "Thank you, Sire. Your praise means everything to me." He bowed to Irulan. "And yours as well, Princess Royal."

Shaddam dismissed him so he could be alone with his daughter. As the door closed behind the officer, he softened his expression. "I admire you for offering yourself to Zenha for the sake of the Imperium. You had the strength of personality and courage to do what was necessary, not what was easy or tasteful."

She did not point out that the entire sequence of events was a direct result of Shaddam's harsh response when Zenha asked for her hand. But the situation itself had been created by the inherent weaknesses and corruption in the Imperial military, an unstable command structure that was bound to fail. She wished her father would see that the underlying flaws still existed, but he had a blind spot toward the pomp he loved so well.

The Emperor rose to his feet to signal that the formal meeting was at an end. "My Imperium is strong," he insisted, as if trying to convince himself. "Come have dinner with me. I am weary and famished."

They walked side by side, father and favorite daughter, down the main-level corridor.

Summoning her courage, Irulan finally asked, "You grew angry at Moko Zenha's impertinence for asking to marry me, but you have declined all other offers of marriage. Please tell me, what plans do you actually have for me? I am already twenty-six. Surely, I must marry an appropriate candidate soon. How much longer do I have to wait to know my future?"

In response he looked at her more coldly than she would have liked. "I will choose the appropriate person, at the appropriate time."

But Irulan did not drop the matter. "I know you value my opinion on political and business matters, so could I not have some say in whom I marry? Would you be willing to hear my ideas on such matters? Have I not earned that right?"

He paused at the entry to the private dining salon. "You are an important adviser to me, Irulan, and I admire your intelligence. But the ultimate choice of an acceptable husband for the Princess Royal is altogether a different matter." He hardened his voice. "And entirely my own decision."

"Of course it is, Father." She sighed. "But do you think I will be happy?"

"Happiness has nothing to do with it." He gestured her into the hall. "Like all of us, you must fulfill your destiny."

To an outsider, my actions may be difficult to interpret, my motivations murky. I must cooperate with friend or foe, Fremen or Imperial or Harkonnen, but there are no doubts in my mind. Even if others are too blind to see my true loyalties, to me my path is as clear as the bright sun in an open sky over Dune.

—IMPERIAL PLANETOLOGIST LIET-KYNES, private journals

On their journey back to Sietch Tabr, Chani grappled with her emotions, rehearsing the words she would use to tell her father, but her throat was thick, her heart heavy. Once the two Tleilaxu craft broke through the storm belt, they had a smooth flight all the way home. The pilots flew low to avoid detection by scanning nets or Harkonnen scouts.

The loss of her brother made everything around her dark.

Jamis sat beside her in the vibrating aircraft, aware of the waves of sadness that came from her. He reached over and said in a gruff voice, "Let me be the one to tell them, Chani. I can give the report just as well as you."

Her instinctive reaction was to brush him away and insist that it was her duty. But Jamis had been Khouro's friend, too. All Fremen would share in the benefits of this operation, and also share the grief.

She felt the heavy burden deep in her soul, and Jamis was offering to lighten it a little. "Thank you," she said. She would add details and repeat the story on her own later, but Jamis could be the first to share the heavy news. She whispered again, "Thank you."

When they returned to the sietch at midday, the people were shocked and grieved about Khouro—yet they celebrated not only the great reward they would receive from the Guild, but also the knowledge that the genetic researchers were eradicated from the pure desert. The Fremen engineers were excited to have the two new Tleilaxu ships, which they would modify for their own purposes. The Bene Tleilax were secretive like the Fremen, and now their secrets and technology would be exposed.

Khouro was celebrated as a hero, just as he deserved. Even with the crowds and constant activity in the close chambers, the sietch felt empty to Chani. With so many people moving about in the cave warrens, few might notice one less young man, but to her, his loss was a loud and resounding blow.

Feeling numb, she slept a great deal, stayed away from others. Upon returning home, she was actually relieved to learn that her father was off doing work at one of the botanical testing stations. She wondered if he had gone away on purpose because he feared knowing what would happen on the raid.

Finally, after the three days of mourning, Chani went by herself to perform a last important duty. She pulled back the spice-fiber hangings at her brother's living chamber and activated a glowglobe. His quarters were small yet comfortable, a cave with fabrics on the walls, a narrow sleeping cot, his own spice coffee service, and a blob of glass from lightning-struck sand, a keepsake he had found on one of their explorations. She had already taken his crysknife before leaving the Tleilaxu facility, but Chani had to honor him in a different way.

She drew the milky-white blade, now cleansed of bloodstains, and held her breath as she looked around the chamber her half brother had called home, where he liked to rest and relax, where he might bring lovers or just while away the hours.

"I miss you, Khouro," she whispered. "Know that we love you and honor what you did." She placed his crysknife on the small rock shelf next to the blob of lightning sand. "I will never forget you."

She sensed his presence here. Even when alone in the desert, or with her father in Arrakeen, Chani had always known Khouro was thinking about her. Now she believed strongly that he was still here, and would watch over her.

She could take what she wanted, to cherish any of her brother's possessions. She needed something to hold in her hands, a tangible memory of him. Soon, the Fremen women would strip his chamber bare and take his possessions into the common area. A funeral would be held, and all would speak their remembrances. His friends might take keepsakes, or perhaps just tell anecdotes. Because of contamination by the Tleilaxu poisons, Khouro's body water would not be distributed among the tribe, as their mother's had been, but his belongings would be shared, the items spread out so that his memory endured.

Yet Khouro would still be gone.

She ran her fingers along the lump of lightning glass, made from the sands of Arrakis, created by wild energy from a storm. She picked it up, felt it in the palm of her hand. Yes, this was what she would keep of him. She could gaze into it and see his face again.

She heard a rustle behind her and whirled, still on edge. Liet-Kynes stood there, his face dusty, his eyes reddened. "I am so sorry," he said.

She steeled herself, swallowing hard. "We did what was asked of us, struck a great victory for the Fremen, and Khouro died bravely."

"But he still *died*," Liet said in a heavy, dry voice. "He still *died* . . . And I am sorry for many things. I grieve for lost opportunities. He and I may have had personal conflicts, but he had a Fremen heart, as do I." He stepped into the chamber, letting the fabric fall behind him. "I wish I'd realized that we carry the same fight." He touched the crysknife on the alcove shelf.

"He questioned whether you did share in that fight," Chani said. "That's why he pushed back." Angrily, she thought of all the times Liet-Kynes worked in the Imperial testing stations, delivered reports to Count Fenring, or went to meet with Baron Harkonnen on Imperial business. "That is why Khouro resisted you—because your interactions with the Imperium made you unreliable in his eyes. He thought you should have used your skills and connections to fight the offworlders, not pander to them." She heard the bitterness in her voice and knew where it came from.

Her father's expression sagged. "You think I would betray the Fremen? *My* Fremen? Is that what Liet-Chih believed?" He sucked in a quick breath. "Is that what *you* believe?"

Chani ran her fingers along the lightning glass, feeling it grow warm in her hand, but it gave her no magical strength. "You serve two masters. We all know it. Which is the real one, should they clash?"

Liet looked around the chamber and locked his eyes on the spice coffee set, undoubtedly remembering that it had recently belonged to Faroula, his lost love. "Come with me, daughter. It is best we have this conversation while we gaze out upon the desert."

From her earliest memories, Chani had never tired of looking out on the dunes. Still holding the lump of glass, she pushed aside the door hanging. She was not leaving her brother behind, just going away for a little while.

Liet led her up stone steps carved into the rock wall, and they climbed to a high point, where they exited through a moisture-seal door out onto an open balcony. The late-afternoon view across the dunes was a spectacular array of colors and shades on the sands and escarpments. They stood shoulder to shoulder just staring, letting their minds expand out like the rolling landscape before them. The sun was behind the rock of their sietch, but still cast a spectrum of colors.

Liet's expression sagged. "Yes, I serve two masters. It is as if I am ruled by a pair of raging wolves, each apart from the other, each vicious and powerful." He lowered his voice. "That is how and why I was able to get you released from the Sardaukar prison."

"I know." Chani was saddened by her own words. "I never thanked you for saving our lives."

"You were only trying to do what was necessary, but in the wrong way," Liet continued. "Yes, I play more than one role, but everything I do is for Arrakis, for my father's great ecological dream. For my dream." He looked hard at her. "The Imperium is merely a tool for me, but the Fremen are a *weapon*."

Standing beside him, Chani touched her own crysknife. The milky blade had been fashioned from the discarded tooth of a sacred sandworm, and there could be no more perfect or deadly weapon for a desert person to use.

"And with enough Fremen as weapons," Chani said in a low, husky voice, "we will have an army."

A faint smile touched her father's bearded face. "When the time is right. When we are ready."

Chani stared at the sunbaked dunes, out toward the horizon, and up to the paintbrush-hued sky, where she saw brown streaks forming, the signs of a distant churning wind.

A storm was coming in.

ACKNOWLEDGMENTS

Princess of Dune is our twentieth book set in the fantastic Dune universe, adding to the legacy of the classic six novels that Frank Herbert wrote. He was himself deeply indebted to his wife of almost four decades, Beverly Herbert, a professional writer herself who provided indispensable advice during the creation of his novels. With deep appreciation, we begin these acknowledgments with a tip of the hat to Brian's father and mother.

As always, our new novel has been a team effort, extending beyond the two of us as authors. Some people have been helping us prepare Dune stories for decades, above all our patient and supportive wives, Jan Herbert and Rebecca Moesta.

Our talented literary agent, John Silbersack, has been tireless and watchful through all of our Dune projects, seeing the big picture while paying close attention to details, working closely with our other skilled agents, Robert Gottlieb and Mary Alice Kier. In recent years, with the adaptation of our collaborative novel *Sisterhood of Dune* to a new TV series, we have been ably guided through the intricacies of Hollywood by the exceptional literary attorneys Marcy Morris and Barry Tyerman.

We have a new editor, Robert Davis at Tor Books, who gave us excellent suggestions to improve *Princess of Dune* and ushered the novel through production. We'd also like to thank the hardworking Kim Herbert and Byron Merritt of Herbert Properties LLC (grandchildren of Frank and Beverly), as well as Marie Whittaker, Tracy Griffiths, Mia Kleve, and CJ Anaya at WordFire, along with our test readers Kris Hamilton and Robert Dickson.

ABOUT THE AUTHORS

Jan Herbert

BRIAN HERBERT, the son of Frank Herbert, wrote the definitive biography of him, *Dreamer of Dune*, which was a Hugo Award finalist. Herbert is also president of the company managing the legacy of Frank Herbert, and is an executive producer of the motion picture *Dune*, as well as of the TV series *Dune: The Sisterhood*. He is the author or coauthor of more than forty-five books, including multiple *New York Times* bestsellers, has been nominated for the Nebula Award, and is always working on several projects at once. He and his wife, Jan, have traveled to all seven continents, and in 2019, they took a trip to Budapest to observe the filming of *Dune*.

KEVIN J. ANDERSON has written dozens of national bestsellers and has been nominated for the Hugo Award, the Nebula Award, the Bram Stoker Award, and the SFX Readers' Choice Award. His critically acclaimed original novels include the ambitious space opera series the Saga of Seven Suns, including *The Dark Between the Stars*, as well as the epic fantasy trilogy Wake the Dragon and the Terra Incognita fantasy epic with its two accompanying rock CDs. He also set the Guinness-certified world record for the largest single-author book signing, and was recently inducted into the Colorado Authors' Hall of Fame.